By AUGUST LI

Coal to Diamonds
Neskaya
On Tinsel Wings • This Same Flower
Steamed Up (Dreamspinner Anthology)

With Eon De Beaumont
STEAMCRAFT AND SORCERY
Boots for the Gentleman
A Grimoire for the Baron
Snowdrop

Published by DREAMSPINNER PRESS
http://www.dreamspinnerpress.com

THIS
SAME
Flower

AUGUST LI

Dreamspinner Press

Published by
DREAMSPINNER PRESS

5032 Capital Circle SW, Suite 2, PMB# 279, Tallahassee, FL 32305-7886 USA
http://www.dreamspinnerpress.com/

This Same Flower
© 2014 August Li.

Cover Art
© 2014 Paul Richmond.
http://www.paulrichmondstudio.com
Cover content is for illustrative purposes only and any person depicted on the cover is a model.

ISBN: 978-1-63216-637-1
Digital ISBN: 978-1-63216-638-8
Library of Congress Control Number: 2014947753
Second Edition August 2014
First edition published by Dreamspinner Press, June 2014

Printed in the United States of America
∞
This paper meets the requirements of
ANSI/NISO Z39.48-1992 (Permanence of Paper).

Author's Note

I started writing this story at a very hopeful and historic point in the equal rights struggle in both the United States and worldwide. As I began writing what I initially saw as a simple story of two young people building a life together and finding their place in the world, eleven of fifty states in my country had legalized same-gender marriages, and France had recognized them not long before. The day I began my first draft, Delaware became the latest state to stand up for equality, and as I write this, I am hopeful many more states will follow. During the course of my work, in an epic first step toward equal rights for all United States citizens, the United States Supreme Court ruled the discriminatory Defense of Marriage Act and California's Proposition 8 unconstitutional. While not an absolute victory by any means, it is a monumental first step.

Therefore, in the spirit of optimism and a rare moment of faith in my fellow humans, I have taken certain liberties. At the time I wrote this book, Japan did not yet acknowledge same-sex marriages as eligible for a dependent visa. Recently, however, Japan did make it possible for Japanese nationals to marry their same-sex partners in countries that allow it, although their union is not necessarily recognized in Japan. The rules at this time are murky and very much open to interpretation, with few legal precedents, but it is still a decent start. Even so, an American in Japan on a work visa would not be able to secure a dependent visa for his husband, even if they had been legally married in a state such as New York.

An American man wishing to stay with his husband in Japan would have a variety of options—it isn't hard for an American national to stay in Japan—such as a student visa, a work visa, or a tourist visa, which can be renewed about every three months. I could have used one of these options for my characters, but I chose instead to imagine a future, one I can only hope isn't too far off, in which Japan would recognize a legal marriage between two men. I hope you'll suspend your disbelief and join me in envisioning a world maybe not exactly as it is, but as it should be.

This book is respectfully dedicated to everyone who made these victories possible: past members of the LGBT community who paved the way for our freedom, present members who are still fighting for equality, our allies, friends, and families. This is for everyone who ever sent a letter or an e-mail, held up a sign, called a senator, or argued the case for equal rights. Patrick would have a quote for what we've achieved. I think he'd choose Sir Isaac Newton: "If I have seen further than others, it is because I stood on the shoulders of giants."

~Gus, May 2013

Gather ye rosebuds while ye may,
Old Time is still a-flying;
And this same flower that smiles today
Tomorrow will be dying.
—*To The Virgins, to Make Much of Time, by Robert Herrick*

Chapter 1

PATRICK HARFORD knew they were outgrowing the little apartment as he looked around at the medieval and Renaissance armor his boyfriend Yu had made hanging on every foot of wall space, along with broadswords, rapiers, maces, and spears leaning in every corner of their living room. Yu's sketches and notes were piled high on the desk beside their computer, and the steel sculptures he'd made in art school—those he felt weren't good enough to show or sell—encircled the fireplace and lined the wall between the hearth and the doorway to the kitchen. Over the past two years, Patrick had acquired so many dresses, wigs, shoes, and pieces of jewelry the closets could no longer contain them all, and the dress forms, Styrofoam heads, and shoe boxes piled five high spilled over not only into their bedroom but into the rest of the space as well.

They were definitely outgrowing the apartment, or maybe they already had, Patrick realized with a nostalgic pang. He remembered working his fingers to the bone to afford what he'd seen as a paradise as if it had been yesterday. He remembered Yu packing his every worldly possession into his car and taking a chance on Patrick—leaping off the edge of the abyss and hoping wings would sprout sometime before he reached the hard ground at the bottom. They'd learned how to live together, and it hadn't always been easy, but Patrick wouldn't trade a second of it, not even the heated arguments over separating metal utensils from plastic or whether bedsheets needed ironing. There had been much more good than bad, more good than Patrick had ever expected to find in life, and this was home—the only one he'd ever known.

Together, he and Yu had learned to fly. They'd both been pushed out of their nests before they were ready, but as long as they held on to each other, they managed to keep from crashing to the ground.

Every item in the apartment, down to the most functional, had a memory attached to it. Patrick and Yu had either chosen it together, picked it up while shopping together (which they always made time to do, despite their hectic schedules), or used it in some significant way. Even the scratches on the walls and the scuffs on the hardwood floor held meaning for Patrick. Every one of them recalled something to him, some smile they'd shared or evening they'd spent just lying on the sagging sofa, when one of Yu's feet had jerked and upset a mug of cocoa, or the time Patrick spilled a tub of paint he had been using to make props for the Faire—

But reminiscing would have to wait. Tonight meant a lot to Yu, and of course Patrick needed to be with him. He finished squeezing the moisture from his long dark red hair and toweled the water droplets from his body. In the bathroom, he dropped the towel into the hamper designated for anything wet, as opposed to the one for dirty laundry, brushed his teeth, and shaved. He dressed in a pair of charcoal trousers, a red shirt that matched his hair, and a gray argyle sweater vest. Then he hurried out into the cool September evening and drove to the University of Pittsburgh to meet Yu.

DOZENS OF people waited outside the University Art Gallery in the Frick Fine Arts Building. While glad to see so many people had come to Yu's show, Patrick also worried. Yu often experienced terrible anxiety around crowds, the noise and chaos of many people talking overwhelming him. Patrick knew Yu had awaited his senior show with a mixture of anticipation and dread; Yu had done something he rarely resorted to, and hated, and taken half a Xanax before leaving earlier that afternoon to set up his pieces. Yu had told Patrick he hated the groggy haze the medicine caused and that he felt it drained his creativity. Usually, Yu suffered through the tightness in his chest and the dizziness when his blood pressure spiked, but tonight he'd seen no choice but to succumb to the minor relief the little pill offered. Patrick walked a little faster, hoping to find Yu quickly and make sure he was all right.

As Patrick crossed the lawn, the grass sheathed in autumn's first frost crunching beneath his canvas sneakers, he responded with waves to the many greetings called out from friends of theirs from the Allegheny Mountains Renaissance Faire and the students he'd come to know. Their frozen breath and cigarette smoke hovered over them in a golden mist backlit by the lampposts. The night was crystal clear, the starlight sharp and bright even in the city. Everything had a pure and brittle beauty, and Patrick couldn't have wished for a lovelier or more magical night for Yu's exhibition. He wanted more than anything to make it a pleasant memory for Yu. Somehow, he'd make tonight something Yu remembered fondly.

Inside the gallery, people stood in small groups around Yu's pieces or the refreshment table, nearly filling the rectangular room. Patrick couldn't believe how many people had come, and he couldn't find Yu among them. He noticed Jen's bright red curls, so similar to his own hair that many Faire patrons inferred that Queen Elizabeth's minstrel boy and constant companion might be a brother born on the wrong side of the bed, and in a way, they were right. Jen had become much more like a big sister than a friend to Patrick over the years. Thinking Jen might have seen Yu, Patrick made his way to where she stood with her longtime boyfriend, Henry, one of the knights from the Faire and Patrick's fighting tutor.

Jen kissed Patrick on the cheek, and Henry clapped him on the shoulder. "Patrick, you must be so proud," Jen said, her blue eyes sparkling. "These sculptures are amazing. This one is my favorite; it's so beautiful."

On a pedestal in front of them stood the steel sculpture Yu had titled *The Lovers*. The two figures, while androgynous, like all of Yu's human depictions, looked more male than female, more angular than rounded. One figure lay sprawled decadently, legs open and head thrown back in ecstasy, while the other lay on top, his face melting into his partner's chest. The entwined legs lost all definition at the knees, their limbs flowing together into a single lump of unworked steel. Both bodies bore the marks of Yu's hammer, his hand evident in every divot and ridge.

Jen ran her fingers over the conjoined legs. "It's so romantic. Even though they don't have any facial features, you can just feel their joy. Their love and connection. And then they just melt into one. Beautiful."

A student Patrick didn't recognize came up to stand beside them. "The way he can capture emotion through gesture is really amazing. Every line expresses passion. I have to say, I'm a little jealous."

An older woman in a black dress took a sip of chardonnay and said, "I adore the contrast between the strength of the medium and the vulnerability of the pose. It's a brilliant juxtaposition, indicative of someone who understands human nature and can capture it. I'd like to show something like this in my galleries. Where is the artist? I'd like to meet him."

Patrick turned to Jen and Henry. "I'm looking for Yu too. Have you seen him?"

"He was with Eric and Rog," Henry said, pointing, "over by his samurai stuff."

Patrick rolled his eyes even as he fought the urge to kiss Henry. He knew Henry didn't mean any offense. He just wasn't the kind of man to attempt to describe art in terms of mediums, poses, and dichotomies, and he wouldn't pretend he was. Patrick felt a little less anxious. At least Yu had Eric and Rog, and they'd look out for him until Patrick got to him. They'd become almost parents to Patrick, and he knew they would make sure Yu was all right. Spotting one of Yu's hannya masks on the wall, Patrick went in that direction. Soon, he saw Yu standing between Eric and Rog, who flanked him like a pair of bodyguards. Yu looked devastating in his black blazer, dark blue shirt, and silver tie, his long hair loose around his shoulders. Patrick could never decide if he preferred Yu clean and dressed immaculately or sweaty and dirty in the tight gray leggings and loose shirt he wore to work his forge at the Faire, his perfect face smeared with soot. He didn't have to choose, though. He had both, and, God, if he didn't know what a lucky man he was.

Tonight, he just hoped he could be worthy of it—make Yu happy.

"Hey, girlfriend," Rog crooned, hugging Patrick and kissing his cheek. Rog possessed a charisma he couldn't turn off, an ease and inherent happiness that made people want to be around him. It served him as well tonight as it did when he performed as Lady Regina. This evening, he looked comfortable and stylish in a light blue shirt that suited his complexion, his tan linen vest unbuttoned.

"Hey, Mama," Patrick said, kissing him back. He reached around Rog to clasp Eric's hand. Eric smiled his mischievous grin that made the women at the Faire weak in the knees when he portrayed the pirate, Sir Francis Drake. Playing to his roguish good looks, Eric wore a dark shirt and pants, with his long dark brown hair pulled back and the perfect amount of stubble lining his strong jaw. Eric leaned in to kiss Patrick on the forehead, and Patrick didn't care what anyone who might be watching them thought. Rog had once told Patrick being ashamed was like admitting to some wrongdoing, and Patrick had nothing in his life to be ashamed of, not anymore. He'd never be ashamed of his family, these people who had nurtured and supported him even if they weren't related by blood. He didn't even want to think about where he'd be if they hadn't been there to hold his head above water when he'd needed it.

He broke free from the arms of his friends and adoptive parents, stepped over to Yu and took Yu's hands in his. He kissed Yu's cheek and leaned in to whisper in his ear. "Are you doing okay?"

Yu didn't mince words, ever, and tonight was no exception. "No. All the words are jumbling together, and my brain can't choose what to focus on. I'm having a hard time, Patrick. I feel like I'm ready to be sick. I want to find a quiet corner and curl up in a ball."

With his nose still buried in Yu's hair, Patrick said, "Everyone loves your work. You're really making people think and feel. Everyone here supports you, but I know that's not what's bothering you. We'll only stay long enough to be polite, but if you need to go, you tell me."

"Thank you," Yu said quietly.

Patrick clasped his hand, and they began to walk around the room, stopping briefly in front of each piece so Yu could speak to those admiring it. As an art major, most of his work was sculptural and abstract, but his professors had embraced his love of traditional armor and weaponry, and some fine examples of his swords, shields, helmets, and breastplates joined the freestanding steel figures. Many of the pieces encompassed the melding of Asian and European traditions, both sides of Yu's heritage. Yu seemed comfortable talking about his work, his techniques, as long as only one or two people questioned him at a time. Forging procedures, Patrick had learned long ago, provided a sort of safe zone for Yu as they were precise, and he could explain them without trying to decipher the subtle social nuances he had such difficulty understanding. There was a right way and a wrong way to make a sword or a piece of armor, none of the gray areas that made Yu so uncomfortable.

When they reached a polished-steel fox mask with a pointy snout that seemed to grin, with elongated eyes and elaborate red-and-white detail, Patrick smiled when he saw, next to the little plaque that read *Kitsune #7* a small tag that said "Not For Sale."

He moved a little closer to Yu, so their shoulders brushed together, and leaned in to speak near his ear, so his voice wouldn't be another Yu had to isolate from the din, and the physical contact between them would soothe Yu. "You didn't have to keep it for me."

Yu turned to smile at him, his warm light brown eyes—eyes like sunlight through amber—crinkling to crescents. "You love that piece, and you said you might want to do some fighting at the Faire, since you've been training with Henry. It's a completely functional helmet, and I can make you an entire set of armor to match if you decide you want one. Besides, it suits you."

Looking at him, talking to him, allowed Yu to ignore the clashing conversations and chaos of the rest of the gallery. It made Patrick glad that, after more than two years together, he could still command all Yu's attention, that when Yu looked at him, the rest of the world faded to insignificance—just like it did for Patrick when he looked at Yu. He liked being Yu's shield.

"Why?" Patrick asked.

Yu leaned closer. When he spoke, his warm breath ruffled the unruly red hair over Patrick's ear and swept across the sensitive skin of Patrick's freshly shaved cheek and chin. "*Kitsune* are very clever, very graceful. In human form, they're exceptionally beautiful, so beautiful they can enchant a person of their choosing into becoming their lover. They can be tricksters, but if someone earns it, they're incredibly loyal and always keep their oaths. They're magical—like you."

Looking at Yu's face, at the expectation mingled with worry, the need for acceptance and to be told he was doing something worthwhile and doing it well, broke Patrick's heart a little. "I love it. But I'd keep everything you made if I had my way. But I guess I have to share you and your talent with the world."

"No, you don't," Yu answered, a hint of dusky rose spreading across his high cheekbones.

"I only mean that I'll be surprised if someone doesn't want this mask."

"They can't have it," Yu said. "It's for you. I intended it for you even before I started making it. Making *them*," he corrected himself. "It took me seven attempts to make it perfect. To get the *kitsune's* expression right. The brows and eyes gave me trouble. I needed to convey all your innocence, strength, wisdom, and playfulness." He shook his head. "I'm still not sure I accomplished it. If I make a better version, I'll sell this one, but until then, it's for you."

Patrick wanted to respond but didn't think he could express how much that meant to him; he knew how much time and how much of his soul Yu put in to every piece he made. Instead, Patrick tugged Yu toward a beautiful, gold-toned mask with serene female features and delicate curling spines radiating around it titled *Amaterasu*. He wanted to guide Yu away from what looked like a gaggle of freshman students in T-shirts and jeans, obviously sent to the show as an assignment, given the way they typed on their tablets. The last thing Yu needed was to be accosted by a loud group of people who didn't really care about his work. Though Yu seemed outwardly composed, Patrick, and probably Patrick alone, knew how hard he worked to maintain the reserved mask on his face.

Patrick and Yu reached the focal point of Yu's exhibition, what Yu felt was his finest and most successful piece to date. *Hope Validated* stood almost life-sized, a clearly male figure with his chest puffed proudly outward, arms up and back, face toward the ceiling. The sculpture's body formed a triumphant curve, and a single foot, balanced on the toes, supported it at the base. The other leg bent at the knee, stretched as if frozen midstep in a dance.

Yu had engraved roses over the figure's prominent ribs, just where Patrick's tattooed roses stretched from his hipbone to his chest. The steel itself was rough—the marks of Yu's hammer clearly visible—yet every crease and indentation added to the beauty and complexity of the piece. Not a scratch or divot looked out of place or accidental. A pair of impossibly delicate steel tines extended from the shoulder blades, and ragged strips of cloth fluttered down from them like wings. Patrick recognized some of the fabric: a scrap of red satin from their bedsheets, a piece of the green gown Patrick had worn on the night Yu had given up everything to be with him, a strip of lace from one of Jen's dresses, a shred of a Jolly Roger flag from Eric's "ship" at the Faire—His eyes stung, and he squeezed tighter to Yu's hand. He'd seen Yu working on the piece when he'd stopped by the school to bring Yu dinner or coffee, but tonight, for the first time, he stood before the finished work, and it was glorious.

Everyone in the gallery gathered around, and the casual conversation dropped to silence. Yu leaned against Patrick, his hand a little shaky in Patrick's, shifting his balance from foot to foot. He probably felt dizzy, like he needed to hold on to something to stay on his feet, and Patrick tried to steady him as phones and cameras flashed, taking pictures of the artist beside his wondrous creation. Slowly, everyone pushed closer, forming a crescent with Yu, Patrick, and the sculpture at the center. Yu looked out over the assembled crowd, and Patrick followed his gaze. Their friends

Aouli and Shawn, Patrick's drag sisters, had made it, along with Tom, the Faire manager and his wife; two knights called Ian and Carlton; Tish and Tracy, who made corsets and other period lingerie for Patrick and many other Faire-goers, and many of the other shop owners and performers. It surprised Patrick to see Wade, the Faire's blacksmith and Yu's mentor, looking almost proud. Well, he'd at least dropped the scowl of constant irritation everyone at the Faire knew well and looked more pleased than Patrick had ever imagined possible.

Patrick's heart swelled with the love and support their friends had shown, but Yu looked disappointed. Since Yu didn't enjoy and often couldn't express himself verbally, Patrick had become adept at reading his body language. The way Yu's shoulder curled slightly forward and his jaw twitched as he fought to keep the corners of his mouth from turning down told Patrick everything he needed to know, but with everyone watching, he didn't know what he could do to comfort his friend.

"Can you tell us a little bit about this piece?" asked the woman in the black dress. "What inspired it?"

Yu flinched, his spine snapping straight as he looked at the expectant faces awaiting his answer. After clearing his throat softly, he said, "The piece is inspired by a poem, 'The Definition of Love' by Andrew Marvell. In it, he calls hope feeble and says it 'vainly flapped its tinsel wing.' I understood that to mean hope is too fragile to hold on to, but I don't agree." Yu met Patrick's gaze and said the next part to Patrick alone. "I don't agree. I think hope is the most important thing in the world, and if you lose it, you've lost everything, so I made my hope from steel. My hope is strong; it can be held without damaging it, but it's also beautiful and delicate, hence the wings."

The people discussed Yu's statement in subdued tones, and a few more cameras flashed.

"The anatomy is gorgeous," the woman continued. "Is it based on a model or purely the product of your imagination?"

"It's based on my partner, Patrick." Yu indicated Patrick with a slow smile and a small tilt of his head. "My hope, and my inspiration."

Now Patrick felt dizzy and light, like he might float away if he didn't find something to hold on to. Like he'd sprouted gossamer wings. The way Yu had acknowledged him without even pausing to consider it, in front of so many friends and strangers, lent a surreal quality to everything.

The lights seemed brighter, the colors more vibrant, the hue of the hardwood floor warmer, and the edges of the sculptures and the people admiring them smudged and hazy, as if seen through rippled old glass. It was as if Yu had cast a spell with those few words. Patrick only wished he had some means of showing Yu the magic, sharing the perfect moment with him, but he knew, seeing the sweat beading above Yu's lips, that Yu only wanted to escape. He was a little like Prospero—the great magician who wanted to give up his spell book. He couldn't appreciate the enchantment he'd woven as his audience did, and he just wanted to relinquish it and be alone.

"Can you tell us a little bit about your process?" asked an older man with wild gray curls and clothing that made him look like a homeless English professor: worn brown corduroys, a burgundy waistcoat and matching bow tie, and a blazer with cracker-leather ovals at the elbows. Patrick smiled at him. He could have been some incarnation of the Doctor. Patrick's years at the Faire had taught him to appreciate unique and eccentric people, and he knew Yu would feel comfortable answering his question, explaining how his vision progressed from salvaged steel to the gorgeous piece no one in the room could look away from.

Yu explained it all in technical terms Patrick doubted most of the people listening would understand, talking at length about metal temperatures, carbon compositions, integrity, and quenching processes. Yu was comfortable with these concrete things, and some of the tension dropped from his posture as he spoke about grinding and polishing. The crowd slowly broke up, as those who clearly didn't understand Yu's explanation wandered over to his other pieces or to the wine, cheese, and crackers on the refreshment table. Soon, only Wade, the woman in the black dress, the professor in the tatty clothes, and their friends remained. Patrick retreated a few steps to allow Yu to occupy the spotlight he'd earned, though he watched the line of his back and shoulders closely for signs of distress—in case Yu needed him.

Wade, a man muscled from years of wielding his hammer over his anvil, approached Yu first, his shorn head reflecting the light from the ceiling, and his thick beard almost concealing the severe line of his mouth. He patted Yu's shoulder brusquely and said, "Not bad, I suppose. It looks like you heard a few things I tried to tell you after all. Just when I thought you had rocks for brains. I'll expect you at work tomorrow. We have to get ready for Halloween." With a single nod, Wade turned and departed, leaving Yu with a wide grin. Patrick and everyone else knew that from Wade, this was high praise indeed.

Jen, Henry, Tom, Shawn, Aouli, and the rest of their friends took turns hugging Yu or shaking his hand. Most of them knew him well enough to keep their congratulations brief and honest. The professor in the bow tie took Yu aside and spoke to him for a few minutes, his youthful smile of excitement looking out of place on his sedate, scholarly face. Some other faculty members Patrick recognized came to speak briefly with Yu. Finally, only the woman remained. Yu stiffened a bit as she approached him and took his hand, so Patrick moved to stand behind his shoulder.

"You're a very talented young man," she said, her white teeth, hazel eyes, and diamond jewelry glimmering.

"Thank you, ma'am," Yu managed. He forced a smile for her and then looked over his shoulder, toward the door to the gallery. Patrick wondered why. Maybe Yu just wanted to get away.

"Please, call me Helen. Helen Weiss. I represent two galleries downtown, one in Philadelphia, two in Manhattan, and another in Washington, DC. I'd be very interested in arranging a tour for you. Do you think you'll have any new pieces soon? I can anticipate at least a few of these sculptures will sell at each showing, so you'll have to have enough in reserve to fill each gallery. Would you be interested in setting something up?"

The way Yu curled and uncurled his fingers told Patrick his anxiety was rising as he struggled to find the words to reply. "I-I appreciate your very kind words. However, making weapons and armor with traditional techniques is my greatest passion."

Patrick hurried in front of Yu, smiling and even batting his lashes a little bit. Not long after he'd started doing drag and coming out of his shell in everyday interactions, he'd realized he could charm older women. Rog teased that they sensed his vulnerability and wanted to mother him. The woman returned his warm smile and took Patrick's hand in her cool fingers. He brushed his thumb quickly over the back of her hand before speaking. "Thank you, Ms. Weiss. You'll appreciate that Yu is extremely busy with his graduation coming up in December at the moment, but we'd be happy to consider your offer. Do you have a business card so we can contact you after everything settles down?"

"Of course." With a flash of her teeth, she reached into her tiny beaded handbag and offered Patrick a card. "I hope I'll hear from you soon. I really think I can sell your work, and if you're looking for an agent to represent you, I have some connections."

"Thank you," Yu said in a strained voice.

"Please excuse us for a moment." Patrick took Yu's elbow and guided him toward the door, noticing the way Yu had trouble walking in a straight line and how he sank his fingernails into the flesh of Patrick's forearm.

When they made it outside and around the corner of the building, Yu doubled over and heaved into the frost-tipped grass. Patrick held Yu's hair back as he retched, though he only brought up a mouthful of foamy liquid. Of course, he hadn't eaten anything all day. He stood and wiped his lips on the back of his hand, and Patrick led him to a nearby bench and put his arm over Yu's shoulders to pull him close. Being held usually calmed him. Patrick had observed that the more anxious Yu became, the less he objected to public affection.

"I'm so pathetic," Yu said in a whisper. "How can you stand me?"

Patrick kissed his temple and rubbed his hand up and down Yu's arm. "No. You're everything to me, and I wouldn't care if you hadn't managed to come here at all. But you did, and you did wonderfully. Everyone loved your work, and they loved your answers to their questions. I... I never knew you modeled the *Hope* after me... my body."

Yu nestled his face against Patrick's chest and reached across Patrick to rest his hand on Patrick's hip. "You're the most beautiful man I've ever seen."

"I guess you've never looked in a mirror," Patrick said, nuzzling against the top of Yu's head and breathing in the ocean and sandalwood scent of his shampoo. "I'm so proud of you. Proud to be with you. I know this wasn't easy for you. Do you want to go home?"

Yu didn't lift his head, but he turned his gaze back toward the gallery door and the parking lot beyond it. His thick black eyelashes sparkled with condensation and cast stark shadows on his cheeks. "I want to go back inside, wait a little bit longer to see if anyone else will come."

"Why do you want to torture yourself?"

"I just want to stay a few more minutes," Yu said, playing with the fuzzy edge of Patrick's sweater, rolling the shedding fibers into little balls between his thumb and finger.

Patrick suddenly understood. He'd seen the invitations to the opening sitting beside their computer as Yu had filled them out. One of them had been addressed to his parents, the parents who had cut him off and severed all ties to him when he'd dropped out of his engineering program to pursue an art degree and study weaponsmithing with Wade. Yu was still hoping they might come, and Patrick wished they would, too, so he could tell them how much they'd hurt the most wonderful man he'd ever met, just because Yu wanted to follow his dreams instead of becoming a mindless, white-collar drone.

Instead of venting his anger, Patrick stood, took Yu's hand, and led him back inside. They waited beside the refreshment table until the janitors finally arrived to clean up and lock the building, and then Patrick led Yu to their Ford SUV and drove him back to their tiny apartment in Shadyside, back home.

Chapter 2

AS SOON as Patrick unlocked the door, Yu hurried to the cupboard above their sink and retrieved his little orange prescription bottle. He swallowed down the remaining half of his Xanax without even bothering to pour a glass of water. Worried, Patrick led him to the sofa in the next room and helped him sit down. He removed Yu's shiny leather dress shoes and tight black socks, then lit a fire in their gas-powered hearth. Soon, orange-and-black triangles with tattered edges fluttered, casting the room in soft light, and the temperature rose to a comfortable toastiness.

"Put some music on." Patrick placed the remote in Yu's hand, though Yu barely seemed to acknowledge it as he stared into the flames.

In the kitchen, Patrick sliced a ciabatta roll and put it on a plate. After spreading some pesto mayonnaise on both sides, he piled it high with prosciutto, smoked turkey, sliced tomato, and aged provolone cheese. Then he selected a bottle of valpolicella from the wine rack Yu had made to look like rose fronds twined together, and filled two glasses. Balancing the plate on his elbow and holding the stems of the glasses in his other hand, Patrick returned to their living room, where Yu still sat holding the remote and staring into the fireplace.

Patrick set the food and drinks on the coffee table and gently slid the remote from Yu's grasping fingers. When he first hit play, Switchblade Symphony's "Witches," a darkwave song he'd contemplated performing to for Halloween came on, but he quickly switched it to Handel's "Water Music." He sat down and moved his back against the arm of the sofa, then grasped Yu's biceps to pull Yu's back against his chest. "I made you a sandwich. You should try to eat something."

Damn, if only he could do more for Yu than make a stupid sandwich! Patrick just didn't know how else to help him.

Yu nodded, letting the back of his head rest against Patrick's collarbone, though he made no attempt to reach for his food. "Patrick, the university wants to add the *Hope Validated* to their permanent collection. They want to buy it."

Patrick slid down until he could rest his head against the arm of the couch. Yu adjusted, wriggling a bit until their bodies lay flush, with the side of Yu's face against Patrick's chest. Patrick opened his legs and bent his knees so Yu lay between them, his old Chuck Taylors resting on the couch by Yu's waist. He ran his fingers up and down the silky length of Yu's tie a few times before he pulled at the knot to loosen it, leaning down to peck along Yu's hairline as he popped the top button of his shirt. "That's great."

Yu reached for his wine and took a few noisy swallows before setting it back down. "I made it for you."

Patrick ran his fingertips over the cords of muscle at Yu's neck, then stopped to pinch his earlobe. It felt like a flower petal, that soft little tab of flesh. "It's okay. You're an artist; you make a living by selling your art. Just because lots of people will look at it and appreciate its beauty doesn't mean it won't be mine. I like the idea of others getting to enjoy it, thinking about what it stands for."

Yu reached up to brush the thick fringe from Patrick's forehead. "I'm so lucky. I love you." He drank a few more sips of wine.

"I love you. I still can't believe you modeled it after me." Patrick slipped his fingers beneath Yu's open collar and grazed his fingertips over Yu's soft warm skin, tracing the subtle furrow between the muscles of his chest.

"All of them," Yu said, his body draped over Patrick's like a warm blanket, clearly growing drowsy. After the combination of Xanax and wine, it wasn't surprising. Yu's anxiety attacks wore him out. He'd told Patrick many times that he never felt as calm as after they'd passed. "Why did you tell that woman I'd consider showing my work in her galleries?"

"I just didn't want to burn any bridges. I thought I could take her card, and you could contact her if you wanted to. If you don't, no harm done."

"Thank you."

"Eat something, Yu."

Probably just to please Patrick, Yu nibbled a little from the edge of his sandwich and washed it down with a few healthy sips of wine. Soon, he'd settled against Patrick's chest again, the back of his head over Patrick's heart and each of his hands draped over Patrick's knees. Patrick could feel the tension flowing out of Yu's tightly wound muscles as he sunk further into Patrick's embrace.

"*Hoshi no tama*," Yu muttered sleepily.

"What?"

"They're-they're gems where *kitsune* keep their souls. Anyone who acquires one gains control of the *kitsune*, and you have my *hoshi no tama*, Patrick. You have my soul."

"You have mine," Patrick said, mashing his lips against Yu's forehead until he could feel the bone beneath the smooth, golden skin.

"I made a fool of myself tonight," Yu said before finishing his wine.

"You didn't. No one knew but me. You were so strong."

"Why—" Yu's voice hitched. "Why didn't my parents come? I sent them an invitation in the mail. Two, actually. And I e-mailed. Why wouldn't they want to see what I've made?"

"It's their loss," Patrick said, his lips grazing the edge of Yu's ear. He pecked softly along the line between Yu's jaw and his neck, bending almost in half and sucking at the sensitive spot between his neck and ear. "Family doesn't always mean blood. Lots of people came to support you. Even Wade!"

Yu finally laughed, though it sounded bitter to Patrick, and he shook his head against Patrick's chest. "Wade. He didn't even berate me or suggest improvements. That was something. But-but I thought my parents might want to see what I could do, that maybe after they saw my art—"

"Shh." Patrick smoothed his hair down before winding his arms around Yu's waist. "Everyone who saw your work was moved by it. You're an exceptional artist." He kissed Yu softly on the temple and set his abandoned plate on the floor.

"I-I know. But I'm their only son. How can they just not care what happens to me?"

Patrick couldn't answer because he'd wondered the same thing so many times. He hadn't heard from his father since the night he'd kicked Patrick out of the house after finding out he had been performing in drag.

Once in a while his mother called from California to brag about celebrities she'd met at dinner parties, but if she asked about Patrick, it was only so she could make herself sound more important and successful or criticize the choices he had made. "*I* care what happens to you, Yu. *I* love you. *I'm* your family. And you're mine. That-that's all I can do."

Yu lifted one of Patrick's hands from his waist, enclosed it in his calloused palm, brought it to his lips, and kissed the back. "I know. It's funny. I expected you to throw me away too, after you saw how much time I spent working and how dysfunctional I am. I worried about it every day for probably the first year or so. Whenever I looked at you, I wondered if today would be the day you'd decide I wasn't worth it. And now it's been more than two years. I still can't quite believe it. I thought you were too good to be true, and I just kept waiting for the bubble to burst."

It had been two years, and they'd outgrown the little apartment. They barely had room for their things, and Yu desperately needed a workspace of his own now that he wouldn't have access to his studio at the school. Patrick liked the idea of a place to sew and work on his costumes; currently, he had to carry the sewing machine out of the closet and put it on their kitchen table. Then after he finished, he had to put it and all his fabric and threads away, because Yu hated the disorder. Sure, Yu never said anything, but any kind of mess ratcheted up his tension noticeably. It would be nice to have a small room of his own where he got to be a bit of a slob. Besides, they had to make a decision soon about renewing their lease. They'd been excellent tenants, so the building manager had given Patrick a few extra months, but when Yu graduated in December, they'd have to make a choice. Yu didn't need to hear that tonight, though. "I don't know how I can convince you I'm not going anywhere," Patrick said.

Yu lifted his head a little to sip from the last of his wine, and his silky hair brushed against Patrick's neck and his forearms where he'd rolled his shirtsleeves up. Then he spoke with a hitch in his voice, like he might cry. Patrick realized he had never seen Yu cry over anything. The possibility scared the shit out of him; he didn't know what he'd do if he saw Yu shatter like that. "It's okay, Patrick. You don't have to say anything. You don't have to cater to my insecurities. I'm being a baby."

"Hey," Patrick said. "You might feel like you have to hold it all in for everyone else, but not with me. You're human and you have feelings. God knows you've seen me at my worst."

"You don't have a worst." Yu turned on his side and nestled his face into Patrick's sweater vest. He spoke slowly, clearly groggy. "I'm going to make you a *hoshi no tama*, and you can wear it around your neck. That will prove I trust you with my soul. That everything I have belongs to you."

"I'll keep it safe for you." Patrick rubbed circles between Yu's shoulder blades, combed his fingers through Yu's hair, and stroked down the length of his arm. Within a few minutes, Yu's slow, deep breathing told Patrick he'd fallen asleep. He roused him by giving his shoulder a gentle shake and said, "Tomorrow's a Faire day. We should get to bed."

Yu nodded and stood slowly, his clothing rumpled and his lids low over his warm brown eyes. Patrick took his hand, led him to their bedroom, and guided him to the edge of the bed. When Yu sat down, Patrick knelt and reached up to unfasten Yu's belt, followed by the button of his dress trousers. Yu fought to keep his eyes open as Patrick slid the trousers down his legs. After climbing up behind Yu, he slipped his blazer off and slid his tie out of his collar. Then he unbuttoned his shirt, and Yu climbed up the decadent red-satin sheets he'd insisted they buy because he liked the way red looked against Patrick's pale skin. Patrick covered him up and bent down to kiss his cheek and breathe the sea-and-incense scent of his hair and the sweet smell of his skin and sweat beneath it. He gathered up Yu's clothes to take them to the hamper in the bathroom, and with them clutched to his chest, he looked down at Yu. He had imagined tonight ending very differently, and he cursed himself for being unable to help Yu enjoy it and make him want to celebrate. What could he have done differently? But Yu was already asleep, his lips slightly parted, so Patrick put out the light. The bottle of Veuve Clicquot he'd bought sat forgotten in the refrigerator.

After taking care of Yu's clothes, Patrick cleaned up his plate and washed the wine glasses. He sat down on the sofa and watched the flames for a while. The little hope charm, the one Yu had made him back when they'd first met, dangled from a hook in the ceiling above the mantle. Back then, Patrick had needed so badly to have a hope he could hold on to, and Yu had made one for him—strong, from steel. Tonight, Yu needed to sleep and forget about his ordeal, and Patrick would take care of everything so he could. Maybe after the Faire ended for the season and Yu graduated, they could go away for a weekend, somewhere quiet and secluded, and bring that bottle of champagne with them. Patrick had been making enough money performing at clubs that he'd been able to save everything he earned at the Faire, and between Yu's commissions and the sales from the website they'd built together, Yu's Armory, they could spare enough for a brief vacation. Two or three days with nothing to worry about but each other sounded like paradise to Patrick.

Patrick turned off the stereo and then the flames in the fireplace. By the light coming through the blinds from the lampposts outside, he watched his hope charm spinning slowly at the end of its ribbon. Somehow, they'd done it. Against almost impossible odds, they'd built a life together, and a good one. Now, maybe, it was time to move on to the next act, and although Patrick knew it would hurt to watch the curtain fall on their first apartment and all the firsts they'd experienced within it, he would hold that hope Yu had given him fiercely and move forward without fear. They had so much to look forward to.

Chapter 3

PATRICK, IN his minstrel costume with the one green- and one gold-legged hose and the muffin-style hat, walked beside Jen in her resplendent ivory gown with its wide, stiff lace collar tipped in faux pearls to match her tiara. She'd pulled her dark red hair back in a severe bun but allowed a few ringlets to stray, dusted her face in white powder that cracked when she smiled, and painted her lips blood red. Over the course of the Faire season, Jen portrayed Queen Elizabeth from blushing young maiden to the coldly perfect matriarch she now embodied, while Patrick's role, as the troubadour and probable spy and assassin to the queen, stayed the same. Though his character had no basis in historical fact, he and the other cast members had built it up over the past few years, and Queen Bess's minstrel boy had become an object of both desire and speculation among the regular attendees. He'd amassed quite a number of fans all his own, something he would have thought impossible before he had the courage to audition for the cast.

"What troubles thee, brother to my heart if not my blood?" Jen asked, resting a gloved hand on Patrick's shoulder.

"Just… nostalgia, I suppose, Your Majesty." He looked at the daub-and-wattle buildings, autumn flowers pouring from the window boxes and fat pumpkins and gourds lined up along their porches. The oak leaves had turned golden and stood out against the muted gray of the sky. "Are you planning to stay on at the Faire?"

Jen dropped her accent as they reached a small hillock that overlooked the idealized Elizabethan village. Below them, vibrant autumn leaves tumbled across the cobbled walkways and drifted on the breeze. "I-I don't know. Henry got a job offer, to play a Viking warrior in a documentary for the History channel. It's not exactly a starring role, but they were impressed with his theatrical combat training, and it could lead to further opportunities for him. He'll have to go to New Zealand for a few months to film, and I want to go with him."

"Then you should," Patrick said.

"I just feel like I'll be letting everyone here at the Faire down. This is more than a job. We've always been like a family."

"A real family wants you to do what will make you happy, make your dreams come true," Patrick said, thinking of Yu, taking both her hands in his, and leaning his face against the stiff fabric of her gown. "*I* want you to be happy. God knows you deserve it. You know I love you, right?"

"I know. God, Patrick. My minstrel boy. My little brother. Shit. I'm going to cry and ruin my makeup."

Patrick hugged her and caught the tear spilling from her eye on his thumb before it could make her eyeliner run. "Please don't cry unless they're happy tears. A while ago, I looked at my apartment and knew I'd have to move on soon, and I was so tempted to hold on to the familiar things, but then I knew I had to welcome the new opportunities in my life. Yu is going to graduate soon, and we need more space. It's scary, but it's exciting. Go to New Zealand with Henry. What's the worst that can happen? You'll always be welcomed back here, both of you."

"I.... Jesus, what would I do without you? Hearing you say it, it all sounds so obvious. I should go with him, shouldn't I?"

"Do you love him?" Patrick asked.

Jen's gaze moved beyond the banners flapping in the breeze atop the shops. "He's the most wonderful man, always thinking of me before himself, always trying to make me happy. Seeing me happy seems to make him happy.... God, yes, I love him. He's a beautiful man. I want to have his babies, Patrick. I... I think he's *the one*. In fact, I know he is."

"Sounds like you've made up your mind."

Jen leaned in to kiss his cheek. "I knew what I wanted to do, but your support means the world to me. I feel so much better now. Patrick, I want you to sit with me in the royal box at the joust today. Don't argue; I'll clear everything with Tom, but I need you with me."

"I live to serve, Your Majesty," Patrick said with an overly theatrical bow.

Jen smacked him on the ass as he turned away, a stinging slap that left his cheek tingling. "I expect you in my box, minstrel boy."

Patrick couldn't resist. "Sir Henry might enjoy it in there more than I, my queen!"

Then he ran down the hill before she could box his ears. Jen lifted her layers of skirts to follow and pursued him. Patrick sprinted ahead before stopping to look over his shoulder and, in a proud moment of maturity, poked his tongue out at her. He knew she'd never catch him in her corset, pantalets, and layers of petticoats; he'd worn such things himself.

When he reached the edge of the village, Patrick stopped to grab his knees and catch his breath. He knew from the heat on his face that his cheeks were probably as red as the chrysanthemums in the pot outside Mistress Hattie's Haberdashery. Yu loved it when Patrick flushed like that, though usually under different circumstances. Lately Yu hadn't had much chance to make Patrick blush, make his skin turn as red as his tattooed roses, what with his upcoming graduation, getting ready for his senior show, and the many commissions he and Wade had to finish before the Faire closed for the season. The blame wasn't Yu's alone; Patrick had been performing days at the Faire and at least three nights a week at clubs around the city. Sometimes he even traveled far enough to necessitate spending a night or two away from home. Right now, he just really missed Yu.

Patrick made his way past the shops and exhibits to the central fountain surrounded by the food stalls and on to the end of the village, where tents stood for the knights to rest and change between matches. Beyond them were the arena and the blacksmith's shop. When Patrick made his way to the forge, Wade moved out front, arranging swords and shields on a rack so they'd be seen by patrons before or after the joust. At first, Patrick couldn't find Yu and supposed he'd gone for something to eat, but then he saw him standing at the very edge of the grounds, staring off into the Faire's wooded border. Aside from his hair fluttering in the wind, he didn't move for a long time. Patrick knew if Yu wasn't working, work being his balm for nearly any ailment, he must really be hurting. He had also learned over the past few years that when Yu needed space, he *really* needed it, so he resisted his instinct to move behind Yu and wrap his arms around his waist. Yu would let him know when and if he was ready to be comforted.

Though Patrick had been a member of the Faire cast for over two years now, he had started out as a humble employee, and he hadn't quite kicked the habit of making his rounds and seeing if any of the vendors or artisans needed anything between his shows. Besides, doing so took his mind off Yu—a little. After he took a leisurely trip around the grounds and caught up with the friends he'd made, he wandered back toward the jousting arena.

The tiered benches were packed with patrons. Their Faire boasted a true tournament; nothing was choreographed, and no one knew ahead of time which knight would prevail. Though the warriors were trained not to injure each other, the competition could become heated. As usual, patrons sat on either the side of Queen Elizabeth or the Duke of Anjou and his retinue of French chevalier. Boys and girls sold roses and triangular banners emblazoned with either the Tudor rose or the fleur-de-lis.

The knights traditionally gave their finest performances for the season's last tourneys, and they always drew a big crowd. Today, though, every person at the Faire seemed to be watching; the cooks, merchants, and even the groundskeepers and janitors had abandoned their posts to attend. Patrick waved to Tish and Tracy as he made his way to the stairs leading to the royal box, surprised they'd abandoned their shop at such a lucrative time. He found Jen seated with her ladies-in-waiting and took his place on the padded bench beside her. To their left, Eric, looking dashing as always as Sir Francis Drake, sat with some of the other cast members, including Grace O'Malley, the Pirate Queen, and Sir Walter Raleigh. Rog sat next to Eric, along with his nieces, Naomi and Melissa. Melissa cuddled against Rog's side while Naomi perched on his lap. Patrick was a little surprised Eric and Rog hadn't told him the girls would be at the Faire, and he cast a suspicious look at Jen.

"You're up to something."

"My sweet troubadour, you have no idea," Jen said with a wink.

"What—"

The trumpeters' horns drowned out Patrick's question, and Jen stood to thunderous applause. She smiled and waved at her adoring subjects until the noise died down. Then she spoke through a wide smile, looking happier than Patrick had ever seen her. "My good lords and ladies, lads and lasses, to say we have enjoyed these festivities held in our honor would not begin to express the love we feel for each of you. As our bard, good Will Shakespeare might say, 'The sight of lovers feedeth those in love,' and 'tis true. How seeing your happiness and glad faces over these years, seeing the bonds that have formed upon these fair lanes and lawns, has fueled our love in turn, we cannot begin to say, for we are no poet. But please, enjoy the joust, and enjoy our revelries as they reach the end all things must come to."

The crowd applauded, though their confusion subdued them, as Patrick's own did him. Jen usually made a few subtle jokes about the lengths of the knights' lances or how well they hoisted them. Normally, she stirred good-natured rivalry between England and France. Today, she just sat down with a subtle smile as her knights—Sirs Ian, Carlton, and Henry—sat on horseback and looked up at her. "Sir Henry, my champion," Jen said, tying a ribbon from her dress to the end of his lance, "if you love us, show us now."

"Aye, Queen Bess," Henry said. "I'll show the whole world what my love of Your Radiant Majesty can inspire me to. Just watch this, my bonny lass!"

As the joust commenced, Patrick realized how much Henry had held back in other competitions. Clearly, he'd let himself be bested on many occasions, but not today. In each joust, he unseated the French knight he faced, sending each to his back in the sand without ever losing the grip on his lance. Upon dismounting, he made such short work of them in hand-to-hand combat it almost wasn't exciting to watch. Henry could really fight; none of the others even managed to land a blow. Every time he knocked an enemy down, he paused to look up at Jen, and Patrick noticed the smiles she returned and the way her cheeks colored beneath her white makeup. After besting them all, Henry threw his helmet to the side of the track and looked up at his queen. "What more, Majesty? Tell me, and it shall be done. Anything you ask of me will be done."

Patrick expected Jen to swoon and offer congratulations to her champion, but instead, she stood and rested her white-gloved hands on the border of the box. "We would see you honor us in hand-to-hand combat, honorable knight. Tell us, valiant sir. Who would prove the most worthy of adversaries?"

For a few seconds, Henry looked confused, but then his easy smile banished all doubt from his face. "If it would please you, Queen Bess, let me match my skills against Sir Ian!"

"Very well."

The audience went wild at the unexpected turn of events, and Patrick watched as Henry blew Jen a kiss before walking with wide strides to the weapons racks beyond the field. Yu waited at the edge of the sward with an assortment of blades, maces, flails, and halberds for each fighter. Henry and Ian chose their weapons and walked back into the arena to face off. Yu stood with a hand resting on the rack and his face pointed toward the horizon beyond the tournament. Weak autumn sunlight lit the planes of his face. Patrick wished he could have seen Yu's expression better and intuited his mood. He discerned only guarded stiffness from the lines of Yu's posture.

Both knights chose sword and shield. Henry's bore the Tudor rose while Ian's showed a stylized griffon. Sunlight glinted off the polished steel as it poked through the gray cloud cover. The two men faced off in the sand, preparing to meet each other's attacks. Patrick balled his fists and held his breath. Both knights were able combatants, and both of them were his friends.

Before they clashed, Jen stood and spoke. "Sir Henry, your reward, should you win this match, will be… quite extraordinary. Commence! For England!"

Henry raised his shield, and Ian's first two strikes bounced harmlessly off Yu's steel. Henry sank into a crouch as Ian's onslaught continued, but when he found an opening, Henry kicked out and caught Ian's knee, sending him to his back. Before Henry could press his advantage, Ian arced his body, landed on his feet, and retreated a few steps. Patrick rested his elbows on the railing as he leaned in to get closer to the action. The knights' athleticism always amazed him; it was so different than what he could achieve as a dancer. Their speed and grace in their heavy armor impressed him to no end. Henry attacked, his blade bouncing off Ian's shield.

The two knights traded blows, and the audience sat silent as steel struck steel with resounding pings. Henry hacked downward, and Ian raised his shield above his head to deflect the blow. At the same time, Ian drove the pummel of his blade into Henry's breastplate, making Henry double over and stumble back a few steps. Ian pressed his advantage, but at the last minute, Henry tucked and rolled away from the downward slice Ian directed at him. Watching, Patrick found it easy to forget both knights had trained in theatrical combat, and while the competition was very real, there was no danger of either hacking off an arm or a head. Watching, it felt like a battle to the death. Patrick's heart beat against the back of his throat.

Henry got to his feet and directed a series of quick jabs at his opponent, which Ian easily blocked with his shield. Ian swiped at Henry's thigh, but Henry dodged to the left and avoided it. Evenly matched, they attacked and dodged, both landing a glancing blow here and there, but nothing decisive, until it became clear to Patrick both had grown exhausted. Their thrusts became slow and lurching, and Henry's blond hair hung around his flushed face in sweaty clumps. Dark blotches marred his face as blood pooled beneath his fair skin. Both knights groaned with exertion as they continued the match.

Patrick tugged Jen's sleeve. "You have to declare a draw," he said when he managed to tear her attention away from the fighters. "They're done for, and at this point the winning blow will be nothing but luck. They're friends; don't encourage animosity between them."

"You're right," Jen whispered. Then she stood, and when she spoke, her strong, clear voice carried above the sounds of clashing steel. "Please be still. It would seem our English knights are all so skilled that determining a champion will be impossible. Sir Ian, Sir Henry, we thank you both for your devotion. It is little wonder ours is the finest kingdom on God's sweet earth, the finest in all of Christendom, when fine young men such as you are willing to fight for her, and for us. Your dedication humbles us."

"Your Majesty, I must protest!" Henry hollered in a rough and tired voice. "I can prevail. For you—"

"Nay, my goodly knight." Jen stood. She held up her layers of skirts as she turned and made her way slowly down the steep steps from the royal box. A few minutes later, she emerged on the field, the train of her gown carving furrows in the sand as she approached her warriors. She leaned in and kissed Ian's cylindrical helmet, saying something to him Patrick couldn't hear. Sir Ian scooped up her hand, kissed the back, and bowed before turning and leaving the arena. Jen approached Henry and stood a few feet away, the two of them just looking at each other as the audience held its collective breath.

To Patrick's surprise—and everyone else's, judging by the unanimous gasp—Jen dropped to her knees in the churned-up sand. Patrick winced, remembering when he'd been responsible for cleaning and maintaining the women's costumes, but he soon dismissed his worries about how hard it would be to get those stains out of the white satin.

Jen reached out and took one of Henry's gauntleted hands in hers. She stripped his chain-mail glove away and let it fall with a small cloud in the sand. She looked earnestly up at his face, framed in blowing blond hair and edged with brown stubble. Patrick knew neither of them noticed the hundred or so people watching; all Jen and Henry saw was each other.

"Henry," Jen said, "you are the finest man I've ever known. I can't imagine my life without you in it. You're brave and valiant but kind and caring. I—"

Jen reached into a pocket of her billowing skirts and then held a small black-velvet box up to Henry. "I want you to be my husband, be my companion through life. Will you? Will you always be my champion? Henry, will you marry me?"

Henry blinked hard a few times, and then he slid the ring onto his finger, his lips pursed tight. "Hell yes!" He pulled Jen to her feet, punched the air, and drew her in for a deep kiss. The audience cheered, many people getting to their feet and throwing flowers at the couple, but Henry and Jen didn't seem to notice any of it. The flashes of cameras never fazed them. They just clung to each other and kissed like it was their last day on earth.

Patrick scrubbed the tears from his cheeks before dashing down the stairs to join his friends. Already, a crowd surrounded them, made up of their friends from the Faire and patrons looking for a photo of the momentous occasion. Patrick pushed his way through the throng and reached Jen just as Tom released her from a long hug. He threw himself into her arms, and both of them buried their faces in each other's shoulders and cried.

"Congratulations," Patrick managed to choke out. "God, I'm so happy for you both."

Jen released him, and Patrick was soon swept up in Henry's strong embrace and lifted off the ground. Cameras clicked and flashed around them, but they didn't stop Henry from kissing Patrick on the cheek. "Holy shit, dude! She asked me to marry her! Jen's gonna be my wife! She wants *me*!"

Patrick pulled away and regarded Henry through the blur of his watery eyes. "Treat her like a queen, or you'll answer to me. She's special."

Henry kissed him again, on the forehead. "Aye, I know it, minstrel boy. I feel like I just won the lottery. Holy shit. I had no idea!"

Patrick stepped away so the long line of people waiting to hug and congratulate Henry and Jen could take their turns. He wandered toward the edge of the arena, weaving through the crowd. Everyone at the Faire seemed to be waiting to speak to the happy couple. Finally, Patrick cleared the mass of bodies and found Yu still standing near the weapons rack. Yu's smile seemed sad as he took Patrick's hand and led him toward the tree line. Soon, they stood squeezing each other's fingers as they looked into the gray woods surrounding the grounds. As they watched, the autumn breeze tore the last of the russet leaves from the oak branches, making the thinner twigs rattle together.

"I think they'll be very happy together," Yu said, just above a whisper.

"Yeah, me too," Patrick agreed. "They really love each other. I'm happy for them. Yu, are you okay?"

"Their parents will come to the wedding," Yu said, his gaze on the horizon beyond the small forest. "They will be so proud."

"Yeah," Patrick responded. "Yeah, and they should be. But I'm proud of you. Of our life together. It's good, isn't it?"

"It is, Patrick."

"Then... what?"

"I hate to admit it, but I wish my parents could be happy for what I've achieved. They've never even met you. They'll never know how lucky I am or how happy we are together. I know I shouldn't be thinking of myself right now—it's Jen and Henry's moment—but I can't help it. I'm sorry, my love. I thought I was over all this."

"I thought so too. What changed?"

Yu tried to pull away, but Patrick held him firm. "I'm acting like a child," Yu said, his disgust with himself plain in his voice.

"Knock it off. Tell me why this is bothering you so much after all this time."

"I… I accepted it when they were no longer willing to pay for my education," Yu said. "I guess, somewhere at the back of mind, whether I acknowledged it or not, I expected them to come around. To see that I'd made it on my own and be proud of me for that. To see the quality of my work and acknowledge I was talented. To see I worked hard and led a good life. I just thought… I thought somehow, even if they disapproved of my choices, they still loved me."

"Yu…." Patrick held Yu, pulling Yu's body tight against his own. "If it means anything, you… you're my world. *I* love you."

"I love you too, Patrick," Yu said in a hoarse whisper. "So much. I—"

"What?"

"Nothing," Yu said. "Let's go congratulate our friends."

"And then what?" Patrick asked, keeping his arms around Yu's waist and holding tight.

"Then… I don't know. We go back to work."

"Okay, Yu," Patrick said, holding Yu's hand as they approached the crowd surrounding Henry and Jen. Yu shied from the loud voices, and Patrick wanted to wrap his arms around Yu's head and protect him, but he didn't want to insult Yu, imply weakness.

Yu kissed Henry and Jen's hands and bowed to them. He promised to make something special for their nuptials, and as soon as he felt it would be acceptable, Yu hurried away. Patrick jogged after him and met him back at the edge of the woods.

"Are you okay?" Patrick asked.

Yu nodded. "It's just… so many people talking…."

"Hey, I know." Patrick folded Yu into his arms. To his surprise, Yu gave his weight to Patrick, going almost limp against Patrick's chest. He would have probably fallen if Patrick had released him, but Patrick had no intention of doing that, ever.

"It's no wonder they don't want me," Yu said, his words like a knife through Patrick's chest.

"They're fools. They don't deserve you. Neither do I. But I'll be here for as long as you'll put up with me, Yu. I'm on my own too, but—"

Yu pulled back so he could lock his gaze with Patrick's, and he moved his hand up Patrick's arm and neck to cup his cheek. "I-I'm so sorry, Patrick. You're estranged from your family too, and I acted like my tragedy was so unique. I'm a selfish bastard, aren't I?"

Patrick leaned into his hand. "No. My family is wonderful. It's you, and Henry and Jen, and Tom, Tish and Tracy, Eric and Rog, Aouli and Shawn. My life is full, and I'm content to share it with the people who want to share it with me."

Behind them, the noise from the crowd lessened as people moved away from the jousting arena. Patrick grinned and said, "The Last Huzzah should be especially vulgar tonight. Will you come?"

"If you want," Yu said, brushing his fingertips over the contours of Patrick's face and never looking away from his eyes. "I like hearing you sing and seeing you happy."

"I wish I could make you happy."

"I have a lot of commissions to finish before next weekend," Yu said, moving his fingers to trace the edge of Patrick's ear, "some really creative armor projects made to look like skulls and bones, but... but I think they can wait. Tonight, I want to make you a meal, have a glass of wine, watch a movie on the sofa, and make love to you. I need that. Would that be all right, Patrick?"

"If spoiling me will make you feel better...." Patrick said, his eyes fluttering shut and his body reacting to the images in his imagination. He leaned into Yu, pressing their bellies tightly together. Then reality intruded. "Shit. I have to perform tonight. No. No, I'll cancel. Say I'm sick or something."

Yu kissed Patrick's closed eyelid. "I don't expect you to do that."

"I want to. I miss you. Need you. Need you to be all right. It's just Joe's, anyway. Not a once-in-a-lifetime show or anything." He angled his head to brush his lips over Yu's. "Just make it worth it to me."

"I'll stop at the store on my way home," Yu said against Patrick's mouth, making Patrick chuckle.

"You could stop at McDonald's, and I'll be happy, as long as I have you."

"Horrifying," Yu said, nibbling along Patrick's lower lip. "I would never subject you to that. Life is too short to eat something like that."

"Foodie," Patrick teased. "Now let me go. These last few hours are already going to be unbearably long without the added nuisance of me walking around with a semi."

Yu groaned as he released Patrick, and Patrick pecked him a few more times on his full, rose-colored lips before turning and running back toward their little Tudor village. As much as Patrick loved the Faire, the day couldn't end soon enough. It had been way too long since he and Yu had had an evening together, and if Yu was willing to put off his work…. Well, Patrick didn't expect that to happen twice in a lifetime.

Chapter 4

AS PATRICK had suspected, the Faire's extravagant musical finale, which the cast called the Last Huzzah, lasted well past twilight. Patrons on the benches kept calling for one last song, and the selections became bawdier as those with children left for the night. Before long, Faire regulars had joined the actors on the stage, all of them draping their arms over each other's shoulders and singing together. Soon, the Faire would close for the winter, and for Patrick, it might be his last season, depending on what he and Yu decided to do now that Yu had finished his degree. Patrick was loath to let it go; the Faire had been the first place he'd ever felt accepted, and most of the people he loved stood beside him, belting out dirty limericks at the top of their lungs and just enjoying being there together.

When the performance on the stage broke up, most of the remaining people made their way to the Faire's tavern, the Saucy Stew, where the drinking, singing, and dancing would continue well into the night. As much as Patrick wanted to get home to Yu and the evening he'd been looking forward to all afternoon, he couldn't deny Jen one drink to toast her engagement when she'd said, "Minstrel boy, how many times do you think I'm going to get married? I'd think my best friend could spare a half an hour to have a drink and celebrate with me."

Finally, though many people tried to delay him, Patrick escaped the raucous pub and made his way to his faithful old Plymouth Horizon, parked on its own in the yellowing grass beyond the Faire gates. He carefully navigated the dirt road to the highway, and then he drove too fast to their apartment in Pittsburgh's Shadyside neighborhood.

Wonderful aromas met Patrick's nose as he unlocked the door and entered their apartment. Yu hadn't turned on any of the lights, but he'd lit candles all over the kitchen countertops, table, the floor leading into the living room, and over the surface of the coffee table in front of the sofa. Small flames flickered in the gas fireplace, and Yu had their meal arranged on the low table beside the couch. He sat on his heels, still in the simple white shirt and tight gray leggings he wore at the Faire, smiling as he arranged the silverware by the china and then filled the wine glasses.

"What did you make?" Patrick asked, sitting on the edge of the sofa to pull off his battered old boots. "It smells wonderful."

Yu smiled, the firelight reflecting off his eyes and deepening the shadows around them. A few strands of hair had come loose from his ponytail and hung around his face, the ends brushing the prominent collarbones his unlaced shirt exposed. In that moment Patrick decided he preferred Yu disheveled. Preferred delight in disorder. Yu was so damn delightful in his disorder. Just… perfect in imperfection.

Yu took Patrick's hand and gently urged Patrick to sit beside him on the floor. They ate like this many nights, and not just because some piece of armor Yu was polishing or a sewing project of Patrick's occupied the kitchen table. Sitting this way, they could lean back against their secondhand sofa and let their shoulders brush together. They could share bites of each other's food and lean in to taste the wine on each other's lips, which, even after two years, they still enjoyed. Patrick smiled as he looked at their hearth. The rug in front of it had seen a lot of action.

"I'm afraid it's a pretty simple meal," Yu said, and Patrick rolled his eyes. Yu cooked like he did everything else: with passion, dedication, and attention to detail, accepting nothing less than perfection. "Just some filet steaks, braised root vegetables, and a wild mushroom risotto with porcini oil. The wine shop was closed by the time I got there, though. I thought maybe we could open one of the bottles we've been saving."

"Good idea." Yu had made them three different wine racks, one in the kitchen and two in here, and not only were all of them full, but bottles sat on the counter and floor around them. Patrick stood up and selected the bottle of Silver Oak Cabernet Sauvignon Tom had bought them two years ago for the combined celebration of Patrick's birthday and their housewarming. He dusted it off on his sleeve and handed it to Yu to open.

Yu looked at the bottle with wide eyes, and then up at Patrick. "But this is for a special occasion."

Patrick smiled indulgently. "Love, we have enough wine stashed away for months of special occasions. For all we know, this might be our last chance to enjoy it. You never know what tomorrow might bring. Let's enjoy tonight."

Yu's lips turned down, and a little crease formed between his brows. Patrick's words had worried him.

Patrick knelt down and brushed a few errant strands of hair out of Yu's face before leaning in to kiss him softly. "Isn't this special, Yu? Celebrating what we've built here together? Your graduation? Our life and being together?" He brushed his lips over Yu's again, then sat down and rested his head on Yu's shoulder. "'What is love? 'Tis not hereafter; Present mirth hath present laughter; What's to come is still unsure.' Let's drink this shit."

With a chuckle, Yu opened the wine, poured some into each glass, and held one to Patrick's lips. Patrick took a small sip and sighed at the complex layers of plum, blackberry, and spice. He let his eyes close as he swished it around in his mouth before swallowing.

"Open," Yu said.

Patrick did. A small cube of steak slid between his lips, and he used his teeth to pull it from the fork and into his mouth. Juice burst across his palate as he bit down, and he groaned with pleasure as he chewed.

"Good?" Yu asked.

After swallowing his food, Patrick tilted his head back and opened his eyes. Yu looked down at him, smiling before kissing him softly. Next he fed Patrick a tiny white carrot covered in what tasted like balsamic glaze, followed by another sip of wine. Patrick sat up and plucked a grilled spear of asparagus from Yu's plate. He lifted it to Yu's lips, and Yu sucked it into his mouth, followed by Patrick's fingers. He flicked the tip of his tongue against the pads a few times before chewing his food. They fed each other a few more bites and shared a few more smoky, peppery kisses before tucking into their meals in earnest. Both of them had worked hard all day and were hungry, and within a few minutes, they reclined against the sofa, holding their bellies and drinking their wine. Not long after, they'd finished the bottle. Patrick nestled closer to Yu, and Yu put his arm around Patrick's shoulder and dropped light kisses across his forehead.

"Are you ready to go to bed?" Yu asked, rubbing the tip of his nose along the bridge of Patrick's before dipping down to nibble Patrick's lower lip.

"I should shower," Patrick said. "I get sweaty performing."

Yu kissed him again, moving his lips along Patrick's jaw, down his neck and back up to trace his tongue over the edge of Patrick's ear. "Go ahead. I'll clean up the dishes."

Patrick raked his fingers up Yu's back, feeling hot, hard cords of muscle beneath the thin cotton. "Leave them. Please leave them, Yu. Come in with me."

Yu sighed out a cloud of hot breath, ruffling Patrick's hair. "You know I'll just keep thinking about them out here dirty. I don't want them distracting me. At least let me rinse them off and put them in the sink."

Patrick pulled away, wishing he could take Yu's attention away from dirty dishes, but knowing Yu didn't mean it that way. He just needed his routine, needed things a certain way to be comfortable. He needed order, and Patrick could accept that. He kissed Yu again and then said, "Please don't keep me waiting. I've really missed you."

Yu nodded and began gathering up the dishes and silverware as Patrick made his way down the hall to their small bathroom. He stripped off his Faire costume and deposited it in the hamper. He ran his palm over his chest and belly, feeling the sandpapery texture of emerging stubble. Since he'd cancelled his performance tonight and wouldn't have to be on stage—other than at the Faire—for a week, he wouldn't need to shave. He didn't really mind shaving, but it took time to do a thorough job. He had better things to do with his time tonight.

Patrick turned on the water and stepped behind the checkered vinyl curtain. It felt nice to wash away the perspiration and grime that built on his skin after a twelve-hour day at the Faire. By the time he heard the curtain rustling and the little plastic rings sliding along the bar, he'd shampooed his hair, soaped up, and rinsed off. It felt damn good to be clean.

Yu smiled as he stepped into the shower, and Patrick moved to the back so Yu could get under the spray. God, he looked so beautiful with his dark hair hanging free around the taut muscles of his shoulders, the ends clumping together and trailing rivulets down the bumps and ridges of his stomach, right into the sparse dark hair framing his pretty uncut cock. Patrick adored that cock. Watching Yu's muscles stretch and contract as he washed himself, the water accentuating the angles of his gorgeous body, made Patrick instantly hard. He thought he might come just from the way Yu's muscles moved beneath his wonderful golden skin, the way his eyes closed and his lips parted slightly beneath the pleasure of the hot water....

Patrick groaned, and Yu opened his eyes, water turning his thick black lashes to curling spikes. His gaze went from Patrick's face to his swollen cock. "See something you like?"

"Something… fuck. You are so fucking hot." Patrick closed the distance between them and rubbed his erection against Yu's belly as he nipped and sucked up Yu's neck, which he knew drove him crazy. The place just below Yu's earlobe, when Patrick sucked on it, could almost finish him. He could feel Yu's pulse and the swish of his blood beneath his lips, and he drew the heated skin between his teeth, careful not to leave a bruise. The bitter taste of soap met his tongue, but Patrick didn't pull away. He ran his hands up Yu's waist, over all that steel-hard but slender musculature, and Yu's cock filled and pressed alongside Patrick's. "I still can't believe you're mine."

"I'll make you believe it," Yu panted against the pale globe of Patrick's shoulder. Patrick watched his lips, dark and exotic next to Patrick's freckled white flesh. He sucked on Patrick's skin, causing a tingling sensation and a purplish-red ellipse when he removed his mouth with a pop. His rough sucking and biting kisses continued across Patrick's collarbone and down his chest and belly, marking him, until Yu knelt in front of him, looking up at Patrick with sparkling, honey-brown eyes as he teased the ticklish places along Patrick's waist with his lips. Water spilled over his face, dripped from the ends of his hair, and meandered over the hills and valleys of his beautiful body.

"Oh my God," Patrick muttered, knotting his fingers in Yu's silky wet hair and letting the back of his head rest against the tiles behind him as Yu cupped his balls and licked slowly up his length. Yu swiped his tongue over Patrick's slit and then circled it around the edge of Patrick's head. Before Patrick could stop him, tell him he didn't want it to end yet, Yu had sucked Patrick deep into his mouth and throat, swallowing around Patrick's erection and drawing it deeper. Almost against his will, Patrick fisted handfuls of Yu's hair to pull him closer, and Yu let himself be tugged until his nose grazed Patrick's emerging treasure trail.

Patrick thrust into the accepting heat of Yu's mouth and throat a few times before regaining his control. "Yu, stop. Please, please not yet."

Yu drew his mouth slowly up Patrick's cock before relinquishing it with obvious reluctance and giving the tip a few last flicks with his tongue. "Why not?"

"I-I want to take care of you too. You know my favorite thing is to—"

Before Patrick could finish, Yu was on his feet and kissing Patrick hard, his tongue pounding against Patrick's as he wound his arms around Patrick's waist and pulled their bodies flush. Without disconnecting, Yu stepped to the side, moved them out of the shower, and turned off the water. They stood, dripping puddles on the tile, as they kissed and circled their hips, grinding their cocks against each other's bellies, wet skin slipping and sliding against wet skin. Yu grabbed a towel, and they did a hurried and incomplete job of drying themselves off before staggering back toward their bedroom. When they fell against the red-satin sheets, their moisture darkened the fabric. Patrick could see it in the amber light spilling through the gaps in the blinds.

Yu stood and turned on the bedside lamp. He liked to watch, liked to look at Patrick's lanky, ivory limbs against the crimson bedclothes. He'd spent way too much on the sheets just because he liked seeing Patrick in, or on, red. His cheeks heating, Patrick stretched his arms and legs across the silky fabric, showing off for Yu, making Yu groan as he pushed himself up on his elbows, spread his legs, and used his hand to lift his full balls out of the way and expose his dark pink cleft. With his other hand, he trailed two fingers lightly over his crease. Yu's lips swelled and darkened, and color stained his cheeks as he watched. His cock pointed straight out, a little pearl welling on the tip, but he just stood looking down.

"Patrick, I wish you could see how beautiful you are, with your red hair and red lips and cheeks… your perfect white skin… touching yourself for me…. Keep touching yourself for me."

"But I don't want to touch myself when I could be getting touched by you," Patrick said, purposely sounding a little bratty even as he circled his wrinkled opening with his finger. Performing in drag at clubs had taught him how to tease, how to ramp up anticipation and desire, though a show like this would only ever be for Yu. He sighed and tossed his hair, tracing the edge of his nipple with the thumb of his opposite hand. Watching Yu's face, he decided to play along, to see how long it might take him to drive Yu into such a frenzy Yu couldn't resist jumping on top of him. Yu could be very disciplined—he liked to prolong the prelude to their lovemaking until he had Patrick babbling and begging like a fool— but Patrick knew he could be very persuasive. Tonight, Yu would be the one falling apart in his desire for Patrick.

Slowly, Patrick dragged his hand over his balls and shaft, smooth stomach, chest, and neck. He traced circles over his lips with his fingers before sucking on them, getting them wet and then moving them back down his body. Yu's gaze followed their descent and the glistening trails they left on Patrick's skin. Yu's eyelids drooped over his dilated eyes, and he lapped at his teeth and chewed his lower lip. Patrick just held his gaze as he scratched his fingernails through the red stubble surrounding his cock and then moved up his length to swirl his precome around the tip of his erection. He lifted his fingers to his mouth to lick away the streaks of white fluid, and that was all it took.

With something between a purr and a groan, Yu planted his knee on the bed and reached for Patrick's hip. Patrick caught his wrist and then his gaze, running his tongue along the edges of his teeth as Yu watched, his pupils almost eclipsing the amber of his eyes.

"You wanted to watch, and you're going to watch." The warm sense of security Patrick experienced as he released Yu's hand to rake his nails down Yu's waist felt different from the power he felt onstage, when every man in the audience stood captivated by him, their pleasure hinging on a twist of his waist or a flick of his wrist. When he performed, he felt a tyrannical control over those watching: the ability to either validate their hopes or crush them with a single glance or smile. With Yu, he felt like a mystical treasure, maybe one of those orbs containing the spirit of a fox, that when revealed could command his lover's attention. Unlike the men who watched him dance, nothing cheap or sordid came from Yu; he radiated only need and a sense of awe. He clearly cherished Patrick, and though Patrick knew he could devastate him with a small gesture, Patrick would never exercise that power. Running his hands over his skin, tracing the length of his cock, raising his hips and plucking his nipples while Yu watched, Patrick felt even more beautiful than he did as Queen Titania.

Yu reached for Patrick again, and Patrick pressed a palm to the center of his chest to stop him. "Watch. I want you to see how I feel with you looking at me. I feel so sexy, so beautiful, with you watching me like that."

A strangled moan escaped Yu's throat, and when he squeezed his eyes shut, a single tear ran down his cheek. "You are. I wish I could capture that beauty. I can't even come close. Patrick—"

Patrick ran his hand up Yu's neck and pressed his fingers to Yu's lips to quiet him. As he took his other hand away from his erection and splayed it across his belly, he said, "See? See what you do to me just by standing there? I'm not even touching myself." Yet drop after drop of pearly seed pooled in and around Patrick's belly button.

A clearish-white trickle ran slowly down the length of Yu's cock, and he grunted. "You *are* a spirit. You must be." His reserved exterior was cracking, his need pouring out like a golden light from the fissures, brighter and brighter as Patrick spread his legs and circled his opening with his finger. Yu trembled all over, pulling apart, the splits in the façade he showed the world gaping wide enough for Patrick to see the hot, raw core of his lust. The soul he only trusted Patrick with. "Patrick, please...."

"Take me now," Patrick said in a whisper that scratched his throat on the way out.

Yu dropped on top of him, thrusting his tongue into Patrick's mouth and cradling the back of Patrick's head with one hand while he pushed Patrick's knee alongside his ribs with the other.

Patrick knew he wouldn't be gentle, not after the way he had provoked him and led him to the edge of desire.

"Want you, Patrick. Need you so bad. Please. Can I—"

"God, yes!" Patrick gripped Yu's hips and pulled him forward. At the same time, he lifted his legs and rested his calves on Yu's shoulders. "Yes, Yu. God, yes! I want you."

Yu lifted himself up so he could look into Patrick's eyes. "Are you sure? I thought you wanted... you love to sixty-nine...."

"I love you, and I want you," Patrick said, arching up and rubbing his crevice against Yu. "I want you now. Inside me. Now!"

For once, Yu didn't stop to consider. He didn't spend forever kissing up and down the insides of Patrick's thighs, taking an eternity on each leg until he reduced Patrick to a molten, malleable heap he could shape into anything he wanted. He didn't spend prolonged moments tracing the lines of Patrick's tattooed roses with his tongue. He just reached into the night-table drawer, fumbling to get it open as he licked with wide swipes along Patrick's jaw and over his Adam's apple. Finally, he managed to get the lube and flick it open. Dollops of cold jelly fell over Patrick's crotch as Yu, in his arousal, the state Patrick had brought him to just by touching himself, aimed the slick where he wanted it while sucking and nipping the skin of Patrick's neck.

Enough of the lube reached where it needed to go, and Patrick felt the oily coolness sliding between his cheeks as he relaxed his muscles. "Yu, I want you in me," he demanded.

Yu complied, pushing past the slight resistance of Patrick's muscles and burying himself in Patrick's body.

It was heaven for Patrick, being connected so intimately, being so filled with Yu's body. The slight burn and stretch just made it more visceral, more intense. He rocked his hips up to meet Yu's hesitant thrust. "What's wrong?"

Yu dragged his lips up Patrick's neck, shuddering as he held Patrick with his cock buried deep inside him. "I-I love you. I don't want to hurt you."

"You're not. I know what to do now." Patrick rolled his hips up as he burrowed his face into Yu's hair, savoring the clean scent. He hooked his knees over Yu's shoulders and pressed his heels against the small of Yu's back to urge him forward. Then he flexed his inner muscles, clenching them tightly around Yu's cock and making Yu practically whimper and drop his forehead against Patrick's. "All you're doing is making me happy. Don't stop. Please don't stop. Just... just fuck me! I need this, Yu. Need you."

"I... okay." Yu pushed into him, his fat cockhead bumping against Patrick's sweet spot. "I-I'll make it good for you... my love.... Patrick...."

"Always do," Patrick muttered. "Give it to me, Yu. Just let go. I need that. Need you to take care of *you*. Just-just take what you need from me tonight."

With a rumbling groan, Yu did as Patrick asked, thrusting into him hard and deep, hitting his prostate with every stroke. "You like that?"

"Jesus, you have to ask?" Patrick panted, throwing his head back and curling his fingers around Yu's shoulders. "More, Yu. All of you."

"Okay." Yu buried his face against Patrick's chest as he pushed into Patrick with long but quick strokes. "How's this?"

"More."

"God, I—" Yu pressed in harder, faster, suckling and nipping across Patrick's shoulders as he gave Patrick everything he had. With his fingers, he kneaded the back of Patrick's neck while he grasped Patrick's cock in his other hand. Patrick wound his hand around the loose, swaying strands of Yu's hair and pulled their faces together. As he circled Yu's tongue and Yu stroked him, his dick hitting Patrick's honey spot with every thrust, Patrick gave in to his pleasure and came all over Yu's chest and belly, along with his own. Yu moaned, skimmed his fingers through the semen pooled above Patrick's sternum, scooped some up, and licked it away. As he did, wet warmth filled Patrick's body, and Patrick tightened his muscles to milk every drop from Yu. Every clench of his opening made Yu bite back a yell, and Yu dropped his forehead to Patrick's chest, trembling all over.

"Patrick…. God, I love you."

"I love you too. You… you make me feel things I would have thought were impossible before. I-I love it when you fuck me. God, sorry. I don't mean to be vulgar, but—"

Yu propped himself up and kissed Patrick softly. "Say what's on your mind."

"I… Okay. I love it when you fuck me like this. God. God, Yu. I've really missed this. You inside me. You letting go and taking me like you can't stop yourself. Needed it. Next time… next time I'm going to make you scream. You won't be able to stop yourself."

"You might kill me, you know." Yu sprinkled kisses all over Patrick's face as he carded his fingers through Patrick's thick hair. "I love to fuck you, and I… I love you, Patrick. It's never been like this for me with anyone else. You make me sloppy, out of control. Are you sure I didn't hurt you?"

Patrick squeezed his muscles around Yu's softening cock and it jerked inside him. The edges of his opening felt rough and puffy. "Only in the really, really good way. The way that'll make me want you to fuck me again in the morning so the tenderness stays with me all day. I like that I can make you lose control. It's good to lose control sometimes."

"You might destroy me," Yu said against Patrick's cheek. "And I don't care. I-I'm so happy."

His orgasm had made him sleepy, and Patrick nestled down into the pillows, then turned on his side with his back to Yu, ignoring the mess on his belly and the backs of his thighs. Yu quickly curled around him and rested his chin on Patrick's shoulder, digging the rounded tip in between Patrick's neck and chest. "Me too. I never thought I could love someone like I love you," Patrick whispered, grasping Yu's hand and kissing the back. He could smell his seed on Yu's skin. "I think I knew it the first time I saw you."

"So did I." Yu edged closer, his chest warm and satiny against Patrick's back as he lightly kissed the tender places he'd left on Patrick's shoulder. "To think I wasted all that time being afraid, afraid I couldn't depend on you. You're the one person in this world I can depend on."

"And now we'll have it forever. It'll always be like this." Yu's words made Patrick tingle with joy as he realized Yu had finally let go of the fear of being judged too much trouble, at least by Patrick. "*Oyasumi nasai*, Yu," he whispered sleepily.

Yu inhaled sharply and stiffened behind Patrick, and Patrick realized the mistake he had made. Yu had told him that was how his mother had told him good night, and with those two words Patrick had reminded him of his recent worries only minutes after having distracted him. Patrick stroked Yu's forearm in the hope of helping him relax again, which he eventually did.

Even after his long work day, Patrick lay awake long after they put out the light, listening to Yu's slow breathing. He couldn't help being angry over the hurt Yu's family had caused. He wondered if they knew what they'd done or what they'd given up by turning their backs on him. Patrick knew what he had to do, he just didn't know if Yu would like it or even if it would work. But Yu had no one else.

Chapter 5

PATRICK HAD never lied to Yu before, and in a strange way, it worked to his advantage now, because since Patrick had only ever been honest, he knew Yu would believe the deception he now told as he packed a wig and some cosmetics into a small overnight bag.

"So, since one of the performers cancelled, and Rog knows the club's owner, they called him to fill in. He's already booked, so he told them about me, and I guess they looked at my site, and Rog said they're really excited to see me perform. It pays great, and this will be a *great* way for me to reach a wider audience. Besides, in this business, you can't do better than get a reputation for being dependable and helping out. That club's owner won't forget that I drove down on short notice and delivered a kick-ass show."

Yu leaned his back on the kitchen counter and blew at the steam rising from his coffee cup. He looked enticingly rumpled, his eyelids low over his eyes and his hair in disarray from sleep. "Washington, DC, has some really bad neighborhoods, Patrick. Exactly where is this club?"

"Oh, uh, I don't remember. Rog texted me the address so I can program it into my GPS. You know Rog is worse than the most overprotective mother, though. He wouldn't send me anywhere dangerous." Patrick finished packing and zipped up his bag, feeling queasy and disgusted with himself.

"Why do you have to leave so early?" Yu asked, glancing at the digital display on the microwave that read half past nine. "When do you go on stage?"

"Not until this evening, but… well, I'll need to shave first, and shower. I can do it in the club's dressing room."

"Why can't you shave here? I don't have class until eleven. We can shower together."

Yu's playful smile only made Patrick feel worse. He had to turn away from Yu's trusting eyes, or he'd spill everything, possibly including the cup of coffee and single piece of toast he'd forced down as breakfast. "But I'll be all sweaty again after all that time on the road. I'm sorry. I-I have to get going. I'll be home late tonight."

The smile fell from Yu's face. "You're driving back tonight? That's crazy. You'll be exhausted. Get a room. We can afford it."

Patrick set his bag on the table and carefully pried the coffee mug from Yu's hands. He wound his arms around Yu's waist, feeling the warmth of his skin through the thin T-shirt he'd slept in. He hadn't washed himself yet, and the remnants of the sweat and semen they'd spread over each other the previous night stretched up like barbs and hooked into Patrick's heart until he felt it tearing every time he moved. As much as he needed to touch Yu, Patrick still couldn't bear to look in his eyes, so he rested his forehead against Yu's and focused on where Yu's collarbones showed beyond the gray cotton of his shirt. Below them, Yu's chest rose and fell slowly with his breath, and his small, dark nipples were slightly hard. Patrick ran his fingers up Yu's back until he could comb them through his silky long hair. "I don't want to sleep in some hotel room all by myself. I don't care what time it is; I want to come home and sleep beside you. Please don't worry. I got a lot of rest last night, and I'm one of the first to go on, so it won't be too late. I can sleep all day tomorrow if I want to. It will be fine. If I'm even slightly tired, I *will* get a room. I promise. Okay?"

"I don't like it," Yu said, inclining his head so his lips moved at the corner of Patrick's mouth. "But I trust you. Always."

Patrick pulled away, ready to abandon this entire ruse. Unlike what he had told Yu, he'd lain awake most of last night considering his decision, and again and again, he'd realized he had to at least try, even if he risked upsetting Yu, or—No, he had to believe he had a chance of succeeding, of helping. Fixing it. But if he didn't get away from Yu now, he'd never be able to keep up his act. He gave Yu a quick peck on the lips, turned, picked up his bag, car keys and phone, and hurried out of their apartment without looking back, calling a final good-bye over his shoulder just before he slammed the door and hurried down the stairs toward the parking lot.

He got into his car, plugged his phone into the charger, and programmed his destination into the GPS app. He pulled out onto the street and followed the robotic female voice as it guided him out of the city and to the interstate. Once on I-76, where he'd remain for many hours and wouldn't need his phone's directions, he rolled the window down and turned the music up. His iPhone selected VNV Nation's "Chrome" before moving on to a recording of "Wild Mountain Thyme" from the Faire. Patrick sang along as the cool autumn air, scented with fallen leaves and piles of sweet, rotting grass struck his face.

FOUR HOURS later, Patrick arrived in Potomac, Maryland. He stopped at a gas station on the outskirts of the town to relieve himself, freshen up as best he could in the restroom, and buy a sandwich and soda for his lunch. Now that he'd neared his destination, his nerves had started to fire and his guts to twist up with anxiety, but he'd come too far to turn back now. He ate his food without really tasting it and got back in the car to let the voice on his phone lead him the last few miles.

He drove into an affluent neighborhood of golf courses and equestrian facilities. Impressive newer homes sat on huge lots surrounded by vast expanses of bright green grass and impeccable landscaping. It all looked pretty enough for a postcard with the sun shining from the cornflower-blue sky and a few puffy clouds casting shadows on the ground as they drifted languidly by. The GPS guided him onto a quiet cul de sac called Split Tree Circle, and after passing a few stately homes, it announced Patrick had reached his destination. Instead of pulling into the long driveway leading up to a large brick colonial, he parked on the street, wiped his sweaty palms on the thighs of his jeans, picked up the envelope he intended to deliver, and took a deep breath to steady himself before getting out of the car.

It was warmer here than in Pittsburgh, and vivid yellow leaves still clung to the branches of the birch tree in the yard. Pots of chrysanthemums sat on the concrete steps leading to the front door, and rhododendrons grew beneath the bay windows on either side, their wide glossy leaves looking cool against the heat of the sun. Before he could change his mind and run back the way he had come, Patrick jabbed the button by the door and heard the bell echo inside the house. He waited a few minutes and then pressed it again. He didn't know if anyone would be home, since it was the middle of the afternoon on a weekday, but it was his only chance. Weekends he worked at the Faire, and he usually performed Friday and Saturday nights at the clubs in the city afterward. Maybe he should have waited until later in the day, after work ended for most people.

Just as he was preparing to slide his envelope under the door and curse himself for wasting an entire afternoon, he heard shoes clicking against the floor, approaching the door. His heart rate sped until he started to feel dizzy, and with tingling fingertips, he gripped the iron railing abutting the porch to keep steady.

A small woman answered the door, and climate-controlled, clean-smelling air rushed out to cool Patrick's heated cheeks. He knew his face must be as red as a beet, and he cursed his fair skin and the way it revealed his every emotion. In stark contrast, the owner of the home wore a chilly, blank expression Patrick recognized only too well. Every detail of her appearance was immaculate, from her tailored navy-blue jacket and skirt to the red wedges on her small feet that matched her lipstick and nail polish, her tasteful makeup, asymmetrical bob, and the subtle string of pearls around her slender neck.

"Mrs. Elion?" Patrick miraculously managed to choke out without stammering.

Only the tiniest nod acknowledged his query before she said, with a barely noticeable Japanese accent, "May I help you?"

"If I could just speak with you, uh, have a few minutes of your time—"

She cut him off in a soft but authoritative tone. "Young man, if you are selling something, I can assure you I'm not interested. Furthermore—"

Patrick held up his hands, one still holding the large manila envelope. "No. I'm not selling anything. Please, just give me a chance. I really need to talk to you about—"

"I'm also not interested in a religious lecture." Yu's mother started to close the door. "Leave, or I'll call the police."

"No! Listen to me! I'm here because of your son, Yu."

Mrs. Elion froze with her hand on the brass doorknob, a tiny crease forming between her perfectly shaped brows—another expression Patrick knew well. "Has something happened?"

"Would you care if it had?" Patrick asked, and instantly her frigid mask slipped back into place and she took a few steps back. Patrick pushed his long fringe off his damp forehead and squinted. He didn't want to seem confrontational; accusing her and picking a fight would accomplish nothing. He had to get a hold of himself. "I'm sorry. Yu isn't hurt or anything, but I really do need to speak with you. Do you think I can come inside? Or… or if you're afraid to trust me, we can go to a public place. I'll meet you anywhere you want."

A subtle look of annoyance crossed her face—no one who didn't know that look would have noticed—and she started to close the door again. "I'm afraid I'm really very busy."

"All I'm asking for is ten minutes," Patrick said, getting desperate. "I've been driving for four hours to talk to you. Isn't your son worth ten minutes of your time?"

"Ten minutes." By way of inviting him in, she turned and walked across the marble floor, heels clicking. Patrick closed the door and followed her through the foyer to a huge kitchen with dark cherry cabinets and granite countertops. She stood on one side of the large central island and rested her palm on the glossy surface, near the sink. Patrick stood on the other side, trying not to gawk at the opulence like a philistine. Everything was arranged and displayed like artwork in a museum, from the copper-bottom pots and pans, to the crystal behind the leaded glass of the cabinets, to the condiments in neat rows above the stove. Even the golden apples in the ceramic bowl on the table by the window looked purposefully placed, as if waiting to be painted into a still life. To Patrick, the formality and perfection just felt cold, like the house was some kind of display model where no people actually cooked, ate, laughed, talked, or… lived. He had a hard time imagining a child here or what it must have been like for Yu to grow up within these walls, probably afraid to touch anything lest he move it an inch from its designated location.

"How do you know my son?" Mrs. Elion's tone was soft, but the impatient demand came through as clear as a bell.

Patrick wondered for a minute what to say, then settled on just telling her the truth. Things couldn't get any worse between Yu and his parents. "My name is Patrick Harford, and Yu is my partner. He-he's my whole world. We're very much in love."

Her face showed no emotion; her fingers on the counter never even twitched. "I see he's not moved past that silly phase, then. What exactly do you want, Mr. Harford?"

Patrick clenched his jaw to keep his anger from spilling out in the form of a string of profanity. If he started yelling, she'd throw him out, her notions about Yu and who he shared his life with reinforced. He had to be better than that, win her over, so he slowly slid the envelope toward her. "Yu and I have been living together for two years. We're—your son is very happy, and he's leading a successful life. He's amazingly talented, and lots of people love and admire him. Maybe I'm wrong, but I just thought, I hoped, as his mother, you might be glad to hear he's happy and doing well. Are you?"

"Frankly, no, Mr. Harford. My son has an IQ of 172, speaks four languages, and could do calculus in eighth grade. Do you honestly expect me to be pleased that he's thrown away all that potential to make pretend weapons in a tent at some filthy carnival?"

"But... don't you want him to do what makes him happy?"

"Yu—my son was on his way to a brilliant and successful career. He turned his back on it, and you expect me to be proud? He could have been well on his way to a house like this at this point in his life, but instead he chose to throw it all away."

"Money isn't everything," Patrick countered. "Yu is full of passion about his work. He's an amazing artist, and has had offers to show in major galleries all across the East Coast." He nudged the envelope a little closer to her, but she made no move to take it. "You should at least look at some of the things he's made. I-I brought some photographs. He's graduating in December, and he just had his senior show. It hurt him very deeply that you and his father didn't come."

"My son made his choice, Mr. Harford. Yu was a difficult child, to say the least. But his father and I did our best to deal with his... issues. We bent over backward to make sure he would succeed in spite of all his flaws, and he threw our efforts back in our faces. It's nothing but a sad waste, both of his potential and our time. He could have been a person who made a difference in the world. An important and worthwhile person.

He's nothing but a disappointment, an embarrassment when he could have been someone we were proud of."

"He is! How can you—" Patrick bit his lower lip and tried to get a handle on his anger even as his blood pumped so hard it made his fingers swell. "Where is Yu's father? Does he feel the same? Doesn't he have any interest in his son?"

"Your ten minutes are up, Mr. Harford. Please leave and don't bother me or my family again."

"Bitch," Patrick couldn't help mumbling under his breath as he turned to leave. He got halfway through the foyer before he turned around and stomped back into the kitchen. "You cold-hearted, selfish.... You think I came here as a favor to Yu, or myself? I came here because I feel sorry for you. I feel sorry for you because your son is a wonderful, talented, dedicated, and hard-working man, the kind of man anyone would be proud to know, to call a friend, and you've got your head jammed so far up your ass you're missing out on all of it. You're missing out on knowing your son, seeing his happiness, and helping him celebrate everything he's earned. You could be there beside him, sharing his joy, sharing yours with him, and life is short, and you can't have those years back.... Oh, the hell with it. Why am I bothering? We don't need you. Yu doesn't need you. He has me, and I love him, and we're going to have a wonderful life. If you don't want to be a part of it, that's your loss. Look at his art or throw the pictures away. I don't care. I never should have come here. You don't deserve to be part of his life. He's too good for you."

He walked out of the house and slammed the door. For a few moments, he just stood in the warm air, listening to the songbirds and the soft hiss of the sprinklers watering the grass, trying to understand. He would walk through fire for Yu and couldn't comprehend Yu's own mother and father tossing him aside like trash. Then he thought of his own parents and realized some people were just so convinced of their righteousness and superiority God himself couldn't change their minds. He tried to assure himself it was their loss. What had he expected to happen? Had he honestly expected Yu's mother to come back to Pittsburgh with him and hug her son, say she loved him no matter what? As he sat down behind the wheel of his car, he realized he had; he'd thought it would all work out like a fairy tale, and everyone would live happily ever after. God, he needed to read less love poetry. He didn't seem able to reconcile real life with the fantasyland in his head. But there was a fantasyland: the one he shared with Yu.

Patrick programmed the address of their apartment into the phone and then started his engine. "Take me home," he told the mechanized voice as he pulled out onto the street. Soon, he left the idealized neighborhood and merged onto the highway. He'd get home early in the evening and would have to make up some excuse. So much for trying to be a hero. This was real life, and he was just an ordinary kid. He couldn't make things better, not even for the person he loved most. No matter how he tried, he was no hero.

Chapter 6

THE NEXT Saturday marked the weekend before Halloween and the end of the Faire season. With the exception of the Elizabethan Christmas weekend, which was more a shopping opportunity and didn't feature the shows and attractions, the grounds would be closed until the following May, and Patrick didn't know if he would be back for the opening ceremonies. He and Yu still had to talk about their plans for the future, and their landlord wouldn't wait much longer for them to either renew their lease or move out.

Patrick tried to put the future out of his mind and concentrate on enjoying the time he had left with his friends, who had become family over the years. God, it was hard for him to believe he'd been working here since he'd begged Tom for a job emptying bins and selling flowers at sixteen—five years ago. Five years, and yet his first day, sweating beneath his cast-off doublet and hoping he wouldn't fuck up bad enough to be driven off, felt like yesterday. He remembered how desperate he had been to sell the roses in his basket and how he'd practically begged the patrons to buy them so he could keep his job. In retrospect, he realized many of those attendees had taken pity on him when they'd bought his overpriced flowers. This place and these people had been the one constant, the one positive, in his short life: a security blanket he feared letting go. He didn't dare think about what could have happened to him without their support. Likely he'd be one of the homeless kids turning to drugs or the bottle, like those at his support group. Maybe worse.

His Faire family had caught him when he'd stumbled, held him up when he was sinking. But was he ready to break free of their comforting hands and stand on his own? He decided it was better to focus on today.

Today, he wore a black-and-white harlequin costume to complement Jen's extravagant white gown as she portrayed an older Elizabeth, the queen in her decline. He'd even painted his face white to match hers, with black makeup accentuating his eye sockets, and his nose and teeth drawn to resemble the death's head. He and Jen had practiced a song to perform spontaneously in front of groups of patrons, and such a group gathered around them now as they stood near the fountain at the center of the food stalls.

Patrick lifted the panpipes he wore around his neck and blew an atonal melody into the reed tubes. Jen, careful of her layered skirts, perched on the edge of the flat stones lining the pool and sang:

> "The wind doth blow today, my love,
> And a few small drops of rain;
> I never had but one true love,
> In a cold grave he was lain.
>
> I'll do as much for my true love
> As any young maid may;
> I'll sit and mourn all at his grave
> For a twelvemonth and a day.
> The twelvemonth and a day being up,
> The dead began to speak:"

Patrick sang:

> "Oh who sits weeping on my grave,
> And will not let me sleep?"

And Jen responded:

> "'Tis I, my love, sits on your grave,
> And will not let you sleep;

For I crave one kiss of your clay-cold lips,
And that is all I seek."

Though he shuddered, and sort of hated the song they performed, Patrick answered her.

"You crave one kiss of my clay-cold lips,
But my breath smells earthy strong;
If you have one kiss of my lily-white lips,
Your time will not be long."

Then they sang together, as the people around them stood transfixed, unsure whether to be enchanted or horrified. Some of them took a few steps back until they could wander discreetly away with sudden feigned interest in one of the nearby booths. Children clung to the legs of their parents, their little mouths gaping open, cheeks red and eyes wide.

"'Tis down in yonder garden green,
Love, where we used to walk,
The finest flower that e'er was seen
Is withered to a stalk.

The stalk is withered dry, my love,
So will our hearts decay;
So make yourself content, my love,
Till God calls you away."

Both Patrick and Jen bowed with a flourish as their audience backed away, clapping out of obligation, clearly disturbed.

Jen leaned into Patrick's hair and whispered, "That's Halloween, fuckers."

"Aye, Your Majesty," Patrick responded, trying not to reveal how the song had bothered him. His emotions had been raw and close to the surface all day, fraying at the edges like old cloth. His time here, at the place he felt most at home, grew shorter by the second. Soon, too soon, he would have to leap out of this nest and hope he could fly on his own, without all the people who'd held him aloft through the years. "Jen...."

"What, my angel?"

"We won't lose touch, will we? You're getting married, and I don't know what we'll do once Yu graduates, but...."

She leaned in and kissed him above the brow, just a light brush of her lips so she wouldn't smear him with her crimson lipstick. "I will always be here for you, my minstrel boy. Hell, Patrick, I think of you as a brother, and I'm closer to you than I am most of my blood family. I'm not letting you go. Let's spit swear."

"Wait—What?"

"Seriously?" She tugged off one of her lace gloves, carefully, a finger at a time. To Patrick's horror, she cleared her throat theatrically and spit into her cupped palm. Then she extended her hand to him. "You've never done a spit swear?"

"No, and I don't want to now. Jesus, that's disgusting." He hurried the few steps to the kabob stand and fetched a pile of napkins, which he thrust at Jen. She looked bizarre—almost like a painted portrait of the queen she portrayed in her elaborate white gown with its puffed sleeves, heart-shaped starched lace ruff, and faux-pearl details—with her bare hand extended and dripping saliva.

Jen took the napkins and wiped her hand with a roll of her eyes. "You are *so gay*, Patrick."

"And you're a delicate flower, Your Majesty. Hell, you just spit a loogie into your own hand. If that's not the very image of a refined, regal lady, I don't know what is!"

"Maybe this." She graced him with the single finger salute and stuck her tongue out.

"Oy!" Tom yelled as he strode by in full Highland regalia, the braids in his white beard tipped with strips of tartan cloth. "Stay in character, you two! This might be the last day, but we're here to give our patrons a show till the end!"

Both Patrick and Jen drooped their heads as if they'd been scolded by a strict but loving father they'd disappointed, which, in essence, they had. Patrick called out an apology, and Tom shook his head, but his thick mustache couldn't quite conceal his grin. The sun had set, and from all the shops and exhibits, the faces of jack-o'-lanterns began to glow in the encroaching twilight, lending their little village an even more magical feel than usual. An almost full, rust-colored moon had just risen above the hills in the distance, and the sweet smells of food, along with roasting pumpkin and clove incense, made Patrick feel like he'd wandered into a deliciously spooky otherworld. Curled brown leaves whispering as they tumbled across the cobblestone walkway enhanced the effect, as did the many patrons making their way toward the main stage in elaborate costumes.

Jen hooked her elbow with Patrick's. "We should get to the Last Huzzah. It might really be our last. This… this could be the last time we'll sing together, Patrick." Her voice cracked a little.

Patrick stepped a little closer to her so their shoulders brushed together as they made their way past the Tudor-style daub-and-wattle buildings draped in artificial cobwebs and adorned with witches, bats, and skeletons. Yu and Wade had cut the shapes of cats, ghostly faces, and twisted, leafless branches into a series of steel drums. Now that the staff had lit fires inside them, they cast strange, shifting images across the ground and the buildings. Burning wood added its aroma to the Halloween perfume wafting on the chilly breeze. The world became all orange firelight and blue-black, undulating shadow. Patrick heard the shrieks of happy children as he stepped in front of Jen and took both her hands in his.

She looked eerie in the gloaming, deep shadows around her eyes and her made-up white face stark against the darkness, but Patrick could see her distress in the downward curve of her painted lips. "What?" he asked her.

Jen shook her head, making the huge fake pearls edging her ruff rattle. Her blue eyes grew so large and sparkling she resembled an anime character. "I-I don't know. My feelings have been on a roller coaster all day. One minute, I look at something simple and feel deliriously happy, and the next thing I see has me ready to cry. I'm scared, I guess."

"I feel the same," Patrick whispered.

"I love Henry, and I want to marry him more than anything in the world, but… but I don't want to grow up yet, Patrick. Does that make any sense? I don't want to have to stop dressing up and getting to sing and pretending to be a queen for a living. I just don't want to let go of this fantasy and face the ugly reality beyond it. I don't know if I'm ready."

He wrapped his arms around her tiny waist, rested his head on her shoulder, and stroked her perfect corkscrew curls. "Growing up doesn't have to mean all the magic drains out of the world. Not if you hold on to it, keep looking for it, let it reveal itself to you. The magic only goes away if you close your eyes to it, make a decision to stop seeing it. This won't be our last song. Even if we're not on the cast, we can come back here and sit on the benches and put whoever takes our place to shame. We can sing anywhere we want, and we will, I promise. I'm not going to abandon you, so let's try to think about everything we have to look forward to instead of what we're giving up."

Someone passing by yelled that they should get a room, which had both Patrick and Jen laughing as they pulled away from each other.

"I'm going to sing my ass off for you," Jen said as she caught Patrick's hand and led him up the steps to the stage. "Let's give these people a show they won't soon forget."

"Yes, Your Majesty," he said with an excited smile. They joined the rest of the cast on the stage. The bleachers below them were filled to the brim, and many more people stood at the edges. The low, flickering light made them all look vaguely skeletal, with long shadows settling across their faces and into the depressions around their eyes and below their noses.

Eric strode to the center of the stage with his signature swagger, and the murmuring among the audience died down. Though his Sir Francis Drake persona had added a little pale powder to his face and dark liner around his striking dark brown eyes, he still exuded much more "sexy pirate" than "scary ghoul," and the ladies—and some of the lads—in the audience cheered their approval. "God save you all on this All Hallows Eve," Eric said in his gravelly, enticing tone. "We intend to leave you shivering, although not necessarily with fright."

A din rose as Eric's loyal fans shouted their love for him but died as soon as he lifted his black-gloved hand. He pressed a finger to his lips and elicited a few more subdued catcalls.

One of the stagehands passed a lute to Patrick, and he strummed it as he stepped up beside Eric to cries of "minstrel boy!"—along with some much more brazen and suggestive declarations. It still amazed him that he'd won his own legion of fans since he'd joined the cast as the queen's nameless troubadour-slash-spy-slash-bodyguard two years ago. He bowed with a flourish, and the memory of being nervous to perform on this stage also felt distant and unreal, like trying to hold on to the fragments of a dream upon waking. Now, tonight, stepping into the spotlight felt like coming home. He'd grown to love the attention and praise he'd once shied away from, and he opened his arm and soaked in the audience's love.

To begin, they performed the old favorites: "Wild Mountain Thyme," "Roll Your Leg Over," and "All For Me Grog." The audience, mostly consisting of dedicated patrons at this point, sang along with enthusiasm. They fell all but silent as Jen and Henry performed the folk song Patrick and Jen had sung earlier, "The Unquiet Grave." It took on an even more tragic aspect when actual lovers relayed the verses, and the crowd sat mesmerized. Patrick even saw some of them wiping at their eyes and noticed a burn in his own. He felt the pain of love cut short, of possibilities ended. He scanned the assembly for Yu, but in the darkness and smoky firelight, he couldn't locate him.

When Jen and Henry finished, Patrick stepped forward to lift the audience's mood with his take on "The Lusty Young Smith," singing, "A lusty young smith by his vice stood a-filing, his hammer laid by but his forge still aglow. When to him a young minstrel boy came smiling, and asked if to work in his forge he would go."

The crowd knew the words well and, despite Patrick's modifications to the song, sang along with chorus: "With a jingle, bang jingle, bang jingle, bang jingle. With a jingle, bang jingle, bang jingle, hi ho!" A collective clap punctuated the refrain, and Patrick continued to scan the throng for Yu as he belted out the rest of the extremely suggestive lyrics. He thought he saw Yu leaning against a lamppost near the edge of the gathering, but in the flickering gloom, he couldn't be sure.

The audience, as reluctant to see the Faire end as the performers, called for song after song. By the time the performance ended, many of them had joined the cast on the stage, while the rest sang at the tops of their voices, often sloshing ale from the mugs they raised. Of course, when the actors finally excused themselves, it was only to invite the others to continue the revelry at the Faire's tavern, the Saucy Stew. Arm in arm with Jen, Patrick led the merry procession up the hill to the pub, though a faint trace of the sorrow hearing "The Unquiet Grave" had inspired lingered in his belly, hollow, like hunger.

Upon reaching the Stew, people scattered to order drinks or platters of greasy snacks. A few people sat inside, around the massive stone fireplace and fake mounted boars' heads, but most of them enjoyed the temperate night beside Yu and Wade's artistic barrels, counting on the

Stew's strong ale to keep them toasty warm against the early autumn chill. They broke off into groups, and Patrick cast his gaze around again for Yu but couldn't find him. Yu hated chaotic gatherings, hated trying to isolate a single voice among many conversations, so Patrick eventually concluded he wouldn't show. Henry brought him a mug of ale, and Patrick slurped the foam off the top as a group of women sang "Where the Roses Grow Wild" beneath the grapevine-wreathed arbor. Patrick settled onto a bench and just tried to relax and enjoy the conclusion of yet another season. It surprised him to see Rog, Aouli, and Shawn leaning against the rough-cut timber railing of the pub's porch. All of them were scheduled to perform in a few hours for Joe's Ballroom's Annual Hallow-Queen Party. Patrick waved, and they returned his greeting, though they didn't come over to speak to him.

Tish and Tracy, the proprietors of the high-end Faire lingerie shop, Madame's Unmentionables, soon joined Patrick, Tish proffering a large plate of chicken wings and fries. The sisters both wore dark jeans and snug black T-shirts. Tracy's proclaimed "I Work Knights" while Tish's read "Wineaux—I Use A Glass." Their disheveled pixie haircuts matched, Tracy's blue and Tish's candy pink. Patrick stood to hug them and kiss each of them on the cheeks. "Good last day?" he asked.

"Oh yeah," Tish said. "We have lots of custom orders to fill over the next few months. We should have a steady income through the off-season. That means we can concentrate on commissions instead of traveling to some of the less lucrative festivals."

"And I think I've finally convinced Sir Carlton to abandon his skirt-chasing ways," Tracy said with a wink.

"That would be something," Patrick said, "but if anyone can tame that boy, it's you, flower of France."

Tracy threw her head back and laughed. "And where's the flower of the Rising Sun tonight, minstrel boy?"

Patrick shrugged as he reached for a wing dripping in red sauce. He shouldn't be eating junk before a performance, but he just needed something to fill the emptiness he felt inside, and greasy pub food and ale usually worked. One day he wouldn't be able to indulge without gaining weight, but he had just turned twenty-two a few weeks back. "Probably working. I honestly have no idea. It's enough to know Yu will be home when I finally make it there." He peeled a few strips of chicken off the bone with his teeth and chewed as the sisters watched him.

Jen and Henry joined them moments later, both of them grinning like they'd had their hands in the cookie jar. Patrick munched on a french fry and washed it down with a sip of ale. "What?"

Out of nowhere, the music Patrick hadn't been paying enough attention to identify died. The first slow notes of his favorite love song, "Helen" by The Cruxshadows, poured from the speakers as everyone gathered in a circle around him in anticipatory silence. All of his friends and acquaintances moved close to the railing and held their drinks against their chests, waiting. Patrick was scanning their faces, hoping for some clue to what might be going on, when Yu walked up the steps and onto the tavern's porch, wiping any concern Patrick had for others from his mind. Yu looked amazing, wearing tight dark jeans, a snug black T-shirt, and a casual gray blazer overtop. His long loose hair still looked a little damp, like he'd showered recently.

Patrick wiped the wing sauce from his mouth with a napkin and then hurried to meet Yu at the edge of the veranda. "I'm surprised to see you here. I thought you'd gone home. Do you want a drink? Something to snack on?"

Yu just shook his head and dragged the back of his hand roughly down Patrick's cheek and neck, his gaze never leaving Patrick's. Patrick had seen passion in Yu's eyes before, but nothing like what he now witnessed; the fire burning behind his golden-brown eyes bordered on violence, the intensity a little frightening to Patrick and all tangled with other feelings: adoration, joy, maybe a touch of worry. He leaned in and brushed his lips across Patrick's, skimming his tongue along the seam where they parted. Then he deepened their kiss, keeping his ministrations gentle and almost worshipful as he explored the edges of Patrick's teeth and the inside of his mouth like he'd never kissed a man before. The freshness and wonder of it spread to Patrick, and he barely noticed Yu guiding him to the center of the porch.

Slowly, Yu pulled away, leaning back in to pepper kisses across Patrick's cheekbones and the bridge of his nose. He pulled away a second time but almost immediately returned to kiss along Patrick's jaw. As pleasant as Patrick found it all, his head started to swim. "What's going on? Are you all right?"

In response, Yu raked his fingers through Patrick's unruly red hair, pinning it out of his face and behind his ears as best he could. Then he ran his hands down Patrick's arms until he could grasp Patrick's hands in both of his. Without breaking eye contact, he slowly sank to his knees in front of Patrick, and in that moment, time seemed to stop. The dozens of people standing in a crescent around them virtually disappeared. The world melted and dripped away until the little porch felt like the entirety of the universe. He saw nothing but Yu, the irregular firelight making the smooth curves of his face glow and his eyes sparkle. He noted the way every strand of hair fell across his shoulders, the small shadows his eyelashes cast on his cheek, the shiny patch his tongue left in the center of his lower lip when it darted out.

Yu wet his lips with his tongue again and rubbed them together, then said, "Patrick. You are the most beautiful man I've ever seen. You have brought me more happiness than I ever expected to find in life. You're the person I can always depend on; I know that now, that no matter what, you'll be there for me, and it has brought me so much peace. If you'll let me, all I want to do is spend the rest of my life making you beautiful things and making you happy. Taking care of you, and letting you take care of me. You've shown me what it means to have a partner in every way."

In blurry slow motion, Yu reached inside his blazer and took out a small black-velvet box. When he flipped the lid open, the tiny band inside caught the light. "Patrick—"

"Oh my God." Patrick could barely manage a whisper. His eyes stung and his face burned, but he didn't care in the slightest. He didn't even care when those tears finally spilled over or what he must look like to those watching with his black-and-white makeup streaked and dripping off his chin. It only mattered what Yu saw in him, and Yu saw something no one else ever had—something he treasured, wanted to call his own, and wanted to keep. Forever. Patrick tried to say something, but he couldn't force enough air out to make a sound beyond a helpless little croak. Instead, he nodded vigorously and pressed his lips together to stop their trembling. A moment later, Yu slid the ring onto Patrick's finger. Then he stood and wrapped his arms around Patrick, pulling him close and kissing him hard, victoriously. Patrick kissed him back, winding his fingers in Yu's hair, scarcely able to believe this brilliant, beautiful man wanted to be all his. The cheers, applause, and stomping around them sounded distant and muffled as Patrick's pulse swished loudly in his head. Though he didn't want to, the need to fill his lungs finally made Patrick break free. Gradually, he became aware of people surrounding them, hugging them and clapping them on the backs. Yu was wiping gray smudges from his cheek from where their faces had rubbed together. Words of congratulations blended into a cacophony, and Patrick began to understand how it felt to Yu. When he looked over at Yu shaking hands with Wade, Yu smiled a little, and he seemed to glow in the firelight. Everything looked fuzzy and dreamlike, bathed in a rosy warmth.

Streaks of pink flesh showed beneath Jen's white makeup where her tears had carved paths down her face. After Patrick had wiped his face with the wet towel she offered, she kissed him on the cheek, followed by Tish and Tracy. Henry almost broke Patrick's spine in a hug. "We are gonna have one hell of a bachelor party, bro. Or do I take Yu to that? How does this go?"

"I don't know," Patrick said with a wide grin at his friend, the sweet, simple bastard. "Maybe me and Yu will take Jen to the gay bar to see the strippers. You're welcome to come with us."

Henry surprised Patrick when he just shrugged and said, "Sure, what the hell. As long as the beer's cold."

"Oh no," Carlton said, looking at Henry as he pumped Patrick's hand. "Our boy here is gonna see some tits before he gets married." Tracy gave him a smack to the back of the head. He looked over at her with mock affront. "What? It's tradition."

"Fine," she said, planting a hand on her upthrust hip, "then I'm going with them to see some cock."

Ian groaned and pushed her aside to pat Patrick's shoulder. "Congrats, man. You landed the best weaponsmith on the East Coast. I'm… almost jealous."

Patrick just shook his head and smiled. He'd have to remember to tell Yu what Ian had said; it would please him.

By now, Eric, Rog, Aouli, and Shawn had made their way through the throng, and Patrick was passed around for another round of hugs. Rog kissed Patrick on the mouth and said, "Honey, I am so happy for you, and I have always wanted to plan a wedding! I have so many ideas already. We'll make it the best wedding ever. An epic wedding. I don't suppose you have a date in mind yet?"

Eric put a hand on the small of Rog's back. "Give the boy a chance to breathe, hon. I'm sure he doesn't want to think about any of that tonight. He probably just wants to take his man the hell home."

"By the time everybody at Joe's hears the news, he'll have so many free drinks in him he won't be able to get home," Aouli teased. "But we'll take care of you, sister. Same as always." He draped an arm around Patrick's shoulder and planted another hard kiss on Patrick's cheek.

Patrick had forgotten all about performing. He'd been looking forward to it, since the costumes and acts he'd come up with for Halloween were fun and creative, but now.... Eric was right. He just wanted to get Yu home. Actually, the car or the grass beyond the light of the pub might be far enough. "Excuse me for a minute," he said to his friends, and then he hurried toward where Yu stood at the edge of the crowd, near the steps. On his way, Patrick waved away at least half a dozen pints of ale thrust at him by his Faire family.

Looking at Yu, Patrick didn't think he'd realized before just how beautiful he was, and how lucky he was to have him in his life. Yu smiled at him and took the hand that wore the ring, lifting it up to kiss. "I hope you don't mind that I made it myself. It's not a diamond or anything."

In the wake of what it stood for, the promise it symbolized for their future, Patrick had forgotten about the actual object and now held it up to have a proper look at it. It was a simple band of polished steel with thin strips of gold around the edges. Patrick marveled at how Yu had managed to make the three kanji on it so crisp and detailed at such a small size. One of the characters Patrick recognized, because he had it tattooed on his ribs next to his roses: hope. Spinning the ring around his finger, he brought another symbol to the front and looked up at Yu. "This one?"

Yu kissed Patrick softly and spoke against his lips. "*Ai*. Love."

Patrick curled against Yu, rested his head on his shoulder, and nibbled at the side of his neck. "And this?"

"Forever. Eternity."

"I wanted to ask if you'd come to the club tonight," Patrick said against Yu's skin. "I know you don't like it, and I don't want you to be uncomfortable, but I don't want to be away from you tonight."

"I will," Yu said softly into Patrick's hair. "As long as we can leave as soon as you're done performing. I have... other plans for us tonight."

"So do I," Patrick said. He pulled away and returned to his friends just long enough to let them know he'd be leaving, and to tell Rog, Eric, Aouli, and Shawn that he'd see them at Joe's. He needed to get there a little early so he had time for a quick shower in the stall in the dressing room. He'd shaved that morning but wanted to rinse off the sweat and dust of the day, along with his ruined makeup. Streaky zebra would *not* be an appealing look for a drag queen.

He caught Yu's hand, and they started down the hill away from the tavern. When they got about halfway, Patrick stopped and looked back at the fuzzy orange glow coming from the Stew's windows and the fires burning in the barrels encircling the small Tudor building. Singing, laughter, and happy conversations spilled out between the wooden shutters. He smiled, feeling full where he'd felt empty, and not from the oily wings. Today might have been his last performing here, but it was okay. All the regret and anxiety he'd felt throughout the day evaporated, replaced by a sense of peace and calm. He might eventually lose touch with some of his friends here, and the wonderful memories of this magical place might grow hazy with time, but Yu would be beside him. Always. No matter what they relinquished or lost, Yu would be there, and everything else that happened would be okay because of that.

THE CLUB was packed to the gills for its infamous Halloween celebration, and Patrick worried about Yu. But Eric had promised to watch out for him and take him outside for some air at the first signs of distress, and as often as necessary. Patrick was excited to perform tonight, because it would be just the four of them, and it was only a show and not a competition, which meant they could have fun and make some money without the stress of a pageant. Also, he had selected most of the music, since his sisters hailed him as the foremost expert on "spooky stuff." They'd be performing to an industrial, darkwave, and electro-medieval soundtrack very different from what one usually heard at a drag show.

Besides, he was just so damn happy he had to let some of it out before he floated away.

Patrick and Aouli went on first. They'd performed together many times since discovering how lucrative their Japanese schoolgirl act was. Tonight, Patrick stood at the center of the darkened stage in a loose, flowing, sleeveless white shift. Soft music, Sarah McLachlan's "Angel"— the depressing song Patrick would forever associate with horrific ads for the ASPCA—began to play as a baby spotlight shone down on him. As he swayed and made slow, serpentine movements with his arms, the audience looked up in utter bewilderment.

The sound of a needle scratching across a record blared out of the speakers, cutting off the maudlin song. A quick but sensual beat replaced it as the Genitorturers's "Flesh is the Law" played at a much louder volume, the lights strobing red, orange, and purple to the rhythm. The audience roared out a cheer, and Patrick knew Aouli—Miss Anita Lei tonight—had appeared in her red vinyl catsuit with the pointed tail, a buckled black corset and black go-go boots overtop. Without turning around, Patrick knew the exotic Polynesian queen wore her thick black hair spiked with red chalk on the tips to match her horns and that she carried a riding crop shaped like a pitchfork.

Miss Anita came up behind Patrick's Queen Titania and grabbed the back of her diaphanous gown. The Velcro strips across the shoulders gave way, and it fluttered to the ground around Patrick's feet. Beneath it, Queen Titania wore a vinyl leotard, open on the right side to expose Patrick's tattoos. The sleeve on that side reached his wrist, while the other side was sleeveless. The thin strip of shiny black barely held Patrick's small fake tits in place. Aouli tugged the long blonde wig off Patrick's head and tossed it away. It wasn't an expensive professional wig; they'd bought it at a discount from Party City, so they didn't mind ruining it.

Patrick shook out his hair. Like Aouli, he wore it natural but enhanced with some glittering gold gel. Symbolically free, Patrick stretched theatrically, strutted to the edge of the stage, and circled and thrust his hips to the tempo of the song. He happily shed his angel persona and became a naughty, wanton sprite, teasing the audience with the bend of his waist and the figure-eight pattern he wove with his groin. Flashing, multicolored lights, sharper and more intense than the firelight at the Faire had been, glinted off his vinyl costume as if it were steel, and illuminated the first beads of sweat forming on his pale skin. Hands moved up his fishnet-swathed thighs, many of them stuffing money beneath the garters. The men in the audience reached up to touch his tattoos, his bare skin, and they slid more bills into the opening on the side of his costume.

After a few minutes, Miss Anita had had enough of sharing her plaything. She grabbed Patrick by the vinyl collar he wore and spun him around, wagging a finger at both him and the crowd. She tugged down on the collar, making Patrick bend almost in half at the waist, and then she beat the asscheeks his thong exposed with the crop—or at least she pretended to; Patrick barely felt a thing. Neither of them was into anything weird in real life, and acts like this one were much more a financial choice than an indulgence of a fetish.

After Anita finished punishing Titania, she strutted over to the left side of the stage and leaned down to run her crop over the reaching arms of the men. Patrick stood and followed, and when Miss Anita turned to face him again, he knelt and pretended to kiss her boot. He couldn't fathom how degrading themselves during actual sex could turn some people on, but their show had crumpled bills raining down around them. Slowly, Patrick moved his face up Aouli's thigh and over his flattened crotch. Aouli grabbed Patrick's hair, pulled his head back, and pretended to slap him. Patrick pressed his hands together as if in prayer, and Aouli looked at the audience and shrugged, seeking their opinion on his pet. The crowd yelled, almost drowning out the music, and threw more money. Aouli helped Patrick to his feet, turned him again, and stuck the handle of the crop between his teeth. They danced chest to back, grinding their hips together, until Aouli put a hand to Patrick's shoulder and "forced" him back to his knees as the song ended and the stage went black. They'd decided to leave the audience hanging, leave them to their own fantasies of what might be happening in the dark. In reality, Patrick and Aouli were scrambling to collect all their tips and escape quietly backstage.

They hurried to change while Rog, or Lady Regina, went onstage to perform to Concrete Blonde's "Bloodletting." Next was Shawn, performing as Sha-Queera to Dead Can Dance, after much persuasion from Patrick. Aouli danced solo to the Birthday Massacre song "Play Dead." Watching from the side of the stage, Patrick knew the poppy but dark song suited Miss Anita, and she looked fantastic in a lacy, Lolita-style dress and violet pigtails.

To end the show, Patrick took the stage in a pointy hat, bloomers, black-and-white striped hose, and a tight black brocade corset. He performed to "Witches," using the slower beat of the song as an opportunity to show off some of the backbends, splits, and walkovers he'd learned from Shawn and worked so hard to master. They always impressed the audience and earned him good tips. He also took advantage of the broomstick he carried as a prop, riding it suggestively, rubbing it between his open legs and even licking the rounded wooden tip.

For their encore, the quartet chose "Spooky Little Girl Like You" by the Zombies. They hadn't really choreographed or practiced it much, so they just had fun, and the audience enjoyed themselves right along with them. The four of them had danced together so many times and knew each other so well that everything just fell into place.

Yu and Eric were waiting when they reached the dressing room. Full of adrenaline and deliriously happy, proud of the strength in his body and the influence his beauty had over others—beauty he hadn't even known he had until he'd first put on one of Jen's gowns in the Ren Faire dressing room—Patrick took off his witch's hat, plunked it on Yu's head, and kissed him. He giggled at the black smear his lipstick left on Yu's mouth and cheek before handing Yu a cosmetic wipe. Yu grinned a little bemusedly and said, "Your show was very entertaining, if much more vulgar than usual."

"Are you upset?" Patrick asked, his warm, buoyant mood fizzling a little.

Yu shrugged. "That every man in this club wants to fuck my boyfriend? Maybe a little." He was never one for subtlety. He turned and looked at Eric. "Do you ever get used to that?"

Eric looked at Roger, his expression full of love, mischief, and banked fire. "No... but you comfort yourself with the knowledge that you're the only one who actually gets to fuck him."

Yu's eyes widened, and color spread across his cheeks and up his ears. "I suppose that's one way to look at it. And it's an act, right? Just something you do for the money." This time, his gaze met and held Patrick's.

"Well, yes and no. This is how I make a living, but it's more than that. It's exciting to perform. It's a turn-on, and it whisks away all my inhibitions. I feel powerful up there, important. Beautiful. Don't you feel that way when someone appreciates one of your weapons or a piece of your art? Special?" He reached out to Yu, and Yu took his hand. For a second, Patrick had worried he wouldn't. Silly insecurity. He should know better by now.

"I don't like attention," Yu said. "I prefer my work speak for itself, but I guess I understand. It's something you need."

"I was just having a good time," Patrick said. The others had fallen into an uncomfortable silence, Shawn and Aouli hurrying to the mirrors to turn all their attention to cleaning up. This should have been a private conversation, but when Yu had something to say, he said it. Unfortunately, it sometimes made others feel awkward. "And I like being appreciated, yeah. I worked hard for it."

"You don't have to defend yourself, Patrick. I haven't expressed myself as I meant to, again. I'm sorry. I'd like to go home now."

"I have one more announcement to make," Patrick said, tousling his hair, glitter falling like gold snowflakes. "I have to tell the club about our engagement, and if you think you can stand two minutes on stage, it would mean a lot if you would come with me."

"Why?" Yu asked.

Patrick squeezed his hand and rubbed circles on the back with his thumb. "Because this is my other family. We told our Faire family, and I'd like to share my good news with the other people who helped me get where I am. Besides, if you want to make sure all those guys know I'm yours, now's your chance."

Yu gave him a single nod of understanding. He even smiled, and Yu's smiles were never fake. "Let's go."

"Just give me a minute. I have to do this as me—as Patrick—not Queen Titania."

He cleaned up and changed as quickly as possible, and then he left Yu waiting by the stage's left entrance with the others while he waded through the crowd in search of Joe, the owner of the club. Before long, he found the huge, bald man with the graying beard standing with some of his brothers from their motorcycle club. Standing on his tiptoes, Patrick whispered to Joe, and the big man—who looked intimidating but Patrick had found gentle and protective over the years—grinned wide and patted Patrick on the shoulder. Joe spoke to the DJ on his way to the stage, and by the time he'd ascended the stairs, the music had stopped and the house lights had come up, leaving the patrons looking around in confusion.

Joe took the mic from its cradle and spoke in a deep voice. "Relax, everybody. Nobody's getting thrown out. It's Halloween, and we're here to party." The crowd hooted and clapped until Joe held up a hand. "But first, I'd like your attention for just a few moments. One of our own has something to say."

As Patrick took the stage, he received a few shouts and catcalls from fans.

Joe passed him the mic.

"I'll keep this short and sweet, so you can all get back to drinking," Patrick said, "but this place is special to me, and some of you are family, so I want to share my good news. Earlier tonight, my boyfriend, Yu"— Patrick reached for him, and Yu joined him on the stage—"the most wonderful man in the world, proposed to me, and I accepted. We're getting married!" He held up their joined hands to thunderous applause, and then Patrick thought, *The hell with it.* He took Yu's cheeks in his hands and kissed him hard. It wasn't something they could do just anywhere, but here, everyone cheered for them and the love they'd found.

It took them a while to escape after that, just as it had at the Faire. Declining drinks and accepting congratulations with politeness but brevity, they made their way toward the door. While it felt good that so many people wished them well and wanted to celebrate them and with them, no force on earth was going to stop Patrick from getting Yu home and showing him how much he wanted and loved him—again and again.

Chapter 7

WINTERIZING THE Faire-grounds and planning next season would start Monday, but everyone took the Sunday after the season's final performance off, most of them to nurse hangovers. Patrick and Yu slept almost until lunchtime, sore and worn out for a completely different reason.

After a late brunch of french toast, roasted apples, and peppered ham steaks, Yu, still in his faded gray sweatpants and thin blue T-shirt, went to the desktop computer in their living room to upload pictures of his recent commissions to his website. Patrick, still in the red-satin robe Yu had bought him last Christmas and his fuzzy black slippers, sprawled out on the couch with his laptop. He checked his social-networking sites and updated his blog, adding some pictures Eric had e-mailed him of last night's show. He had to admit he looked really slutty in some of those shots, but the results of the little bit of possessiveness it had ignited in Yu, well—Patrick shifted on the couch, still slightly sore. He surfed through some sites that sold wigs and high-heeled shoes in larger sizes. Then he pulled up eBay and shopped for bargains on vintage gowns. After looking at some costume jewelry and cosmetics, he grew bored.

"Yu, do you want to go out tonight? Like to dinner, since we both have the day off?"

"I should go to the blacksmith's shop. I have half a dozen requests for new commissions. I'll send some estimates, but I should also make sketches for these customers and try to finish the projects I have outstanding, in case they want to work with me. I expect most of them will."

Patrick scooted down the couch, a little disappointed. Still, he knew what he had signed up for back when he'd started seeing Yu. Yu was passionate about his craft, and it took a lot of his time. Patrick had promised to accept him as he was and not try to change him. He meant to keep that promise. Patrick scrolled through a few more web pages before he lost interest in shopping. He considered streaming a movie through Netflix but decided he'd rather read. He went to the site of a publisher specializing in fiction with gay main characters, clicked on the link to the fantasy genre, and began looking at the covers and reading through the blurbs. He wanted to download a book he could lose himself in, but one that would be fun and full of action—nothing too deep. This particular publisher had a lot to choose from, and the art was gorgeous, and Patrick had a hard time deciding on one or even two books. Soon, he had four in his basket and was still looking, marveling at the painted covers.

He was still considering when an instant message appeared at the corner of his screen.

Evan: Can U talk?

Patrick knew Evan Welliver from the support group he ran at the LGBT center. Though he knew he was no replacement for a licensed counselor, after all the support he'd received from others, Patrick wanted to pay it forward. So, every second Tuesday, he bought cookies, doughnuts, and coffee and helped the lost kids who wandered in fill out job applications, find places to live, and seek out help beyond what he could provide. He saw that the ones who were hungry got a meal and those unwilling to go to a shelter got blankets and secondhand coats he bought with his own money. Mostly, he told them they were all right, that there was nothing wrong with them. He told them the story of how he'd fought, worked hard, and found his place, hoping it would inspire them to do the same. The psychologist Patrick had trained under briefly said that was the most important thing: that the kids felt accepted, normal. That they knew someone cared. So Patrick told them, over and over again, that they were fine, perfect, just as they were. He told them he loved them, and he meant it. Sometimes it helped, though Patrick was only a few years older than most of the kids.

Most of the kids, despite overwhelming odds, wanted to fight for themselves and eventually secured employment and undertook the uphill battle to find their place in life. Some had bigger problems, like Charlene, who had been born Charles. Patrick had helped her with clothing and makeup, and they'd become friends. They spent a lot of time shopping and seeing girly movies Yu wouldn't be interested in, even if Yu would agree to go. When Charlene had told Patrick she was no longer afraid of others seeing her, that she felt beautiful and no longer wanted to hide, he'd never been so proud. Sometimes Charlene grew depressed about the cost of the surgeries she wanted, but like most of the others in the group, she worked hard and wanted to make a good life for herself.

Evan was an unusual case, and Patrick didn't know much about him. He knew Evan had left home at sixteen—either thrown out or to escape abuse—and that the young man had high walls around him. Patrick suspected he attended the meetings mostly for the free food and condoms. He knew from the gossip Charlene had shared that Evan liked pain pills, especially OxyContin, but wouldn't turn down the harder stuff. He also suspected Evan, now seventeen, of selling himself for drugs or to make ends meet. He hurried to respond.

Patrick: Not busy. How are you?

Evan: Feeling down.

Patrick looked up from his monitor to see Yu drawing. Watching him draw was eerie; Yu made no sketch lines or rough shapes beneath his final pencils, but drew light, tight finals instantly, perfect on his first try. Patrick spared a few moments to watch an intricate breastplate for a woman appear, as if by conjuration, on Yu's easel, and then he turned his attention back to the computer.

Patrick: Where are you?

Evan: Public library.

Patrick: Want to get some dinner? Talk?

Evan: Yeah, that would B nice

Patrick: Okay, I'll meet you in an hour.

He gave Evan the address of a diner not far from the library before signing off. He shut his computer down, set it on the coffee table, and stood up to stretch. "I'm going to shower and head into the city," he told Yu. "You'll be busy anyway, and one of the kids from my support group wants to meet up and talk."

Yu nodded without looking away from his easel. "I'm going to scan these sketches in and send them to the clients. Then I'm going to Wade's to try to finish up my outstanding projects."

Patrick went to stand behind him and rested his hands on Yu's shoulders. Yu's muscles twitched furiously beneath Patrick's hands as he drew on the paper, every line perfect and precise, his vision coming to glorious life as Patrick watched. Patrick kissed him on the top of his head and spoke against the part of his hair. "Will you be home for dinner?"

Yu let his pencil come to rest against his thigh, turned his head to look up at Patrick, and smiled. "I promise. I'll cook for you. Eight o'clock?"

Patrick kissed him. "It's a date. After all, I'm sure I'll be expected to put out after an expensive dinner."

Yu prepared to answer, but Patrick stopped him with another kiss. They nibbled at each other's lips and twirled their tongues together for a few moments before Patrick pulled away, hesitant to relinquish the silky strand of dark hair he'd unknowingly grasped. When he let it fall, Yu returned to his easel, and Patrick headed for the shower.

PATRICK PARKED on the street about a block from the diner. The weather had turned sour, the chill mist rising from the pavement mingling with the light but cold drizzle. Patrick bunched his shoulders up, glad he'd donned his brown wool peacoat and the gray-and-green scarf Jen had knitted, and hurried toward the inviting light beyond the fogged glass door. Once inside the diner, he located Evan at a booth in the corner. Evan had blond hair so light it almost looked artificial and contrasting dark brown eyes. He was waifish—almost feylike in Patrick's eyes—even smaller than Patrick's five foot eight and 145 pounds. Since Patrick had talked to him about skin care, most of Evan's acne had cleared up, though his hair hung in greasy clumps and some pale-gold stubble covered his face. His complexion looked pallid and a little waxen, making Patrick hope he wasn't high on something. He really wasn't equipped to deal with that.

Patrick slid into the booth, and a waitress handed them both laminated menus. "Order whatever you want," Patrick said. "My treat."

The kid's hunger trumped any feigned pride—a feeling Patrick remembered only too well—and when the waitress returned, Evan asked for a bacon double cheeseburger, fries, and an order of battered mozzarella sticks. He hurried to add a chocolate milkshake as she scribbled on her pad. Patrick, still full from brunch, ordered a side salad and chicken fingers. While they waited for their food, they drank coffee, and Evan poured three packets of sugar into every cup. He'd learned to take advantage of the free calories, something a kid his age should never have to worry about. Patrick remembered gorging himself on his free high school lunches, because he'd known his father had nothing in the refrigerator but greasy bologna and questionable hot dogs. After a few nights of puking from the spoiled meat, Patrick took what he could get from the school, filling his pockets with anything he couldn't finish, including free sugar packets and even ketchup.

"So, where have you been staying?" Patrick asked, gladly thinking of something besides himself at Evan's age. At least he'd had a roof over his head.

"The stupid shelter," Evan grumbled. They'd tried to get him into public housing, but, as a minor, Evan wasn't eligible, and he'd made it clear he wouldn't consider foster care. Too many of the questions on the housing application forms had scared the shit out of the kid, and Patrick preferred to have him come to the center now and then to disappearing into the streets for good.

"Any luck finding a job?" Patrick continued hopefully, but Evan just shrugged. Patrick decided on a more direct line of questioning. "When you messaged me earlier, you said you were feeling down? What's wrong?"

"I am," Evan muttered, staring into his mug.

"No, you're not," Patrick said automatically, reaching across the white plastic tabletop for Evan's hand. Evan flinched at first but then let Patrick grasp his fingers. His skin felt cool and waxen in Patrick's grip. The psychologist at the center had told Patrick that was what these kids needed to hear: that there was nothing wrong with them. Many of them were desperate to be touched, to feel a human connection.

"That's what all of you say. But it's not true. I've been on Grindr, looking for a guy, but no one is interested in a person like me. Their profiles all say 'no fems, no queens, interested in a masculine, fit man.' Some of them even say they want a 'straight-acting' guy. What does that mean? They're gay men. How do you suck a dick and act straight? Whatever 'straight-acting' means, I know it's not me. I'm small and skinny. I've got a pretty face. Gay men don't want someone like me, do they?"

Patrick didn't know what to say, so he asked, "Evan, what are you doing on Grindr? You're seventeen. You should be looking for a way to finish your GED and get a job." God, that sounded like a lecture, and that wouldn't make the kid any more comfortable. "I mean, is a relationship really your goal right now?"

Evan's dark gaze met Patrick's. His eyes looked tired but clear. "Of course. What else am I going to do? I need to find a successful man to take care of me. It's just—none of them seem interested in someone like me. They all want these bronzed, muscled guys who can pass as straight. I don't get it."

Patrick hung his head, the tips of his hair grazing the greasy tabletop. "Oh no. Oh, honey, no. You can't expect someone else to look out for you. They'll disappoint you every time." He couldn't help thinking of Yu and his older roommate, James, the man who'd wanted to "help" Yu with his art, just in exchange for—"You have to find your own way in the world, be able to provide for yourself. Don't look for someone to take care of you. Even if you find someone, it's going to come with a price."

"So what?" Evan pulled his hand free of Patrick's grip. "It's better than sleeping in that fucking shelter! Or on the street. What else am I going to do? I don't got much to offer, but I'm pretty and I'm easy. You saying I shouldn't use what I have?"

"Yes!" Patrick said. "You can make it on your own. I did. I worked, and I saved, and now I have a life I'm proud of, and it's mine. I don't owe anyone. Believe me, Evan, you don't want to owe anyone. Because they'll want to collect. You're better off getting it yourself, even if it's harder. I'm not going to lie to you—it's hard, but it isn't impossible. You *can* make it. I did. You certainly don't have to sell yourself to the highest bidder. You're worth more than that."

Evan arched a fair brow. "Am I? Are you? 'Cause I'm sorry to say, Patrick, but you make your living letting men stuff money down your panties. How are we so different?"

"I-I'm a performer," Patrick said, the sight of the breaded chicken the waitress set before him turning his stomach. "What I do is an act. The men pay for the fantasy, the same as someone buying a ticket to a movie. I'm no different than a musician or an actor."

"Sure," Evan said as he picked up his burger and took a few large bites. After he swallowed, he added, "I bet you let them feel you up. Grab your ass a little when they stick the money down your pants. Especially if it's a fifty. What do you let them do for a hundred?"

"That's not the same as fucking them for money." Goddammit, as much as Patrick wanted to help this kid, half of him wanted to backhand that smug smirk off his face. Had he been such a little prick at seventeen, thinking he had the world all figured out and knew everything? "I'm not a whore."

"No?"

"No! In fact, I'm getting married. I have a wonderful partner, and—" Patrick stopped himself. This wasn't about him. Evan didn't need to hear him boasting about his wonderful life. "But that's beside the point. We need to find you a job and a permanent place to live. Then we need to get you enrolled in night school so you can get an equivalency diploma. After that, we can check out some of the community colleges. Do you have any idea what you might want to do as a career?"

After Evan swallowed the handful of fries he'd stuffed into his mouth, he swallowed and said, "Gay men aren't interested in someone like me. They see me as too feminine. It's not my fault I'm small, or not 'straight-acting', but they don't want me. No successful man is going to be in a hurry to move me in. Too bad I can't stand pussy. Maybe I could find a rich old lady."

Patrick sipped his Diet Coke while he wondered what to say. God, this poor kid. Presumably rejected by straight parents, only to be found lacking by the gay community, the community that should have embraced him. He tried to collect his thoughts and wished he'd been trained to handle a situation like this. Maybe he was in over his head and he should get Evan to a licensed counselor. But the kid had reached out to him, seen him as someone worthy of trust, so Patrick would do his best. "Listen, Evan. I'm not burly or... or 'straight-acting', but I've worked hard and made a place for myself. I have a wonderful man in my life, and we're getting married. My dad kicked me out too, but I fought. I didn't give up, and I made it. So can you. You aren't defined solely by what others think you'll do sexually. You are a complete person, and right now, you need to go after what you want out of life, and you need to do it on your own. There's nothing wrong with you the way you are, and you don't need to change. Your dedication and will are going to be what will carry you to success, not the way you look or the way you talk. Show people you're dependable, and they won't care about any of that. I think I can find you a job, if you want it."

"Doing what?" Evan looked skeptical as he shoveled fries into his mouth.

"Mowing grass, weeding flower beds, raking gravel, and maybe shoveling some dirt. Washing buildings, maybe a bit of painting. Not afraid of hard work, are you? You'll be paid fairly. If you're interested, I can pick you up tomorrow morning."

Evan hesitated, a handful of fries held a few inches from his mouth. He narrowed his arresting dark eyes at Patrick as if waiting for the catch. When it didn't come, he smiled, looking incredulous but relieved. "I— yeah. That sounds great, Patrick. I have to ask, though. Why are you doing this for me? What do you get out of it?"

Patrick took a sip from his soda; his throat felt parched. "I'm helping you because some wonderful people helped me when I was in your position, and I think you have a lot to offer. Others saw that in me when I didn't see it in myself, and I guess... I guess I'm returning the favor. I want to see you succeed, and I'm here for you, Evan. I... I know how it feels to be abandoned, and I want you to know you haven't been, at least not by me. You're not alone."

"We'll see," Evan said. Then he turned his attention to devouring the rest of his food like a stray cat.

Chapter 8

THE FOLLOWING day, and for weeks afterward, well into November, Evan surprised Patrick by working hard to winterize the Faire-grounds and repair the buildings. Patrick introduced him to Yu, Eric, Tom, Jen, Henry, Ian, Carlton, Tom, Tish, and Tracy, hoping Evan might find a sense of family here as Patrick had. He wished he'd thought to bring the kid here earlier in the season, as Evan seemed entranced by the old-fashioned buildings and especially by the horses. When his workday ended, he could often be found at the stables, helping the knights care for their mounts on his own time. Evan considered getting to brush a horse or work the knots out of a tangled mane a treat. He had also been attending night school to prepare to test for his equivalency diploma, and as far as Patrick knew, he'd been leaving the pills alone. Patrick could ignore the occasional joint Evan smoked to relieve some stress if he didn't turn to anything worse. After all, plenty of his Faire friends could occasionally be found burning one out behind the storage sheds when the workday ended.

After today, they would shut the Faire-grounds down for the winter. Patrick was worried because he had yet to find a job for Evan in the off-season. Evan swore he'd been saving his earnings and would soon have enough for an apartment, but to keep making his rent, he would need employment—a steady, reliable job.

Patrick finished at the main stage, and after watching the curled brown leaves skitter across the polished wood for many moments, thinking they mirrored the chaotic movements of his thoughts, he made his way to the blacksmith's shop. Yu had just completed his work and was scrubbing the soot from his hands and arms. When he saw Patrick, he dried off and came to put his arms around Patrick's waist. Patrick kissed him softly, drawing comfort from Yu's warm, solid body against his and the sweet, smoky fragrance clinging to Yu's hair. Even the pungent smell of the gritty green soap he used comforted Patrick, stilled the erratic tempest of his worries.

"Are you okay?" Yu asked, petting Patrick's cheek.

Patrick shrugged. "I'm worried about Evan. He really fit in here, just like I did, but now that the season's over... I don't know. Just feeling tossed up inside, about him, about leaving the Faire, about the future.... Do you think we could ask Evan to dinner tonight?"

Yu kissed the center of Patrick's forehead. "Sure. I have fresh prawns, and plenty of them. I was planning on making scampi, and it won't be a problem to cook a little extra pasta."

"Thanks. You're good to me. I love you. You know that, right?"

Yu grinned. "I could stand reminding."

Patrick wove his fingers into Yu's hair, drew his face close, and reminded him, letting all the love and gratitude he felt spill from him into Yu as he swirled his tongue around inside Yu's sweet mouth. He finally pulled away, reluctantly, and said, "Let's go find him."

Hand in hand, they strolled slowly toward the stables, not hurrying, taking time to enjoy the stark beauty of the bare oak branches against the steely gray sky and the brittle leaves crunching beneath their feet. The chill air smelled of maple and distant fires. Before they reached the barn, Patrick saw Eric repairing a section of fencing. Since one of his many cousins ran a contracting company specializing in residential improvement, Eric worked as a carpenter and painter in the off-season, at least when he wasn't performing at other faires, and Tom invariably put his talents to use. Patrick tugged Yu in Eric's direction.

Eric stowed his hammer in one of the canvas loops on his belt and emptied the nails in his left hand into a pocket. He tilted his head from side to side to work out the kinks in his neck. "What's up, princess?"

Princess. After all these years, Patrick rarely contemplated Eric's pet name for him, but in the wake of his many conversations with Evan, he couldn't help but consider it. After talking with the kid, he'd gone to Grindr and a few other gay hookup sites. What Evan had described had proved true. Most of the eligible men sought "Masculine, in good shape.

No fems. No lisps. No queens." Patrick had even seen profiles specifying "No girly, emotional twinks." As if having feelings and expressing them somehow made one less of a man. No wonder Evan was confused. What gave these men the right to define masculinity? Or to condemn femininity as somehow inferior? Did they have any idea of the damage they caused to a sensitive kid like Evan? Kids like him didn't need any more people telling them they didn't measure up. They'd heard it all their lives. Frankly, it pissed Patrick off, and a few times, after a couple of glasses of wine, he'd had to fight the urge to respond to them.

Eric, "straight-acting" Eric, said, "Earth to Patrick."

"Sorry. I just wanted to ask you if it would be okay if I invited Evan to Thanksgiving dinner. He doesn't have anyone, and I'd hate to see him all by himself for the holiday. I'm trying to show him he's not alone."

"Oh, of course he's welcome," Eric said, wiping the sweat from his forehead with his sleeve. "He's a good kid. Reminds me a little of you, back when."

"Thanks," Patrick said. "I can't wait to tell him. What he really needs is a family." He patted Eric on the shoulder and turned back toward the stables. Eric nodded once before resuming his task.

As they made a slow journey toward the main barn, Yu said, "You know, what you are to Evan, what Eric and Rog were to you, James was to me."

Patrick stopped. Even the mention of that man's name turned his stomach and made him want to hit something. "Hardly. I'm not helping Evan so I can keep him on hand for a convenient fuck."

Yu pulled his hand free of Patrick's grip. "I'm sorry I said anything. You'll obviously never understand."

Patrick raked his hair back and pinned it behind his ears. "No, I'm sorry. That was out of line. I'm sorry, Yu, but... why would you bring him up after all this time?"

Yu stood with his feet apart and his palms pressed against his thighs, his gaze on the yellowed grass. "I... just want you to know I wasn't like Evan. I wasn't looking for a sugar daddy."

"How can you judge him?" Patrick responded before he could consider his words. "He wants the acceptance more than he wants the security money can provide. He just wants to be loved."

"I shouldn't have said anything," Yu repeated.

"Why did you?"

"James contacted me. He wants me to make something for him, a sculpture."

Patrick contemplated. "Well, so what? If he's a customer hoping to commission a piece, then take his money."

"I think he sees it as an investment. It's kind of flattering that he thinks my work will be worth something one day and wants some of it. James thinks in terms of the future, always. He's always speculating on how he can increase the value of things. I think he's hoping I'll make a name for myself, and he can sell the piece for twice what he paid. That wouldn't bother you? Wouldn't feel like charity?"

"I—No. But if it feels like that to you, turn him down. I trust your judgment. We're fine, though. We don't need the money, if you don't want to do it. What does he want, anyway?"

"A self-portrait in steel," Yu muttered. "Me. He wants me."

"It's up to you," Patrick said again, but as the minutes passed, a larger and larger part of him hoped Yu would say no. He didn't want James having even a tiny piece of Yu—he didn't deserve any of him. Patrick consoled himself with a reminder that Yu made him things all the time, without him even asking. Out of love. He looked down at the ring he wore.

"Okay. I'll think about it. I just didn't want it to be a secret. I don't want to fight." Yu lifted Patrick's hand and kissed the back. They'd come to the entrance of the main barn, and Ian met them in the doorway.

"Can I have him?" Ian asked.

"Wh-what?" Patrick responded.

"Your boy, Evan. I want him."

Patrick raised his eyebrows. "Well, he is underage. You might have to wait a year or two, noble Sir Ian, but it will probably be worth your while. You can court him chastely meanwhile."

Ian shoved Patrick's shoulder. "Smartass little shit. I want him to work in the stables. That kid has been busting his ass, and if he can keep it up, we could use him. If he proves himself, I might consider taking him on tour, on the circuit to other faires."

"I could kiss you on the mouth," Patrick said.

Ian held up his hands, fingers spread and palms toward Patrick. "Hell no. As cute as you are, I'm into tits and gash."

"Your success with the ladies must be unprecedented, using such romantic language," Yu said.

"Fuck you, Elion. And I don't mean it like that. Whatever." Ian waved a hand between them. "Can I hire this kid to help with the horses or not? The horses don't exactly stop eating and shitting during the off-season, and they need their exercise. Without Henry, we'll need someone extra when we move on from here. If this kid keeps working like he has been, we could use him when we go south after Christmas."

"I think Evan will be ecstatic," Patrick said. "He really needs a job, and he likes it here."

"Cool." Ian turned and walked into the barn, his boots raising clouds of sawdust as he made his way down the aisle to where Evan arranged bales of straw into a pile. He tapped the kid on the shoulder, and Evan turned to face him. Sweat had carved lines through the thin layer of dirt on his face, and his pale cheeks bloomed pink. Patrick smiled. Evan looked healthier than he had ever seen him—and happier. "I'd like to keep you on, caring for the horses over the winter, at least until Christmas," Ian said. "One of us can pick you up in the mornings and give you a ride home. What do you say?"

"Really?" Patrick wondered if the grin on Evan's face and the way his eyes misted would be considered "too gay" by the men on the Internet. "I love working with the horses. I-I would be happy to. Thank you so much. Wow. Do you mean it? Of course!"

"Right," Ian responded. "All these stalls need mucked out by the end of the day. We clean them morning and evening, and we strip them once a week and lay new straw. Get to work. Make sure you scrape up any of the sawdust that's wet with piss and replace it. If the water buckets are slimy, they'll need scrubbed out. Then you can fill the mangers with hay."

"Yes, sir," Evan said, eagerly taking up the pitchfork leaning against the wall.

Patrick stopped him before he could begin the grueling task Ian had set. "How are you doing?"

"Awesome," Evan responded. "This place is so cool."

"Good. We're all hoping you can join us for Thanksgiving next week. What do you say?"

"Gee, let me check my social calendar," Evan said with a roll of his dark eyes.

Patrick wanted to smack him at the same time as he wanted to hug him. "I'll drop by the shelter and pick you up. In the meantime, work hard. Ian will have high expectations."

"Thanks, Patrick. I will. I want to stay here, and I want to save up for a sword."

"Really?" Yu asked.

Evan nodded. "I watched you work a few times. It's so cool, and I want something you made. Plus, the idea of having a weapon makes me feel strong, like if I have one of your swords at my side, nobody can fuck with me. I know I can't walk down the street with it or anything, but I like the idea of having it. I'm going to save for one."

"I see," Yu said. Patrick caught the conspiratorial glint in his eyes. Yu *sucked* at trying to hide *anything*. "And I think everyone should have a sword. At one time, all important men carried one, and I'm sorry that has changed. I'll make a special one just for you."

"Sweet," Evan said, barely containing his glee and anticipation. "Henry said he'd teach me how to use it before he leaves to start working on that show."

"He's a good teacher," Patrick said. "Listen to him, and you'll win every tournament and be able to defend yourself in a street fight. He taught me some fancy moves for the arena, but he grew up on the North Side, and he also taught me some dirty tricks for when I was unarmed, in the real world."

"Thanks," Evan said, happiness radiating from his face. "For everything, Patrick. I'm going to start saving right away."

Grinning back, Patrick said, "I'm happy to do it. I'll pick you up next week, Evan. It might sound lame, but I'm really proud of you." He expected a sarcastic, teenaged retort and braced for it.

"I won't let you down," Evan said as he took up the pitchfork and went into the nearest stall. The big gray gelding Carlton usually rode in the tournament nickered softly and rubbed his forehead on Evan's back, almost knocking the small young man over but eliciting a chuckle. Evan gave the horse a scratch behind the ears before he started scraping the straw aside to look for the presents the animal had left him.

"Well, finish up, and then you can come to our place for dinner, if you want."

"Yu's cooking?" Evan said. "Hells to the yeah!"

"So what are you going to make for him?" Patrick asked Yu as soon as they left the barn.

"Katana," Yu said. "I need more practice making them, and I think it will be perfect for him. He's small, so he won't want something too heavy. A katana requires speed and skill over brute strength. I'll have it by Christmas and give it to him then, if he's still in our lives."

"What? Why wouldn't he be?"

Yu turned to look at him, frowning a little as he scooped up Patrick's hand. "You've done a lot for him, but he's a very troubled young man. There's pain behind his eyes I'm not sure I want to know the reasons for. You just can't…. You can't blame yourself if everything doesn't go the way you think it should. I know you'd try, but you can't always save everyone and fix everything."

"Yeah," Patrick said, thinking of his conversation with Yu's mother. Though he knew it was illogical, he couldn't help shouldering the responsibility for that failure.

"You have to take care of yourself too," Yu reminded him, as he often did. "Not just everyone else. You've got your hands full, dealing with me. You have to look out for yourself too."

Patrick chuckled and leaned in to kiss him. "No, I don't. I have you looking out for me. But I really hope I can help Evan."

"*We* can only try our best," Yu said. "A lot of it will have to come from him."

"Thanks," Patrick said.

"For what?"

"Giving me hope. Making me happy. Have you thought about when you want to have this wedding, and where?"

Yu arched his brows and the right side of his mouth quirked up. "I assumed we'd have it here, at the Faire. This is where all our friends are."

"I like that idea."

"Maybe during the Lovers' Hideaway?" Yu suggested. "Do you remember? That was when we spent the night together for the first time. Maybe we could even stay in a tent, just like we did back then. If you don't think that's too plain, of course. If you want to be treated like a princess, I'll make it happen. I mean, if you want a honeymoon suite at a fancy hotel—"

"No, I love that idea," Patrick said dreamily, remembering their first magical night together and all the trouble Yu had gone through to make it perfect. "I'm just not sure I want to wait that long. I guess I imagined early spring, when everything's in bloom. Early May, maybe. Late April, even. Before the Faire opens for the season."

"Should we set a date?" Yu asked. He fished his phone out of his pants pocket and pulled up the calendar.

"Maybe not yet," Patrick said. "You know what we have to do."

"What?"

"We have to call our parents and tell them, at least give them the chance to come. If they choose not to, which I guess is likely, at least we'll have extended the olive branch. I just don't want to start our lives off with a missed opportunity. Life's just too short not to even try. Isn't it?"

"Of course," Yu said, looking a little sick. "I-I guess we should renew our lease. Even if we decide to move, it will take a while to find another place. We should try to sign a six-month lease."

Patrick shook his head. "That won't go over with the manager. Leases are by the year, and she's already given us an extra month to decide."

"You should talk to her. Mrs. McCreary loves you."

"It's my red hair," Patrick said, shaking his head and tossing his bright unruly locks around. "She likes to make me tea and scones and pretend she's back in Ireland. It's kind of nice, like having a grandmother. She even complains I'm too thin. I think she's just lonely. I guess it can't hurt to talk to her."

They wandered over to the edge of the woods and sat in the crinkly grass. Patrick edged close to Yu against the increasing cold coming with the approach of evening. Yu draped his arms over Patrick's shoulders, and Patrick leaned back against his chest and his warmth. They talked about everything from eventually buying a house, to getting a cat, to what kind of cake they wanted at their wedding, until Evan finally found them. From the smell of the kid, Patrick was willing to wait a little longer so Evan could visit the shower house. He didn't want to breathe horse shit during the entire forty-minute drive to their apartment.

THE SUN hadn't even thought about rising when Yu woke Patrick with a kiss to the forehead and a gentle shake to the shoulder. Patrick grumbled, rolled away, and hid his head beneath the pillow. Now that Faire season had ended, he finally got to catch up on his rest, and he'd been having the loveliest dream about him and Yu swimming in a tropical reef, surrounded by colorful fish. Naked, of course. Everything had been bright and alive, the colors so vibrant they almost hurt his dreaming eyes. Neon afterimages of the fish and the coral flashed across his vision as he blinked, and he just wanted to sink back into that warm water.

"Come on, love," Yu persisted.

"Can we go to the beach for our honeymoon?" Patrick grumbled, throwing his arm across his eyes and trying to catch those brilliant fish by the tails as they flitted out of his imagination. "Somewhere tropical? Secluded?"

"Anything you want. But right now, you have to get up. You know I promised I'd help Roger cook."

"Forced him to accept your help, more like," Patrick muttered. "What time is it, anyway?"

"Almost four."

"God, Yu, that's… that's sacrilege." Patrick wriggled farther beneath the covers and clutched them tight around him. Still, he looked forward to celebrating Thanksgiving with his extended family, and he gradually managed to peel his head off the pillow. "There'd better be coffee."

Yu patted his butt. "You know it."

Patrick couldn't help it. He dropped his head back to the pillow and curled into a ball, his back to Yu. "Five more minutes."

Cool air accosted Patrick's bare body as Yu whisked the comforter and sheets away. He grasped Patrick's hips and rolled Patrick to his back. "I guess I'll have to wake you up the proper way." Yu gripped Patrick's thighs just above his knees and pulled his legs apart so he could crouch between them. In the darkness, he looked like little more than a blob, but Patrick could tell from his silhouette that he'd already dressed in trousers and a button-down shirt. Absently, still half-asleep, Patrick hoped it was the teal-blue one—the one the color of the water in his dream. Yu looked really good in that shirt....

All distractions flew from his mind when Yu cradled his balls in his hand and gave them a gentle tug. A moment later, he closed his warm, petal-soft lips around the crown of Patrick's cock, rubbing his tongue furiously against the groove on the underside. Pleasure shot from Patrick's root up through his body, awakening him almost instantly. He wound his fingers in Yu's silky hair as he tried to lie still and resist his body's instinct to thrust into the tight heat of Yu's throat. He groaned and stretched his neck, keeping his body still and content. Yu would take care of him.

Yu slowly slid his mouth down Patrick's length until he had Patrick's cock comfortably seated in his throat, and then he swallowed. Patrick bit his lips to muffle his cry as he almost shot. His reaction made Yu chuckle, and the sound sent wonderful vibrations through Patrick's dick and up his body. Goose bumps rose when Yu started moving, sucking hard while gliding his tongue along the underside of Patrick's erection and over the slit at the tip. He shuddered as Yu bobbed his head, and soon, way sooner than Patrick would have liked, Yu finished him spectacularly. Patrick saw stars and felt like he'd pass out as he came buckets down Yu's throat, his whole body convulsing. When his euphoria subsided enough for him to form a coherent thought, he grasped Yu's collar and drew Yu up to him, wrapping his arms around Yu's back and starting to doze again as Yu pecked across his jawline and chin, Patrick's seed sweet on his breath.

"The whole point of this was to wake you up," Yu said, nibbling Patrick's earlobe.

"I'm awake. I'm just really relaxed now, but I'm up."

"Get out of bed, then."

"It'd be easier if you weren't on top of me," Patrick said. "Not that I'm complaining. Want me to return the favor?"

"Yes," Yu said, his decisive, hungry tone making Patrick's mouth water, "but I'm afraid there isn't time. You need to get in the shower. You can have coffee as soon as you're dressed."

"Coffee first," Patrick complained.

"Oh no, my love. I know you better than that. If I bring a mug of coffee in here, you'll nurse it for half an hour. Get cleaned up, and you can drink it in the car. Come on; Evan will be waiting for us."

That thought finally compelled Patrick from his wonderful, warm sanctuary and into the bathroom.

DESPITE THE early hour and the cold that had left frost in runic patterns on the windows, Evan had been waiting for them outside the shelter. The three of them arrived at Eric and Roger's house in Mount Lebanon just after 5:00 a.m.

The warmth and aromas of food cooking already filled the house when they entered. Yu went into the kitchen, and Patrick slumped next to Eric on the sofa in front of the TV. Eric, in a Pittsburgh Pirates jersey over a thermal shirt and a pair of black track pants with a silver stripe up the sides, lay almost on his back as he sipped coffee from his mug. He shot Patrick a sympathetic look, and both of them smiled. The holiday feast at Eric and Roger's house was hardly a formal affair, and people wore what they felt comfortable in. Being together was what mattered, not appearances. Patrick took another sip from his travel mug as Evan sat on his left. Dishes clattered in the kitchen, and after a while Rog brought another carafe of coffee, three mugs, and a box of donuts. The three of them who weren't cooking settled down to watch a movie while they shared breakfast.

The quiet and calm lasted for a few hours, until Rog's sister, Kate, showed up with her husband, Leo, and their two young daughters, Naomi and Melissa. Kate carried a casserole dish into the kitchen while both girls dove on Eric. Their high, delighted voices competed to tell him everything they'd been doing at school, at their ballet lessons, and around the house. They'd recently adopted a pet bunny called Sam, which they talked about at great length, right down to detailed descriptions of cleaning up the creature's poo. They spoke so quickly Patrick could hardly keep up, but their happiness infected him, and he smiled, though he felt a little sorry for Sam the bunny as he imagined the girls hauling her around the house with her haunches dragging on the ground. Both girls took a turn on Patrick's lap, where they repeated what he'd heard them tell Eric, and then they ran screeching though the house in search of Uncle Roger. Leo, looking tired, draped his coat and scarf over the back of the recliner and sat down. Before long, he'd fallen asleep, and not even the thunder of his daughters stomping up the stairs to the room Eric and Rog kept for them caused him to stir.

Evan looked a little overwhelmed, sitting with his back straight and looking around the house with wide eyes.

Patrick set his coffee down on the low table in front of them and rested his hand on Evan's arm. "Are you okay? I take it this is different from the Thanksgivings you're used to."

Evan curled his lips like he'd just tasted something sour, maybe even caustic. "You could say that."

Patrick waited to see if Evan would elaborate. He knew next to nothing about Evan's life from before he'd come to the support group at the center. Had Evan been thrown out of his house for being gay? Had he run to escape abuse? Or was there another reason he now called a shelter home? When Evan remained silent and stared into the dark depths of his cup, Patrick didn't press him. Most of the kids he had worked with wanted to talk, to tell their stories, but they wanted to tell them in their own time, and Evan would likely do the same. He even seemed to relax a little and leaned back against the sofa when he realized Patrick didn't intend to grill him.

"Ever have a pet bunny?" Patrick teased.

Evan looked wistfully into the steam rising from his mug. "No. That would have been cool. I really like animals. They're just... good. If you're nice to them, they accept you."

"Yeah," Patrick said. "I always wanted a pet growing up. Even a hamster. I really wanted a dog, but I knew there was no way in hell my dad would allow that. I think now I want a cat."

"Did you come from a big family?" Evan asked Patrick.

"No. It was just me and my dad. He has a pretty bad drinking problem, so we never really celebrated holidays. We didn't have the money." Because he thought it might help Evan see his situation, whatever it was, wasn't so unique, Patrick proceeded to tell him about his life: how his brother had died when he was three, his parents had split up, and his father found solace in the bottle. He went on to tell Evan how he'd found friends and people who cared about and supported him at the Faire and how Rog had become his drag mama and taught him the nuances of the craft. It had been hard for Patrick and Yu at first, with money tight and both of them working almost constantly to make a place for themselves. But they hadn't given up, and things gradually got easier.

"I know it's what everyone says, Evan, but it really *will* get better, and you'll find people who'll help you up if you stumble. But you have to keep fighting; you can't give up even when it seems impossible to take another step. I can't sugarcoat it. You're going to have to bust your ass. But at the end of the day, you'll be able to say it's all yours."

Nodding slowly, Evan met Patrick's gaze. "How did your dad know you were gay?"

"The man who'd been stalking me sent him pictures of me performing in drag," Patrick said. "I think he hoped if my dad kicked me out I'd have no choice but to turn to him."

"But before that," Evan said. "You said he called you names before you started performing. You don't act *that* gay. How did he know?"

"I don't know if he really did," Patrick said. "I wasn't sure for a while. It took me a long time to come to terms with all of it."

"So you don't see your family anymore?" Evan asked. "Do you miss them?"

"Yes and no. They are still my parents, but they usually just made me unhappy. I have a new family now, with Yu, and Eric and Rog, and my drag sisters, and all my friends at the Faire. I wouldn't trade it for the world. I have to admit, I love holidays now, all of us getting together like this. I never knew what I was missing. We all have a lot to celebrate, to be thankful for."

"Yeah, I guess," Evan mumbled before turning his attention back to the television.

Shawn and Aouli arrived a little later, both with more food and wine to share. Tish and Tracy stopped by on their way to their grandmother's house, and Yu emerged from the kitchen with a platter of fancy appetizers: prawns wrapped in bacon, smoked oysters, mushroom toast, and warm artichoke dip with sweet-potato chips. Both he and Rog took a break for a snack and a glass of chardonnay. Henry and Jen, who planned to eat with Jen's family, arrived in time to partake, and even Tom stopped by, though all five of his children and their families and offspring waited at his farmhouse outside the city.

Finally, the time came to serve the meal Yu, Rog, and Kate had worked for hours to prepare, and Patrick, Evan, and Leo went into the dining room while Eric went to retrieve his nieces. After they finished the meal, which consisted of a soup course, two starters, and turkey with half a dozen sides, they retired to the living room to rub their distended tummies and watch football. As they picked at their pumpkin custard or one of five different kinds of pie and sipped wine, Melissa, age seven, conscripted Shawn into braiding her bouncy blonde locks into cornrows like his. Naomi dozed on Kate's lap, and Rog, who had been quiet through the meal, nothing like the eager host Patrick had expected and knew well, rested his head on Eric's shoulder. Patrick and Yu sat on the floor, with Yu leaning against the wall and Patrick reclining against his chest. Kate watched them with a smile as Patrick held Yu's hand, and Yu toyed with the ends of Patrick's hair.

"Roger told me the two of you are getting married. I'm so happy for you. It's just a shame you can't make any babies. They'd be beautiful," she said with a wink.

Patrick winced at the thought. Trying to help Evan was frustrating enough. Yu squeezed Patrick a little closer and chuckled softly into Patrick's hair. It surprised everyone when Rog pulled away from Eric, got off the couch, and hurried through the house. The back door opened and then slammed shut a minute later.

Patrick looked at Eric, and Eric shook his head. "He's been upset all week. Another surrogate fell through, and he's starting to worry we'll never have a child of our own. I told him it's fine—he's enough for me, and I'm completely content with our life—but he feels like something's missing."

"Oh, sh—sugar," Kate said. "Me and my big mouth. I had no idea. Have you thought about adopting?"

"We talked about it," Eric said, "but Rog really wants me to father the child. I guess I should go talk to him, though I don't know what I can say that I haven't already. It kills me to see him hurting, but I just don't know what else I can do."

"Let me?" Patrick asked, reluctantly pulling away from Yu and standing.

When Eric nodded, he crossed through the house and went out the back to the yard. Though the rain had tapered off, a cold drizzle, almost a fine mist, lent the hedges surrounding the lawn a smudged quality. Rog, standing next to the grill they'd covered for the winter, seemed oblivious to the moisture soaking his burgundy plaid shirt. Patrick bunched his shoulders up in a vain attempt to keep the cold rain from running down his collar as he crossed the soggy grass and laid a hand on Rog's shoulder. "Hey, Mama."

Rog turned and offered a smile Patrick could tell was forced. Then he hugged Patrick and kissed him on the cheek. "Hey, baby girl."

Since he had nothing relevant to say and couldn't even begin to offer advice on something like wanting a child to raise, Patrick did the only thing he could—he let Rog know he was there for him. As the drizzle soaked their hair and raised goose bumps on Patrick's skin, he slipped his fingers around Rog's hand and gave it a squeeze, which Rog returned along with a small smile, more sincere this time. Though the muddy water and tall wet grass soon saturated Patrick's ivory canvas high-tops, Rog made no move to retreat from the elements, so neither did he. It was the least he could do after what Rog and Eric had done for him. They'd accepted him when he'd been broken and floundering and helped him put the pieces back together—helped make him whole. For several moments, they stood in silence, watching the rain clump the yellowed grass and carve brown rivulets in the dark loam of the flower beds and beneath the hedge, cold water collecting at the ends of their hair and streaming down their faces.

Water dripped from the tip of Patrick's nose as he leaned his head to the side and rested it against Rog's shoulder. His hair darkened Rog's shirt in a reverse halo around his head. He sighed as his mind replaced the somber gray landscape in front of him with memories of happy summer days, barbeques, and nights around the fire with sparks spiraling into the darkened sky like faeries frolicking above them. "I've spent some of the best days of my life here with you, Mama. Remember that first night, after the cookout, when you and Aouli and Shawn taught me how to dance and walk in heels?"

Rog chuckled softly. "You were so cute. You reminded me so much of myself at your age. All I wanted was for you to find your place and be happy. Remember how you tried to say you weren't gay?"

Patrick shook his head, remembering how silly he'd been, thinking his friends at the Faire would turn their backs on him when he came out. "I was lucky. I don't know what would have happened to me if you and Eric hadn't looked out for me, convinced me there wasn't anything wrong with me. I'd probably be homeless like Evan, or worse. It would have been worse, Mama, I—"

"It's great what you're doing for him," Rog said. "We're all in the same boat together, and if we don't stand up for each other, no one will."

Patrick shook his head. "It's just so hard to know what to say to him. How did you know how to help me?"

"Girlfriend, you were easy. You *wanted* to do the right thing, work hard and get your own. All you needed was someone to tell you you could, and I was happy to be that mama, because I believed it from the first time I met you. I have a sneaking suspicion you would have made it with or without me and Eric. You are fierce, and not just as Queen Titania. Honey, I am so proud of you."

"Evan—He thinks the only way he'll get anywhere is if he gets a rich man to take care of him. How can I convince him he can do it himself? How can I make him know he's worth more than that?"

"Baby girl, those are answers I don't have. I don't think any parent does. You do the best you can, I guess." Rog's voice softened to less than a whisper as he finished the sentence, and he swiped his palm over his face, shedding water onto the front of his shirt and spattering it against Patrick's forehead and dripping-wet fringe.

"Eric told me what's bothering you. Not that there's much I can do."

"Sometimes I think I'm making too much of it all," Rog said, his gaze on the dark clouds in the distance that promised the rain would turn to snow if it got any colder. Patrick could almost taste the storm on the air, the impending deep freeze waiting to cripple the city. "I just think me and Eric have a lot to offer a child. I don't claim to know everything, but I know that child would be loved, and that he or she would always have support in whatever he or she wanted to do. I can promise nothing would make me turn my back on a child or to give less than everything I have to make one happy. When I think of the way some kids have to grow up, kids like you…. Eric tries to console me with all the trips we'll be able to take if we don't have the responsibility of a child, and he always makes sure I know his life is full because I'm in it, and he doesn't need more. I love him for that, but I can't get the idea of a baby with his beautiful brown eyes off my mind. I feel so empty sometimes, sitting in this quiet house after Naomi and Melissa have left. Patrick, honey, what should I do?"

"Rog, I'm twenty-two. I've never even considered raising a child. I don't think I'm ready for that kind of responsibility. I can barely take care of myself. Or Yu."

Rog turned to face Patrick, moisture beading in his eyelashes and one dirty-blond brow quirked up. "Oh, and what about Evan?"

"Evan just sort of happened."

"Yeah, well, babies just sort of happen to straight people all the time. Just ask my sister."

"Okay, Rog. If you want my advice, here it is, for what it's worth. Don't give up on your dreams. If I know one thing, it's that hope favors those who keep chasing her, keep reaching and trying to catch her in their hand like a butterfly. She might slip away 99 percent of the time, but eventually you'll grab that fickle bitch. In the meantime, though, I guess be happy with what you have. Right now, you have a house full of family who loves you. It's more than a lot of people have. You have that, that *warm* house.... That *dry* house."

"All right, all right, you little tart. Real subtle, bitch. I can take a hint." Rog, still clasping Patrick's hand, led him back toward the house. Only when he got back inside did Patrick realize how hard he'd been shivering. "I'm going to get changed. If you go down to the laundry room in the basement, you'll find some of Eric's sweatshirts in the basket. Put one of them on and put your shirt into the dryer. And Patrick, thanks. In spite of all the poetry, you said just what I needed to hear. It's just like Eric always says—you're too damn clever for your own good. You've grown into a damn fine man, and I'm proud to call you my baby girl. Go get changed. I'll make some hot chocolate."

"Um, Rog?" Patrick clutched his wet shirt away from his trembling skin as water dripped onto the kitchen tiles around him. Both of them looked like they'd just emerged from a lake. "You might give adopting a second thought. After all, nobody who I consider family is related to me by blood. None of the people who have been important in my life are. You and Eric, my sisters Aouli and Shawn, Jen, Henry, and everyone at the Faire—you're my family. Maybe there's a kid out there who really needs someone like you. *I* needed you."

Rog just nodded as he turned and went to retrieve some mugs from the cupboard above the stove. "Go get changed."

Patrick made his way down the stairs to the finished basement that served both as a laundry room and extra storage for Lady Regina's many costumes, accessories, and props. As he always did, Patrick glanced at the racks of sequined gowns with longing. He'd never be able to amass such an impressive collection of drag until he and Yu had a house of their own. That was what he wanted, he realized as he looked at the trio of cacti in their small clay pots lined up on the windowsill and the small wire basket holding change and other things that had been removed from trouser pockets before washing: a place to put their mark on, make their own, and put down roots. He'd never considered his father's hovel a home, and maybe that was why he yearned for one so keenly. As Patrick stripped off his sopping red button-down shirt, brown tie, and the undershirt beneath, he decided he'd talk to Yu about looking into buying a home. With what he earned performing and the profits from Yu's website and commissions at the Faire, they could afford it if they found the right place. Patrick didn't know if he'd ever want a child as Rog did, but he'd always wanted a pet since his father would never consider even a hamster. Yu had always had a cat growing up, and he adored the creatures. The sudden vision of two tricolored calico cats curled on a loveseat beneath a bay window, a book lying open next to them, drove some of the chill from Patrick's body.

God, he wanted that. A safe place, where he'd always be accepted. A place that belonged to him—to them—and where they belonged.

As Patrick opened the dryer to toss his wet garments inside, he heard hesitant footsteps on the stairs leading into the cellar. Expecting Rog, he ignored them, put his clothes in the machine, and turned it on. When he turned, it surprised him to see Evan standing there, his dark gaze glued to Patrick's bare torso.

"Everything okay, Evan?"

"Oh yeah. I've been looking for you. I wanted to thank you for bringing me here, for everything."

"You don't have to thank me," Patrick said. As Evan drew nearer, his wine-scented breath bloomed around Patrick, and his eyes looked glazed, the lids drooping languidly. Patrick knew the red stain across his cheeks and the bridge of his nose hadn't come from the warmth of the full living room. Apparently he'd been helping himself to the wine Eric and Rog usually provided to accompany meals. Since the rest of them only ever enjoyed a glass or two, no one had thought to monitor how much Evan imbibed, and he'd obviously gone as crazy as a kid set loose in a candy store.

"But I want to. I like small, slender guys like you." Evan reached for Patrick's face and squashed his lips against Patrick's before Patrick knew what was happening. The tang of alcohol coming from his mouth was strong and even stronger on the tongue he tried to push past Patrick's teeth. He had to practically pry the boy off him to get away.

"I don't expect this," he told Evan firmly. "I'm helping you because I think you're a great kid, and I want you to have a chance at a decent life. Not everyone who's nice to you has ulterior motives."

"Yeah, right. I might be young, but I'm not an idiot." Evan reached for the waistband of Patrick's corduroys and hooked his fingers beneath it before Patrick could catch his hands. He rubbed the heel of his hand down Patrick's length and cupped his balls. "Everyone wants this. Everyone likes this. Just give me a chance."

Patrick grasped Evan's shoulders and pushed him back, holding his upper arms to keep Evan a foot away. Evan looked up, and their gazes locked. "I don't want this from you," Patrick said. "You don't owe me this. Me, or anyone else."

"Come on, Patrick." Evan tugged so hard against Patrick's trousers he popped the button, and the zipper opened halfway. Evan dropped to his knees and rubbed his cheek against the bulge held within Patrick's black boxer-briefs. "I can be what you need; I know I can. I can be masculine and quiet like Yu. Give me a chance, and I'll make myself into the man of your dreams." He ran his wet lips and tongue over the cotton covering Patrick's cock, darkening the fabric with his saliva. "I know I can make you want to keep me."

"Evan, no!" Patrick grasped the collar of the younger man's worn T-shirt and pulled Evan away from his crotch. "You don't have to do this to make me like you. I like you, just not like that. You're more like a little brother to me, I—"

Evan got to his feet and brushed at the knees of his threadbare jeans. "Yeah, sure. I'm just not good enough, not enough of a man. If I was Yu or Eric, you'd let me suck your dick—"

"Yu is the only one who gets to do that," Patrick said, buttoning up his trousers. "Jesus, we're getting married."

"Whatever." Evan wiped his mouth on the back of his hand and scowled at Patrick before turning to hurry up the steps.

Patrick sighed and rooted through the clothes in the basket on the wooden bench until he found a plain brown hooded sweatshirt and slipped it on. Though it warmed his skin, it couldn't banish the chill Evan's actions and words had left in his heart. How could he make that young man understand he didn't have to trade his body for affection? His reaction today had likely only made Evan feel worse about himself. Though he hadn't intended it, he'd made Evan feel inferior. Dealing with him, trying to predict his responses, was beyond Patrick. Not for the first time, he wondered if he'd bitten off more than he could chew and if he should hand Evan off to a counselor trained to handle his skewed view of life. But no, Patrick decided, Evan had chosen to place his trust in him, and he'd do his best for the kid, just as others had done for him. Even so, he took a few minutes to himself in the quiet, lavender-scented laundry room before facing Evan again.

When he reached the top of the steps, Patrick took the hot chocolate Rog offered him and inhaled the sweet steam wafting from the mug. He thanked Rog and made his way back toward the living room and the certainty and comfort of Yu's arms. Eric and the others, filled and sedate after their fine meal, reclined, watching the game. Patrick cast his gaze around, but he didn't see Evan. Though the others didn't notice his concern, he hurried to check the kitchen and then the rooms upstairs. When he returned to the living room, probably pallid with stress and out of breath, every gaze focused on him.

"Evan is gone."

Chapter 9

PATRICK AND Yu spent the rest of the afternoon and evening driving around the quiet streets of Mount Lebanon, looking for Evan among the snow-caked brick houses and idyllic gardens. The snow fell harder after the sun set, sticking in thick clumps to the windshield like spitballs shot from a schoolboy's straw. Their SUV's headlights barely cut a swath through the swirling white, and the tires carved ruts in the slippery carpet thickening over the pavement. No one seemed to want to brave the first real storm of the winter, and save for those clearing sidewalks with shovels or snowblowers, Patrick and Yu didn't see anyone on the street.

Patrick's worry increased by the minute. When they'd picked Evan up that morning, he'd been wearing only secondhand sneakers, jeans worn thin, and a ratty flannel over his equally ratty T-shirt. No hat, no gloves. No decent coat. And it was fucking cold. Despite the heat blasting through the vents on the SUV's dash, Patrick's fingertips froze when he touched the windows. Beside him, Yu looked worn out, tired to the point his eyes on the road seemed unfocused and faraway, but he kept driving in silence, and Patrick was thankful. He'd told Yu what had happened in the laundry room, and while a sliver of him expected anger, Yu's nod felt soft and familiar, like walking into his cramped living room and sinking into the well-worn couch. It made him feel like he was home even as they braved the ever-worsening conditions.

The beep of a plow truck sounded behind them, and Yu pulled over to let it pass with a grating sound and a spray of dirty snow fanning around the heavy metal scoop. The SUV's tires spun, struggling for purchase against the slick road, but Yu eventually managed to halt the fishtailing of the back wheels and continue their slow process up the street.

"I think I really fucked up with Evan," Patrick said softly.

"How?" Yu didn't look away from the road. "What were you supposed to do? Let him blow you in Eric and Rog's basement?"

Patrick rubbed his stinging, tired eyes. His head throbbed. "Something I said made him feel... undesirable. Not good enough. I should have considered my words better."

"You won't do him any favors by coddling him," Yu said. "No one else is going to cater to his insecurities."

"You're angry with him."

Yu clenched his teeth and hissed a breath out between them. "Yeah. He has you sick with worry. After everything you've done for him.... It just seems ungrateful."

"He's just really hurting, Yu. I.... Yu, do you try to act straight?" Almost as soon as the question left his lips, Patrick realized how stupid it sounded. Of course Yu didn't. Yu couldn't even manage to act when social graces demanded it; he had a hard time picking up on subtle cues and reacting accordingly. He had never learned—or was incapable of knowing—when to tell the brutal truth and when to hold his tongue. Patrick loved that he never had to wonder if Yu's words were authentic. "No. Never mind. Do you think I act gay?"

"You are gay."

Patrick reached up to try to rub some of the knots out of the back of his neck. "That's not what I mean. Everyone seemed to know I was gay before I did. How did you know?"

Patrick saw Yu's small smile from the corner of his eye. "That night when you came to the blacksmith's shop, you watched me working like you wanted to eat me alive. Even *I* couldn't miss the way you looked at me."

The memory of Yu's sweaty, chiseled torso beneath his leather apron made Patrick smile too. "I did. I wanted to lap up the streams of sweat I saw running down your body. I had never seen anything so beautiful."

Yu looked away from the wheel long enough to offer Patrick a wide grin, one that reached his eyes and crinkled them to crescents.

"But Evan. He's… small, delicate. He thinks he's too effeminate for other men to be interested. I remember you saying you didn't think you'd like a man completely shaved. Is it true, what he thinks? I don't like to think of gay men, of the community I'm a part of, judging each other like that when we should be supporting each other."

"I can't speak for anyone else," Yu said, reaching over to drape his hand across Patrick's knee, "but I fell in love with *you*, not your body hair. I've never found you effeminate, even though you perform in drag. You're a beautiful man, and a passionate, intelligent, and sensitive one."

"Could you have fallen in love with someone like Evan?"

"That's an unfair question, Patrick. I hardly know Evan, and he's a child. And I'm in love with you. Have you considered that his insistence that no man wants him is his way of protecting his heart? That if he convinces himself no one will want him, he doesn't have to take a chance on anyone, risk the difficulty of a relationship? Risk being hurt again?"

Patrick hadn't, but he could see how it might appear that way to Yu. "I wish I knew more about his life, what's led him to think all he has to offer is sex."

"For a long time, I told myself no one would put up with me, with my long hours of work and awkwardness in social situations, because if I believed that, I could blame others and not myself. I was afraid to be told I wasn't good enough again. I stayed safe behind the walls I'd built, until you came along and took a battering ram to them. Until you, uh, insisted, I didn't have to take the risk, because I'd convinced myself no one would want me."

"How do I make Evan see that?"

Yu chuckled. "Just be as stubborn as you were with me. He'll have no choice."

"Am I that domineering?"

"I needed it, Patrick. If you'd given up, I'd still believe no one would ever accept me."

"You don't worry anymore, do you? That I'll change my mind?"

"No, not anymore." Yu squeezed his thigh. "You've become the one thing I can always depend on. It means more to me than I can adequately express."

Exhaustion and anxiety brought the frayed edges of Patrick's emotions near the surface, and Yu's declaration rubbed against the exposed ends, almost making Patrick tear up. He hated how weepy he got when he was tired, but he knew Yu had seen it before and wouldn't slink away. Patrick could think of only one thing to say. "You're everything to me. Thank you."

Yu shook his head. "Let's find this kid so I can get you home and into bed where I can hold you."

Another hour passed, and Patrick was almost ready to give up hope. The shelter where Evan was staying was all the way back in Pittsburgh. He wouldn't have tried to walk there, would he? Had he taken shelter somewhere else against the increasing snow? Patrick didn't dare consider what else could have happened in the hours Evan had been exposed to the elements with little protection. Conditions were quickly getting so treacherous they were putting themselves in danger by continuing to navigate the unattended suburban streets. "Maybe we should just head home. If Evan doesn't want to be found, we won't find him."

"We'll give him a few more minutes," Yu said, guiding their vehicle along the road in front of the high school. Sure enough, Patrick noticed a figure, little more than a streak of darkness cut against the white veil of the snow, moving along the sidewalk with his shoulders pressed nearly to his ears and caps of ice over his head and shoulders.

Yu pulled over, and Patrick jumped from the vehicle almost before it came to a sliding stop. He slipped through the snow to reach Evan and grasp his shoulders. Evan turned around, and the bluish tint to his lips and the chattering of his teeth hardly surprised Patrick, though they did worry him. He hurried to fling open the rear doors of the SUV and push Evan onto the backseat, then climbed in behind him soon as he sat down and wrapped his arms around Evan to share some of his warmth.

"Please don't take me back to the shelter," Evan bit out from between clenched and rattling teeth.

"Okay," Patrick said, drawing Evan's frail, cold body against his chest and meeting Yu's eyes in the rearview mirror. "We'll just go home."

Evan shook hard enough against Patrick to truly scare him. As cold as he'd ever gotten working at the gas station in the winter, Patrick had never jerked that hard, not even when he'd been cold enough to cry. When he touched the skin of Evan's face, it felt as frozen and inanimate as the glass of the window had, like it would break as easily against something fine and pointed. Living out of his car had proved a hard habit for Patrick to break, and he felt glad as he reached into the compartment behind the backseat and found a green fleece blanket to wrap around Evan's quivering body. He tucked the edges tight behind Evan's back as he smoothed the pale, wet hair off Evan's face. Evan's skin temperature didn't seem to be rising.

"You were looking for me?" Evan choked out in chilly puffs, as if he'd been running a marathon through the blizzard.

Patrick nestled closer, draping a leg across Evan's lap, trying to cover him in his body and keep him warm. "Of course. We care about you."

Evan clutched the arm Patrick had draped across his chest. "But you don't want me. I don't get it, Patrick. What do you get out of this?"

"Hopefully a friend, a man we can be proud to call a part of our family," Yu said without turning his attention from the dangerous stretch of highway they'd reached.

Evan curled into a ball and rested against Patrick, still shaking hard. Yu drove faster than was probably safe given the conditions, and before long, they pulled into the secure lot of their building and parked the car. Yu killed the ignition and pocketed the keys, and then he came around the vehicle to open the back door for Patrick and Evan. Patrick stepped gladly into the six inches of snow, happy to be home, but Evan's legs buckled when he tried to exit the vehicle. He would have slipped and landed on his ass if Yu hadn't caught his arm. Together, Patrick and Yu supported the frozen and exhausted young man, guiding him into the building and up the steps to their apartment. Evan had some difficulty on the stairs, as lifting his feet came at a great effort.

Once inside, Patrick helped Evan to the couch while Yu went into the kitchen to make coffee and call Eric and Rog to let them know everything was okay and that they wouldn't be returning to the party. When he got Evan situated and covered with the knitted blue blanket Jen had made, Patrick went to the inglenook to light the gas-powered fire. The open flames always made Patrick feel warmer when he was chilled to the bone, and though it might have been psychological, he hoped watching the fire flickering in the hearth would help to banish the cold gripping Evan. Just in case it didn't, he stretched out on his side next to Evan and wrapped his arms around Evan's waist. When Evan touched the nape of

Patrick's neck, his fingers felt at least a little warmer than a corpse's. They held each other close, and although Patrick felt Evan's arousal pressing against his belly, he neither pulled away nor pressed against it. "I just need to get you warm, Evan."

"Can I stay here tonight?" Evan asked, his brittle voice cracking with desperation. He still shook so hard a hail of chill droplets flew into Patrick's face from his hair, and the blue tint hadn't left his lips. Patrick was starting to wonder if he should take Evan to the hospital.

"Yeah, tonight," Patrick said, "on the couch."

Evan made a disappointed sound, and when he tried to grind his erection against Patrick's belly, Patrick stood up and tucked the blanket under Evan's chin. He raked the wet, white-blond hair off Evan's face just as Yu appeared with a tray containing three mugs and a carafe of coffee.

Evan sat up, but he was still shivering. Patrick knew he had to get out of his wet clothes. He pushed the blanket back and grasped the bottom of Evan's T-shirt, so soaked it was almost translucent, before pulling it up over Evan's head. Evan toed off his sneakers and drenched socks, and then he stood to shed his thin jeans between the sofa and coffee table. Patrick choked on a gasp as he witnessed what lay beneath Evan's clothes.

A crisscrossing network of scars, some healed over to pale pink strips, others still an angry, puffed-up purple, lay like a tangled net over the boy's chest, back, belly, and the backs of his legs. Evan's skin was still fish-belly white, and it made the marks stand out in stark contrast. Patrick quickly looked away; the last thing Evan needed to see was the dismay on his face—Evan would just add it to the long list of things he found wrong with himself and his body. When Patrick looked up and met Yu's gaze, Yu looked like he wanted to pick up one of the weapons decorating their living room and find the person responsible for the scarring. The serene anger on his face scared even Patrick. Since Patrick didn't want Evan to notice Yu's flared nostrils or the way his lips pulled back to reveal teeth clamped tightly together, he hurried to ask Yu to find Evan something to wear. When Yu went into the bedroom, Patrick turned his attention back to Evan's scrawny body, trembling in his too-large, worn-out blue boxer-briefs. Evan actually had a nice body—lean, compact muscles showing prominently because he was a little too thin, but good proportions and a natural grace to his posture. Patrick hoped Evan would come to realize the beauty he possessed. It hurt his heart to think Evan could look at himself and find disgust in what he saw.

He stood and draped the blanket around Evan's shoulders, rubbing his arms briskly to try to help get his blood flowing. Evan pulled the blanket tight around him and looked over it to meet Patrick's gaze. Patrick hated the shame he saw in Evan's dark eyes, and he knew Evan knew he'd seen the old wounds. Something else flitted across Evan's expression: gratitude, maybe, for Patrick not grilling him on what he'd seen. Evan brushed his lips against Patrick's, but Patrick pulled quickly away, though he continued to hold Evan's shivering body.

"Patrick, I'm sorry for what happened back at Eric and Roger's house. I really just thought I could make you happy, pay you back for everything you've done for me. It's really all I have to offer."

Patrick squeezed Evan tighter around his shoulders. The boy was little more than pale skin and fine, brittle bones within his embrace. He could break so easily if Patrick wasn't careful. "That's not true, Evan. You have a lot to offer. And you can pay me back by getting your life on the right track. All I want is to see you find your place."

"I just... hoped I could make you want to keep me."

"I'm your friend, and that's not going to change."

Evan just nodded, and then he slowly pulled on the thermal underwear and gray sweats Yu handed him. He still seemed a little unsteady, so Patrick helped him back onto the couch, covered him, and added the extra blanket Yu had also brought. Evan curled on his side and propped his elbow against the armrest so he could sip at his coffee. Patrick took a seat near Evan's feet at the other end of the couch, and Yu sat on the floor between Patrick's knees. They turned on the television and spent the next hour watching a late-night variety show. By the time it ended, Evan lay curled in a tight ball, fast asleep, cheeks and lips returned to a healthy rose.

"HE CAN'T stay here," Yu said, picking apart the buttons of his teal shirt when they reached the bedroom. It felt like years had passed since Patrick had thought about that shirt while Yu curled over him in the dark. "We barely have room for ourselves."

"I know." Patrick toed off his canvas sneakers without untying them and kicked them toward the foot of the bed. Yu had been quiet for the past hour, and not his usual, contented quiet that meant he didn't have anything meaningful to say at the moment, but a strangled quiet. Patrick could almost see the words churning inside him, wanting to boil up and erupt, but unable to make it past Yu's constricted throat. He pulled off Eric's sweatshirt, tossed it into the hamper, went to stand behind Yu, and gently removed Yu's stiff fingers from his buttons. Leaning into the curve of Yu's back, fitting perfectly against him as he had since the first time they'd held each other, Patrick took over undoing his shirt. When he finished, he slid the shirt off Yu's shoulders and pressed a light kiss to the golden skin he revealed. "What is it?"

Yu sighed and leaned back against Patrick, consenting to let Patrick help him shoulder his burden. He granted that permission more easily every day. "I was very angry at Evan earlier, when we were driving around looking for him. I thought he was just being selfish, and he had you so upset.... Then, when he took off his shirt, and I saw what had been done to him... I'm the selfish one. I spent days moping around because my parents didn't come to my senior show, but compared to what that boy has obviously gone through, their not supporting my career feels so insignificant."

"Hey." Patrick worked his hands beneath the bottom of Yu's white tank top and ran his fingers up the subtle bumps of his abs. "It hurt you. It's not insignificant. Not all scars are on the outside."

Yu rested his head back against Patrick's shoulder, giving Patrick access to peck and nibble up and down the side of his long, graceful neck. As he did, Patrick moved his fingers up to Yu's nipples and grazed them with the pads of his fingers. Yu moaned softly, and his buttcheeks clenched. Patrick moved his hands back down Yu's belly until he could pick apart the buckle of his belt. Soon Yu's pants dropped and pooled around his feet. He stepped out of them, bent to shed his shoes and socks, then turned, took Patrick's hand, and led him the few feet to the bed.

Patrick sat on the edge and then fell back on his elbows, letting Yu slip his trousers and briefs over his legs, then lying naked on the red satin sheets. Yu stood staring down at him until Patrick reached out his hand and caught Yu's wrist. He moved up toward the pillows as Yu lowered himself onto Patrick's body, the sparse trail of hair meandering down from his belly button to his pubic patch catching delightfully against Patrick's shorn skin. They found each other's mouths and let their lips weave together, bumping tongues. Patrick felt pain and desperation in the movements of Yu's mouth and body, and he soaked up what wafted off his partner as he exposed his own raw, tangled core to Yu. They were good at this, both of them: taking the scraps of things and sewing or forging the cast-off pieces into something beautiful and worthwhile. Both of them took the scrapings others cast aside and constructed beauty, art. They lay against each other, volleying the confusion and regret between them until they'd broken it into pieces small enough to be brushed aside, and then, liberated, Patrick opened his legs and wrapped them around Yu so they could make love. They took the shards and reforged them, sewed them together into something wonderful. Life had taught them how to use what they were given, both of them: taking discarded things, pulling them apart, and reassembling them into something unexpected and beautiful.

As Patrick lay panting and sweating after disengaging from Yu's body, he realized what they were building from all the scraps they melted down: armor. They needed steel to protect their hearts.

Chapter 10

PATRICK AND Yu slept until almost lunchtime the following day, when the aromas of coffee, toast, and sausage finally compelled them from their warm bed and the security of each other's arms. They found Evan in the kitchen, seated at the table, where he'd set three plates amidst the steel rings, wire, and tools Yu had been using to make a chain-mail cuirass for one of his clients. The boy had piled Yu's sketches and notes neatly out of the way to make room for a platter of what looked like microwaveable sausages, scrambled eggs, and toast. Patrick realized Evan must have woken before them and braved a trip to the store, and Evan's sneakers, sitting in a pool of water in the corner, confirmed his suspicion.

Evan looked up from the Sunday paper he'd been marking with a pink highlighter and smiled at them as they sat down. He still wore the sweats Yu had given him the previous night, but from the look of his hair and smooth face, he'd showered and shaved either before or after his trip to the market. His dark brown eyes looked alert, and most of the lines around his mouth and eyes had smoothed and disappeared after a good night's rest. Patrick thought he actually looked like a kid, sitting there in comfortable clothes and enjoying a holiday morning. It made him smile.

"Wow, Evan. This is so great. Thanks for doing this," Patrick said.

Evan batted his pale eyelashes, but for once, it didn't seem sexual. He looked like a little boy praised by a parent. "Well, I'm sure it won't compare to what Yu would have made you for breakfast."

"You shouldn't do that." Yu reached across the table to squeeze Evan's hand. "You shouldn't trivialize it when you do something wonderful. It's okay to take credit when you've earned it."

Evan grinned wider and nodded, while Patrick looked at Yu with a measure of surprise. While Yu wasn't as selfish as he often criticized himself for being, he rarely offered encouragement to others; Patrick suspected Yu didn't think his praise worthy of sharing. When he'd started helping Evan, decided to stand beside him and help him find his way, Patrick had expected to do it alone. Yu had more than enough on his plate already, and this wasn't his crusade. That he'd given his support without Patrick even asking meant so much. Though he wouldn't have thought it possible, he loved Yu even more. How had he gotten so lucky? Was Yu's fate the universe's way of compensating Patrick for how shitty his life had been up until they'd met? If so, Patrick thought it a fair trade and then some.

Evan served them the food he'd made, and they ate it quietly. Patrick was hungry in spite of the feast the day before, and though the microwaved sausages were greasy and overly salty, they hit a spot when washed down with coffee with plenty of sugar and half-and-half. After he cleaned his plate, he worried the amount of fat and carbs—something his body was no longer accustomed to having two days in a row—might send him back to bed. He refilled his mug so he wouldn't waste a day off. He had to perform later, at Joe's, but he didn't want to squander his free time lounging around.

"What are you planning to do today?" Patrick asked Evan.

"I'm looking for a second job. Based on the paper, a lot of retail stores are hiring seasonal help. The malls are out, since I don't have a car, but I found a bunch of places in the city. It won't be a permanent solution, but at least I'll be able to make some extra money. I need to find something in the evenings so it won't conflict with my work at the Faire. Patrick, we're about the same size. Do you think I could borrow a shirt? You know, so I can make a good impression. And could I print off a few copies of my résumé on your computer?"

"Yeah, of course." It sounded to Patrick like Evan had understood what he'd been trying to tell him about making his own way, and the kid seemed ready to take on the world. "I don't have to be anywhere today, so I'd be happy to take you to some of these places, if you want."

"That will work out nicely," Yu added. "I'd planned to go to the forge. I have some commissions to finish up and a few special projects I want to get underway. Now I won't have to feel guilty about leaving you alone and bored. We should meet up for dinner."

Evan groaned with anticipation. How could he still be hungry? "You're cooking?"

Yu grinned. "I thought we might go out. Do you like sushi?"

"Love it," Evan said, making Patrick wonder where a homeless street kid had tasted the expensive cuisine.

"Umi, at eight?" Yu suggested. "One of my customers just paid me for a full set of armor, so my treat."

Patrick stood and patted Evan on the shoulder. "Come on. Let's find you something presentable to wear."

EVAN CAME out of his third interview of the day, this one at a chocolate shop, looking dejected. Patrick, who had waited by the car, offered a sympathetic smile when Evan shook his head.

"What's the problem?" Evan looked great in the tan shirt and paisley tie Patrick had loaned him, very professional.

"It's that I don't have a permanent address," Evan said, kicking at the dirty ice built up around the base of the parking meter. "The lady in the candy shop said that makes me a liability. Do you think I could use your address? No one will know."

"I… I guess so. Sure." Patrick wanted to offer to let Evan stay with them, but they just didn't have the space. "Where's our next stop?"

Evan pulled out the piece of newspaper he'd marked up with pink streaks. "There's a club looking for a bar-back. It's walking distance from the shelter."

"Bar-backing is really hard work," Patrick warned. "It's lugging kegs and cleaning up puke a lot of the time."

Evan looked over his shoulder and smiled at Patrick. "It's a gay bar. If I work hard and learn what I can, maybe I can move up to bartender. Ian and the other jousters are leaving after Christmas to perform at faires down south, so I'll need something. I think I'd like this job. Can I use you as a reference? Queen Titania will go a long way."

"Really?"

Evan rolled his eyes. "I'd heard of her before I ever met you, Patrick. Queen Titania, Lady Regina, Miss Anita Lei, and Sha-Queera are Pittsburgh drag royalty. So, can I drop your name?"

"I had no idea so many people knew who I am," Patrick said. "Do you want me to come with you?"

Evan seemed to consider. "Do you think that'll help? Or will it look like I need my mama for support."

"I… don't know if I'm ready to be anyone's mama," Patrick said. He remembered how proud Rog had been upon assuming that title, but Rog had been so much more ready for it than Patrick. "I'm not ready, but I'll be your mama, Evan. I'll stand by you, if you want."

"Yeah. I do."

Together, they went down the stairs into the dank, cramped establishment with the purple walls and porn playing on the TVs at the corners of the room. It reeked of stale smoke and old booze, reminding Patrick of his father's house. They met with a chubby, older man named Pete at one of the tables in front of the bar.

Pete took short puffs off his Virginia Slim as he eyed Patrick and Evan from across the table. "Are you willing to work with your shirt off?"

"Wait," Patrick said, halting Evan's positive response. "Why would he do that? He won't be receiving tips. If you want to hire him on as a shot boy, then maybe we can talk, but there's no reason for a bar-back to work without a shirt."

Pete took a drag from his slender cigarette and exhaled a cartoon-perfect puffy cloud of smoke. The eyeliner he'd used to accentuate his eyebrows had started to melt, sending watery blackish streams of sweat mixed with kohl toward his sagging eyes.

"All right, all right. Don't get your panties in a bunch, Queen Titania. The shirt can stay on. It pays ten dollars an hour, cash under the table. Can you start tonight?"

"Tonight?" Evan smiled wide.

"Yeah, honey. It's Black Friday. We'll be busy. If you still want the job, be back here at eight."

"Great!" Evan reached across the table to shake Pete's hand. "Thank you so much."

Pete waved his long, nicotine-stained fingers in front of his face. "Yeah, well, maybe get your friend there to come perform, and we'll call it even. Queen Titania would do wonders for this shit hole."

Looking around, Patrick didn't think he'd have room to dance in his cage bustle, and he wouldn't feel even remotely safe. This was the kind of dive where bad things happened in the bathroom. With some effort, he kept his thoughts to himself and took Evan's elbow to hurry them up the steps toward the door.

After the stale air in the bar, Patrick welcomed the cold wind and light flurries that met them outside. "Evan," he began cautiously. He didn't want to burst the kid's bubble, but he had a few things he needed to say. "It's great that you got another job and you'll be making some more money. You're going to have to be careful, though. That guy, Pete, didn't even ask for your age or social security number. The place is a little shady. Some of the guys, the customers, are probably going to try to take advantage of you. They're guys who can smell naïve and vulnerable like bloodhounds. You... you're going to have to be very careful not to mistake a guy trying to fuck you for real affection. Some of these guys can be pretty convincing."

"How will I know?" Evan asked as they strolled slowly back toward where Patrick had parked his car.

"Well, for starters, a decent guy is willing to wait until you're ready. He won't try to pressure you. And any kind of a decent man will ask how old you are, and he won't try to sleep with you when he finds out you're underage. That is, as long as you don't lie."

Evan stopped walking and took Patrick's hand. "I won't lie. I promise. I'm going to go there and empty ashtrays and carry kegs. It's probably going to be disgusting and suck ass, but I'm going to do it the best I can. You're the first person who's ever wanted to see me succeed. I'm going to make you proud of me. And... and thanks for standing up for me to Pete. No one's ever done that for me, and it felt really good."

Patrick remembered saying almost those exact words to Eric and Rog a couple of years ago, and he remembered how validated he'd felt when someone had found him worth defending. "I was happy to do it. Like I said, you're going to have to make sure nobody tries to take advantage of you, because I won't be there next time."

"I will. I promise."

"And no drinking," Patrick said firmly. "Anybody offering you alcohol or encouraging you to drink probably doesn't have your best interests at heart."

"Duh," Evan said. "You can trust me. I can take care of myself."

Patrick didn't know if that was entirely true, but he also knew what Yu had said made sense. If he coddled Evan and never let Evan fight his own battles, the kid would never learn how. Even as his mind knew he had to give Evan distance, his heart just wanted to stand in front of the boy and shield him from the world. He wanted to take all the broken bits and make them into armor for Evan. He couldn't imagine how confused, how torn apart, he'd be if Evan was his son instead of a kid who'd come into his support group a few months ago.

"Look, if anybody gives you trouble or makes you feel uncomfortable, even if it's just a feeling, you call us," Patrick said. "Don't wait to see if you're right. It can be too late by then. Believe me; I know. Call. Anytime. I'll be there."

Evan opened his mouth like he might argue, but then he bit his lower lip and threw his arms around Patrick's neck, almost knocking Patrick over. He buried his face against Patrick's shoulder and hugged Patrick so hard Patrick could hardly breathe. As soon as his surprise subsided, Patrick hugged him back, held him, because he needed it, and to hell with the people gawking at them as they walked by.

EVAN DECIDED to go back to the shelter to get ready for his first night of work instead of returning to Shadyside with Patrick and made Patrick promise to get a rain check from Yu on the sushi. The slow drive through the holiday traffic gave Patrick time to think. While the thought of Evan having access to alcohol and dozens of men willing to provide something like the affection and acceptance he craved worried Patrick, he had to trust the kid. He had to let Evan live. He had no idea what Evan's upbringing had been like, but Evan was smart, and he'd seen what Patrick, Yu, and the people at the Faire had achieved through hard work.

It surprised Patrick when he reached their building, climbed the stairs, and heard soft music coming from inside the apartment. He'd expected Yu to stay working at Wade's until well after dark since they weren't going out for dinner. He liked Yu being around, even if both of them were working and not talking or even paying much attention to each other. The world just felt right when Patrick could look up from something he was sewing and see Yu bent over a piece of armor with a file. They needed a house so Yu would have work space and Patrick would have storage for his costumes. Patrick really wanted what Rog and Eric had—a place to make their own, a place to have dinners and entertain friends. He wanted to come home to two cats napping on the bookshelf and Yu cooking in the kitchen. Maybe they could have a small garden out back, grow herbs and tomatoes. The idea of a real home was important to Patrick, and the time had probably come to let his soon-to-be-husband in on his plans.

First, though, they needed to do something much less pleasant.

At the table in the kitchen, Yu sat fitting steel rings together, making chain mail. Some vaguely Celtic music, flutes and drums, drifted in from the living room, and the scent of coffee greeted Patrick as he took off his wet boots and left them on the mat by the door. He placed his coat and scarf on a hook nearby.

"How was your day with Evan?" Yu asked without looking up from his work.

"Successful, I guess. He found a job bar-backing at a sleazy little place downtown. It's not the best atmosphere for him, but...."

"He's practically an adult, Patrick. You can't make his decisions for him."

Patrick stood behind Yu, rested a hand on Yu's shoulder, and leaned down to kiss the part of his silky hair. "I know. He's just so starved for love. I'm afraid he'll see some dirtbag trying to fuck him for something it's not."

"You've done everything you can to show him otherwise. For what it's worth, I think he'll be okay. He has strength, deep down. If he didn't, he wouldn't have survived whatever gave him those scars. Now, forget about him for a few minutes and take time to take care of yourself. At least make yourself a sandwich before you start getting ready for the show."

"Actually, I thought we might call our parents," Patrick said. "We might as well get it out of the way. When we know how they feel, we'll be able to get past it and start planning this wedding for ourselves and the people who will be happy for us."

"It doesn't sound like you're expecting a positive response."

"Are you?" Patrick asked.

"No," Yu said as he stood up and stretched his arms over his head. "I'm dreading it. My mother has an uncanny ability to make me feel like the most worthless thing to ever exist. I'm not looking forward to being reminded how much of a disappointment I am."

"I won't force you to call them, but… but what if they've changed their minds? Do you want to miss the chance to know that?"

"And maybe your father quit drinking," Yu said. "But I agree. Let's go into the living room."

Patrick followed him, and they sat together on their sagging old couch, watching the flames flicker low in the hearth. Patrick fished his phone out of his pocket. "I'll go first."

He dialed his father's number, and the ensuing message in the electronic, feminine voice telling him the line had been disconnected came as little shock. "I guess the old man quit paying the phone bill. Ugh. That means I'll have to go over there in person."

"I'll go with you," Yu offered.

"The place is a real shit hole," Patrick said, suddenly embarrassed for Yu to see the conditions he'd grown up in, especially after seeing the palatial home where Yu had spent his childhood.

"Do you think I'm going to hold that against you? Give me a little more credit than that. Besides, I'm not letting you go alone. You forget I saw what your father did to your face the last time you two talked. If he tries laying a finger on you again, he's going to find out why I'm the second best swordsmith on the East Coast."

"The caveman side of you is sexy sometimes," Patrick said, snuggling closer to Yu and resting his head on Yu's shoulder. "But I can take care of myself. Maybe I couldn't back then, but I've been training with Henry and the knights for almost two years, and I can now."

"I know you can. But taking care of you is still my job." Yu wriggled a fingertip against the ticklish spot on Patrick's waist, making Patrick shriek and giggle.

"So, who's first?"

"What?" Yu asked, moving his hand up Patrick's side so he could twist and toy with the ends of Patrick's hair.

"If you're the second best swordsmith on the East Coast, who's first?"

"Wade, of course. Though he finally admits my work isn't utter garbage."

"That's the ultimate compliment, coming from him," Patrick said.

"It is! I never thought it would happen when he took me on as an apprentice, but I've become quite fond of the nasty old bastard. If we decide to leave, I'm going to miss the way he comes up behind me while I'm working and grunts over my shoulder. That's his way of telling me I'm doing a good job. Most people would have probably picked up on that right away, but it took me years. It takes a long time for me to understand people. Especially the things they don't say."

"I know. Even if we leave, we'll come back to visit," Patrick said. "First things first, though."

With dread, Patrick dialed his mother's number. It would be a little after three in the afternoon in Los Angeles, and he hoped dropping a few grand in designer boutiques might have put her in a good mood.

She picked up her cell on the third ring, and her artificially sweetened voice was loud on the other end. "Patrick? Well, isn't this a surprise. Hi, honey. How *are* you?"

"I'm good, Mom. Do you have a few minutes?"

"Sure. The girls and I are just having a late lunch and some cocktails at Nobu. We all got up early to get a start on our Christmas shopping. You *know* how exhausting that can be, what with finding gifts for everyone and then dresses for all the different holiday parties Stan gets invited to. You don't want to be seen in the same gown twice, not when you're going to dinner parties with movie producers and directors. Honey, guess who invited us to a luncheon?"

"I don't know, Mom. I actually—"

"Well, guess, honey. Think about the most talked-about action movie of the summer."

"I don't want to play this game, Mom. Do you want to hear what I called to tell you or not?"

"I haven't heard from you in over a year," she responded as glass and silverware clinked softly in the background. "Forgive me if I thought you might want to catch up a little bit, hear what's been going on in our lives. I thought you might wonder how your sisters and brother are doing. Chelsea just got a modeling contract, and Zane will have his film debut as a student in a new sitcom—"

"I'm really happy to hear that," Patrick lied. "Do you want to hear about *me*?"

She made a small sound of exasperation, clearly telling Patrick nothing he could possibly say would compete with the achievements of her perfect family. "Go ahead, honey."

He braced himself and squeezed Yu's hand, needing skin, bone, something solid. "Well, it's good news. I-I'm getting married."

"Oh my God, Patrick. Did you get some poor girl pregnant?" She spoke loudly, no doubt so her friends would hear and she could lament her suffering to them when the call ended. "This doesn't have to ruin your life. How far along is she? Can she get rid of it? Do you need money? You're what—twenty?"

"Jesus. Do you really not remember how old I am? I'm twenty-two."

"That is still far too young to take on the responsibility of a baby. One of the biggest mistakes I ever made was having children so young."

"Thanks, Mom."

"Oh, honey, you know that's not what I meant," she crooned, the false sweetness oozing insidiously over the connection, as if Patrick had been the insensitive one by implying she'd said something she hadn't. "So, how much do you need to make this little problem go away? A few thousand?"

"No. Just stop talking, please. Stop for a second, and just be quiet until I finish. Please."

"There's no need to be rude, Patrick. I'm offering to help you, after all."

"I don't need help! There's no pregnant girl! There's no girl at all. I'm getting married because I'm in love. *His* name is Yu, and we've been living together for two years now. We're hoping to get married in the spring."

"Is that even legal?"

"Well, not in Pennsylvania, but we're planning to—"

"So it isn't a *real* wedding, then. Thank God. I still think you're too young, and you still have no education. At least you don't have to be worried about being saddled with kids."

"It is a real wedding," Patrick said through clenched teeth. "We're going to get our marriage license in Maryland and have the ceremony at the Faire. Do you want me to send you an invitation or not?"

"Well, that will mean yet another dress and gowns for your sisters. Though I suppose any old thing we throw on will be impressive at a Pennsylvania Renaissance Faire. There's hardly a need for Jimmy Choos when wading through horse droppings. I hope we'll be able to find a decent hotel."

Patrick sighed loud enough to make sure she heard, but, of course, she ignored it. "There are plenty of five-star hotels in Pittsburgh, and you know it. But if all you plan to do is come and brag about how much better you are than everyone else and try to make my friends, the people who have supported me for years, feel inferior, then please don't. If you want to come, you won't get to be the center of attention for once."

"Well, maybe I won't come if I'm not wanted."

"If you want to come and see me happy marrying the man I love, I'll send you an invitation. But this about *me*, me and my husband, not you and Stan or your perfect kids."

"Well, I'll check our schedules. We're all very busy, you know."

"Okay. Well, I guess I'll talk to you later, Mom." Patrick touched his screen and ended the call before she could say anything else.

Yu shook his head. "That was brutal. Are you all right?"

Patrick shrugged. "It actually wasn't as bad as I expected."

"Do you think she'll come?"

"It's hard to say. I can't imagine her passing up an opportunity to show me how much better her new kids are than me." Patrick felt a savage delight as he imagined his mother looking at Yu. She'd be jealous; he was ten times more beautiful than Patrick's half siblings. It would *kill* her not to have anything to criticize.

"Chelsea and Zane," Yu said, making soothing circles on the back of Patrick's hand with his thumb. "Those are such Hollywood names."

"They were the lucky ones. My youngest half sister got stuck with Venice Rogue."

Yu's eyes widened, and he grimaced. "No. It sounds like the name of a pizzeria."

"Yeah. Listen, Yu, I don't want to seem impatient...."

"But you have to get ready for work soon," Yu finished for him. "All right. Time to man up, I suppose. But I'm putting it on speaker."

Patrick caught Yu's hand as he reached for his phone. "There's.... I have to tell you something first." As nervous as it made him, he couldn't let Yu face his mother at a disadvantage. "I-I spoke to your mother. Took her some pictures of your work from the show. I thought maybe, if she saw it, she'd reconsider. The whole thing had you so upset—"

"You went to my parents' house? When?" Yu interrupted him. Yu *never* interrupted anyone.

"When-when I told you I was going to DC to perform."

"Oh God. I can't believe you did that. I can't believe you *lied* to me."

"Let me explain." Patrick reached for Yu's hand, but Yu flinched away from him, something he had hoped would never happen. It struck him like a kick to the groin and made his stomach lurch into his throat.

"You don't know what you've done," Yu said. "My mother will see this as weakness, like I sent someone else to fight my battles. You've just made it worse. So much worse!"

"How?" Patrick asked. "How much worse can it get? She talks about you like you're some annoying telemarketer wasting her time. I shouldn't have gone behind your back—I know that—but you were hurting, and I thought I could help. I really thought if I showed your parents some of your work, told them the kind of man you are... I don't know. I just couldn't imagine anyone not being as proud as I am to call you theirs. I'm sorry. I just didn't like seeing you upset."

Yu crossed his arms over his chest and rubbed his shoulders. "I can't believe you lied to me. I know you were trying to help, to fix things like you always do, but now, when you tell me something, I'll have to wonder if you're being honest. I've never had that doubt before. We have never lied to each other."

"Yu. Okay, yeah. I lied about where I was going, but it's like lying to keep a gift secret, or at least, that's how I hoped it would turn out. I'm stupid and immature, and I honestly thought I could smooth things over between you and your family. I had this silly notion everything would work out, have a happy ending, like in a fairy tale. I was an idiot. I-I guess I still need to grow up. I just wanted you to know. Maybe there's still a chance."

Yu looked at him with that cold expression of anger and disappointment that hurt more than being yelled at or even hit. "You're about to see exactly how much of a chance there is."

He dialed and set his phone screen-side up in his thigh. It rang twice before his mother answered. "Hello?"

"*Okaa-san?*" Yu sounded like a frightened child, his voice high-pitched and trembling. "Mom?"

"Yu?"

"Yes, it's me."

"Is there something I can do for you?"

"Can we talk?" Yu practically pleaded. Patrick struggled against the anger building inside him as he rubbed the tense muscles at the back of Yu's neck.

"I don't know what we have to say to each other. You know how your father and I feel about the way you've chosen to live your life. We can't support your making such poor decisions and throwing away your potential."

Patrick almost came to Yu's defense, but he choked it down just before the words passed his lips. What the hell was wrong with this woman? How could anyone not be proud to call Yu her son? Patrick had a hard time not bragging about Yu to anyone who would listen.

"I'll only take a few minutes of your time. Although I doubt you'll be interested, I felt it would be a courtesy to call and tell you I'm getting married."

"If this is a joke, it isn't funny."

"It's not a joke. I've met someone I love very much, and I asked him to marry me. He accepted."

She said a word Patrick didn't understand, but was quite clearly a profanity. "Please tell me it's not that obnoxious redhead."

"Wh-what?"

"So did this Patrick tell you he came here and insulted me? I'm not surprised. As for you, you just continue to disappoint me. I wonder if you're doing it intentionally. Do I even have to point out that he isn't good enough for you? Why would you settle for a person like that?"

"I'm not going to discuss this with you," Yu said, glaring at Patrick. "I expected you to react just as you are. I won't bother sending you an invitation, but I would like *'baa-san's* address."

"Do you honestly expect your grandmother to fly here from Japan for this... farce?"

"I believe she has the right to make that decision for herself."

Yu's mother recited the address, and Yu entered it into his phone. Then he ended the call without saying good-bye. After placing his phone on the table, he turned to Patrick. "Do you see what you've done?"

"Yu, you don't understand—I'm silly and childish, and I really thought this could end happily, like in a story. I need to grow up and stop living in a fantasyland, and I promise I'll try."

Yu looked up and met Patrick's gaze. While obviously still conflicted, his features had softened, and a small smile even graced his wonderful, pouty lips. "Don't you dare. The way you believe in hope and happy endings is one of the things I love most about you." Yu opened his arm, stretching it across the back of the sofa, and Patrick hurried to fill the space, curling up beside Yu and resting his head on Yu's chest. When Yu wrapped his arm around Patrick, the tension and cold dread that had filled Patrick instantly flowed out of his chest, banished by Yu's warmth. "My mother is the scariest person I know. She makes Wade look like a teddy bear. It must have been terrible for you."

"I had to try," Patrick said, nuzzling his cheek against Yu, trying to sift past the scent of detergent on his shirt and the lingering smell of metal and unearth the sweet fragrance of his skin. As Yu carded his fingers through Patrick's hair, he dropped his lips to Patrick's forehead and peppered Patrick's hairline with light kisses. "If it meant making you feel better, I had to try. Stupid. I thought I could be some kind of hero and make things okay."

"I guess I have to let it go," Yu said. "Thank you for trying. Next time, just let me be a part of your plans. We're in this together, right?"

"Right. So, your grandmother. Has she always lived in Japan?"

"No. She grew up in America and was one of the first translators for the United Nations. She went home about fifteen years ago, after we lost my grandfather. I was very young then."

"You think of Japan as home?"

"Oh, I don't know. I always liked going there. I loved spending time at my 'baa-san's house. I'd like to take you. But I think of home as anywhere you are."

"So do I." For the next half hour, Patrick rested against Yu, content to listen to Yu's heartbeat and breathing and feel Yu's light touches. He loved talking with Yu, but he also loved the comfortable silences between them, when just being together was more than enough. Between them, the silence wasn't awkward, as if they couldn't think of anything to discuss; it was peace, home, security, a feeling similar to sitting outside and feeling connected to nature, feeling like a part of something greater and having found a place to belong. It was a simple yet profound magic. "Yu, I am sorry."

"It's okay. It was a brave thing to do, and you had good intentions. I'm just glad the calling the parents is over and done."

"Kind of," Patrick said. "We still have to talk to my father."

"Patrick, I'm sorry if I'm out of line here, but you know your father isn't going to be happy about us getting married. He'll probably just insult you. He might even get violent again. Why subject yourself to that?"

"I have to. I have to give him a chance—one last chance. It will probably happen just like you said, but I have to give him the option. Then I can move on."

"I'll be right beside you."

"I know." Patrick closed his eyes and let Yu's warmth and scent envelop him a few minutes more. Soon, he'd need to shower and get ready to perform, but he wasn't quite ready to stand on his own. He needed a few more minutes to submerge himself in Yu before he faced the world, put on his Queen Titania mask. "I just want to start our lives off with a clean slate, no missed opportunities, no what-ifs."

"I know, my love."

They'd taken a few steps toward that fresh start, but the worst was yet to come. They'd need the steel they'd forged together to protect their hearts. Luckily, it was solid and strong.

Chapter 11

THE NEIGHBORHood where Patrick had grown up looked even smaller and shabbier than he remembered. Kids played in the small yards as he drove slowly past before eventually parking in front of his father's house. Weeds and grass grew high in the yard, breaking through the wide cracks in the cement sidewalks and even the dirty snow, and the notices Patrick had hated when he'd lived here—those neon-orange and green pieces of paper announcing the water or gas would be turned off if the bills weren't paid—almost covered the door. Patrick killed the Horizon's engine and got out of the car, meeting Yu near the passenger-side door. As much as the thought of Yu seeing where he'd lived shamed him, he needed Yu's strength and reached out to take his hand as they made their way over the jagged cement of the walkway toward the front door.

Letters overflowed from the little mailbox bolted near the door, and some of the paint on the siding had flaked away, adding to the snow packed between the house and the concrete of the stoop. A layer of grime, left by the exhaust of passing cars, coated everything in oily black. With a shaking hand, Patrick rapped three times on the flimsy aluminum storm door. When no one answered, he knocked again. Still no one came to the door.

Patrick turned to Yu, who looked worried and on guard, but without the disgust and pity Patrick had expected. "It's almost three o'clock. Dad should be awake by now. Even if he's hungover. Do you think he's ignoring me? Should we go?"

"Maybe we should," Yu said. "You tried, but if he's not willing to come to the door, what more can you do?"

Patrick let his gaze wander over the notices stuck to the door. "No heat, no telephone, no water—How is he surviving?"

"Patrick, he's a grown man—"

"I was always the one who made sure the bills were paid," Patrick said. "What do you think he's been eating?"

"That's not your responsibility," Yu said a little more firmly. "He was supposed to take care of you."

"Yeah. We should probably leave, I guess."

"You tried," Yu assured him. "It's more than what most people would have done."

"Yeah."

Yu tucked a strand of hair behind Patrick's ear as he turned to head back to the car. Patrick followed him, because he didn't know what else he could do. If his father sat inside that crumbling house, watching a football game while he drank himself into oblivion…. If he wouldn't even come to the door, what could Patrick do?

As much as he hated to admit it, avoiding the conflict with his father was a relief. Though it might be cowardly, turning back toward the car to leave, to forget about this filthy hellhole, felt liberating. Maybe this time, he could leave the house and all the bad memories it contained behind for good. He didn't need it hanging like a ball and chain from his ankle as he tried to move forward. They'd almost reached the old Plymouth when Bernie, one of Patrick's dad's drinking buddies, staggered up the street to meet them. The old man with the yellowed skin seesawed from foot to foot as he regarded Patrick and Yu.

"You looking for your old man?" Bernie slurred out.

"I was," Patrick said, his memories of the drunk spilling into the present and overlapping the bare trees and coal smoke rising from the chimneys of nearby houses. He took a step back from the man's rancid breath and body odor. "He doesn't seem to want to see me, though."

"He ain't there." Bernie gestured toward the house. The skin below his eyes sagged, exposing bright red crescents below his yellowed orbs. "He's sick. Took 'im to the hospital early this week."

"Which one?" Patrick asked.

Bernie gave them the details, and soon, sooner than Patrick could process what was happening, they were back on the highway. Everything blurred past him until Yu parked the Horizon in the hospital lot. He felt ephemeral, insubstantial, as Yu led him across the street to the hospital's main entrance. It all felt like a nightmare, and like he did in dreams, Patrick felt as though he couldn't influence the physical world. His boots on the slippery pavement felt disembodied, like he floated over it. Nothing seemed solid. If he drove his fist into the stones of the wall, he felt sure he'd make no impact. Only Yu's hand holding his felt corporeal as they entered the hospital lobby and went up to the desk, and he held onto it for all he was worth.

Patrick had to speak; he knew that, but it took an effort. "I'm looking for Patrick Harford's room."

The attractive Asian man behind the computer typed a few lines. "Room 506, sir," he said, offering them a tired smile.

Yu guided Patrick toward the elevators and hit the buttons. He held Patrick in silent solidarity as they ascended, and he didn't release Patrick's hand as they stepped onto the fifth floor. Together, they made their way to the nurses' station, and once again, Patrick gave the information he had. They followed the nurse's directions to his father's room.

The door was ajar, halfway open, so Patrick went inside with Yu close behind him, still clasping his hand. It smelled of hospital antiseptic, with the stench of urine and decay barely concealed. Patrick's father, lying in the narrow bed beneath the stiff white blanket, didn't seem to notice them. He appeared asleep. His skin, which had had a yellowish cast for as long as Patrick could remember, now made him look like a character from *The Simpsons*. Tubes ran into his nose, into the veins of his arm, and beneath the covers to places Patrick couldn't see. A monitor near the bed displayed his heartbeat in a rhythmic pulse of jagged neon-green lines.

Looking at his father lying in that bed, hooked up to those machines, Patrick knew—his father was dying. He could smell death in the air of the chilly little room. Feeling a little dizzy, he stepped closer to Yu and grasped his sleeve in his fist. He had never imagined a human body could look the way his father did. It reminded him of something out of a horror movie, and he wanted to run away—back to the elevators and across the parking lot to his car—and try to wipe the image from his mind. He wanted to curl up in a ball somewhere and just shut it out.

"He's sleeping," Yu noted. "Do you want to wait?"

At the soft sound of Yu's voice, Patrick's father opened his eyes. The whites were the same orange-yellow as his skin, and the once bright blue, the same color as Patrick's eyes, had turned a clouded gray.

"Dad?"

His father seemed confused at first, looking around the room as though he couldn't locate the source of the voice. When his gaze finally landed on Patrick, he squinted and shook his head. He seemed surprised Patrick didn't disappear. "What the hell are you doing here, boy?"

"I…. Bernie said you were sick, that they brought you here."

Patrick's father retched and gurgled. He held his distended stomach with his hand until the spell passed. "And why the hell did you come? Did you think I'd want you to?"

"Maybe I did," Patrick answered pitifully, suddenly feeling twelve years old and torn between wanting his father's love and fearing his wrath. Torn between wanting to slink off and crumple in on himself and wanting to stay a little longer and maybe, finally, say the right thing, the thing that would make his dad recognize he had some worth. All the self-confidence and pride he'd built since leaving home abandoned him, and he wanted to find a small, dark corner and disappear. "I thought you might not want to be alone. I could keep you company. I mean, we're family."

"Not anymore." His father looked away in disgust. "I told you before no son of mine will be a cocksucker. I told you I got no son. Now get the hell out of here."

"Dad—"

"I said get out! I can't stand to look at your face. I don't want you coming back here, Patty. Go."

"I wanted to tell you I'm a good man. I lead a good life. I've worked really hard, and—"

"I said get the fuck out of here!" Patrick's father fumbled for the small white remote and pressed the button. "Nurse!"

"Patrick, he doesn't want us here," Yu said. "We might as well go. You tried. Nothing more can be expected. This isn't your fault."

"I know. I just…. You're right. Let's go." Patrick took Yu's hand again and turned toward the door. He reached for the handle and stopped, resting his fingers on the cold metal. He didn't look at his father when he spoke, but kept his gaze on the pale skin of his knuckles and the slight dusting of freckles. "I don't know if you care, but I came here to say something, and I'm going to say it. I have a good life, a nice apartment, friends who support me, and work I love. I'm happy. I have Yu, and I love him. We're getting married in the spring. Maybe you'll be able to find it in your heart to be glad I've found happiness and love. Maybe not."

"You make me sick. Get the hell out of here, Patty, and don't come back. Jesus, can't you finally leave me in peace? Ain't I wasted enough of my life worrying about you? Leave me alone."

With a nod, Patrick stepped into the hall. A nurse, an older black woman with short hair and whimsical angels on her baby-blue scrubs, came around the corner just as Patrick and Yu left the room. Her kind but tired eyes met Patrick's.

"You a relative?" the nurse asked. "Everything okay in there?"

Patrick forced a smile. "Yeah. I think my dad just called for you because he wanted us to leave."

"Your dad? I didn't know Mr. Harford had any family."

"I think he wishes he didn't," Patrick told the nurse—Gloria, according to the plastic badge pinned to her shirt. "Can you tell me what's wrong with him? He looks pretty bad. How long will it be before he gets out of here?"

Nurse Gloria gently took Patrick's free hand. Her palms were warm and smooth, and the concern in her dark eyes felt genuine. "Honey, your dad's not getting out of here."

"What's the matter with him?" Patrick repeated.

The nurse shook her head. "His liver is almost completely shut down. Nothing but scar tissue. It's led to some complications. He has a serious respiratory infection, some bleeding in the stomach, and impaired cognitive functions. Aside from a liver transplant, there's nothing we can do. He's on the waiting list for a liver, but… but so are lots of other people."

Yu asked the question Patrick couldn't force out of his throat. "How long?"

"It's hard to say," Nurse Gloria answered. "Could be two weeks, could be three days. We're trying to keep him comfortable. I'm glad he won't be alone at the end."

"He will," Patrick said, staring down at the square white tiles flecked with metallic bluish-gray, watching the light bounce off their polished surfaces. "He's made it very clear he doesn't want me to come back."

"Now why on earth would he do that?" she asked.

"He has a problem with me being gay," Patrick said.

The nurse shook her head. "Sad. You'd think at the end of the day, little shit like that wouldn't matter anymore. I'd better check up on him. You take care, honey. I'm really sorry."

"If I leave my phone number, will someone call me if… if there's any change?" Patrick asked.

"Sure thing. Just leave it at the desk." She went into the room, and Patrick let Yu lead him to the desk, the elevator, through the lobby, and back out to the car. They drove home without exchanging a word, and when they got to their apartment, Yu plugged in the kettle and made tea while Patrick traded his clothes for a comfortable pair of sweats and a *Gears of War* T-shirt. He started the fireplace and wrapped up in the blanket Jen had made. It smelled like Evan. Soon, Yu curled up next to him, resting his head on Patrick's shoulder and draping his arm over Patrick's belly. Patrick hadn't even realized he'd been rocking as he held onto his knees.

For a while, they sipped their holiday-spiced chai in silence. Finally, Yu asked, "Do you want to talk?"

"I don't know what to say." Patrick wriggled his fingers under the thermal shirt Yu wore beneath his black polo and ran the pads of his fingers through the soft sparse hair of Yu's arm and over the smooth skin underneath it. "He reacted just the way I knew he would. I just thought… I thought, eventually, he'd accept me, realize I'm his only son. I've worked hard, and I've done everything right. I thought it would mean something to him. I'm gay, yeah, but I'm more than that. I thought he'd see."

"I thought the same about my parents," Yu said. "After a time, you have to stop living your life to please them. Especially if it's impossible. You have to let it go."

"Have you let it go?"

"No, but I'm trying. I have you, and my mind and my heart say it's enough, but there's still a little voice telling me I haven't been a good son, that I should try harder to honor my parents. Some part of me wants that validation, even while I know I don't need it. Neither do you."

"Even on his deathbed," Patrick said, more to himself. "He'd rather die alone than have me with him. He really finds me that worthless."

"It's his choice," Yu said, "and his loss. He's missing out on knowing a remarkable person. The best person I've ever known."

"I just thought there'd be more time," Patrick said, feeling drained to the point where he could hardly lift his head from the back of the old sofa. "I thought, given time, he would understand. I just feel numb. Floating. I don't like it. Can we go to bed?"

"Yeah," Yu said. He stood and took Patrick's hand. When they reached the bedroom, they undressed each other almost solemnly, leaving their clothes strewn in a trail from the door to the bed. When they touched skin to skin, Patrick felt his nerve endings firing again, sensation returning to his body. He, *they*, were young and alive tonight. It wouldn't last, he knew, just as he knew when he lay dying, he wouldn't be alone. Yu would be there, like he was here now, dragging his lips over Patrick's hipbone, up his waist, and back down to nuzzle at the emerging hair between Patrick's inner thigh and sac. Yu moved to suck Patrick's balls into his mouth, and Patrick forgot about everything that had come before or would come after, and reveled in the perfect moment: the two of them, in the home they'd made, making love and just setting their feet on the meandering path of life. He chose to seize that moment, because he knew how fickle fate could be, and soon he and Yu were on the bed, the red sheets twisted around them.

PATRICK'S FATHER died a week later. Patrick got the call early Wednesday morning, while he and Yu were having breakfast in bed: chocolate-chip pancakes and bacon, because Yu had been catering to Patrick's preferences since they'd been to the hospital. Making sure Patrick was surrounded by his favorite things was Yu's way of comforting him. In a detached, formal tone, the doctor informed Patrick his father had passed peacefully in his sleep. It did little to reassure Patrick, and his appetite slipped away until it was gone. He spent most of the day in bed, with Yu beside him, curled up, both of them too drained to move.

THE NEXT few weeks flew by in a blur. Arrangements had to be made for his father's body. The house, which came to Patrick as next of kin, had to be cleaned and sold. Together, he and Yu shampooed the filthy carpets, washed the walls, and mowed the lawn. Here and there, Patrick noticed a stain or a scuff on the wall and remembered how it had been made. If he were honest with himself, though, most of those memories were unpleasant. Nothing within the crumbling walls with their peeling paint reminded him of a time when he'd been happy. Most of his father's furnishings and possessions weren't even good enough to donate, and so they filled a rented dumpster and had all of Patrick Senior's life hauled off to a landfill. By the time they finished, there was nothing left of the man who'd lived and slowly killed himself in the small house on the outskirts of Pittsburgh. Anything that proved he'd ever existed had been scrubbed off or thrown away. It was as if his life had never happened, hadn't mattered.

"It'll be Christmas soon," Yu told Patrick as they locked the door on the house where he'd grown up for the last time. "Do you want to go shopping?"

Patrick's smile rose up and cracked the shell of misery and indifference that had encased him since he'd learned of his father's condition. "Yeah. I want to get gifts for all our friends. Henry and Jen are leaving. Eric and Rog will hopefully soon have a child of their own to worry about. This might be the last Christmas we all spend together, and I want it to be special. You *hate* shopping, though."

"I'll manage," Yu said, taking Patrick's hand and leading him toward the car.

"The mall will be packed with holiday shoppers," Patrick argued without much passion. "It'll drive you out of your mind, all those people and their chattering. I don't want to subject you to that."

"We'll just stay for a little while. I don't want to waste this time either. I'll enjoy it if it means I get to see you happy. I miss being able to make you smile. I bet you won't say no to a jalapeño pretzel with cheese dipping sauce, and one of those toilet-bowl-cleaner-colored slushies. Let's go to the mall."

"You're the best thing, Yu. I'm happy. How could I not be when I have you?"

Chapter 12

FINALLY, LESS than a week before Christmas, the Realtor called to tell Patrick his father's house had been sold. According to Patrick's wishes, the Realtor had acted as his representative and made sure the money was deposited into Patrick's account. After his fees and the back taxes owed on the property, Patrick had received a little over twenty-five thousand dollars. He felt guilty being happy to have the money; it would make a reasonable down payment on a home of their own, one they could choose together, put their mark on, and where they'd have the space they needed to pursue their careers. He wandered out of their room and sat down on the sofa, staring at the phone he still clutched in his hand. Was his father looking down on him, disgusted that the sale of his home would help Patrick and Yu start their life together? Was he in heaven? Did Patrick even really believe in such a place?

He sat in a daze, too tired to lift his arms, watching the flames flicker in the hearth. As the sun went down, they became the only light in the small room, pulling peculiar shadows from Yu's sculptures, making it look like a procession of dancing figures wreathed the room. Patrick thought about heaven and all the good, selfless people his father's views didn't allow there. He imagined losing Eric, Rog, Jen, Shawn, Aouli, or, God forbid, Yu. Just thinking about it hurt more than the fact that his father was gone, the urn holding his ashes sitting beside the picture of Patrick's brother, Dylan, who'd died when Patrick was three. Growing up, the idea of Dylan's absence hurt more than this. What was wrong with him? Why couldn't he manage a single tear for his father?

He thought of a line from *Macbeth*: "Nothing in his life became him like the leaving it". Though he was ashamed, it was true. Leaving Patrick that money had been the only thing his father had ever done for him. He only managed to keep Patrick clothed and fed when it didn't cut into his drinking money, and he never let Patrick forget what a burden he was.

Right. Time to gather the scraps and quilt them into something shiny and promising.

Soon after full night fell, Yu returned home from working at Wade's forge. He'd spent a lot of time there recently, trying to finish all the gifts he wanted to make for their friends along with commissions his customers wanted by the holidays. Patrick heard him in the kitchen as he set down his bag of tools, slipped off his boots, and hung his coat and leather apron on a hook. In his socks, Yu padded quietly across the hardwood floor and sat down next to Patrick.

"What are you doing, sitting all by yourself here in the dark?"

"Thinking." Patrick moved closer to Yu and nestled against him, breathing the smells of smoke, metal, the scratchy green soap he used, and his sweat underneath. Those smells, to Patrick, meant love, security, and certainty. They meant he could be himself and always be accepted. They meant home, family, and they wrapped around him like a physical embrace as he rubbed his face against the damp exposed skin above Yu's collar.

"About?"

"The Realtor called. Dad's house is sold. The money should be in my account by tomorrow."

"Missing him?" Yu put his arm over Patrick's shoulders and pulled him closer.

"No, but I feel like I should be. I'm happy to have that money. It can do a lot for us. I... can't be sad he's gone."

"He's been out of your life for years now. If you hadn't contacted him, you would have never known anything until you got the call that he'd died. If even then. You gave him a chance to have his family with him at the end, and he turned it down. It was his choice, not yours."

"I knew this was coming," Patrick said, remembering his father throwing up on himself and passing out on the floor. "I tried to tell him to get help. Do you think... do you think, if we'd had more time, he might have eventually wanted to know me? Been happy that I'm leading a good life? Do you think I might have encouraged him to get help? Saved him?"

"I don't know," Yu said, petting down the outside of Patrick's arm. "It doesn't matter."

Patrick caught a strand of Yu's silky hair and rolled and twisted the end between his thumb and finger. "Yu, do you believe in life after death? God?"

"No, I don't think so."

"But what about spirits, *kitsune* and things?"

Yu was quiet for several moments, and then he sighed and spoke wistfully, in a tone Patrick rarely heard from him. "Most of the time I don't believe in them. I see them as personifications of human emotion and values, but…. Sometimes, when I've walked in the forest in Japan, got so deep into the woods that I couldn't see any evidence of humanity at all, I felt like the spirits were all around me. It was scary and magical. Of course, sitting here, I feel silly even mentioning it."

Patrick leaned his head back to kiss Yu beneath his jaw. "Don't. I see magic all around."

"I love that about you. It's like, all the things we believe in as children—hope, fairies, angels, magic, and happy endings, all the things we become blind to as we get older—you can still see. I'm envious sometimes, but I have started seeing the magic again since I met you. Like you're tearing down the veil between the worlds thread by thread. It's come through in my work. You've made me better."

Patrick put his arm across Yu's chest, and they held each other tight, watching the flames flickering in the fireplace and listening to the cars swishing by on the wet road outside. It was nothing special, just an average night at home, but Patrick relished every second. He felt immersed in magic, and every second that ticked by was gone, lost forever to time. Each one deserved appropriate appreciation. They wouldn't get even a second back.

After a while, Patrick straightened and sat up, though he kept his shoulder leaning against Yu's. "Look at this place," he said, his gaze roving over their possessions. "We have so much stuff we hardly have room for ourselves. I'd love to have a sewing room, and if you had a place to work, you wouldn't have to drive all the way to Wade's. Could you build a forge?"

"I know how it's done," Yu said. "Why?"

"I've been thinking a lot lately about a place of our own, a place we could make our own. Now, with the money my dad left me, we could afford a down payment. I think we should start looking for a house, a place to spend our lives. What do you think? Someplace out in the suburbs with a big yard, like Eric and Rog's? Or a farmhouse like Tom's? That would give you plenty of room to work. We could build you a shop."

"I don't know about that, Patrick."

"Well, we could find something in the city. Warehouse space we could make into a loft and work area. That would be cool."

"Buying a house is a huge step," Yu said. "It would mean staying where we are and a big financial commitment."

An unpleasant little shiver, like spider's legs on his skin, moved up Patrick's arms. He remembered Yu refusing to move in with him because he feared taking such a big step so early in their relationship. But he couldn't mean that now; they were getting married. He was probably just worried about the money. "The Realtor who helped me with the sale of my dad's place was really nice. We talked a little bit about buying a house. He said it can take a while to find the right place within your budget, but with patience, we could find the perfect place. I think we should at least start looking. Our mortgage might not be much more than we're paying for rent, and we'd have a place to put down roots. That's important to me. Isn't that something you want?"

Yu reached over to the coffee table and picked up a commissioned dagger he'd been working on with an ornate, serpentine blade. Somehow, the steel had a reddish tint. He'd formed and hammered the weapon but hadn't ground it down or polished it yet, so its edges were still blunt. Yu ran his fingers over the hilt and turned his blade over and over in his hands. He had to have something to do with his hands when he was thinking, and that worried Patrick. Only in the most serious situations did Yu weigh his words or plan how to say something. Normally he just said whatever came to his mind. Usually, he couldn't help it.

"I don't know if I'm ready to settle down yet," Yu finally said, his gaze intent upon the dagger in his hands. "At least not in terms of buying a house. I want to settle down with you, of course. We're in it together for life, I hope."

"Of course," Patrick said.

"The thing is, I've been talking to someone online, and—"

"Oh God."

"Patrick, no. How could you even think that? You are the only one I want, and it hurts me that you still doubt it. The person I've been talking to is a swordsmith, one of the few men in the world who knows the traditional method for forging katana, working with Japanese steel. I've been sending him pictures of my work for months, and after I showed him the pieces from my show, he agreed to take me on as a student."

"That's great! But it's all the more reason for you to have a place to work," Patrick said.

Yu slowly set the dagger down, carefully, so it didn't clatter against the tabletop, and took Patrick's hand. "Patrick, he lives in Japan."

Before he could think about it, Patrick pulled his hand out of Yu's grip. He felt cold despite the cozy blaze in the fireplace, and his stomach felt like it was collapsing in on itself. "You mean, you're leaving? You're going to marry me and take off to Japan?"

Yu shook his head. "You really don't understand what you mean to me, do you? Of course not. Patrick, I was hoping you would come with me. We can go to Japan together. I have family there, and I'll have the sponsorship of my sensei. You can get a visa—as my spouse."

Patrick slipped into one of those moments when he mistrusted reality. He kept expecting for Yu to say it was a joke, or to wake up and realize he'd dozed off on the couch. Yu just kept looking at him expectantly, his long lashes casting shadows on his cheekbones.

"When were you going to tell me?" Patrick asked.

"What? I'm telling you now."

Patrick had so many questions, yet he didn't want to sound accusatory. After all, Yu had just achieved his lifelong dream. "Did he offer to take you as a student before you asked me to marry you?"

"Yes."

"Is that the reason you asked me?" It sounded harsh, even to his own ears, but Patrick needed to know.

"I asked you to marry me because I love you more than anything in this world, and I can't imagine spending my life without you. I'm getting a little upset by you constantly doubting that. Have I given you a reason to?"

"No, of course not. I guess it still feels surreal that someone like you chose me."

"It feels that way to me too, sometimes," Yu admitted. "I can't believe you've put up with me as long as you have, but you have. And you will, and I believe that now. If I catch myself worrying you'll decide I'm not worth it, I curse myself for an idiot. You need to start doing the same."

"Cursing myself for an idiot?"

"If you think I don't love you or that I'll ever let you go, then yes," Yu told him.

Patrick thought about Japan. Everything he knew of it came from video games and anime. The thought of going there exhilarated him and scared him to death at the same time. "How long will we be staying?"

Yu smiled wide. Patrick thought the only time he'd seen him happier was when he'd put his ring on Patrick's finger. "You'll go?"

"I.... This is a lot to process. My life is here. My drag sisters and my job. Evan, and my friends. The Faire. My family. I have to think about it. How long?"

"At least a couple of years."

"Years," Patrick echoed. Years away from everything he knew and the family he'd built for himself. The life he'd built. "If I didn't want to go, would you still go?"

"No," Yu said, the bitterness of regret tainting his answer. "I wouldn't go without you, but I would hate to miss this chance. It's a once-in-a-lifetime opportunity. This knowledge is so close to being lost forever. It's my dream to carry on this tradition."

"I know," Patrick said, threading their fingers together. "I've just been dreaming of a cute little house with two cats and maybe a vegetable garden. Here, with all the people I love close by."

"We can have that eventually," Yu said. "Put your money into an account or invest it, and when we come back, we'll buy a house. I have enough to pay for the trip, especially after the sale of the *Hope Validated*. I really think you'll love Japan."

"I need time, Yu. I'm sorry."

Yu kissed him softly on the forehead. "I understand." Still holding Patrick's hand, he stood and led Patrick into the bedroom. They undressed slowly and put their clothes into the hamper before getting into bed. The satin sheets felt cool against Patrick's skin as Yu enveloped them in the scarlet bedding. His calloused hands felt rough as he traced them over the outsides of Patrick's thighs and up his waist. His skin was warm and smooth against Patrick's chest and belly, his weight above Patrick solid and comforting. "I'm sorry I didn't tell you sooner," Yu said, nipping at Patrick's lips between words. "I wanted to wait until it was set in stone. I don't ever want to be without you. Not even for a day. Nothing is more important to me than you."

"I know. I want you to have what you've always dreamed of. I just need to think. Can we let it go for now?" Patrick grasped Yu's hips and pulled Yu against him, making their hardening cocks bump and slide against each other.

"No." Yu, holding Patrick tight to him, rolled to his back and shifted Patrick on top of him. He spread his legs and curled his body so his hot cleft brushed against Patrick's shaft. He crossed his ankles over Patrick's lower back and rolled up against him. "I need you."

"Okay." Patrick understood that Yu wanted to be taken, that Patrick having him would somehow restore his faith that he belonged to Patrick. He needed this, and Patrick was more than willing to give it to him. He knew Yu didn't want it gently; Yu wanted to be claimed and marked. It excited Patrick, and not because they usually did things the opposite way, but because Yu needed him, needed the reassurance that they belonged to each other.

Patrick fumbled with the night-table drawer until he found the lube and flipped the cap open. He managed to squirt a dollop of clear liquid onto his fingers and spread it along Yu's crack. As he began to ease his middle finger into him, Yu grabbed his wrist and pulled his hand away. "No."

"Yu?"

Yu grasped the base of Patrick's cock and guided it to his opening. His muscles relaxed and spread as Patrick pushed forward, and soon they'd joined, Patrick buried to the balls inside Yu. He stilled, looking down at Yu's face and enjoying the tight, pulsating heat around his cock. It took all his willpower not to shoot into Yu.

"Come on, Patrick. Show me I'm yours."

"Okay." Patrick thrust, angling his hips to hit Yu's sweet spot, and Yu threw his head back and keened.

"More. Make me believe it."

"I will. You're mine, and I'm yours. Yu—" Almost against his will, Patrick snapped his hips quick and hard, driving into Yu and making Yu moan and whimper in the most enticing way.

"Yours. No matter what. I need you to believe that. Show me."

Patrick did. They clung to each other and pumped against each other, hard and fast, savagely, Patrick claiming Yu's body and Yu willingly submitting, until both of them began to pant. They rubbed their sweaty faces together, too distracted to even kiss, as they furiously slammed their bodies together. Yu sank his fingernails into Patrick's hips, and the slight sting spurred Patrick on. He drove into Yu for all he was worth, trying to somehow express the love he felt physically, but it didn't seem enough. He would never be able to properly show Yu what he meant to him. But he tried, curling his hips up and pounding Yu's spot until he could hold off no longer.

"Yu... I can't. I love you so much."

"Give it to me, Patrick. I love it when you come inside me."

As he rocked into Yu's tight, delicious heat, Patrick grasped Yu's cock and stroked it in time with his thrusts. Soon, both of them were flushed, heaving, and desperate for release. Patrick tightened all the muscles of his body, forcing himself to wait until Yu found satisfaction. As soon as he felt Yu's hot seed splatter his belly, he emptied himself into Yu, coming so hard he saw stars and had to lower his face to Yu's chest and clutch his hips to ground himself. They stayed joined long after they'd spiraled down from the pinnacles of their pleasure, two souls sharing a body, as close to each other as they could get. Only when Yu started to doze beneath him did Patrick pull out and fall to his back next to Yu. He kissed Yu's flushed and sweaty cheek before letting his pillow mold around his head and draw him toward blissful rest and peace. Questions about the road he should take in life fluttered at the outskirts of Patrick's mind, but he kept them at bay. They were minor considerations; the important thing was that he had Yu, and Yu had him. But... Japan? Did he dare turn his back on the familiar and risk something like that? Did fortune truly favor the bold, or did it favor the responsible?

Chapter 13

ON THE morning of Christmas Eve, Patrick and Yu loaded all their gifts into the back of the Horizon and picked Evan up at the shelter. A fresh layer of snow had fallen the night before, covering up the gritty black crust that inevitably formed over the compacted layers of ice and snow along the city streets and in piles in the parking lots. To Patrick, the scenery passing by beyond his frost-framed window looked both pure and enchanted with the new powder glittering in the stark morning light. Ever since meeting Eric, Rog, and the rest of his friends, he had loved Christmas and had endeavored to make up for all the celebrations he'd missed growing up. Several tins of the cookies he and Yu had spent the past several days baking sat next to Evan on the backseat. Since Yu's graduation earlier in December, they'd had more time to spend together. Probably just to indulge Patrick, Yu wore a pine-green V-neck sweater over his crisp white shirt. Even Evan had dressed for the holiday in a new-looking mint polo shirt and dark jeans without a single tear. Of course, Patrick wore a scarlet button-down shirt with a Fair Isles cardigan over top. They looked so festive, Patrick couldn't resist asking Yu to stop in front of Trinity Cathedral on Sixth Avenue. The Gothic structure, decked out in holly, evergreen fronds, and red and gold ribbons made a perfect backdrop, and Patrick convinced an older woman walking a Yorkshire terrier to snap several pictures of the three of them.

Their first stop was Jen and Henry's apartment, not far from the church, in an old brick building on Liberty Avenue. They parked on the street and climbed the stairs to their friends' third-story loft. Jen answered the door in a sparkly champagne-colored dress with a lacy collar and a row of pearl buttons down the front. Combined with her upswept red ringlets, held in place by a few rhinestone-covered combs, it made her look like a glamorous 1950s housewife to Patrick. In stark contrast, Henry sat at the kitchen table in a Led Zeppelin T-shirt and a pair of faded sweatpants that had probably once been navy. Thick light brown scruff covered his cheeks and chin, and his long blond hair was held back from his face with a pink plastic clip that probably belonged to Jen.

Savory aromas of ham, cloves, roasting potatoes, and something chocolate filled the small kitchen. Jen and Patrick hugged and kissed while Yu found a place in the living room to deposit his armload of packages. Evan stood near the door, looking uncertain.

Henry, bless him, got up from the table and tapped Evan on the elbow. "Hey, man. There's a game on." He tilted his head toward the flat-screen TV mounted on the brick wall a few feet away. "Or we can play some *Duty*. Come on."

With a bright smile, Evan followed Henry to the beige sectional beyond the industrial-looking concrete post that delineated the kitchen from the living room.

"Go easy on him," Patrick called to Evan. "And no camping." He'd played *Call of Duty* with both Evan and Henry, and, well, Henry excelled at actual combat, but Patrick had no doubt Evan would take him to school in the game.

Yu followed them and perched on the arm of the sofa while they sat on the floor and picked up their controllers. "I'll play the winner."

Both of them groaned. Though he had never touched a video game before meeting Patrick, Yu possessed some freakish talent for them, to the point where other players signed off of Xbox Live when they saw his gamer tag appear. Maybe it was that high IQ Yu's mother had mentioned.

Patrick took the seat Henry had vacated, and Jen sat down across from him. She poured some champagne into two flutes and slid one over to Patrick.

"Isn't it a little early?" he asked, pinching the stem between his thumb and finger and watching the little bubbles swim up through the pale gold liquid.

She rolled her eyes. "Come on. It's Christmas. Besides, I want to talk to you about something. I've had the best idea."

"Go on, then."

"Well, how would you feel about getting married together? Like, a joint ceremony? You're my best friend in the world, and I'd want you there anyway, so we might as well split the cost, right? Neither of us is exactly rich. You were planning on having yours at the Faire, right?"

Before Patrick could answer, Henry's cry of "Son of a bitch!" had them both chuckling and shaking their heads.

"Come on, give it over," Patrick heard Yu say, followed by another strong oath from Henry.

"Anyway," Jen continued, "I would love it if we could stand up there together and start our lives—our grown-up lives—side by side. As long as you aren't planning on coming in drag, that is. I can't have you being prettier than me on my wedding day."

Patrick rolled his eyes even as he smiled at her. "I love that idea, but what about your and Henry's families?"

"What about them?"

"Are they going to be okay with a gay couple getting married alongside you and Henry?"

"If they're not, they can go to hell. You guys are my family too."

"Then, yeah. Let's do it. As long as Yu doesn't mind, but I doubt he will. Neither of us really have any family attending, so I guess we'll only be making it more convenient for our Faire friends. When were you thinking?"

"Jesus, dude," Evan said from the other room. "You have the fucking reflexes of a fighter pilot."

Yu chuckled. "Want to play me, Henry?"

"No. Absolutely not. How about a good old-fashioned sword fight?"

"Okay," Yu responded. "I started studying kendo at five."

Patrick hadn't known that about him. He realized there might be a lot he didn't know about Yu; two years just wasn't long enough to find out everything, and Yu kept secrets, like planning to go to Japan. Like James. "This is a big step, Jen. I'm scared as hell. Are you?"

"A little." She leaned across the table and spoke in just above a whisper next to Patrick's ear. "Are you having second thoughts? Not sure about him?"

Was he? Yu had been his only boyfriend, the only man he'd ever dated or been with. He had nothing to compare it to. Could he be missing out on something better? No, he couldn't believe that. He was just shaken up about Japan and feeling uncertain as to why Yu hadn't told him sooner. He looked over his shoulder at the three men huddled around the TV and game console.

Jen understood. "I need a cigarette. Patrick, will you come outside with me?"

He got his coat and followed her down the stairs. Together, they leaned against the outside of the building.

"So you're getting cold feet?" Jen asked.

Patrick considered how to answer. He wanted to marry Yu; he really did. "It's just so final."

Jen lit a cigarette and exhaled a white plume into the chilly air. "It is, isn't it? I don't think I ever saw so many interesting, fuckable guys as I did on my way to pick out my dress last week. But they're all off-limits now. But... I'm okay with it. I'm sure of Henry. But you. You've never had a chance to date or play the field. Is that it?"

"I don't think so. I see a hot guy now and then who piques my interest, but when I compare them to Yu, they never measure up. God, I wanted him from the first minute I saw him, and I still kind of can't believe I got him. Maybe it just feels too good to be true. I guess I just keep expecting something to come along and ruin it all."

She squeezed Patrick's shoulder. "If that's all you're worried about, don't be. Anyone can see he adores you."

"He wants me to move to Japan with him."

"Cool!"

"I'm scared. Until I started doing drag shows, I'd never been outside Pennsylvania. I'm afraid of not having you, and Rog and Eric. No one to fall back on."

"You'll have your *husband*," Jen said. "And if you don't think you can depend on him to support you, you need to call this off right now. I like Yu, but you're my little brother, minstrel boy. You come first, Patrick. And I'm sorry to be blunt, but it's always seemed like you give him more than he gives you."

"He's trying. Yu has a lot of issues. I love him."

"If you don't want to do this, you don't have to. You won't be alone. Not ever."

For a second, Patrick wished he could draw the comfort others did from smoking, but the smell had always made him feel sick. "I'm not afraid to be alone. I made my own way, and I can do it again. It isn't that. I just keep thinking back to how miserable my parents made each other, what a clusterfuck that excuse for a marriage turned into. What if I fuck it up like they did? I don't want us to end up hating each other. I don't want to resent him because I never had the chance to date and mess around. He doesn't deserve that."

"Well, what means more to you? Banging a bunch of random guys and exploring, or building a life with Yu? Think about it. I won't judge you either way. What you want and what you feel is legitimate."

Patrick thought about it while Jen finished her cigarette. Sleeping with a never-ending parade of men held little appeal for him. He only wanted Yu, had only ever wanted Yu. But ever since the topic of moving to Japan had come up, he'd felt a little like an accessory or a security blanket: something Yu wanted to carry with him as a reminder of home. But maybe he was being unfair. Hadn't Yu said he would give up his dream if Patrick didn't want to go to Japan? Meaning more to Yu than the fulfillment of his life's goal had to count for something, and the idea of a life without him made Patrick's stomach hurt and his chest constrict. "I think it's just me. My insecurity. Being let down again and again by people who were supposed to love me. It isn't fair to project all that onto Yu."

"No," Jen agreed. "It sounds to me like you're doubting yourself. You shouldn't. You rock, Patrick. You are absolutely worthy of him, and if you want to marry him, you should do it without hesitation. But if you don't—if you think you're too young and want to test the waters—well, I can understand that too. I'm your friend either way."

"I do want to marry him."

"Then for God's sake, be happy. Be proud. Yu is getting quite a catch, and so are you. I'm freezing. Let's go back inside."

"Thanks, Jen."

She turned her head toward him and grinned. "This wedding is going to *rock*. Tom's an ordained minister; he can perform the ceremony. Do you think your friend Aouli might do my makeup?"

"Oh, he would love that. I should warn you, though—Rog is all about helping me plan my wedding, so he's probably going to have some, um, suggestions for you too. He'll probably want to color coordinate the dresses for our bridesmaids. Not that I'll have any. I don't even know who to ask to be my best man."

"What about Rog or Eric?" They'd reached the top of the steps, and when Jen opened the door, the warm, welcome air of the apartment wrapped around Patrick. The smell of the food reached right into the pit of his stomach. They hung their coats and went to join the others in the living room.

"They're more like parents to me," Patrick said, sitting down next to Yu. Yu looked over and smiled. He brushed a strand of hair away from Patrick's eye and let his fingers linger on the cold-reddened skin of Patrick's cheek. Patrick felt guilty for doubting Yu's devotion, but he couldn't imagine any man about to get married, especially one as young as himself, went into it without any reservations. He just wished they'd be settling down, making a home together. Maybe he was boring, but a home and a family had been all Patrick had ever wanted, and now, to follow Yu's dream, he'd be walking away from those things. He wished they were alone, because out of nowhere, he felt like it had been unfair for Yu to ask that of him, and he needed to know if Yu realized how much Patrick needed stability. If he just didn't know, that would be different. It wasn't like he could expect Yu to pick up on subtle cues; he needed to say how he felt. The topic of conversation quickly turned to all things wedding as soon as Yu agreed to Jen's plan: clothing, flowers, food, cake, and even gifts for attendees. Yu, with a pink magic marker and yesterday's newspaper, drew an arbor he wanted to make for Henry and Jen. The flowing, organic lines and floral details reminded Patrick of something out of Lothlórien in *The Lord of the Rings* movies. Though everyone liked the design, they became more and more lost as Yu explained the techniques he would employ to produce it. Jen continued to nod politely, while Henry's gaze wandered back to the television screen. Patrick looked over at Evan, who sat at the end of the couch, apart from the rest of them, looking dejected and picking at a thread on the bottom of his shirt.

Patrick felt like a tool, rejoicing about the upcoming wedding while Evan sat alone, afraid he'd never find anyone to love. He reached over and clasped Evan's hand. "You'll be at the wedding, won't you?"

"Yeah," Evan muttered without looking up. "I don't have anything better to do, and you know it."

Patrick made a decision. "Evan, I don't have a lot of friends or people who are important to me. Would you consider being my best man?"

Evan raised his head slowly and met Patrick's gaze, unshed tears making his dark eyes glitter. "What—me?"

"Unless it's an imposition," Patrick said, "I'd like you to stand beside me."

"I don't know why you'd want that," Evan said, his pale cheeks pinking.

"I do, but if you're uncomfortable, I'll understand if you say no."

"No!" Evan looked like someone had just handed him one of those oversized checks when he hadn't even entered the contest. "No. I mean yes! You want *me*? Are you sure?"

"Positive."

"Thanks, Patrick."

"I'm thinking of asking Wade," Yu said, and all of them groaned.

"Maybe you should put on one of your helmets when you do," Henry said. "God help you."

"Still, he's important to me. By taking me on as an apprentice, he helped me realize my dream."

They spent another hour or so discussing the wedding, with Evan smiling the entire time, reassuring Patrick that he'd done the right thing. Originally, he'd planned to ask Shawn or Aouli to be his best man, but he didn't want to show favoritism between his sisters, and now he didn't have to. They could be part of his wedding party—as either men or women—as equals. The more they talked, the more excited Patrick became about declaring his love for Yu and having it celebrated. They still needed to talk, but Patrick knew he'd never want anyone else. He'd just been nervous about taking such a momentous step.

Gifts were exchanged over coffee and chocolate cake. Jen had knitted Evan a pale wisteria sweater that suited his faerie coloring perfectly. She'd also made matching rust-red hats for Patrick and Yu. Since Jen and Henry planned to move, Yu and Patrick had opted for gift cards, and while they weren't especially exciting or personal, they appreciated them. Patrick and Jen made plans for brunch after the New Year, to continue planning their celebration, and they all kissed and hugged before saying good-bye.

They made their next stop at Eric and Rog's. Rog liked to keep Christmas Eve exclusive to close friends, since he and Eric spent Christmas with their families. Not long after they reached the suburban home, all of them sat around the TV watching *A Christmas Story* and sipping hot cocoa. Unlike he had at Thanksgiving, Evan looked comfortable and at ease, tucked into the corner of the sofa and wrapped in an old patchwork quilt. Patrick was glad to see Rog looking happier, too, and he wondered if it had anything to do with the adoption pamphlets he'd seen on the kitchen table. When the movie ended and one of the old stop-motion animation kids' films came on, Eric turned the volume down, and Patrick filled the others in on what he and Jen had discussed in regards to the wedding.

"Oh my God," Aouli said, "you tell that beautiful girl that I'll be honored to do her makeup. I promise I'll make her look *sickening*. Don't tell her I said this, but I've thought on a few occasions that she could use a few tips from a professional."

"A professional what, bitch?" Shawn asked, elbowing his friend and drag sister in the ribs.

"Ask your father," Aouli teased back.

"You guys will be in my wedding party, right?" Patrick asked. "Evan will be my best man, but I hope you'll be... groomsmen... or bridesmaids. Whatever you want."

"Oh, honey, of course we will!" Aouli said, answering for Shawn as he often did. Shawn just rolled his eyes. "I'd love to dress up, but how will your families feel about a bunch of drag queens in your procession?"

"What family?" Patrick said, sounding a little more bitter than he'd intended. "You guys, and the people from the Faire, are it." Talking about the wedding again should have cheered and excited him, but it just sent questing claws digging into the mire of his thoughts and dredging up everything he'd buried there. Soon the waters of his mind muddied as a result, making it hard for him to see clearly. He looked at Eric and Rog, sitting together on the recliner. "How come you guys have never thought about making it official? You've been together seven years."

Eric shot Patrick a quizzical look; then he turned toward Rog, and Rog commandeered all his attention. As he traced a fingertip down Rog's neck, he said, "What makes you think it's not official?"

"Haven't you ever wanted to get married?" Patrick pressed, more to understand his own feelings than their situation.

"We don't need a piece of paper, and we don't have anything to prove to anyone else," Rog said, eyelids drooping and cheeks coloring at Eric's attention.

Patrick turned to look at Shawn and Aouli. "Do you two ever plan on settling down?"

"I don't," Shawn said. "I have my sisters and friends, and I can get laid anytime I want. I have no desire to give up my freedom. I'm having too much damn fun."

"Doesn't that feel"—Patrick searched for the word—"empty?"

"Little sister, we're gay men," Aouli said. "I'm happy for you and what you have, and I'm happy for Eric and Rog. Believe me, I support equal rights, but I also don't think we have to emulate the straights if we don't want to. I like getting to bang lots of guys without any strings attached. But I don't need to trade freedom for sex. I'm just not into subscribing to that antiquated model. It was designed to oppress women and ensure a guy's actual biological son inherited his property. Monogamy just isn't in my nature. Oh hell. That sounded totally bitchy, didn't it?"

Patrick looked into his mug, where a ring of brown globs had congealed just below the lip. A milky skin had formed over his cocoa, and he set it on the floor, feeling a little sick. "But don't you want someone special?"

"If someone ever comes along who makes me want to give up having my pick of the guys at the club, I'll worry about it when it happens," Shawn said. "I could maybe do an open relationship. I always kind of suspected the only reason straight boys are exclusive is because women make them do it. Lots of gay men don't feel the way women do."

Dammit, they were supposed to be making Patrick feel better, not stirring up more doubts from the slimy soup at the back of his mind. "Do you think Henry feels that way? About Jen? He really loves her."

"And you don't think if she gave him permission to bang other girls and still stay married to her, he'd take it?" Shawn asked. "Boy's only human."

Patrick turned back to Eric and Rog. Their devotion gave him hope. "You guys don't feel forced, do you? You've been committed, right?"

Eric and Rog looked at each other and shared a moment. "We've dabbled," Rog said. "It hasn't made us any less committed to sharing our lives. Sometimes sex is just sex."

Patrick scrubbed a hand over his face, trying to rub away the tingling numbness settling like a web over his skin. Yu hadn't said a word the entire time, hadn't even moved his hands from where they rested on his knees. Looking at his face, Patrick couldn't intuit his opinion on it all. Did he want to "dabble" as well? Or had the conversation finally laid bare to him the doubts Patrick had? Except he didn't have doubts about wanting Yu—only about Yu's motives for proposing.

A pall fell over their gathering like someone had thrown a moldy wet blanket over a glittering buffet. For a long time, no one said anything, and only the squeaky saccharin cartoon voices broke the silence. Patrick wanted to choke the damn elf who dreamed of becoming a dentist. He felt like he'd ruined the holiday for everyone, and it had brought him no closer to untangling the jumbled undergrowth in his head. He felt like a fairy-tale knight lost in a dark forest, unable to hack his way through the bracken or break whatever dark enchantment had gripped him out of nowhere.

Evan finally broke the silence. "Um, I have some small gifts for all of you. I'm afraid they aren't much." He reached into his pocket and pulled out some awkwardly wrapped parcels, each about the size of a sugar packet. He checked the names written on each in blue ink and passed them around.

Patrick carefully pulled the single piece of clear tape up with his fingernail and opened the little package. Inside he found a bracelet woven from colored threads with a little fairy charm dangling down. The others unwrapped similar bands and smiled as they held them up. "Did you make this?" Patrick asked.

Evan stared at his hands, clenched tightly in his lap. "Yeah, sorry. I didn't have a lot to spend."

Yu reached over and clutched his wrist. "Evan, there's no more profound way to show you love someone than making something for them. You think of them as you work." He was looking at Patrick. "Every stroke of your hammer, or in this case, every knot you tie, is an act of love. It's almost a spell, a way to channel your feelings into a physical object. It imbues what you make with a unique strength, almost a magic. That reminds me. I have something for you. I'll be right back."

Yu went outside and returned a few minutes later with a gleaming sword. He turned it in his hand, cutting silvery arcs through the fuzzy light in the living room, and presented it, hilt first, with a bow of his head, to Evan, who stood to accept it with a look of sheer disbelief on his face. He turned the blade so he could look at it lengthwise, his reflection distorted back at him from the polished steel. "I-I don't know what to say, Yu. I didn't expect this. I know what this is worth. I feel like I shouldn't accept it."

"Nonsense," Yu said. "I made it with you in mind. That means it won't be happy with anyone else."

"Is that true?" Evan asked.

"I believe so," Yu told him. "I imagined you as I forged it. Every stroke of my hammer put my feelings for you into the steel."

"I don't know how to use it," Evan said, his voice weak and cracked. "I don't deserve it. I can't take it, Yu. It will get stolen at the shelter. Unless... can you keep it safe for me and maybe teach me how to take care of it?"

"But it's your sword," Yu said, looking a little confused. "It should be with you."

Patrick reached up to tug on the hem of Yu's shirt. "You can keep it safe for now, though," he said, meeting Yu's eyes. "Until Evan has a place of his own. A place worthy of it. And until then, you can teach him how to use it when the two of you get together. Does that sound good?"

Yu nodded. "Come on. Let's go out back, where I can show you a few things."

They retrieved their coats and made their way through the kitchen toward the backyard, Evan grinning and looking more like the kid he was than Patrick had ever seen. As soon as he heard the door close, Patrick said, "How great is he? I'm lucky, aren't I?"

"That was a really nice thing he did for Evan," Eric said carefully. "The sword is beautiful."

"Yu is very talented," Aouli said.

"Oh hell," Shawn said. "I'm not dancing around it. Patrick, you're not happy. You don't want to get married, do you?"

"I do," Patrick said. "I really do."

"But?" Rog coaxed.

"Yu wants me to move to Japan with him. He has family there, and he found a swordsmith to accept him as a student."

"That sounds amazing," Aouli said. "I'm totally jealous."

"He wants to stay for a few years," Patrick said. "I feel like my life is here."

"It is," Rog said, untangling himself from Eric so he could sit up. "You're making a name for yourself as Queen Titania, and if you leave for a few years, you'll be all but forgotten. If you come back and want to do drag again, you'll be starting from scratch. I hate to be blunt, be it'll be harder on the wrong side of twenty-five than it was at nineteen, honey."

"But this is his lifelong dream," Patrick protested. "He said he'd give it up if I didn't want to go, but I don't know if I can do that to him."

"So you give up your dream instead?" Rog's protective mother tone had emerged. "How's that fair?"

"Do you want to go?" Eric asked.

"I don't know. It's exciting, but I'm scared to leave everything I know behind. When Yu proposed, I had these stupid storybook visions of a little house, a garden, and two cats. Maybe I'm just being a coward."

"There's nothing stupid or cowardly about that," Rog said. "Your desires and dreams are just as legitimate as his."

"But you are really young, Patrick," Aouli argued. "You have plenty of time for the picket fence later on. This could be a real adventure. For what it's worth, I'd go in a heartbeat."

"It's a shitty situation," Shawn said. "One or the other of you has to sacrifice your dream. That sucks no matter how you slice it, but it doesn't always have to be you, Patrick. Yu's a good guy, but you're my sister. I'll be there no matter what you decide."

"Jen said that too." Patrick stared down at the bracelet Evan had made. He still held it, palm up, in his hand. "It makes me feel sorry for Yu that everyone supports me and is so willing to toss him aside. Everyone's on my side, and he's all alone. Part of the reason he was afraid of a relationship with me was that everyone had always decided he wasn't worth the effort. Worth the sacrifice. He's worth it to me, though. I have all of you, but he only has me."

"That's no excuse for him to be selfish," Aouli said.

"Amen," Shawn agreed.

"Hold on," Eric said, his clear, deep voice drawing everyone's attention. "It seems to me there's one question you have to ask yourself, Patrick: Which is more important to you—doing drag here in Pittsburgh and buying a house or staying with Yu? Which one can you live without?"

"I can't live without Yu," Patrick said, feeling the sediment clear from the murky waters of his mind for the first time all day. Eric, good old Eric, had made it so obvious. He'd managed to skim away all the flotsam clouding the surface of Patrick's thoughts.

"So he should give up his career for what Yu wants?" Rog countered.

Eric chuckled and kissed him on the forehead. "Babe, I gave up the Faire circuit because you didn't want me gone for months at a time. I loved traveling with the Faire, but you meant more."

"Ooh, you traveled with the Faire?" Aouli asked. "I bet you got so much ass."

With a shake of his head, Eric said, "I could tell some stories. But I don't regret giving it up."

Though Patrick felt better than he had since talking to Jen, he still had concerns. "I'm worried about leaving Evan."

"Evan seems to be doing fine on his own," Shawn noted. "I thought he'd be traveling with the jousters, anyway. Kid'll have the time of his life."

"Mmm," Aouli said. "All those hotties in tight leggings and their *long lances*. Maybe I should follow the Faire."

"I guess Ian hasn't decided yet," Patrick said. "He hasn't mentioned anything more about it. He was waiting to see how Evan did with the horses, but I can't imagine he's not satisfied with Evan's work. I hope Evan will be okay on the road."

"It'll be fine," Eric said. "Getting to see some different places will do wonders for Evan, open up his perspective. It did for me. And if he gets laid a couple times along the way, so much the better."

"I just don't want to abandon him." Patrick knew how much it hurt to be tossed aside.

"You can't let guilt rule your life," Shawn said. "You have to do what's right for you. You deserve that."

Linoleum squeaked in the kitchen, and by the time Patrick turned around, Yu and Evan waited at the edge of the living room, their cheeks nipped red by cold air and exertion. Evan had his sword hand resting against his shoulder like a character from a video game, though the smile had fallen off his face. How much had they heard before Patrick realized they'd entered the house?

The rest of the gift-giving and cookie-eating proceeded with a shallow frivolity. Eric and Rog delighted at the crib mobile Patrick had made: fuzzy felt unicorns and sprites circling a crescent moon covered in glow-in-the-dark paint. He and Yu received mostly wedding-related gift cards, for floral services or tuxedo rentals, and everyone simply gave Evan money, because he needed it. By the time they hugged and kissed each other good-bye, Patrick felt like his world had returned to normal.

Outside, lights twinkled against the brick houses and the frost-edged ivy snaking over their walls. To Patrick, it mimicked the stars flickering above them. As much as he coveted a house like those they passed on their way to where they'd parked, he felt ready for adventure, ready to meet uncertainty with Yu by his side.

Evan had to work, so they dropped him off downtown near the bar. As soon as he shut the door and waved them off, Yu said, "Patrick, if you're interested in an open relationship... I don't think I can be okay with that."

"I'm not."

"Are you sure? You sounded like you were having doubts today. Have you decided I'm too much effort?"

"I'm so sick of you falling back on that, holding it over me. Yu, if I thought you were too much work, I'd have said something before now." Out of nowhere, all the doubt returned to descend on him like an avalanche and leave him clawing his way back to clarity through the dirty, cutting ice.

"I'm sorry."

"Stop doing it, then. I'm tired of having to measure every word to validate you. It isn't fair. I have other things to worry about besides making you feel like I'm not leaving, when you should know by now I'm not."

"Maybe you should," Yu said in an arctic tone. "It certainly sounds like you find me a burden. Or maybe you just want to go out to clubs and let a bunch of strangers fuck you."

"Jesus. Fuck! I.... Do you want me to leave? Prove your theory? Is that what you've been after all along? An example to prove what a tortured and misunderstood artist you are? If that's what you want, then take me back to Eric and Rog's. I'm not going to be the one who proves you're not worth holding on to." Patrick's eyes stung. Goddammit, he was so tired, and his emotions were stretched so thin they could only tear at the seams. Everything was pulling apart, and no matter how Patrick clutched at the edges, he didn't know if he could hold it together.

"Yu, if you truly doubt I would walk through fire to stay beside you, that I'd do anything, please turn around and take me back to Eric and Rog's. If I haven't proven myself to you yet, I never will."

The tires squealed and threw up plumes of dirty snow as Yu skidded to a stop next to a row of closed shops and restaurants.

Yu got out of the car and slammed the door. Patrick sat, shocked, as he stomped up the snowy sidewalk with his fists balled beside him. Then he snatched the keys out of the ignition and got out of the car to chase after Yu. When he reached him and grabbed his shoulder, Yu shrugged out of his grasp and spun around to face him.

"If you don't want to marry me, why did you say yes?" Yu asked.

"I do want to marry you," Patrick said, white vapor freezing between them as he huffed to catch his breath.

"It didn't sound that way. It sounded like you want to be a normal twenty-two-year-old and go out and party and date other guys—just like I always worried you would. And it's normal of you to feel that way. I did it, in a way. I can't even be angry with you, but—"

"But you are."

Yu shook his head and thrust his shivering hands into his coat pockets. "I'm angry at myself. No one thinks I'm good enough for you, and they're probably right. I tried so hard to make you feel important—loved. I love you so much. I tried to do as much for you as you do for me, but it looks like I failed. Again."

Patrick closed his eyes and covered them with his hand. He just wanted to sit down on the frosty cement and wrap his arms around his knees. Everything had been going so wonderfully for him, and now it was all crashing down around his head, and he couldn't think of anything to do but try to shield himself against the debris. Should he have expected this—expected the other shoe to drop as soon as things got too good? He drew in a fractured breath and forced himself to speak. "I love you. I don't want anyone else. I don't think you're more trouble than you're worth, but I also don't know why I should keep repeating myself if it doesn't do any good. How else can I phrase it to make you understand? You have your insecurities and doubts piled so high around you that my words can't make it through. Okay, I'm a little nervous about taking this step. I think everyone who gets married probably is. It's a huge change in your life, isn't it? But that doesn't mean I don't want to do it. I'm totally ready to leap off that cliff, and I'm sure the wings will sprout. *I'm sure.* But you aren't. Why do you want to marry me when you're so convinced I'm going to give up eventually? Sometimes I think you'd be happier by yourself, with no one to interrupt your work, with no outside expectations. If that's true, tell me now. It's only fair."

Yu wrapped his warm fingers around Patrick's wrist and gently pried Patrick's hand away from his face. "Patrick, I'm sorry. My heart knows you won't give up. You don't give up on anything, ever. But my mind… my mind keeps telling me what's happened every other time I've been sure I could believe will happen again. It's telling me it's my fault, that I'll disappoint you."

"Then tell it to shut the fuck up," Patrick choked, his voice cracking at the tears glittering in Yu's eyelashes. "I just… I just need to know you believe in me. In us. I can't—" His stomach jumped, making him hiccup. "I can't go into this if I don't think you believe in me."

Yu bit his lower lip and scrunched his eyes shut, forcing the tears that had gathered down his cheeks. "I just don't believe in *me.*"

Patrick hadn't realized how deep Yu's self-doubt ran, and he really hated Yu's parents as he reached out to wrap his arms around Yu's head and pull him close. Yu stiffened at first before relaxing against Patrick and swallowing a few dry sobs. Patrick petted the back of his head and said, "I do. I swear I do. And I'll come to Japan with you."

Yu lifted his head to meet Patrick's gaze, eyes glittering and lips pinched together. "No. We should stay here, buy a house. It was selfish of me to expect you to give up your dream for mine. I can still forge weapons, and I can see you have what you need. It was selfish of me not to consider it before, and I'm sorry. Aside from you, I don't have any ties here, but you do. A home is important to you. I understand that now. I should have thought of your feelings before I even asked. You are *not* an interruption to my work. I'm sorry I made you feel that way. I can spend less time working—"

"I've made my decision, Yu. I want to go. I'm scared, but I'm excited too."

"What about your career? Your dream?"

Patrick took a step back and let his arms fall. He walked a few feet to a wooden bench and brushed the snow away before sitting down. "I don't know that doing drag was ever my dream, at least not like making swords is yours. I like doing it, and the money is nice, but I can live without it, at least for a while. I just really like clothes. I like making things, making an illusion that completely enthralls people. But I have to decide what I want to make of my life. I can't be doing this when I'm fifty, at least not professionally."

"Isn't that all the more reason to do it while you can?" Yu rested his hand on Patrick's shoulder but didn't sit down. "Show the world your beauty before it fades?"

Patrick reached up and covered Yu's hand with his. Yu's fingers were cold where they curved around the seam of Patrick's wool coat. "There's no way to know what the future will bring, if there'll even be a future. Maybe that's all the more reason to take this chance. We might not get another opportunity to go to Japan. I don't want to leave it as a what-if. But I'm scared—scared of being on my own without Rog and Jen and everybody else. I've always hated being alone, but I need to grow up, stand on my own feet without their support."

"You'll have me," Yu said, sounding miserable. "Although I can see why you feel like you can't depend on that. I haven't given you much reason to feel like you can. When you need someone, you turn to Jen or Roger, Eric, or even Evan. Because I'm not there, or my mind is too occupied with my work. I'm going to change that, start putting you first. I never thought I'd find someone I was willing to put my work aside for, but—"

"I don't want you putting your work aside." Patrick pulled Yu's hand down and kissed his chilly knuckles. "It will make you miserable, and I really don't mind you working."

"What do you need from me?"

"I just need you to believe I love you. To stop thinking it's only a matter of time before I throw you away, because it's not going to happen."

"I do." Yu kissed Patrick on the top of the head. "I've… never experienced unconditional love. All of this still seems too good to be true. Not even my parents—"

"I know," Patrick said. With everything going so well, he couldn't shake the feeling something terrible waited just around the next bend. That was the pattern his life had followed up until he'd met Yu; as soon as he built something up, something happened to bring it all crashing down, leaving him to pick up the pieces and start over. Dammit. He was good at picking up pieces. Making something exquisite from scrap. "But we have to stop projecting our past disappointments onto each other. I do it to you too. Maybe it will be good for us, going to Japan and having only each other to worry about."

"We'll talk more about going later." Yu turned his hand over beneath Patrick's, wrapped his fingers around Patrick's hand, and urged Patrick to his feet. "We'll decide together if going is the right thing for both of us. For now, let's just go home." They walked back toward the car. "Patrick, are you sure you're satisfied with me? You aren't curious about other men? You never think about it?"

Patrick elbowed him playfully in the ribs. "Everyone thinks about it. But when you win the lottery the first time you play, you don't burn the ticket and try again, right? I *know* there's nothing better out there."

"I want to prove it," Yu said. "Again and again."

"Okay," Patrick said, feeling a tingle across the base of his body. "Let's go home. I still have to give you your gifts."

"I have a few things to give you too."

Chapter 14

YU SHOWED Patrick his love through concrete things, things he could touch, quantify, and understand. He showed Patrick through grand, romantic gestures like the one Patrick woke to on Christmas morning. As he stumbled from the bedroom scrubbing sleep from his eyes, he was met by the glow of dozens of candles, their light bright and golden against the gloom of the overcast snowy sky outside. They burned on the ledges of the windows, surrounded by fragrant sprigs of evergreen branches and ivy. A tree, between two and three feet tall, stood on the center of the coffee table, covered in white lights, shimmering ribbons, candy canes, and angelic little figurines Yu had made. Packages wrapped in silver paper sat beneath it. A fire burned low in the hearth, and two red-velvet stockings overflowing with presents and candy hung above it.

Yu was in the kitchen, standing over the stove while coffee dripped rhythmically into the pot. Patrick smelled bacon and chocolate. He stepped up behind Yu, wrapped his arms around Yu's bare torso, and dropped a few light kisses across his shoulders.

"Merry Christmas," Yu said. "Breakfast is almost ready. Why don't you go sit down and I'll bring it out to you?"

Patrick couldn't imagine how early Yu had gotten up to get all of this ready, especially after the make-up sex of the previous night. It felt like a Christmas morning from a storybook, and no one had ever done anything like it for Patrick before. As soon as he caught himself wondering what might go wrong, Patrick pushed the doubt away. He was going to let himself be happy. He deserved it; they both did. They'd planned to spend Christmas Day alone, relaxing and enjoying each other, and that was what they'd do. Patrick peppered a few more kisses over Yu's back before returning to the living room and nestling into the couch, wrapped in the blanket Jen had made.

After they ate a breakfast specific to Patrick's preferences—Yu was the only person he'd ever met who didn't like chocolate—of chocolate-chip pancakes, smoked bacon, scrambled eggs, and poached pears, they pushed their plates aside and sat on the floor to lean back against the sofa. Patrick held his full belly. He couldn't stop smiling at Yu. "We'd better enjoy eating like this while we can—while we're young. If we keep it up, in a few years, we'll start getting fat."

Yu brushed Patrick's hair aside and kissed his neck. "I'll still love you."

Patrick chuckled and grinned even wider, because he knew Yu didn't—couldn't—say things he didn't mean. "Will your customers love sculptures with potbellies and saddlebags?"

"I don't care." Yu pulled Patrick's T-shirt aside to nibble across his collarbone. He brushed the fingertips of his other hand over Patrick's ribs and across his chest until he could circle Patrick's nipple. "Let's go back to bed."

"What about the gifts?"

"They'll still be here. The ham is in the oven, but it needs to cook for a few hours. Let's go work up an appetite."

FULL AND sated, they fell asleep and didn't wake again until the afternoon. They spent a leisurely half an hour or so in the shower before dressing in comfy sweats and making their way back to the living room. Yu made more coffee, and they cradled their warm mugs close as they sat in silence on the floor, watching the lights twinkle on their little tree.

"How boring are we?" Patrick joked.

"Pretty boring," Yu agreed. "Isn't it wonderful? Patrick… I've never been this happy. Just relaxing, eating, making love… just being with you. You really accept me. You really don't want me different."

Patrick rolled his eyes. "Idiot. Of course not."

"I never thought—No. It doesn't matter. Can I give you your gifts now?"

"I thought you'd never get to it," Patrick said. "Come on. Treat me like the princess I am."

Patrick unwrapped and opened the first box Yu handed him to discover a floral-printed shirt he'd admired at Urban Outfitters—but had thought too expensive. More clothes followed, along with a few books and a wooden sewing box bearing a brass plaque that said Patrick's name. Finally, Yu handed Patrick his final gift: a cylindrical box small enough to hold in his palm. Slowly, Patrick untied the gold bow and then peeled the shiny silver paper back until he could open the box's lid. Inside he found a delicate silver chain with a thimble-sized, onion-shaped charm dangling from the end. Though it was beautiful and delicate, Patrick didn't quite understand. "What is it?"

"*Hoshi no tama*," Yu said. "My soul. Look." He pressed on the top of the charm, and the six petals slowly opened to reveal a tiny piece of amber suspended by a thin wire at the center. Then he closed the pendant, and anyone who hadn't seen it open wouldn't know it wasn't a solid piece of metal. "For your eyes only. Only for you."

Patrick closed his fingers around it. "Thank you. I hope my gifts won't seem too inadequate after this."

"Do you know what I got for Christmas as a child?" Yu asked. Patrick shook his head. "Language-learning courses and math workbooks. Soap and toothpaste. A few pairs of socks if I was lucky. In middle school, I got a scientific calculator."

"Well, I guess I did better than that." Patrick went to retrieve the gifts he'd hidden beneath their bed. He'd wrapped them in gaudy paper featuring snowmen and angels, nothing as sophisticated as Yu's presentation. After two trips, he'd fetched all the packages and piled them around Yu—except for the two small ones stashed in the pockets of his sweat pants.

When he'd been shopping, trying to find the perfect thing to make Yu smile, Patrick had worried his selections had been too frivolous, but after hearing about Yu's disappointing gifts as a child, he thought maybe they were perfect. Yu seemed to like the bright red set of professional-quality pots and pans, as well as the handmade metal chopsticks and ceramic teabag holders shaped like hedgehogs. As soon as he opened it, he began leafing through the thick book on the history of arms and armor with clear enthusiasm. Though Yu looked like he'd be content to spend the rest of the afternoon with the book, Patrick pushed the final lumpy package across the floor toward his knee. It was the first gift Patrick had prepared, and after almost two months under the bed, it looked a mess, the paper creased and crumpled and the shiny blue ribbon twisted up. Yu eyed it skeptically, like it might be a joke gift. Patrick just hoped he wouldn't feel that way when he opened it, but he couldn't be sure.

Patrick waited as Yu carefully picked away the clear strips of tape and unfolded the paper. He lifted what he found inside with a bemused but not unhappy expression.

Patrick had made a pillow from white fleece. While basically square, he'd cut it into the shape of a fox with a pointed snout, legs, and curling tail. He'd appliqued red and black accents to form the features and had attached a little golden tassel to the tail. On the back, he'd sewn in some pockets and filled them with blank and lined tablets and pencils and pens. Yu pulled a pink highlighter out and shifted his eyes in Patrick's direction.

Cheeks burning, Patrick tried to explain. "You're always making beautiful things for me. I-I wanted to make you something. I'm not skilled like you, but I'm learning to sew all right. I just thought… I don't know. Maybe, on nights when I'm away performing, you could hold it and think of me. I would be with you in a way. And if you were in bed and had an idea—I get ideas in bed a lot—you could draw it or write it down. Is it stupid? Childish?"

Yu blinked a few times and hugged the fox pillow to his chest. He looked impossibly young and innocent as he rubbed his cheek against the soft fleece, closed his eyes, and smiled. Patrick had never seen anything so endearing. "No. No one has ever made anything for me before. I…. Thank you. I love it. You're so special, and so is this."

Tears stung Patrick's eyes, and he scrubbed at them with the heel of his hand. At first he felt stupid, until he noticed the glimmer in Yu's eyes. "We're a couple of losers."

"Yeah." Yu kissed each of Patrick's eyelids. He wound his arms around Patrick's shoulders and pulled Patrick to his chest with the pillow squished between them. For a while, they just held each other in front of the fireplace, by the light of the flames, the glimmering strands on the tree, and the candles quickly being reduced to pools of wax. It was perfect, like magic flurried down over Patrick and covered him in a blanket of enchantment. Then Yu whispered, "I love you," and the tears perched on the rims of Patrick's eyes spilled out and down his cheeks. "Don't be sad."

"I'm not," Patrick told Yu. "I'm so happy I can't hold it in."

"Good." Yu slowly trailed the tip of his tongue up Patrick's face, following the path of his tear. "If I can, I'll make you this happy every day. Nothing is more important to me."

Patrick turned to meet Yu's lips, and they kissed slowly and almost reverently for a few minutes. When they broke apart, Patrick rested his head against Yu's shoulder. He brushed his lips against Yu's neck as he spoke. "I have more for you."

"What?"

Patrick reached into his pocket and pressed the little black box against Yu's palm. Yu adjusted so he could open it and look in without disturbing Patrick. When he opened the lid, he gasped. He lifted the ring and held it between his thumb and finger. "Patrick, you shouldn't have done this. This is too expensive." Firelight glinted off the square, half-carat diamond set against the simple white-gold band. A few filigree details gave it an antique look, which had attracted Patrick to the design, but the setting of the stone looked masculine and subtle, which he thought Yu would appreciate. It was the perfect mix of their personalities, but Yu looked at it with discomfort. "The one I gave you is nothing compared to this. It makes me feel ashamed."

"No," Patrick told him. "You made mine. I wish I could do that for you, but I can't. Still, I want you to wear it. I want everyone to know you're mine. No, that's not right. I don't care what anyone else thinks. I want *you* to know you're mine and be reminded every time you see it."

Yu slipped it onto his finger. "Thank you, my love."

Patrick kissed him. "It's so good when it's just the two of us, without anything outside intruding. I love this."

"Well, then—" Yu started to say, but Patrick interrupted him.

"I have something else for you. One last thing." He reached into his pocket and pressed the little blue booklet into Yu's waiting hand. Yu opened it and flipped through the pages.

"Your passport?"

Patrick nodded. "I just got it. It was a bitch. And expensive. The birth certificate I had wasn't the official one, and I had to go to the records office—"

"You should have let me help you. I know what a pain it can be, filling out all those forms. You didn't have to do it alone."

Patrick shook his head. "I wanted it to be a surprise. You… you understand concrete things. I wanted something I could put in your hand, proof I'm beside you in this. I'd have got our plane tickets if I'd known when you wanted to leave. I'm all in, Yu. No looking back. Carpe diem."

Slowly, Yu set Patrick's passport on the table beside bits of colored paper and strips of shiny ribbon. He took both of Patrick's hands in his and met Patrick's gaze. For a long time, he just looked at Patrick while flicking his gaze from side to side, searching. "Do you mean it? If you don't, I won't be able to tell. Others can, but not me. I can only go on your words."

"I know," Patrick said, pinning a strand of hair behind Yu's small round ear. "I mean it. Japan will never be the same."

"What about your career? I know what Rog and the others think."

"I can perform anywhere and anytime I want. Yu, I don't see this as a loss. I see it as an opportunity. Laugh if you want, but it's like a quest in a book or a video game. You don't get to play, don't get to have a part in the story, until you agree to go on the adventure. I'm excited to do something big. It's a little scary, but if you'll be with me—"

"I will," Yu said with a wide smile. "Always. Even if you don't want to go."

"Dammit. Are you listening or just hearing what you expect me to say? I *want* to go."

"Sorry," Yu whispered.

Patrick just smiled and nodded once. It sucked—and it hurt him— that Yu still had so much trouble accepting someone wanting to be with him unconditionally. He resolved to just keep showing Yu how much he wanted him until Yu could no longer question it. Talk would do no good with Yu; he needed empirical evidence, and Patrick would provide it. For an artist, Yu had such a scientific approach to life. The thought made Patrick laugh.

"What's funny?" Yu asked, eyes narrowing.

"I'm just happy," Patrick responded. It wasn't a lie.

Yu leaned in to press their lips together, and soon they'd opened their mouths and twined their tongues tight. Not long after, they stumbled, groping each other, unwilling to relinquish contact, back to the bedroom. They remained there until Yu had to leave the sweaty, rumpled sheets to check on his ham.

As they dined on the pineapple-studded ham, along with lemon-pepper green beans, sweet potato puree, and spinach, leek, and feta bread pudding, both of them received a number of calls on their cell phones. Rog, Eric, Henry, Jen, Shawn, and Aouli all phoned to wish Patrick a quick happy holiday. Yu's conversation when he called his grandmother lasted much longer. They talked excitedly in Japanese for almost a half an hour while Patrick stared at his cookies and hot cocoa without the will to shove one more crumb of food down his gullet. Finally, Yu disconnected the call, smiling serenely.

"What was all that about?" Patrick asked, flipping through the same holiday specials on TV without paying much attention to what appeared on the screen.

"'*Baa-san*, my grandmother, will come to our wedding." Yu looked happier than Patrick had ever seen him, but still with that lingering fear in his taut frame and the way he clutched his phone in his tight, pale fist, like the iridescent soap bubble would burst at any moment. "I told her all about you, and she's happy I found someone to love. She's really happy for us. When I told her how much we liked just staying home together, being alone, talking, she said we reminded her of herself and my grandfather. She said… she said if we love each other that much, nothing will stand in our way. She believes we're going to make it. I believe that too."

Patrick smiled, though inwardly he wondered why Yu's grandmother's assurances meant more than his own. His musings scattered when Yu fell on top of him, laughing and nibbling against Patrick's neck while he rubbed a renewed erection against Patrick's root. Yu caught Patrick's earlobe between his teeth and slid his hands beneath Patrick's T-shirt. Though tired and sore, Patrick was about to consent to round three on the couch when his phone blipped. Irritated, he picked it up and saw Ian's name on the screen. Planning for a short and sweet holiday greeting, he answered the call.

"Hi, Ian."

"Hey, Patrick. Merry Christmas and all that shit."

Above Patrick, Yu rubbed his cock alongside Patrick's through their sweats and continued licking and sucking up and down his neck and across his jaw. He worked his nimble fingers to Patrick's nipple and circled the hard bead before giving it a playful squeeze. Patrick swallowed the moan and managed, "You too."

"So, I need to talk to you about Evan."

"Okay."

"I'm not gonna beat around the bush, brother. We're thinking of taking him on the Faire circuit with us, and I need to know where he's at in life."

As Yu bunched Patrick's shirt up to his armpits and drizzled soft teasing kisses down the exposed flesh of his waist, Patrick clutched his phone hard in his trembling fingers. He curled his hips up toward Yu, and his eyes rolled back as he struggled to concentrate on the conversation. He knew Ian's words were important, but as Yu traced the outlines of Patrick's tattooed roses with the tip of his tongue, he wanted to be selfish and tell Ian he couldn't talk. He just wanted to experience Yu's clever mouth without distraction, but Ian's questions continued.

"Look, I know the kid was using. Is he still?"

"I don't think so," Patrick managed as Yu rubbed his chin along the stubble of Patrick's emerging treasure trail. Patrick's cock strained against the cotton of his pants just a few inches lower.

"He's a good worker, but I can't play babysitter," Ian said. "I just need your assurance that this kid will do what he's supposed to do and keep himself clean before we take him on the road. I don't wanna deal with his shit. Can you give me your word, as family, that I won't have to?"

Yu rolled the waistband of Patrick's sweats down his hips until the head of Patrick's cock poked free. As soon as it appeared, Yu began lapping at the sensitive groove beneath the crown and running his tongue over Patrick's leaking slit. Patrick groaned into the phone as his head rolled back over the arm of the sofa.

"Patrick? You okay, man?"

"Yeah, I'm… really great. Listen, take a chance on Evan. He's doing everything he can to lead a respectable life. As far as I know, he hasn't touched anything but some weed occasionally. I believe in him. He needs people to believe he can make it."

"We've always been friends," Ian said as Yu continued swirling his tongue along the ridge where the base of Patrick's dick met the head. "But I ain't operating a charity. If you tell me I can count on this kid, that's all I need. I know you wouldn't fuck us over."

"No," Patrick gasped as Yu teased his asshole with a finger, his pad catching against the wrinkled skin. "I-I stand behind Evan. He's trying so hard. This chance is just what he needs. He won't let you down." Yu slid his finger inside him, and Patrick tried to stifle the moan, but couldn't completely prevent its escape.

"You sure you're all right?" Ian asked.

"I—ah. Yu and I are enjoying some time to ourselves."

"Oh jeez. That's—Oh, uh, well... have a good time, man." Ian quickly ended the call, and Patrick grinned up at Yu as Yu peeled his pants slowly down his legs. He let his phone drop to the floor and slide beneath the sofa. Then he met Yu's lips and opened his legs.

Chapter 15

A SOFT brush of lips across his shoulder as he lay sleeping on his belly awakened Patrick. The mattress groaned as Yu sat up, his hand still draped over the small of Patrick's back.

"Stay," Patrick growled in a voice rough with sleep, curving his ass up into Yu's hand.

"I can't, you enchanting, temping creature. When I called her last week, I told Ms. Weiss I'd have at least six more pieces ready for my gallery tour. She seems very optimistic that I can sell at least one sculpture at each of the five galleries she's planning to contact. I'm hoping to schedule my first opening in early March, which leaves me only about a month and a half to have everything prepared. Working on the sculptures at Wade's forge will be more difficult than when I had the studios at the university at my disposal. Wade's workshop is designed to make weapons and armor, not art."

"Weapons and armor are what you love," Patrick said, scrubbing the sleep from his eyes with the heels of his hands. "You want to make swords. You hated talking at your show at the university. I'm kind of surprised you even called her, let alone agreed to a tour. Why are you doing this?"

"Look here." Yu went to where his laptop sat on top of the dresser in their bedroom, and pulled up the image of a small, Japanese-style house surrounded by woodland: evergreens and red maples. He sat down on the edge of the bed to give Patrick a better view. A rustic fence enclosed a small garden, and a curving little stone path led to the door. It looked like something out of a fairy tale or a Miyazaki movie.

"What's this?" Patrick asked, sitting up to have a closer look. Yu brushed away the lock of hair that fell into Patrick's eyes.

"It's a house for rent near the village where we'll be staying. I know how important it is to you to have a home. This one won't be forever, but it can be ours while we're there. We can put our own touches on it, just like you wanted. You can even grow herbs and vegetables."

"And that's why you agreed to do the gallery tour?"

"It's not a big house. We won't have much more space than we do now, but I want to do this for you. You're giving up a lot so I can have my dream. I just want to make sure you'll be happy. With the money I hope to make from the tour, I can do that."

"Yu, I don't know what to say."

"Well, then, just smile, and give me a kiss. I have to get to work."

"Okay. I love you."

A few minutes later, Patrick heard the door close softly. The apartment was quiet after that; the swish of cars going by on the street below sounded distant. For a while, Patrick just lay staring up at the ceiling, relishing the fact that he had nowhere he had to be today. The time between Christmas and the New Year and the arrival of springtime always gave him a respite. With the Faire closed for the season and the furious partying that went on in the clubs over the holidays concluded, he had the chance to rest and spend his days at his leisure, working on projects he had to neglect while he was busy. He'd gotten better at spending time alone, had come to realize it didn't mean Yu or anyone else didn't care just because they weren't physically in his presence. He'd come to understand he didn't need to depend on others to entertain him or validate him. Though he always missed Yu when they weren't together, he no longer dreaded a day on his own as he once had.

Patrick contemplated getting up, making himself coffee and something for breakfast, but he decided it could wait a bit. He pulled the bedclothes around him and tucked the edge of the comforter under his chin. The blankets still held Yu's scent and the lingering aroma of the love they'd made the night before. Patrick thought about the little Japanese house and what it would be like to live there. He tried to imagine the rooms inside, how they'd set up their things. He couldn't help but wonder if it would ever feel like home, the way the apartment did, but then he had a vision of waking up next to Yu on a futon on the floor, with the morning sun peeking through the maple leaves, and he smiled.

Home was anywhere they were together. Why had he ever resisted the idea of going to Japan? If someone had asked him a few years ago, he'd have said he never expected to get out of Pittsburgh. They'd be flying. Patrick tried to imagine what that would be like. For at least an hour, he let himself wander through pleasant daydreams, and then he finally got out of bed and went into the kitchen.

A full pot of coffee waited on the counter, and a chocolate-chocolate-chip muffin from the bakery nearby sat in a small brown bag. He really wouldn't be able to eat like this forever, but right now, a double dose of chocolate sounded divine. When Patrick picked up the bag, he found a little note beneath.

My Beautiful Patrick,

It was hard to leave you this morning. I left you breakfast. Thank you again for standing by me while I pursue my dream. I never imagined I'd find anyone to walk this path with me. I'll be thinking of you all day, so I hope you'll be ready for me to show you how much I love you when I come home.

Yu had signed his name in kanji and drawn a little heart. Patrick traced a fingertip over the delicate characters before pinning the note to the refrigerator with a magnet. He poured a cup of coffee and took it, along with his breakfast, to the couch in the living room. He wanted to think of a way to surprise Yu. Maybe he'd cook. With that idea in mind, he took his phone from the coffee table and pulled up the web browser to search for recipes.

He noticed a message from Evan: *We R in GA! So cool! Filled in in the joust yesterday when Carleton sprained his wrist. Me! Ian kicked my ass, but still. Having the best time. Wouldn't be here if not 4 U. Thnx, Patrick. I really owe you. ~E.*

Patrick replied: *I'm glad you're having fun and working hard. You earned it.*

It surprised Patrick when Evan wrote back right away. *Patrick, I met a boy.*

Yeah?

Evan typed a smiley face and three hearts. *He's really hot. And no sex yet, so don't flip out, Mama.*

I don't have anything against sex. Tell me about him.

Evan typed: *He's a drummer in a Celtic band that follows the Faires. He's a little older.*

How much older?

26. But he said he'll wait till I'm legal. Patrick, I don't want to wait. He's really sweet to me.

Take it slow, Patrick advised. *If he really wants you, he'll wait.*

I know. But I'm going crazy!

Just be safe if you do anything, Patrick wrote. If Evan had found the person he wanted to be with, why should he wait? Nothing in life was certain, and Evan might as well enjoy his youth. Eric had once told Patrick something similar, about how he was at the most exciting point in his life, and he'd never experience anything as wonderful as falling in love for the first time. He really hoped Evan was feeling what he had when he'd met Yu, that Evan had acquired the skills to tell real affection from false. He worried, but he had to trust Evan. *You'll know if it's right.*

Thnx, Mama. Good talking. Miss U and LOVE U. Thnx 4 everything. Have 2 get 2 work now. Horses R hungry.

I love you too, Patrick wrote. *Have fun and take care.* He considered for a moment, then typed, *Slap Ian's ass and tell him it's from me.*

Evan responded: *LOL. Will do.*

A small smile remained on Patrick's face as he searched for what to make for dinner. He'd worried about Evan leaving, but the boy—the young man—seemed like he'd be fine. Patrick pulled up the Food Network site and searched through recipes for roasts. He wanted something that would cook a long time, warm the apartment, and scent its air with the aroma. After a long day of working at the outdoor forge, Yu would appreciate it. He'd also be surprised; Patrick almost never cooked. Patrick wanted something that would wrap around him and welcome him home as soon as he stepped in the door. He'd realized long ago the kind of magic a good, lovingly prepared meal could weave. Magic existed all around, and it could burn bright over a perfect evening at home with good food and better company. He just had to assemble the ingredients for his spell.

Patrick decided on a Provence-style beef stew and was making a list of what he'd need to buy when an incoming call interrupted him. Seeing it was Aouli, he answered.

"Hey, gorgeous. How's it hanging?"

"Just fine, baby girl," Patrick said. "What's up?"

"Well, we talked about doing a show and doing some touring at Christmas at Rog's. If you're still interested in something like that, I think I can line us up a few stops, if you're not opposed to some traveling."

Patrick considered. If Yu would be away during his gallery tour, he'd much rather be on the road with Aouli than sitting home alone. Besides, he could make some money to help them on their upcoming adventure. "I'm down. When are you thinking?"

"We'll need some time to make costumes and rehearse. Your wedding is, what, April 24? And then you're going to Japan in May? Maybe we can book some venues for a few weeks in March."

"Cool. We should get together and talk about the show," Patrick said. "You busy today?" When Aouli told him he didn't have plans, Patrick suggested he come over.

"Okay, sister. I'll be there in an hour."

Patrick straightened up the apartment and put on a fresh pot of coffee. Aouli arrived just when he said he would, and Patrick took out a notebook to jot down their ideas as they sat together on the sagging old couch. He brought out a plastic container of chocolate-covered cream puffs to thaw. They were orgasmic with the filling still a little frozen, and Patrick could never deny his sister the guilt he felt over indulging in them. They gave Aouli the perfect excuse to solicit a comment about how slender and beautiful he was from Patrick. His sister seemed to need those affirmations, and Patrick didn't mind. Making his sister feel good made him feel good. Plus, the compliments went both ways.

"Well, don't you look well-fucked, glowing, and so beautiful it makes me sick?" Aouli asked when Patrick opened the door to let him in. "I guess this monogamy thing agrees with you."

"Yeah, I'm happy." They moved into the living room to sit down, and predictably Aouli rolled his eyes at the pastries and made the expected comments about trying to get him fat. Patrick just supplied the requisite, "Please. You're, like, the hottest bitch I know."

"Aw. Thank you, honey."

"Aouli, do you really not hope to find somebody special and settle down someday?"

"Not anytime soon. I'm not in a position yet where I have to trade freedom for sex. As you so keenly observed, I'm working with all this." He swiped his delicate fingers theatrically down the length of his body.

Patrick set the cream puff he'd picked up back in the container. "Is that what you think I'm doing?"

Aouli turned to face Patrick and took his hand. "Sister, I think you're scared to be alone."

"I am, or at least I *was* scared to be alone. I had nobody growing up. I can't remember a time when I didn't have to take care of myself. It's nice having somebody take care of me. But I don't think I'm trading my freedom for it. It's not like Yu tries to control me."

"He seemed awfully jealous that night at the club."

"He was. But he trusts me. He's never asked me to stop performing."

Aouli parted his lips like he had more to say but quickly pressed them shut.

"What?" Patrick asked. "We're sisters, so if you've got something to say—"

"Okay, honey, but remember you asked for this. He might not have asked, but he's sure putting a stop to you performing by dragging you to Japan. What are you going to do over there while he's making swords, anyway? You are too fabulous to be a housewife."

All of a sudden, the little house didn't seem so idyllic. What *would* he do all day? He'd have no friends, no one who even spoke his language to talk to. Patrick shook his head. No. He wouldn't let these doubts worm their way back into his head. It shamed him how easily questions about Yu's true motives wiggled into his thoughts and how tenacious their barbs could be. It wasn't fair to Yu. Yu hadn't been one of the people who had hurt or abandoned him growing up. "I… I thought you liked Yu."

Aouli pressed his eyes shut and held them that way for a few seconds. "Oh, honey, I do. I'm just worried about you. You'll be so far away. Who are you going to turn to if things don't work out? We, your sisters, the people who will *never* let you down, are here."

Patrick, ready to say Yu would never let him down, left the words unsaid as he looked at Aouli's face, his eyes warm and wide, a little crease between his perfectly plucked brows. It occurred to Patrick, and he didn't know how he'd missed it before, that Aouli had been abandoned too. Patrick didn't know when or by whom, but he knew with certainty it had happened. Aouli trusted no one but his drag sisters; he wouldn't even attempt a relationship with a man. For the first time, Patrick saw the other queen's vanity and frivolous surface personality for the armor they were. It made him sad, and he leaned forward and hugged the other man. "Someday, I hope you find someone you won't have to worry about letting you down. Yu is that person for me. I had a hard time believing it—I mean, life has taught me otherwise—but some things are worth the risk. You have to leave your heart exposed sometimes in spite of everything sharp pointed at it."

Aouli nodded and hugged Patrick back. When he spoke, his voice was lower, less lilting. "I don't know if I'm that brave. And I am happy for you, Patrick. It's just like Eric always says, you're too smart for your own good. But you also have a lot of courage."

"Someone hurt you, didn't they?" Patrick already knew the answer. He felt it in the desperate clinging of Aouli's slender arms. "If you want to talk—"

Aouli pulled away and swiped beneath his eyes with his fingertips. "Hell with that. You're *my* little sister. I might not be brave, but I am strong. Now enough of this chick-flick sob fest. Let's suck down some chocolate and figure out this show. Actually, doesn't wine pair pretty well with chocolate?" He very obviously turned his gaze to the many dusty bottles in the rack.

Patrick let out a sharp laugh, mostly to dispel the tension tightening his chest. "It's ten in the morning!"

"Oh, all right, honey, but when we get on the road, I am going to teach you how to party."

They spent the next few hours sketching, jotting down ideas, and looking up songs on Patrick's phone. When they got hungry for something a little more substantial than the cream puffs, they walked a few blocks to a neighborhood deli. Over fat Reuben sandwiches, coleslaw, and fries, they discussed the finer points of the two-person show they planned to take on the road. By the time they finished their lunch, they'd made plans to get together later in the week to start shopping for their costumes. Patrick felt better than he had in weeks as he returned to the apartment to get ready to host his support group at the LGBT Center.

By the time he returned from that meeting, he felt more miserable and hopeless than he ever had.

THE APARTMENT was dark. Patrick didn't bother turning on the lights or even removing his wet sneakers. They squeaked against the hardwood and left grimy little puddles as he moved on autopilot toward the couch. He let his body drop, let his head fall into his open hands. Why wasn't Yu home yet?

Patrick had no idea how long he'd been sitting with his face covered when he felt his phone vibrating in his coat pocket. He pulled it out and stared at the screen, barely registering his friend's name until it was almost too late to answer the call. "Eric."

"Hey, princess. There's a game on pretty soon. You wanna come over for some beer and wings?"

Good old Eric. Thank God. "Yeah, I could really use a friend."

THE CRAFTSMAN-style house in the Mount Lebanon suburb felt different when Patrick let himself in the front door—colder, somehow less alive. Maybe it was just his mood after the devastating news he'd received at the support group. At least he wasn't stuck at home alone waiting for Yu.

The TV was on in the living room, and Patrick noticed some empty pizza boxes stacked beside the couch and some dirty socks discarded on the floor. A few beer bottles sat on the coffee table. Missing were the several other people Eric and Rog usually invited over to watch a game.

Patrick found Eric alone in the kitchen. More beer bottles, along with some Chinese take-out boxes and empty bags from fast-food places littered the counters. Eric stood near the sink, dumping wings from a Styrofoam container onto a plate. He turned when he heard Patrick's still-wet canvas sneakers squeaking on the tiles. Eric's normally sexy stubble now made him look more like a mountain man than a seductive pirate.

"Jesus, princess. You look like shit. Have you been crying?"

He had, at the center. The entire meeting had consisted of little more than the members holding each other and crying. Since then? Patrick wasn't sure.

Eric abandoned the plate of wings and came to grasp Patrick's shoulders. "What the hell happened, Patrick? Is Yu okay?"

"Yeah. He's fine. Could we go sit down?"

Eric nodded, retrieved two beers from the fridge, followed Patrick to the living room, and sat very close to him on the couch. Patrick rested his hands on his thighs, palms up, and looked down at them. They seemed weak and frail, just slender bones covered in white skin and dusted with freckles—hands without the strength to hold anything together.

"Baby?" Eric urged.

Patrick looked over at him. Eric had been the closest thing he'd ever had to a father. "If I ask you to hold me, you'll know I don't mean anything inappropriate by it, right?" He was scared as he awaited Eric's response, scared shitless of being turned away again. Luckily he didn't wait long.

Eric opened his arms, pulled Patrick down against his chest, and wrapped him up so tightly Patrick could hardly move. Patrick just rested his head beneath Eric's chin and closed his eyes, breathing the scent of Eric's soap and the fabric softener on his soft old T-shirt. Eric reached up to pet the back of Patrick's head. "What happened, Patrick?"

Patrick sniffled. "I-I volunteer at the LGBT Center, running a support group for kids. Most of them are okay; they just need someone to tell them so, to tell them they aren't alone. Mostly I help them look for jobs and fill out applications. I-I'm not any substitute for a licensed counselor, but I try to be a friend. I mean, after what you and Rog, what everybody did to help me, I just… I just…. God, I don't know what I'm trying to do."

Eric dropped a kiss into the part of Patrick's hair and let his chin rest on top of Patrick's head. "What you're doing is important."

"I'm not doing it good enough." Patrick nestled his face against Eric, trying to soak up strength from the man who had supported him from the beginning. "I—One of my kids… she died. She killed herself, Eric." A sob cut off Patrick's next words, and Eric just waited for him to recover, rubbing soothing circles on the back of Patrick's head.

"Her name is—was—Charlene. I thought she was happy. She worked so hard. Thought she was doing well. I knew she was depressed because of her hormones, and the surgeries she needed were expensive, and she didn't make enough working at the makeup counter, but—

"How did I not know how much pain she was in? She was such a sweetheart, always with a smile for everybody. How did I not know? She was hurting so bad she couldn't keep going, and I didn't see it. What the fuck is wrong with me? I should have been able to help her. She's fucking dead! Because I couldn't see she needed my help. I failed her. She was only nineteen years old, and I let her die when I should have been there to help her."

Patrick could no longer keep the sobs erupting from the pit of his body, and he clutched fistfuls of Eric's shirt and cried. "How could I have not known she was in that much pain? She was in pain, and I didn't help her. I left her alone. And she couldn't go on. Couldn't face it. I should have been there. Faced it with her—I—I failed her. I was all she had, and I failed her."

Eric just held him and nuzzled his face into Patrick's hair until Patrick got a hold of himself. Then he held him in comfortable silence while their beers sat ignored on the coffee table and the game continued on the TV without either of them paying it any attention. Finally, Eric said, "Sometimes you can only do your best, baby. And it isn't always enough."

"I'm not qualified to do this work. I should probably stop, leave it to someone who's trained to see the signs, to know what to do."

"And abandon all the kids you *can* help because one slipped through your fingers?"

"Dammit, Eric. I hurt, and I'm tired, and I'm confused."

"I'm sorry. Maybe you should take some time off. Take care of yourself. You always put yourself last. You've never been any different, but maybe that needs to change now, princess. What does Yu say about all of this?"

"He was still working when I got home. He's... he wants to get me a house."

"Did you even call him? Ask him to come home? Baby, you're not on your own anymore. Why do you have so much trouble asking for help?"

"I don't know. I just want to make things better for the people I love. Um, Eric? Where's Roger?"

Eric sighed and stiffened slightly beneath Patrick. "He's spending some time at his sister's house."

"What? What happened?"

Eric hugged Patrick a little closer, not to comfort Patrick, but to draw comfort from having Patrick in his arms. Patrick could feel it, just as he had when Aouli had held on to him so desperately. "Eric?"

"We had a fight. He doesn't know how much it hurts me to see him looking at me and finding me lacking. I shrugged it off for as long as I could, but then, then he outright asked me if I wanted a baby as much as he did, and I told him no. Because it's the goddamn truth. I never wanted kids. I don't want that responsibility. I just want the man I love and free time to spend with him. I had so many plans for when Rog retires from doing drag—traveling, cruises, whole weekends just staying in bed. He's all I want. He's enough. I'm not enough for him, and honestly, I don't understand it, and it fucking hurts. He got pissed off and called me a selfish bastard, and then he went to his sister's. Christ. I want to make him happy, make his dreams come true, but how much am I expected to give up?"

Patrick nodded, understanding better than he wanted to.

"I mean, I entered into a partnership with a gay man. I never imagined kids would be part of the equation. Then Rog said he wanted a baby, and I supported him. I'd do it for him, you know? To make him happy. And of course I would love the child and be the best father I could. But it just wasn't working out with the surrogates, and I was fucking sick of jerking off into a dish, and I just wanted it to be like it was, when we loved each other and were enough for each other. We have a good life. I feel complete. He doesn't, and it fucking stings."

"Sorry," was all Patrick could offer as his world cracked a little more. The pieces raining down were becoming too big for him to dodge. Suddenly he wanted Yu, wanted him fiercely, wanted to hold him in his arms and know he was whole and unhurt, that he wouldn't run away. He needed to feel Yu's skin and bones pressed against him, and though he hated to leave Eric, he wriggled out of Eric's arms. "I have to get home. If there's anything I can do…."

"You can take care of yourself for a change."

Patrick nodded as he stood. Then he bent down to kiss Eric on the forehead. "I love you."

"I love you, too," Eric whispered wistfully as he stroked Patrick's arm. "Go on. I'll be fine. Just gonna drink these beers and watch the rest of the game. You don't have to worry about me."

"Please call if you need me."

"I will, princess. I promise."

"YOU THAWED a roast," Yu said as Patrick stumbled into the kitchen. Patrick barely remembered driving home. He felt numb and lost inside his head. "Did you have plans for it, or can I—"

God, Yu was beautiful in his worn flannel shirt and ratty jeans. Patrick just needed to hold him, feel the certainty of Yu against him. He crossed the kitchen, threw himself against Yu, and buried his face in the loose hair spilling over Yu's shoulder. "You're so beautiful. Oh God, Yu."

He couldn't hold his weight up anymore, and Yu supported him as he backed into the living room and settled them on their wonderful, worn-out, shitty sofa. He held Patrick against his chest as Eric had, but it felt even better, more permanent. Safer. Patrick choked out the story of poor Charlene, and of Eric and Rog, whose love had always been his inspiration, and he looked at the picture of his brother Dylan, who'd died when Patrick was three, sitting beside the plain bronze urn holding his father's ashes. "None of them. Couldn't—couldn't save any of them."

He cried, letting himself fall apart into pieces, because Yu was here, and Yu would pick up those scraps, melt them down, and forge them into something better and more beautiful than they'd been before. Patrick could trust him not to discard any fragment he dropped, and goddammit, he needed this. It had been too long coming. He needed to fall apart and be remade into something new and better, so he cried there against Yu's soft flannel shirt. He cried for Charlene and Dylan, who'd never had a chance, and for his father, who had thrown his life away. He cried for himself and his failure to save them. Yu held him, safe in his strong, slender arms, and Patrick cried for Eric and Rog. If they couldn't make it, how could anyone? He cried because finally, he knew there were no fairy-tale endings. Not for anyone. Life was not a storybook or a love poem, no matter how much he wanted it to be.

"I couldn't—I tried. I wanted to save everyone. Fix it. I just wanted everyone to get their happily ever after. There's no such thing. Is there?"

"There is for me," Yu whispered as he raked his fingers through Patrick's hair.

"I failed them all. Charlene, Dylan, my dad… even you. I-I wanted to save everyone, but—"

"No." Yu grasped Patrick's chin hard enough to hurt and tilted Patrick's head up until he could look into Patrick's swollen, stinging eyes. His gaze was as hard and sharp as the katana he wanted to learn to forge. "You did not fail me."

"I—your parents—"

"No. Before you, I thought I would spend my life alone, that I was too much trouble. Everyone I've ever known has told me I'm not good enough. Until you. You did not fail me, and I won't let you say you did. I can't."

"Yu, I…."

"Come to bed. Let me take care of you. I know you don't believe it, but I'll always take care of you. No matter what, you're not getting rid of me."

"I believe you," Patrick said as he let Yu drag him from the sofa and tug him toward their bedroom. "But I'm scared. If Eric and Rog can't make it, what are our chances? How can we make it?"

"We love each other. I would do anything for you, Patrick."

"Eric and Rog love each other too."

"They're not us. Not me. I don't know if you have any idea how much I love you, Patrick."

"Show me. Let me keep believing in fairy-tale endings. I-I don't want to think they're impossible, so… show me?"

Yu did.

Chapter 16

THE WEEKS before they would have to separate passed too quickly. As if they knew what they'd be giving up, Patrick and Yu stayed in almost constant physical contact; if they weren't making love, they sat on the sofa with their thighs pressed together, Patrick sewing beads onto his gloves while Yu made sketches for his customers. They ate, slept, and showered with their skin and bones pressed together, and it almost physically hurt to separate when Patrick had to perform or Yu went to the forge.

On the day he planned to leave, Patrick stood looking around their small, cramped living room. Yu had mailed all but one of their wedding invitations: the one addressed to his parents. Patrick picked it up and flipped it over and over in his hands. He wanted one last chance to repair the rift between Yu and his family, because he knew how short life could be, how abruptly it could end. Yu, as well as his parents, deserved another chance—a chance for the fairy-tale happily ever after Patrick had started to doubt but couldn't quite dismiss. There was always hope. He just couldn't keep going if he couldn't believe that. But ultimately the decision fell to Yu. He didn't dare risk making things worse, and he'd sworn to Yu he'd never lie to him again. He intended to keep that promise, so he set the envelope down, ran his fingers along the embossed lettering, and then turned away and tried to forget about it.

Patrick and Yu had made love, with Patrick topping and giving Yu everything he had. Yu had grasped Patrick's hips, dug his nails into Patrick's skin, compelling Patrick to slam against him as if they could hammer them together like two pieces of heated malleable steel, before Patrick had packed his things, kissed Yu, and met Aouli at the bus station.

In ten hours, they'd be performing in a club in Harrisburg. Patrick let the excitement wash away his loneliness as he sat looking out the window. Beside him, Aouli had fallen asleep against the woven blue upholstery of the bus's seat with his lips slightly agape and a thin string of drool running over his chin. Patrick shifted uncomfortably, unable to find a suitable position. The pain he'd felt over the past few weeks when he wasn't with Yu intensified, almost like someone had cut away a part of his body, like a piece of him was missing. As the bleak winter landscape blurred by beyond the window, all dirty white and somber gray, Patrick wondered if he was being weak.

They arrived in Harrisburg and dragged their luggage from the bus stop to their hotel a few blocks away. Patrick closed his eyes as he stretched across his expansive bed. Unlike Aouli, he had trouble falling asleep when he wasn't alone, with Yu, or safe behind a locked door. At his father's house, he'd only ever been safe in the tiny space he had claimed, with the door locked. He struggled to fall asleep without Yu curled around him. Especially now. He looked over at Aouli on his bed, sitting cross-legged as he flipped through the channels on the TV, and tried to breathe slowly and evenly. He was here with his sister, and he was safe. It had never affected him like this before. He closed his eyes and pictured what the house in Japan would be like in the spring. His heart rate slowly returned to normal with his visions of a tidy little kitchen with a flower garden beyond the small window. It might be nice—peaceful—not to have anyone to worry about for once. Yu would be happy; there would be nothing Patrick had to fix, no one for him to fail.

Patrick managed to sleep for a few hours and woke to a smiling Aouli holding a huge cup of coffee. "Double caramel mocha with an extra shot and whipped cream. You know that's, like, eight thousand calories, right?"

Patrick couldn't even roll his eyes. It was such a sweet gesture, and he needed that coffee. "You want the shower first?"

"You go ahead," Aouli said. "I shaved this morning, and, well, there are some good aspects to being Hawaiian. Like very little body hair. Take your time."

Looking at the clock on the table between their beds, Patrick saw they still had three hours before they had to perform. He had time to lean against the bouncy, overstuffed pillows and enjoy his drink. Soon, blessed caffeine ran through his veins, sugary goodness burst over his tongue, and eventually he made his way to the bathroom to wash off. He shaved and did his makeup at the hotel, and then they were off to perform their show for the first time.

THE CLUB was called Stallions, and it seemed higher class to Patrick, not a dive or a meat market. Soft white lights shone down on him as he made his way to the center of the modest stage. The sound of birds chirping echoed through the speakers as Patrick sat down, the metal wires of a fake dove's foot wound around his fingers. Patrick brought the bird's black beak close to his lips in a Disney-like semblance of a kiss. He wore a baby-blue satin gown that would make Jen drool, with a stiff, heart-shaped lace ruff, white gloves, a blonde wig, and a pearl necklace to match his tiara. He and Aouli had gone all-out on costuming, and Patrick knew he looked exquisite even though they had cobbled most of the pieces together from thrift-store finds. With his fair complexion and blue eyes, Patrick looked almost as convincing as a blonde as a redhead. Since Yu had needed the SUV to transport his pieces, and Patrick's old Horizon provided less space than the bus, they'd improvised on the set. They just couldn't transport large pieces, so Patrick swooned over a set of folding metal chairs draped in purple velvet with a few silk flowers strewn around the base.

"If only my prince would come," Patrick said to the fake bird. "But wait! Maybe he's already here." Patrick rose and surveyed the audience clustered close to the stage. "Which one of these is destined to be my true love?" Ignoring the most beautiful men, he chose a plainer guy, gangly, with a slight overbite and mousy brown hair hanging in his eyes, and led him up the steps to the stage. This guy was a guaranteed twenty-dollar tip, and besides, Patrick liked making him feel good, feel beautiful. This guy had as much right to his moment in the spotlight as his more conventionally good-looking friends. Patrick remembered only too well how it felt to be invisible and ignored. He led his reluctant volunteer to the draped chairs. He stroked his cheek and fondled the collar of his pale blue polo shirt.

"Oh, my prince. Now that I have found you, we'll be happy forever." The man's awkwardness was cute as Patrick fondled his cheek and chin. His face colored adorably.

The tinkly fairy-tale music cut off as Aouli stepped onto the stage in a clinging, black satin gown with puffy sleeves and a plunging neckline.

His wig had been twisted into a pair of bull-like horns wrapped in beaded wire and silver ribbon, and he held a riding crop.

"Oh, I don't think so, princess."

"You? What are you doing here? Why?" Patrick wailed. He crossed his arms over his volunteer's chest. "Why do you want to ruin my happiness?"

"Why? Why, honey? Well, it's simple," Aouli said, cutting figure eights in the smoky air with the riding crop. He grabbed Patrick's prince by the front of his shirt, pulled him to his feet, and gave him a gentle push toward the steps leading offstage. "I'm a *bitch*."

Music began to play, and Patrick covered his face in his hands as the space around him went dark. Aouli sang the lyrics to Meredith Brooks's "Bitch," as he moved provocatively to the music. Men ran their hands over his long black satin gown as he swiveled his hips at the edge of the stage and belted out the lyrics. The slits in the sides of the dress exposed his fishnet-clad legs and garters, and the audience stuffed them full of bills. He and Patrick had decided they would sing all the songs in their show, since they both had strong voices. The audience seemed to appreciate it. Aouli pretended to smack Patrick across the face when he wandered near the bench and Patrick lifted his head, and Patrick dropped his head into his folded arms as Aouli strutted behind the curtain.

Patrick sighed theatrically. A soft baby spot shone down on him. "I miss my prince, and I love him. No other will do. If I can't be with him, whatever shall I do?" He couldn't help thinking of Yu as the next song began to play. It helped Patrick to spread his legs, hitch up his layers of skirts, and run his hand up his white lace-hosed legs and over his garter belts and satin panties. Soon he sang along to the Divinyls' "I Touch Myself." Just as the song said, Patrick didn't want anybody else, and as he sang, he strutted across the stage, touching his buttocks, his tucked-in groin, his waist, and his small faux breasts. Someone had once told him that no man masturbated to visions of his partner, but for him, nothing made his arousal soar like imagining Yu's face when he came, with his eyelids fluttering and his amazing lips parted. The men in the audience stood, entranced, even as they knew they weren't the man of Queen Titania's fantasies. But watching Patrick, they could imagine him singing and dancing for them, wanting them, making them the focus of his universe. Patrick just grinned and took the money they waved at him, leaning down to let them touch the exposed skin between his gloves and sleeves. Without even showing much skin, he held these men in the palm of his hand and it… it was empowering.

After the two songs, Patrick felt sure he and Aouli had made the money it had cost them to come here back and then some. The rest of the show would be pure profit. Hopefully by the end of the night, they'd pay for their costumes and props, and the rest of the stops on their tour would be just as lucrative. Harrisburg was a small city, and the reaction of the audience here gave Patrick high hopes for Philadelphia and Baltimore.

As his number ended, Patrick stood beneath the spotlight holding the hems of his skirts. He sighed theatrically enough for the audience to hear him and shook his head. "Maybe I'm going about this all wrong. Look at me. Maybe-maybe handsome princes aren't interested in innocent girls like me. What do you boys think?"

He paused for the audience to answer, though their response sounded like a garbled shout, neither negative nor affirmative. Patrick could work with that. He lowered his head, looked up through his fake eyelashes, and flashed a mischievous grin. "You know, I think you're right. No more sweet little princess for me! That's no fun. From now on, I want to be *bad girl*."

The men in the audience hooted and applauded as Patrick shook the fake bird from his hand and tugged on the sides of his dress. The Velcro he'd strategically placed easily gave way, and soon he left the gown in a sapphire pool near the back of the stage. Underneath, he wore a white bra, a white waist-cincher, bloomers, and thigh-highs topped in little white satin bows. He dragged his palms from his knees to his hipbones as "Bad Girl" by Rihanna played over the sound system.

The song had a good beat for dancing, and Patrick took advantage of it, strutting around and kicking his legs up parallel with his body. It also had some slower segments, giving him an opportunity to show off his more acrobatic moves, like backbends and walkovers. He became so entranced with performing that he forgot he had an audience. He just moved to the music, bending and stretching his body to its limits. When the song ended, it surprised Patrick to see the wrinkled bills surrounding him, to hear the paper crumpling beneath his little white shoes. When the lights went down, he scooped up what he could and tucked it beneath the velvet draping of the chairs so he and Aouli could collect it after their performance. He wasn't sure, but it seemed like a lot. The audience had really liked him, and that made him feel good, worthwhile.

Patrick and Aouli performed the rest of their show, at one point facing off with rapiers in a duel while Wagner thundered in the background. Henry had helped them choreograph their fight, and they knew their unconventional show would either be a huge hit or it would bomb spectacularly. That was okay with Patrick. He preferred love or hate—some form of passion—from his audience over indifference. Sure, he wanted to make a living, but he also wanted to make art, and art was risky. Art meant venturing beyond the safe and formulaic. It meant a duel instead of covering songs by Cher and Liza Minelli. It meant the unexpected, and not everyone was comfortable with something new. But for Patrick, clashing swords with Aouli was exhilarating. He knew he wasn't Yu, presenting beautiful pieces in a gallery, but he wanted to make the men watching him think. As they performed, he didn't know how the audience felt, but none of them were lounging against the bar, playing video poker, or scrolling through the songs on the jukebox. The all stood with their attention glued to the stage as Patrick and Aouli shouted witty insults at each other.

By the end of their sword fight, Aouli stood in faux-leather hot pants, a halter-style top that exposed his stomach, and knee-high, stiletto-heeled boots. Throughout the duel, Patrick had carefully used his blunt blade to open several strips of Velcro on Aouli's gown, cutting it away piece by piece. They stood facing each other, swords crossed at the tips, Patrick in frilly ivory and Aouli in shiny black. Bright white light washed Aouli's side of the stage, blurring away everything but his black costume and headdress. A black light shone on the darkened portion of the stage Patrick occupied, so only his white costume and UV-reactive wig glowed against the heavy shadows. Patrick was especially proud of this segment of their show: the yin and yang of it, the symbolic light in darkness and darkness in light. Visually, he knew it must be stunning. They'd practiced hard, so everything fell into place just so, and in the end, Patrick defeated Aouli, and Aouli fell to his knees. Patrick stood with the edge of his blade at Aouli's throat.

Aouli looked up at Patrick, pressed his palms together in supplication, and said, "Please don't kill me."

"Why should I spare your life, after everything you've done to me?"

"You don't understand." Aouli bowed and shook his head, and Patrick let his sword fall a few inches.

"What don't I understand? You ruined my chance at love. Why would you do that?"

Aouli took Patrick's hand and rubbed his cheek against the back. "Don't you see? I want you for myself. I always have!"

Patrick, feigning shock, staggered back a few steps and let his rapier fall to the stage with a resounding clang. He covered his mouth with his hand as Aouli got to his feet.

"I've been searching for something," Aouli said, taking a tentative step toward Patrick as music began to play in the background.

"But you think I'm fragile," Patrick said, letting his voice waver and break before he began singing Stevie Nicks's part of the "Leather and Lace" duet. It taxed his vocal range, but his voice rang out clear and strong as he let the meaning of the lyrics wash over him, the emotion they inspired creeping into his vocals. Aouli joined him, and they sounded better together in the spacious room than when they'd practiced in Eric and Rog's backyard. As they sang, they clung to each other, caressed each other, danced slowly and ground against each other. Overwhelmed with the feelings the old song inspired, Patrick nearly forgot they had an audience—again. When the song ended and Aouli knelt on the stage with his arms wrapped around Patrick's waist, Patrick had to blink and force himself to remember they'd been performing.

The men below the stage just stood, staring, and Patrick couldn't tell whether they were intrigued or just confused and indifferent. He remembered he had one final part to play, and he bent down and kissed Aouli's forehead, even though they hadn't planned it. Then he stepped out of his friend's strong, supple arms, strutted to the edge of the stage, and bowed with a flourish, batting his blonde locks over his shoulder.

> "If we shadows have offended,
> Think but this, and all is mended,
> That you have but slumber'd here
> While these visions did appear.
> And this weak and idle theme,
> No more yielding but a dream,
> Gentles, do not reprehend:
> if you pardon, we will mend:
> And, as I am an honest Puck,

If we have unearned luck

Now to 'scape the serpent's tongue,

We will make amends ere long;

Else the Puck a liar call;

So, good night unto you all.

Give me your hands, if we be friends,

And Robin shall restore amends."

With the famous soliloquy completed, Patrick dragged his hand over his blonde wig and it fluttered to the floor. Beneath, a pair of tiny horns protruded from his red hair. He reached down to unfasten the busk of his corset and let it fall. Then he carefully stepped out of his lacy underpants and stood before his audience in nothing but a faux-fur thong. In an instant, he transformed from the archetypal princess, the blushing virgin, to the trickster, the grinning faun who'd taken the audience as unknowing accomplices in his delightful deception. Whether the men in the club understood, Patrick couldn't be sure. He had a feeling his bare body commandeered most of their attention.

Finally, hand in hand, Patrick and Aouli took their final bows. The moment of truth had come. The men would either appreciate their daring and original show or they would say, "What the fuck was that?" and return to drinking and dancing. Patrick clutched Aouli's sweaty palm tightly as he waited for their reaction.

There was silence, and Patrick hung his head. They'd gone too far, pushed too hard against the boundaries of what was expected in their genre. He'd known failure was a distinct possibility with a show as weird and risky as theirs, but it still stung. Dammit, they had worked so hard.... Patrick had put his heart and soul into every aspect of this show; he'd even expressed some of his most personal fears about vulnerability and rejection, but they didn't get it. He'd failed, and not only himself, but Aouli too, who'd trusted him. What would happen now? Would the other venues who'd booked them want to cancel? Would all of their time and effort have been for nothing? What the hell had he been thinking? A sword fight in a drag show? Shakespeare?

Slowly, the lights on the stage grew brighter, bathing Patrick and Aouli in cold, unforgiving light. Patrick tried to tug on Aouli's hand and guide him toward the exit and escape from the audience's indifference, but Aouli resisted.

"Come on." Patrick gave Aouli's hand a desperate yank. "They didn't like it. I thought…. They didn't get it."

As the full light of the stage fell on them, the audience went wild, clapping, shouting, and stomping until the whole venue vibrated. Tremors moved through Patrick's kitten heels and up his legs as he stood in disbelief. Men pressed their chests against the edge of the stage, waving money and shouting.

"They want an encore," Aouli said in Patrick's ear.

Patrick just shook his head. He couldn't believe they'd liked the show.

"Patrick…."

"Okay. They want more; then let's give it to them."

Aouli winked and kissed Patrick at the corner of his mouth. He signaled to the DJ, and the music began to play. They sang, "Somebody That I Used to Know," by Gotye and Kimbra. It was a challenging duet— timing was everything, but it gave both of them a chance to show off their range, and they sounded terrific. It bothered Patrick a little to end their show on the idea that the fantasy relationship hadn't lasted; he'd always been a fan of happily ever after. But as the audience sang along to the chorus, Patrick knew they felt the way he did: true love was one in a million, and usually the attempt ended in a messy disappointment.

Both Patrick and Aouli were tired after traveling and performing. They spent as little time as they could at their merch table, selling T-shirts and signing headshots. For once, Aouli preferred his bed to free drinks and unlimited male attention, so they cleaned up, packed their costumes and props, and prepared to walk the few blocks back to their hotel. Despite how well the show had been received, Patrick felt melancholy and introspective. That last number had really taken it out of him. He still wondered if any relationship could prevail. Eric and Rog… they'd seemed like a fairy-tale couple, and yet…. Yu could never be just a memory, a dalliance. Could he? Somebody he used to know? What if Patrick had decided to stay in Pittsburgh doing drag and Yu had insisted on going to Japan to learn to make katana? After a few years, would Yu think of Patrick as just a boy he used to know?

Aouli stripped naked and fell into bed as soon as they reached their room, but Patrick lay awake after washing up and changing into a pair of light sweats, his arms folded beneath his head. The plaster ceiling of the hotel room had been carved into swirls and coated with something sparkling that made Patrick think of open sky and constellations. He wondered what Yu was looking at just then. He wondered if Yu wondered what he was looking at before he decided he was being melodramatic and a bit of a baby. They'd only been apart for a little over a day. Patrick knew he got emotional when he was tired, and he tried to sleep, but couldn't manage to quiet the constant monologue of his thoughts.

Patrick's phone rang, and he touched the button to accept the call. "Hey."

"Hi, love. How was your first show?" Yu sounded tired; his voice was scratchy, but his tone was interested.

"Awesome. I kept thinking about you. Everything reminded me of you. How was your show?"

"Hard."

"What do you mean?" Silence. Too much silence. "Yu?"

"I got through it. I don't like the chaos."

"Where are you now?"

"Home. My first opening was here in the city. The apartment feels wrong without you." Yu's voice still sounded strained. "Patrick, I don't like people. I don't understand their expectations or know how to react to them. People—they're not honest. Beneath the surface, they always want something, and I can't understand. How can I give them what they expect when I don't know what that is?"

"You're there to show your art, nothing else. You don't owe anyone anything more."

"They want more, though. They want things I don't understand. I wish you were here to help me make sense of it."

"Yu, I can be there. Tell me if you need me."

"I do. I need you, but you have your own goals to achieve. I won't stand in your way."

"I can be there in a few hours if you need me."

Yu sighed loudly into his phone. "No. I already feel better, just hearing your voice. Tell me about tonight."

Patrick talked about the show and the audience reaction, trying to stay quiet so he wouldn't disturb Aouli even when he got excited. "And at the end, the guys lined up at our table to get autographs, and… well, I got quite a few offers."

"Offers?"

"You know. For sex. Does that bother you?"

Yu remained quiet for a few seconds. "It bothers me, but it doesn't worry me. I trust you. I… got a few offers myself."

"I'll bet." Patrick chuckled softly. "You are the hottest guy I've ever seen. Anybody who isn't straight or dead is going to notice."

Yu finally laughed, and he didn't feign laughter like some people. He only laughed if genuinely amused. "Some of them were straight, Patrick. I received quite a few invitations from women."

With a smile, Patrick said, "Those poor ladies. I guess we can't expect them to know they can't suck your pretty cock like I can."

Yu groaned. "I miss your beautiful mouth already. I miss everything about you. I can smell your hair on the pillow. I always thought I preferred being alone. I was always happy alone, working, but now—now I feel like half of me is gone, like my greatest treasure, my soul, has been taken."

"It's only for a couple of weeks," Patrick said, trying to be reassuring even though he felt the same way. "I can't wait to marry you, tell the whole damn world you're mine and I'm yours." His dick was hard just imagining Yu in bed next to him, his breath on Patrick's skin as they spoke. It was either engage in some dirty phone sex—which Patrick didn't want to do with Aouli sleeping a few feet away—or change the subject. "Tell me about your show."

"I sold two sculptures: *Alone* and *Compromise*. One to a private collector, but the other will be going in the lobby of a bank. I'm not sure how I feel about that, but I made twelve thousand dollars. Well, not made. After the cost of my materials, I made a few thousand, though. Money I can use to assure you have a real home."

"My home is anywhere you are." Patrick nestled into the mattress and pulled the crisp, bleach-smelling sheets over his body. "I made money too. I'm too tired to count my tips, but I know we did okay. We'll be okay, Yu."

"I know. I just feel diminished. You have my soul."

Patrick reached beneath the blankets and closed his hand over the small charm he wore around his neck. He hadn't taken it off since Yu had given it to him for Christmas, not even when he performed. "I'll take good care of it."

"I know. That's why I gave it to you."

For a long time, Patrick just held his phone pressed to his cheek, listening to Yu breathe. Neither of them needed to fill the silence with meaningless chatter, and it almost felt like Yu lay beside him in companionable quiet. Patrick's eyelids closed against his will, and his arm shot out in search of Yu in the bed.

"Still awake, my love?"

"Not really," Patrick said in a rough voice. "It's been a long day."

"I should let you go."

"No. No, Yu. I never want you to let me go."

"Okay."

"I love you."

"I love you too, Patrick."

With a tired smile, Patrick burrowed his head further into the pillow as he turned on his side and pulled his knees up against his belly. He could hear Yu adjusting in their bed and breathing into the phone as he fell asleep.

Chapter 17

WORD OF their show spread like wildfire on the Internet. Often, as they traveled on buses and trains, Aouli read snippets of reviews to Patrick while staring intently at his phone. They contained words like "risky, unexpected, brilliant and unique" that made Patrick smile as he tried but failed to get any rest while in transit. He could just never manage to get comfortable when he couldn't stretch out.

They arrived in Philadelphia for their second-to-last show. They stepped off the bus into the early morning air, and Patrick detected the green scents of spring over the smells of garbage, bus exhaust, and wet asphalt. The sun shone bright and warm for a day in early March, and it warmed Patrick's shoulders. Some snowdrops pushed their way through the dirt and bunched sandwich wrappers surrounding the trees, and Patrick smiled. He had a good feeling about today. There was always something beautiful to appreciate, always some subtle magic just waiting to be noticed. Today would pass and then be gone forever, and Patrick wanted to enjoy it. He grasped the handle of his large and somewhat unwieldy wheeled bag with one hand and Aouli's wrist with the other. "I've never been in Philadelphia. We have a lot of time before the show. We should drop our stuff off at the hotel and walk around for a while. Look for cool little shops. Get a cheesesteak. Get a feel for the city."

"Okay, hon. That sounds nice."

They made their way to their Hampton Inn near Philadelphia's Chinatown. After leaving their luggage and cleaning up a little, they wandered through the small neighborhood and eventually made their way to South Street. Patrick enjoyed browsing the boutiques and made a few purchases before they strolled slowly back to their hotel to get ready for the show.

When Patrick and Aouli approached the club, men were lined up around the block, many of them wearing the tour T-shirts Yu had designed and Patrick and Aouli had sold at previous shows and via their website: Patrick's white silhouette against a black background and Aouli's contrasting black shape opposite him on white. A pair of bouncers in tight black shirts hurried them to an entrance around the side of the building, then led them up a narrow staircase to the small dressing room.

Backstage, Patrick turned to Aouli and rested his hands on Aouli's waist, just above his hips. "Thanks for an awesome day, sister. I feel really good."

"That's awesome, babe. We don't have our last show for another four days. We should get totally fucked up tonight and go to a spa for some pampering tomorrow."

"Okay." Their tour was almost over; they had a photo shoot to do for a new cosmetics company specializing in makeup for queens and other performers, and then their final performance on Fire Island. Then he'd go home to Yu, and they'd get married, declaring their love for each other in front of all the people that mattered to them. It felt right, like he'd completed the arc in some story he hadn't known he was part of, and he was ready to move on to his next adventure. "Hey. Tonight, if the audience wants an encore—"

"You mean *when*."

Patrick shook his head and smiled. "Okay. *When* they want an encore, I want to do something positive. Not a break-up song."

Aouli grinned indulgently. "Not a break-up song. How about something sexy?"

"Like what?"

"Wanna do 'Don't go Breaking My Heart'?"

Patrick considered, then smiled shyly and shook his head. "I want to do 'Summer Wine.' The Ville Valo version we practiced."

Aouli canted his head to the side and squinted at Patrick. "It'll be impressive if we can pull it off. You up to those vocals?"

"Yeah. Today, I'm up for anything."

"Okay, then. We should probably go start getting ready. Tonight's going to be big." Aouli caught Patrick's hand and swung his arm as he walked with a bounce in his steps toward their makeup stations to prepare for their show

As they brushed glittering cosmetics over their skin, transforming themselves into their regal personas, Patrick hummed the song they'd perform later.

THEIR PHILADELPHIA show sold out, and they stayed at the club until long after it should have legally closed. They spent the next day sleeping off their hangovers and getting facials and massages at a spa in Chinatown. Then they were back on the train and headed for New York City, where they had three days to relax and explore.

Patrick couldn't help gawking like a tourist when they reached Times Square. He was hardly a farm boy, but he had never envisioned anything like the glittering billboards. And all the theaters they passed, with people in beautiful suits and gowns lined up to see the shows! He couldn't even imagine the costumes those performers got to wear. As they passed one venue after another on their way to their hotel, Patrick realized costuming, the creation of character, enthralled him even more than depicting that character on stage. As much as he loved to sing, dance, and bask in the warm light of love his audience exuded, he liked to comb thrift stores and create a beautiful character from nothing even more. He felt like a queen on stage, but when he made things, he felt like a magician.

Since they had a few days before the photo shoot with the cosmetics company who'd contacted them through the tour's Facebook page after their first show, Patrick and Aouli rested, ate at famous restaurants because they could afford it after the success of their tour, saw the sights, and even attended a performance of *Wicked*. They checked out some of the city's famous gay bars, but they didn't drink very much so they wouldn't be dehydrated and their skin wouldn't look sallow for their ad campaign. Even though the company was small and the products for a niche market, they'd offered Patrick and Aouli a handsome amount of money to model for them, and they didn't want to arrive haggard and ruin their chances at a second photo shoot.

The shoot itself was surreal; everyone seemed in such a hurry. Patrick was shoved into a chair, and a moment later, a trio of stylists began attacking his face and hair. Then he and Aouli were shoved in front of a green screen with brutal white light beating down on them while a photographer barked orders. He tried his best to comply, and before he knew it, the shoot was over. He couldn't believe how tired he was as he stumbled into their dressing room to wash his face.

"Do you think they liked us?" Patrick asked Aouli as he collapsed onto a stool and grasped the end of a false eyelash to peel it away.

"I have no idea. They seemed so angry and rushed. I don't know if 'liked' is in their vocabulary." Aouli looked exhausted as he wiped his burgundy lipstick off with a tissue. "Though I doubt they would have let us go if they hadn't gotten something they could use. Fucking hell, they were relentless."

Patrick dropped the eyelashes in the bin, where they looked like dead centipedes curling on top of the color-smeared tissues. He drew a few cosmetic wipes from the plastic container and dragged them over his face. The makeup felt inches thick, even thicker than he applied when he performed. "My skin hurts from them tugging on it. I need a shower. A long one."

"What do you want to do after?" Aouli asked as he flicked away the small gems glued above his eyebrows.

"I want to order a pizza and watch HBO in the hotel," Patrick said, pulling out another handful of wipes, wondering if he'd ever get the glittery blue liner off his eyes. "Sorry if I'm boring, but I feel like I'm going to fall over."

"Baby girl, that sounds like heaven. We'll get a pizza, some cheap red wine, and curl up and watch *Eat Pray Love*. I could use a girls' night before we have to perform. They have cheesecake here, right?"

"I'm sure we can find something. New York has everything, right?" Patrick muttered as he tried to remove the long, electric-blue nails they'd glued on him. If he wasn't careful, he pulled up his real nails and it hurt like a bitch. "Wait. *You're* going to eat cheesecake? You aren't worried it will make you fat?"

"It's not gonna make me fat by tomorrow, bitch," Aouli said with a haughty expression, looking down at his own tangerine claws.

Patrick held up his hands in surrender. "Okay, okay. If we're going to indulge, I want a double mocha almond latte with whole milk and whipped cream."

Aouli raised his hand, and they high-fived each other before they finished cleaning up, made their way back to their hotel, changed into soft T-shirts and worn sweats, and turned on the TV. They lay close together on Patrick's bed, Aouli's head on Patrick's shoulder, as they watched *Memoirs of a Geisha.*

"I don't think this is accurate," Patrick mumbled at the TV screen, feeling drowsy. Aouli didn't answer, and Patrick knew he'd fallen asleep, so he pried the huge glass of wine from his sister's hand and set it on the floor. Then he scooted down until he could rest his head on the pillow, wrapped his arms around Aouli, and fell almost instantly asleep.

PATRICK HAD been so content and peaceful, sleeping so deeply by his sister, when his phone rang, he barely managed to fumble for his phone on the night table and answer it before it went to voice mail. "Yu?"

"Patrick?"

It wasn't Yu's voice on the other end of the line. Patrick recognized it, even through the exhaustion that wanted to drag him back down into blissful sleep. "Ian?"

"Bro, I need to talk to you."

Patrick inched up in the bed, trying not to disturb Aouli, who rested against his chest. The hotel room was completely black except for the bluish glow from the screen of Patrick's phone and a few slivers of orange streetlight seeping through the cleft in the drawn curtains. Aouli grunted and stirred, and Patrick ran his fingers through Aouli's hair until he fell still. "Go ahead," he told Ian.

"It's Evan."

Patrick's skin bunched to goose flesh. "What about him?"

"He's gone, man. We were working a Faire in South Carolina. Evan was acting weird, moping around, but he wouldn't tell me what was bothering him. After I took care of the horses, I went to check on him, but he was gone, along with some of his stuff. I asked around, and some of the other performers and merchants told me Evan had seemed drunk and really upset. He told some of them he had to go home. I—I like the kid, and I'm worried. I think maybe he's on his way back to Pittsburgh. Can you see if he turns up? I don't know what happened, but he hasn't been himself the past few days. Shit. I don't want anything to happen to that poor kid, Patrick. Maybe he'll come to you. He talks about you all the time. He trusts you. He likes all of us jousters, but I think you're the only one he really has faith in. If he calls you or comes to your place, will you let me know?"

"I-I'm in New York City."

"Shit," Ian hissed. "I tried Eric and Rog's place but got no answer. Should I call Tom? We can't leave him—"

"No, no, Ian. I'll go back. I'll find Evan. He's my responsibility. Just please don't worry," Patrick said even as his guts knotted up with anxiety.

"Wait, man. If you're busy, just see if he calls. I'm not even sure if he's on his way back to Pittsburgh. It's just a feeling based on some things he's said lately. You don't have to drop what you're doing."

"No. Even if there's a chance he's going to my place, I don't want him to show up there and find it empty. Then he won't have anywhere to go. Even if it's only a slim chance, I want to be there if he needs me."

"You sure, dude?"

"Yeah." Patrick was already out of bed and throwing his garments and toiletries into his bag. "I'll get the next train. Do you have any idea what could have upset him? I thought he was doing great."

"He was," Ian confirmed. "Then... it was like somebody flipped a switch. Jesus, man. I don't want anything to happen to that kid. I wish I could come home, but we have a show tomorrow morning. I was just kinda hoping you'd heard from him."

"I'm heading back. I'm already almost packed," Patrick said. He'd never experienced as much terror as he felt as he threw his costumes haphazardly into his bag. He just wanted to find Evan; nothing else mattered.

"Thanks, man," Ian said.

"Yeah. I have to go." Patrick quickly finished packing and leaned over the bed to shake Aouli's shoulder. "Baby girl...."

"Mmm?"

"I have to go."

"Got a hot date, Patrick? About time." Aouli burrowed his face into the pillow.

"No, dammit. Shit, I have to walk out on you, sister. I'm sorry. Evan is in trouble, and I have to go back to Pittsburgh."

Patrick's words seemed to wipe away Aouli's contented slumber, and he sat up and rubbed his eyes. "Honey, what's going on?"

"I don't know." Patrick put on his hooded sweatshirt and zipped it up. "Evan left the Faire messed up, and Ian thinks he's on his way back to Pittsburgh. He's in trouble, and I have to find him. Fuck! I know we agreed to do this tour together, and I don't want to let you down, but Evan…. Evan is in bad shape, sister. He needs me. If—if I don't find him…."

Aouli got out of bed and took both of Patrick's hands in his. He kissed Patrick at the corner of his lips. "Honey, hush. I know. I know you. I'll take care of everything. I have some solo acts I can perform at Fire Island if that's what they want, and honestly, I won't mind having the boys to myself. Or the room, if you know what I mean. Get your ass home."

"Aouli, I have an obligation to you…. The show…."

"Patrick, it's a drag show. We're not saving lives, honey. But maybe you are. Look, I pretend to be shallow and materialistic, but if you can help that poor boy, you need to do it. I was that boy, once. Don't let him be lost. Go find him, and I'll take care of the rest. Get going."

Patrick's eyes stung as he regarded Aouli's sincere smile. How had he been blessed enough to find people like his sister? After growing up with his father, selflessness always surprised Patrick. "I love you, baby girl." He kissed Aouli's forehead.

"And how could you resist? Get your ass moving, Patrick. I'll take care of everything. Try not to think of the men I'll get if I don't have to compete with you, and get your sweet little ass home to Evan. And, honey, call me as soon as you know anything."

Patrick swiped the grateful tears from his eyes and blew his sister a kiss. Then he dragged his bag from the room to the elevator. A few hours later, he was on a train back to Pittsburgh.

"WHERE ARE you?" The sound of Yu's voice made Patrick's throat close up and his eyes sting. He'd been carefully concealing his distress, trying to be strong, his hands barely shaking as he bought his train ticket. As soon as he heard Yu, he wanted to let all his fear and guilt out. He wanted to sob into the phone, because he knew with Yu, it would be okay. "Patrick? What are you doing up so early? Is everything okay, my love?"

"Yu—" Patrick's voice came out in a dry croak. "I'm on my way back to Pittsburgh. I'm on Amtrak right now."

"Oh my God. What happened? Are you hurt?"

"No, not me." Patrick leaned closer to the window and spoke in a soft voice so the other passengers wouldn't overhear as he relayed what Ian had told him a few hours ago.

"You're giving up your biggest show when you don't even know for sure if Evan's coming here?"

"What am I supposed to do?" Patrick's voice rose before he even realized it, and the plump woman across the aisle from him lifted her head from her zebra-printed travel pillow and shot him a glare. "What if he needs me? Am I just supposed to leave him out there somewhere on his own?"

Yu sighed. "You found him a good job, and he walked away from it. Patrick, what about your career? Your reputation? Don't you think you're overreacting? You have no idea where he's planning to go."

"I have to save him if I can!"

"Patrick, saving him won't bring back your brother. Or your dad. Or Charlene. It won't—"

"How can you say that? Think that? I care about Evan, and he has nobody. I had nobody. If Eric and Rog…."

"Patrick, just stop. I'm not judging you. Maybe I am, but I'm finding you too good, not questioning your motives. You… I worry about you. You're always putting everyone ahead of yourself: those kids at your support group, Evan, Eric, Rog, Jen… even me. Especially me. I shouldn't have said that." Patrick heard muffled sounds, maybe drawers opening and closing, in the background. "I should try to think before I speak. I just want you taken care of also."

"It's okay." Drained, Patrick slid lower in his stiff seat and turned to watch the grayish-pink dawn scenery blur past beyond the train's window. "You say what's in your heart; I've always known that. But if there's a chance I can find Evan, get to him before something happens, I have to try. I might fail—it's happened before—but I have to try. Eric and Rog didn't give up on me because I was too much trouble. Neither did you."

"I know," Yu said. Patrick thought he heard a car door. "I'll meet you there, and we'll find him."

"Meet me there? Yu, what do you mean?"

Yu chuckled without any real mirth. "I'm not leaving you to go through this alone. I'm your partner. I'll meet you at home. I'm packing the car now. It should take me about five or six hours to get to Pittsburgh from Washington, DC."

"Yu… your show. I don't know what to say."

"Well, someone has to take care of you, if you won't take care of yourself. Besides, I think I've had all I can take of dealing with people and trying to figure them out. This crowd is so pretentious. They never say what they mean. I never want to do this again. If people want my work, they'll have to get it from the website or from Wade." A car door slammed. "I'll call Ms. Weiss later and make my excuses. I already sold almost everything I have, and maybe the rest will move whether I'm there or not. I really don't care. I need to get back to making weapons." The SUV's engine hummed to life. "I'm going to get on the road. I'll see you soon, love."

Patrick scrubbed at his eye with the heel of his hand, both numb with exhaustion and acute enough to feel every emotion magnified. "Thanks, Yu. You never let me down. Please be careful, driving. I love you."

"I love you too."

After they hung up, Patrick clutched his phone tight enough to crack it and looked at his reflection in the glass. Beyond his waxen complexion, red-rimmed eyes, and the bags underneath, the countryside began to brighten from muted grays to soft shades of green dotted with the color of the earliest spring flowers. The sky lit to a cornflower color that promised to blossom into brilliant sapphire. Since Patrick could do little at the moment, he let himself appreciate the rolling hills and the first leaves and blossoms emerging from the barren trees he passed. No matter how bad things got, the world didn't stop being beautiful. Beauty seemed able to ignore the ugliness around it. Beauty endured. Hope endured. If Patrick couldn't believe that, he had nothing. It was going to be a beautiful day, one the world would never see again. Everything would be okay. It had to.

Chapter 18

PATRICK COULD barely lift his feet. In spite of his pride, he draped his arm over Yu's shoulders and let Yu drag him up the steps to their apartment. Once inside, Patrick collapsed on the couch and covered his face with his forearm. He couldn't even summon the energy to move while Yu worked in the kitchen, or the energy to lift his head when savory aromas filled their small space. When Yu set a bowl of canned soup and a cheese sandwich he'd made in the panini press on the coffee table, Patrick thought his appetite would abandon him, but it didn't. He was hungry, and he ate. The Campbell's beef vegetable soup combined with the melting cheddar comforted him in the perfect way, though he couldn't quite relax.

"Is it okay?" Yu asked.

"It might sound lame, but it tastes like love," Patrick answered. "Thank you. For taking care of me."

Yu sat next to him on the sofa, put his hand on Patrick's knee, and rested his cheek on Patrick's shoulder. "Someone should. You deserve it."

Patrick shook his head. "I haven't done anything useful. I don't know where else to look for Evan. We've tried the shelters, the gay bars, the places homeless kids hang out. God, we've been in crack houses looking for him, and no one has seen him. I've let him down."

"Love, for all you know, he never came back to the city."

"No," Patrick said. "He's here. I can feel it. I just know."

Yu combed his fingers through Patrick's hair and tucked it behind his ears before pressing his lips to Patrick's forehead. "We've filed reports with the police. They're checking the hospitals for anyone matching

Evan's description. We've talked to anyone who might know where he is. We've done what we can, love. Please rest. Please, don't make yourself sick over this. For all we know, Evan never came back to Pittsburgh. He could be anywhere."

"I feel like I've let him down," Patrick said, cradling his bowl of soup next to his chest for its warmth. "Failed him."

"Just rest," Yu repeated. "You won't do him any good by getting yourself so exhausted you end up in the hospital again. I'll never forget when you fell asleep driving. I don't want either of us going through something like that again. Here, let's find something on TV." Yu picked up the remote and finally settled on a rerun of *The Labyrinth*, a movie he knew Patrick loved. "First thing in the morning, we'll try to think of some other ways to find Evan."

Patrick set his dishes on the table, turned on his side, and snuggled against Yu. He tried to lose himself in the story of Sarah and the Goblin King, thinking, as he had as a child, that he wished he'd been given the opportunity to save his baby brother through a quest. Not that he could have forced his drunken mother to strap Dylan into his car seat properly when he'd been only three. Another part of him had wished, as a lonely young man, for an exotic prince like Jareth to find him special enough to take him away from the pain and drudgery of his daily life. When he'd first seen the movie, he'd wondered why Sarah didn't just stay. He wondered if he would have stayed, stayed in the perfect little world inside the Goblin King's crystal ball, been content with the delusion. Now he knew he wouldn't have stayed. He'd have sacrificed his own happiness for a chance to save his brother. He would have done anything, given up anything to keep Dylan safe. He would do the same for Evan.

Yu pulled a blanket over Patrick's shoulders as Patrick hummed and mumbled along with songs he knew by heart. Yu petted his hair and kept him close, and Patrick wondered how he had survived his first nineteen years without anyone to hold him like this. How had Yu survived without being held? His mother certainly didn't seem the type. She seemed more like the kind of person who *might* shake her son's hand if he got a good grade on an exam. It didn't matter anymore; they'd found each other, and Yu's touch eased some of the strain in Patrick's overwrought muscles. As the movie reached its conclusion, he felt his eyelids drooping. He felt safe and cherished next to Yu in a way he'd never dared to hope for. He was warm beneath the blanket Yu had tucked around him, full from the soup

Yu had cooked, and he must have fallen asleep. "Within You" played somewhere far off, and the music carried Patrick into dreams of dancing in a gorgeous ivory gown, surrounded by frightening but beautiful creatures, clinging to Yu, who wore a grotesque mask and a wicked smile....

He decided he wanted to do a show with the songs from *The Labyrinth* and dreamed of making the dresses, getting to be both the beautiful damsel and the hero for once....

YU BOLTED upright just as Patrick lifted his head, awakened by the persistent pounding on their door. The infomercial on TV provided enough light for them to stumble to their feet. Patrick crossed the kitchen, so exhausted he almost didn't care who stood outside their apartment. He just wanted them to go away so he could go back to sleep.

"It's the middle of the night," Yu grumbled. "Who would be here?"

Too tired to answer, Patrick unlocked the door and opened it a crack. When he saw Evan standing in the hall, yellowish-white to match the streetlights on the chilly sidewalks, Patrick wondered if he was still dreaming—or having a nightmare. He removed the chain from the door, and Evan staggered into the kitchen, colliding with the counter and almost pulling their CrockPot down in his attempt to get back on his feet. For a moment he seemed okay, but when he attempted to take another step, he fell over a chair and landed on his hands and knees. Patrick grasped him by the arms and hauled him up, holding Evan at arms' length to get a better look at him. Evan's pupils were completely blown, and black rings underlined his eyes. He seemed to stare at Patrick without seeing him. He'd lost weight, and pale gold stubble covered his jaw.

Patrick disregarded all the questions he wanted to ask Evan and said "What are you on?"

"I.... Patrick. Mama, I want you to keep me. Please let me come home." Evan collapsed against Patrick and sobbed on his shoulder. Then his sobs turned to gagging and retching, and Patrick steered him to the garbage bin to throw up, holding Evan's greasy hair back as he clung to the edges of the plastic container. After he'd emptied his stomach, Evan remained half bent over, crying, with his head hanging in the bin. Out of instinct, Patrick rubbed his back. "Please keep me, Patrick. Let me stay."

Patrick didn't know what to say or do. It all still felt like a dream. Yu moved between Patrick and Evan and grasped the front of Evan's shirt, spinning him around as he lifted him to his feet. After guiding Evan to a chair and telling him not to get up, Yu went to the refrigerator and filled a glass. "You need to drink some water." Evan obeyed and took a few small sips as he looked up at Yu with red-rimmed eyes.

"Yu, please—"

Yu held up a hand to interrupt Evan. "You have caused a great deal of worry and pain to the person I love. And after Patrick went out of his way to help you. Drink the water."

"Yu, are you going to throw me out? I know I deserve it, but please."

"Evan, shut up." Patrick had never heard Yu so angry. Even though he suppressed it and kept his voice soft and even, a hot, sharp edge of rage glowed beneath his words. "You have behaved like a child and thrown away every opportunity you've been given, but... but I won't abandon you. You're important and worthwhile no matter what mistakes you've made. You can stay here, but I want to know what you're on. Do we need to take you to the hospital?"

Evan shook his head. "I had a lot to drink. Smoked some weed. Scored a couple of Darvocet. I just... it hurt. I needed it not to hurt. I didn't want to hurt you or Patrick. I swear."

Though his hands shook and his knees felt ready to buckle, Patrick took the few steps to the table and pressed his palms to its cool, solid surface. He looked into Evan's dilated eyes. "Do you need to go to the hospital?"

"No, no, please. Jesus. I puked most of it up. I doubt the pills even got into my system yet." Evan clasped Patrick's hand. "Just let me stay somewhere I feel safe. Just for a few days. Then-then I won't bother you anymore. I'll figure something out. Please. Just a few days."

Patrick looked at Yu, met his gaze, and Yu nodded once. Patrick patted the back of Evan's hand. "Finish your water. We'll get you set up on the couch."

"Thanks. You don't know what this means."

"I'll go find some extra blankets," Yu said. He seemed glad to get out of the kitchen.

"Can I have a fire?" Evan asked, his head dipping down, as though he might pass out.

Patrick shook Evan's shoulder until Evan opened his eyes. "You scared the fuck out of me, Evan. I'll let you stay here, but tomorrow, when you're sober, we're going to have a talk, and you're going to tell me the truth or you're out. It's only fair."

"Yeah." Evan held the edge of the tabletop to stand and turned to hug Patrick. "Just keep me. I'll do anything."

"Tonight you'll sleep. Tomorrow we'll talk." Patrick guided Evan into the living room, where Yu waited with the extra blankets. Patrick and Yu helped Evan settle in. They lit the fire, and before long, Evan snored softly, curled on his side.

YU WAS already up and dressing by the time Patrick opened his eyes the next morning. "I'm going to the forge," he said as he walked briskly from the bedroom to the living room, where he gathered up his sketchbooks and shoved them into his bag. "I'll be back this afternoon. In time for dinner."

Patrick understood. Yu was angry and confused, and dealing with such emotions taxed him. He would be better after a good day's work, so Patrick just kissed him and let him go. Yu tucked his jeans into his boots and slipped into a light jacket, and then he was gone.

With nothing else to do while he waited for Evan to wake up, Patrick made coffee and took out a box of pumpkin-flavored pancake mix they had left over from the holidays. He beat eggs and milk into the batter and melted butter in the skillet. Soon he had a stack of only slightly deformed cakes piled on a plate and sprinkled with cinnamon and sugar.

"Smells good." Evan entered the kitchen in the clothes he'd slept in, Jen's knitted afghan draped over his shoulders like a cape.

"Hungry?" Patrick asked.

"Yeah, thanks."

Patrick canted his head toward the cluttered kitchen table and set the pancakes down as Evan sat. He poured two mugs of coffee and took maple syrup from the fridge. Evan tucked right in, so Patrick took a seat opposite him and picked at his breakfast, though he had little appetite. After Evan had eaten his fill, Patrick started the conversation. There was no use in putting it off.

"Evan, what happened at the Faire?"

Evan shrugged and dragged the tines of his fork through the syrup remaining on his plate, making swirling patterns in the golden-brown sauce. "I-I met someone. I had hopes for it. It didn't work out, and I took it pretty hard. Harder than I should have. I'm sorry. There's no excuse for the way I worried you, and I should have been stronger."

Patrick slammed his fork down so hard he rattled everything on the tabletop. "Goddammit. Don't tell me what you think I want to hear! I'm not a therapist; I'm your friend, or I'm trying to be. If you can't be honest with me, I don't know what we have to discuss."

"I'm sorry." Evan pushed his empty plate away and folded his hands in his lap.

"Can we start at the beginning?" Patrick dared. "Can you tell me about your life before you ran away? You can trust me, Evan. I won't judge you. I want to help. But I have to know what we're dealing with. Can you believe in me? Trust me?"

"I guess it's the least I owe you," Evan said, sounding like he'd just agreed to his own execution. "Do you think I could take a shower first? I can't remember the last time I had one."

"Yeah. I'll find you something to wear."

Patrick cleaned up their breakfast while Evan showered, and when Evan emerged from the small bathroom in a pair of Patrick's sweatpants and a *Rocky Horror Picture Show* T-shirt, they sat down together on the couch. "Evan, I need you to help me understand what's going on with you."

"I—Okay. What do you want to know? That my dad died in Operation Desert Storm when I was ten? That my mom lost it and couldn't take care of me or herself?"

Patrick nodded and reached across the table to close his hand over Evan's elbow. Evan continued, talking fast, as if finally glad to get it all out. As he spoke, he tapped his fingers on the worn knees of the sweats and stared straight ahead, toward the fireplace.

"Dad was gone a lot. You know, deployed. I thought he was a hero. We lived out in the country, more toward eastern Pennsylvania, and it was dusty in the summer. Dry. I had this yellow truck I used to fill up with dirt and rocks. I'd pretend I was building barricades for the soldiers to hide behind. Like I could keep them safe. The whole time, I'd watch for my dad to come up the dirt road with a candy bar for me. He always brought me a Snickers when he came home, and he sat with me and made little houses out of the rocks and sticks on the ground. Roads for my trucks. He always brought me a treat. I was so young and stupid, all I thought of was getting a candy bar."

Patrick wanted to say that wasn't stupid, but he didn't want to interrupt Evan or dam the flow of words that had had been so long in coming, so he just nodded.

"Dad never came with that Snickers bar, and my mom never told me why. I know he died in the line of duty, but I still don't know exactly what happened. She just started drinking a lot of wine and forgetting to feed me dinner. Sometimes she didn't get out of bed for days. I was scared to leave her, so I stopped going to school. Then the social worker showed up and took me to live with my mom's sister, my Aunt Mandy, and her husband.

"They had three other kids, two boys and a girl. I never felt like family. I don't want to whine or feel sorry for myself, but they never even tried to include me. I was a charity case, and they made sure I knew it. At every meal. Every time they bought me clothes at Walmart. It felt like a favor. I knew Mark, my stepfather, was disappointed in me. I wasn't the kind of man he wanted to raise. I wasn't big enough to play sports, and I preferred drawing. I wanted to make a comic book. I wanted to play an instrument in the school orchestra not play football. He told me my dad would have been disappointed, and he liked to smack me around for the smallest mistakes. He never hit any of the other kids, and he told me he was trying to make me into a real man. Anyway. I knew he didn't approve, but Amanda, his wife, was worse. She acted like she wanted to help me, be my friend, improve me. God, I almost thought she really had my best interests in mind, but then—

"They were a religious family. Before I went to live with them, I didn't know much about religion. We never went to church or talked about God or anything. Then I found myself living in a house where I had to spend an hour reading the Bible before bed and saying a prayer every time I ate anything. Whatever. I didn't believe in any of that stuff, but I knew I had to do it to keep a roof over my head and food on my plate. Even asking why meant missing a meal, and I figured it out quick. I just had to suck it up and pretend until I turned eighteen, and then I could get the money my dad put aside for me and go to school or something. I thought I could deal with it, play along, just keep my head down."

Patrick nodded again. He understood. He'd felt the same way living with his alcoholic father, and he'd tried so hard to make himself invisible he'd eventually succeeded. Afterward, becoming solid again, having the confidence to take his rightful space in the universe and let other people look at him, see him, had been a difficult struggle.

"I learned pretty fast that drawing much attention to myself brought on judgment, ridicule, and sometimes worse," Evan said, echoing what Patrick had been thinking. "I knew I was gay. I knew it when I was eleven and I saw Viggo Mortensen in *The Lord of the Rings*. Of course, I had to sneak away to watch the movie. *Harry Potter* too. Mandy and Mark thought that kind of stuff was evil. Anyway, I thought if I just didn't say much, stayed out of the spotlight, other people might not notice there was something wrong with me. I hoped they'd just ignore me, that they wouldn't figure it out. But they did.

"Mandy acted like she wanted to help me, like she was on my side. Every morning she took me aside to pray with her. She said if we kept praying all my sinful desires would go away. I knew it was bullshit. Besides, I didn't want them to go away. I was thirteen by then, and I wanted to touch other boys. To kiss them. You know what I mean. I didn't think there was anything wrong with me, but I went along with them, just counting down the days until I would be free. I didn't get any bigger or bulkier as the years went by, and I stayed just as pretty. Mark looked at me with so much disgust. It was hatred by then, I think. They made me keep my head shaved because my hair made me look too feminine. They forced me to sign up for a sport, so I chose to run track. It turned out I liked it and was pretty good at it. It got me out of the house and away from my aunt and uncle. I also met Kyle Fenstemaker. He was openly gay and had the support of his family. He was even pretty popular at school.

"Becoming Kyle's friend put attention on me, though. We spent a lot of time training together and just hanging out, and that led to some rumors. It wasn't even true. I wouldn't have minded if it was—I thought Kyle was hot—but he was interested in someone else. It's the oldest story in the book after that. I was told I wasn't allowed to hang out with Kyle. I was making their family look bad. Kyle was a bad influence. I was forced to join the youth group at the church, and a few months later they pulled me out of school because of the rumors that I was gay. That's when they started trying to beat it out of me, all the while acting like they were doing me a favor. My Aunt Amanda, that sick bitch, would hold my hand and pray while her husband beat me with a leather belt."

Patrick closed his eyes tightly against the threatening tears. He'd heard a lot of stories like Evan's, but it never got any easier to accept that people who were supposed to love and cherish the children placed in their care hurt them and threw them away.

"I ran away," Evan said in a scratchy whisper, "not even because of the beatings. I could take those. But they were starting to get to me. I was starting to believe there was something wrong with me, like maybe I would be better if I could change, make the things I felt go away. Like maybe I shouldn't act on the things I wanted. I didn't want to believe that, and I knew there were people who didn't feel that way. People like Kyle and his family. I didn't want them messing with my head, making me think I was wrong. All I've ever wanted was to find a man to love me and take care of me."

Patrick cleared his throat. "You'll find that person. You'll find a person who will take care of you, that you'll want to take care of too."

"So you see, it's pretty typical. Nothing you haven't heard before."

"Evan... what you went through, it was horrible. Just because other people have suffered doesn't diminish what happened to you. How—Do you want to tell me about the drugs?"

Evan shrugged and picked at the inner seam of his pants, tugging a loose thread with his thumb and finger. "Aunt Amanda had gall-bladder surgery when I was thirteen. One day, it was the anniversary of the day my dad died, I was really hurting. So I took one of her pills to make the pain go away, and it did. It made sense to me. If I was in pain, I took pain medication. I took a lot of it over the next few years, especially after they pulled me out of school, when I didn't have running and Kyle to make me feel better. Luckily for me, that bitch was overweight and it aggravated her back and her joint problems, so I usually had plenty of shit to pick from: pain meds, muscles relaxers, sedatives, antidepressants. And Uncle Mark liked his Jim Beam. I needed it, Patrick. I needed something so it wouldn't hurt so bad, some escape. Do you think I'm weak?"

"No. But I do think you have to stop. You have to find other ways to deal with the pain."

"I know," Evan muttered. "It's just so easy to wash an OxyContin down with a few beers and let it all go away."

"Life isn't easy, hon," Patrick said, turning his head to look into Evan's dark eyes. "It's hard as hell. It's a struggle. A battle. But you have to fight. You're worth fighting for."

"You're the only one who's ever thought so. You know, all the time I was stuck in that hellhole, my mom never even called to ask how I was doing. She just signed me over and walked away. No one but you gives a damn what happens to me."

"That isn't true. What about Ian and Carlton? They were worried sick when you disappeared. Evan, what happened at the Faire?"

Evan drew in a shaky breath. "Can we open some wine?"

Patrick shook his head. "Hon, you have to deal with this without hiding behind booze. Stay here. I'll go make us a cup of tea." He patted Evan's shoulder and stood to go into the kitchen. A few minutes later he came back with two mugs of vanilla chai and some shortbread cookies. Evan thanked him, wrapped his long pale fingers around his cup, brought it to his face, and stared into the steam.

"Remember the guy I told you I've been seeing?" Evan asked. Patrick nodded. "I really like him, and I wanted to be with him, but he wanted to wait until I turned eighteen. Well, that was last Wednesday. Dan took me out to dinner, and then we went back to his trailer at the Faire. It was going great. Better than great. It was like a dream, like every cheesy romantic chick flick I ever saw, with flowers and candles and music. I was so excited; I'd been wanting him like this for months, and it was finally happening. See, I've never been with a guy I liked that way. Before, it was just sex. Dan took my shirt off and saw the scars. You've seen them. They're... they're pretty bad. I was afraid he would be disgusted, but he got mad. Really mad. Like, shaky angry. He wrapped his arms around me and told me he'd like to kill whoever hurt me like that. He told me he'd keep me safe; he'd protect me and never let anyone hurt me again.

"I should have felt safe, happy. Taken care of, like I always wanted. But I just felt scared, and I didn't know why. I ran out of there, went into town, found a bar and a guy who'd buy me drinks all night in exchange for a blow job in the john. When I went back to the Faire, I couldn't even stand looking at Dan. I felt like such a piece of shit. And an idiot, walking away from this great guy who cared about me. And then I realized it. That was what scared me. Having feelings for Dan. If I let myself love him and he tossed me away like my mom, it would hurt. I'm tired of hurting. I... I don't know if I can give someone the power to destroy me. What if I can't ever let myself love someone? It scared me, and I took what I'd earned at the Faire and came back here, where I know where to score drugs. Where I know which bars I can drink in and find a guy to give me a place to stay for the night, if you know what I mean. I didn't know what else to do."

Evan trembled and tears ran down his face. Patrick pried the tea cup from his hands and pulled Evan tight against his chest, wrapped his arms around him, and kissed him on the top of his head. "I fucked up. I wanted a rich guy to take care of me, but I didn't want to have to care back. I wanted somebody who would be happy with my body. But Dan wanted my heart, and I couldn't give it to him. I-I couldn't even let him see it. What if I can't ever love anyone? What if I'm that fucked up?"

"Nobody's that fucked up," Patrick said softly into Evan's hair. "The people who were supposed to protect you hurt you, and you're scared to trust anyone. That's only natural. But if this guy Dan is worth it, take a chance. Take it slow, but if you feel like he deserves it, take a chance. I'm not going to tell you you won't get hurt, but it might be worth the risk."

"Can I stay here with you for a little while? Please. Just until I figure out how to get the money my dad left for me. When I do, I'll pay you for letting me stay."

"You don't have to do that," Patrick said. "You can stay. But you have to stay clean. I really think you should think about going to some NA meetings at the center and maybe finding someone to talk to about what you went through."

"Thanks, Patrick. I don't know why you're doing this or what you get out of it, but thanks. No one has ever wanted to help me without wanting something in return. What should I do?"

Patrick picked up his cell phone and pressed it into Evan's hand. "You need to make some calls, let the people who care about you know you're all right. I'll go into the kitchen and get dinner started, give you some privacy."

"Does Yu hate me?" Evan asked.

"He's just protective of me," Patrick said, standing. "He doesn't want to see me hurt. Probably like this Dan guy feels about you. Yu will come around. He would understand everything you told me better than you know."

"Thanks," Evan said again as he looked down at the screen of the phone.

Patrick went into the kitchen to look for something special to make for dinner. They deserved a celebration; today had been a victory of sorts, but it was only the first step up a very long and steep slope.

Chapter 19

FOR THE next week, Patrick watched Evan carefully for any signs of a relapse. Evan seemed fine, but he had seemed fine before. Patrick didn't know how he could have missed how much pain Evan was in, how hard he was struggling. After what he'd gone through, it made sense for Evan to be confused. It made sense that he still seemed depressed and spent a lot of time sleeping. He also had nightmares and woke up crying more than once, unable to go back to sleep unless Patrick held him. The first time, he had asked for sleeping pills, just over the counter, but Patrick hadn't thought that was a good idea, so he'd remained on the couch until Evan went back to sleep.

Tonight, Evan slept peacefully though it was still early. In the kitchen, Yu washed the dishes, and Patrick dried them and put them away. When they finished, they sat down at the table, and Yu opened a bottle of merlot. He closed his eyes as he held his first small sip in his mouth. "I've missed having wine with dinner."

"Sorry," Patrick said. He had more he needed to say, but first he thought he'd be a complete hypocrite and finish a glass of wine or two to give him the courage. "It's nice to have some time alone. To talk."

Yu reached across the table and took Patrick's hand. "I miss our quiet nights."

"I know."

"It will be quiet in Japan, in the country, and just the two of us. I'm looking forward to that, to just sitting outside our little house and looking up at the sky," Yu said with a small smile. "I guess I just have to share you for another month and a half. I can do that."

"Yu.... Yu, I can't go to Japan in May."

"What?"

Patrick took a few more gulps of wine. "I can't. I can't leave Evan here until I know he's going to be able to support himself and be okay. I think I'm the only person he really trusts, and after what happened to him.... He let himself trust me. Imagine what it will do to him if I turn my back on him now. He might never let himself trust another person. He might go back to drugs."

"You can't be serious," Yu said softly, his eyes narrowed. "You're not going with me now?"

"Not until I know, know for a fact he'll be all right. I-I just can't, Yu. I wouldn't be able to look at myself in the mirror if something happens to him. I have to be the one person in his life who doesn't let him down."

"But what about us? Our plans? Patrick, what about what you want? Why does it always have to take a backseat to everyone else? This is our life. I was really looking forward to taking you to Japan, living with you, being married to you. This is devastating. I-I don't know what to say to you. When were you going to tell me you'd changed all the plans we'd made for our lives?"

"Yu, the kid doesn't have anyone else!" Patrick wanted to yell, but he kept his voice down so he wouldn't wake Evan. "Can you honestly not understand that he needs me?"

"I do understand," Yu said, hanging his head in defeat. "I just wanted this. I wanted it so much, and I wanted it with you. I imagined it like a two-year honeymoon we'd remember all our lives, something we'd be talking about when we were old and gray and looking back on the best parts of our lives. I won't get another chance like this."

"I want you to go," Patrick said, rocking in his chair and rubbing his arms. "Go, and get started with your training. I'll stay here. I'll get Evan back on his feet. When I know for sure he'll be okay, I'll come to Japan. I just need you to wait for me for a while."

"This just keeps getting better," Yu said. "You want me to marry the man I love and then go off to live without him? For how long? Six months? A year? Longer? For how long, Patrick?"

"I don't know!"

Yu stood up and ran his fingers through his hair, then began pacing the kitchen as he yanked on his locks. "I need you!"

"But you'll be okay. You'll be so busy working, I bet you won't even miss me very often."

Yu stopped walking and faced Patrick with a snarl. "That isn't fair, and you know it! I didn't need anyone before, but I do now. I need *you*. How can you say I won't miss you?"

"It was a shitty thing to say," Patrick admitted. "I'm sorry. I don't know what to do. I don't know how to do this so everyone gets what they need. I just know Evan needs me, and he might.... Something really bad could happen if I'm not here for him."

"I'm going to be your husband," Yu said in a broken whisper. "I'm supposed to come first. I'm sorry to be selfish, and I don't want anything to happen to Evan, but there must be another way. I want to start my life with you, and I want Evan to be all right, but I want, I need you by my side."

"I know. I need you too. But I don't want you putting your dreams on hold. I don't know how I can make everything okay for everybody."

"Maybe you can't save everybody," Yu said as he took his jacket from the hook by the door. "I understand what you want to do, and it's a noble thing, but it hurts to be your second choice."

"You know I don't mean it that way," Patrick protested. "If you have another solution, please tell me!"

Yu just shook his head. "I need some space. I'm going to the forge. You might as well not wait up."

Patrick wanted to beg him to stay, to help him figure everything out, but when Yu needed to be alone, he really needed it, so Patrick just watched him walk out the door and close it quietly behind him. He stared at the door for a few minutes, feeling numb, and then he sat at the table and finished the wine in the bottle. He felt tipsy and even more miserable when he rose to put his glass by the sink and head into his room to go to bed. Alone. In the living room, he paused behind the couch and looked down at Evan sleeping. His face looked peaceful in the flickering light of the fire he enjoyed so much, but Patrick knew how much pain hid behind his closed eyes, and he knew the lengths Evan might go to to get rid of that pain. He couldn't leave him to face it alone.

But what if Yu decided he didn't want to marry Patrick anymore? What if he didn't want a husband who couldn't put him first? In a way,

Patrick wouldn't blame him, but losing Yu would kill him. But letting Evan destroy himself when he could have saved him would kill Patrick. He couldn't conceive of a way to save everybody, including himself.

Yu's art and weapons, along with Patrick's drag and sewing projects, cluttered their bedroom, but it still felt huge and empty as Patrick undressed to get into bed. The feeling intensified when he laid down and pulled the covers up, the sheets cold against his skin. He couldn't imagine going to sleep for the rest of his life without Yu lying next to him or waking up every morning without Yu by his side. Did he really have to make this choice? To choose between a man who loved and needed him, his life's companion, and a hurt and broken boy who might not survive without Patrick's help? God, if Evan had anyone else....

Yu didn't have anyone either, but Yu was strong, capable, independent. At least on the outside. Underneath, Patrick knew how much Yu needed acceptance, someone to love him for all his quirks, to tell him he was good enough, just perfect as he was. Patrick had sworn he'd be that person, no matter what they faced together.

"I don't know what to do," Patrick whispered into the darkness. What if Yu didn't come home? He wanted to call someone, but he hated to burden Jen with all the stress her own wedding and move across the world had heaped on her, and Eric and Rog had enough drama of their own. He tried calling Shawn but got his voice mail. Then he tried Aouli, who picked up right away. "Baby girl?"

"Patrick, honey? Are you okay? You sound like you've been crying."

"I'm okay. I just need somebody to talk to. Are you busy?"

"No, just watching some TV and doing my nails. I always have time for my little sister. What's up?"

Aouli knew by now what had happened with Evan leaving the Faire and showing up trashed at Yu and Patrick's apartment. Patrick swore Aouli to secrecy and divulged everything Evan had told him about his childhood and his potential boyfriend at the Faire. "I think his addiction to pain meds is a lot more serious than he let on at first. He's in so much pain, he just doesn't see any other way to get relief. If I leave him now, I think there's a real chance he could harm himself, or worse. But Yu needs me too. I think I broke his heart tonight when I said I couldn't leave Evan to come with him to Japan right away. He left to work at the forge, and... and what if he doesn't come back? Honey, what should I do?"

"Oh shit, sister. What a mess. I don't know what to say, but don't let your imagination run away with you. Yu looks at you like you hung the stars. I don't think he's going anywhere. Besides, he thinks no one else would want him."

"Don't remind me," Patrick said. "I'm not going to take advantage of his insecurity. I feel like I've told him he can't depend on me."

"Give him a little credit, Patrick. Maybe he just needs some time to process everything. Two weeks ago you guys were set to go live this wonderful, exotic life together, and now you're not."

"It hurts me too, but what would you do?"

"Patrick...."

"What?"

"I'm not you," Aouli said. "There's a reason why I don't have a permanent man in my life, why I don't want one. It's because I never have to take anyone else into consideration when I make decisions. I don't have anyone depending on me or expecting things from me. I know it isn't what you want to hear, and I know you guys are crazy in love with each other. I also know I was Evan once, and so were you. Except Evan is in a worse position than either of us."

"And what would have happened to me if you and Shawn and Eric and Rog had turned your backs on me?"

Aouli blew out a puff of air. "You would have worked your ass off and been fine without us."

"I don't know," Patrick said. "Yes, I always worked hard, but I needed you guys more than you know. I needed to be told I was okay, to not be alone, and Evan needs it even more. He's never been able to depend on anyone, and I know how that feels. Or I did, until I found you guys. What should I do?"

"All I can say is talk to your man, honey. If what you have with him is worth keeping, you'll find a way to get through this. If not, well, shit. Then you'll get all slutted up and come out clubbing with me, and we'll get a record number of ass. I still need to teach you how to party."

Patrick forced a laugh. "God help every single gay man on the East Coast if that day ever comes. Thanks, baby. I think you're right. Me and Yu will figure something out. What we have is strong." *Strong like steel but delicate and magical, like gossamer and hope.*

"I'm here if you need to talk." The high-pitched lilt dropped from Aouli's voice, and his tone grew deep and serious. "Day or night. I mean it, Patrick. We're blood."

"Thanks. Love you, hon. I'll see you tomorrow."

"And I'm taking you out for ice cream after the photo shoot, so wear loose pants so we can pig the fuck out."

"Okay, baby. I will."

"Good night, Patrick."

Patrick hung up and stared at the ceiling for a while, at the way beams of light moved across it as cars passed on the street below. He felt a little better after talking with Aouli, and the bottle of wine he'd had mostly to himself made him drowsy enough to gradually drop off.

YU CAME home late. No cars passed the apartment as Yu undressed and left his clothes strewn across the floor in a very uncharacteristic way. Smelling of smoke and steel, he got into bed, grabbed Patrick's hips roughly in his calloused hands, and turned Patrick from his side to his back. He rolled on top of Patrick and shoved his thigh between Patrick's legs, pressing his hard muscle against Patrick's cock and balls. He smashed his lips against Patrick's in a bruising kiss, and Patrick returned it, wrestling his tongue against Yu's until they had to break apart to gasp for air.

As they lay panting against each other's wet and swollen lips, their hearts hammering against each other, Yu breathed out, "I love you. I'm not going to lose you. You're mine, always mine, even if we're separated by half of the world."

"Yu, I know I let you down—"

"Don't talk. I need to know you're mine." Yu sat up on his heels and whisked Patrick's boxer shorts off. Then he grabbed Patrick's thighs and pulled them open. After fumbling with the night-table drawer and then the cap on the lube, Yu pushed inside Patrick with a single, smooth thrust. Patrick stiffened at the sudden penetration and tried to relax his muscles as Yu began to move, and soon the sting subsided and Patrick curved his body up to meet Yu's thrusts. Skin slapped against skin. Patrick reached for Yu's waist, but Yu caught Patrick's wrists and pinned them above Patrick's head as he drove into him. Patrick's erection throbbed and his balls drew up, but the brush of his cock against Yu's sparse treasure trail wasn't enough. He broke his hands out of Yu's grip. With one, he grabbed Yu's hair and dragged him down until their lips met. He wrapped the other around his pulsing dick and stroked, coming until he saw stars moments later. Yu repeated Patrick's name like a prayer as he emptied his seed deep into Patrick. They lay together, dragging in heaving breaths, forehead to sweaty forehead, until Patrick's thighs started to cramp and he had to move. Both of them turned on their sides and faced each other.

"I love you, Patrick," Yu said. "It's time I made some sacrifices for you. I'll do what I need to do. We'll get through this."

"I thought you might leave me," Patrick said. "I should have known better. We—what we have is too good to throw away."

"You should have known better, my love. I'm not going anywhere, and I understand why you have to do this. I'm still not happy about it, because I want you with me, but we have the rest of our lives. I am going to miss you every single day, and when you get Evan on his feet and come back to me, I'm afraid I might destroy you."

"What a way to go," Patrick said dreamily, happy, sated, and drowsy. "How did I get so lucky? You—you're amazing. Yu, you want to go again?"

Yu moved closer and rubbed his renewed erection against Patrick's thigh. "Are you sure?"

Patrick nibbled along Yu's chin and across his jaw. "Yeah. Make love to me. No. On second thought, fuck me. Show me I'm yours."

With a hard kiss and a chuckle, Yu tossed Patrick on his belly and pulled his hips up.

PATRICK WOKE up sore in the best possible way, found his boxers on the bedroom floor, tugged them on, and went to the kitchen in search of coffee. He found Evan sitting at the table reading a magazine about horses. A full pot of blessed french roast waited on the counter. "Where's Yu?"

"He left early," Evan said. "All smiles. I, uh, I heard the two of you making love last night."

Patrick's cheeks felt hot enough to blister. "Oh fuck. I'm sorry about that. I thought you were asleep."

"It's okay, Patrick." Evan smiled even though he sounded somehow sad. "What's wrong with making love? You love each other, and it's beautiful. Like something out of a story. You're really lucky. Both of you."

"Yeah," was all Patrick could manage. He hurried to finish his coffee and decided against breakfast. He showered quickly, packed the clothing and props he'd need into a garment bag, and paused beside the door. "I have some work to do today, but I'll be back in time to make dinner. Maybe I'll pick something up. Anything you're in the mood for? Thai?"

"No." Evan stood and hugged Patrick, resting his cheek on Patrick's shoulder so his lips brushed Patrick's neck when he spoke again. "I don't want you worrying about me. You found me worth a damn when no one else did, and it meant a lot. I just want you to live a wonderful life and be happy. God knows you deserve it. And Patrick, tell Yu I'm sorry about the mess."

Patrick looked at the few dishes in the sink in confusion, but he was running late and had to go, so he kissed Evan on the forehead. "See you tonight."

"Yeah. I want you to know I appreciate everything you've done for me, okay?"

"Okay, Ev. See you later." Patrick hurried down the stairs to his car.

AT THE photography studio downtown, Patrick changed into his pale gray suit and blue paisley tie. Yu had helped him pick it out because Patrick had no sense when it came to men's clothing. Along with Rog, Shawn, and Aouli, he went to have his picture taken in front of the green screen. The cameramen and director recorded some video footage as well: Patrick making a heart with his hands, making a peace sign, and saying things like "It's what's on the inside that counts" and "Be true to yourself."

The slogan of their charity campaign, sponsored by the LGBT center and some local business, including Joe's Ballroom, was "The Same on the Inside." Pictures of the four men in their suits would appear on billboards, the Internet, and in magazines alongside photos of them in drag. All of them hurried to get ready. Patrick played to his fairy persona as Queen Titania, wearing a mint-green wig, a little silver dress with an asymmetrical tulle skirt, high-heeled Roman sandals, and a pair of shimmering wings. The shoot's director had him pose and throw some glitter around, and then he recorded a few sound bites. "Be fabulous," Patrick said, winking into the camera as he pursed his lips and blew sparkling confetti off his palm. "Never forget you're magical."

Shawn performed next, in a black mesh halter top and a pair of leopard-print spandex leggings that made his ass look amazing. The photographers scored some choice shots of Shawn showing off his acrobatic prowess. Patrick thought the one of him doing a handstand in his gold heels and canary-yellow Afro wig would possibly win some awards—the lines and angles were so artistic.

Aouli strutted into the spotlight in a tiny lavender kimono and an elaborate Geisha wig. True to his style, he soon shed the silky, floral-printed robe and stood in nothing but a pair of black lace panties and stockings. The photographers got some sexy shots, but Patrick didn't think they'd be able to use them in their public-service campaign.

Finally Rog, Patrick's drag mama, emerged from the dressing room looking like a golden-age film star in a strapless red gown covered in iridescent beading. Waves of blonde hair cascaded over Rog's slender shoulders, and satin gloves covered his arms to his elbows. His pearl-and-diamond necklace and matching earrings enhanced the decadent impression of his ensemble, as did the little rhinestones on his cherry-red fingernails. He'd outlined his commanding blue eyes in smudged, smoky grays and blacks, and his expressive lips in crimson. Patrick was filled with professional jealousy and admiration as he watched his mentor walk to the screen, the train of his exquisite dress trailing behind him.

"Jesus, the camera loves this guy," Patrick heard one of the men say.

"If you're going to do anything, do it the best you can. Be beautiful, inside and out." Rog's sultry drawl would have put Marilyn Monroe to shame. "Don't be ashamed to shine, darling. You're a diamond. Let your beautiful light out."

Before they went to the dressing room to clean up, the director showed them the shots she hoped to use of them in their suits beside them in drag, with the tagline "The Same on the Inside" running across both. Patrick liked his shots. In his suit, he looked a little like a slacker at a job interview with his unruly red hair gelled back, but in drag, he looked like a wonderful sprite, a magical, androgynous creature. His mama Rog looked like a 1950s film goddess, Shawn looked like a fierce urban Amazon, and Aouli…. Aouli looked like a slutty Geisha.

"Oh, I look like such a little tart," Aouli said, his hand on Patrick's shoulder as he regarded the photos on the screen. "I love it. It's just what I was going for!"

They changed, cleaned up, and left the studio. It surprised Patrick when he found a crew from a local news station waiting for them on the sidewalk. The anchorman asked Patrick to say a few words about why he wanted to donate his time and talent to the campaign.

"I believe everyone, every young person, should express themselves in the way they feel most comfortable," Patrick said into the camera. "I believe in the message behind this campaign, and I would ask everyone out there to look at what's on the inside. You might find someone who really needs you, or you might find a friend who will support you for life. Don't jump to conclusions, and don't judge people. You might not know what that person has been through, so just be there. Look for the beauty, and find the magic. The magic is there, just waiting to be noticed. Live today like it's your last, and love each other." Patrick blew a kiss into the camera.

They went to Cold Stone Creamery for ice cream, and Patrick indulged in a cup of chocolate filled with chunks of peanut butter cups. He sat next to Rog in the booth, and it gave them a chance to talk while Shawn and Aouli teased each other. "I came to the house. Watched some football with Eric. How are you guys doing?"

Rog licked some strawberry ice cream from his spoon. "I love the guy. He pisses me off sometimes, but I can't imagine my life without him. We're working it out."

"And the baby?"

Rog circled his mound of ice cream with his spoon and didn't look at Patrick. "I don't know. I still want a child, and I think we have a lot to offer to one, but if it's not in the cards…… I'm happy with Eric. He's my great love. You understand that, right?"

"Yeah."

"I still want a baby, but we're getting through it. For a while there, I guess I forgot how blessed I was to have a man who loved me like Eric does. We'll see what happens, but I'm not giving up on him. Thank God he didn't give up on me."

"I'm glad," Patrick said. "You guys give me hope."

"Hope's not enough, baby girl. It—a relationship—is a lot of talking and a lot of compromise. You know, you have to understand how he feels as much as you want him to know how you feel. You have to put yourself in his position and see things through his eyes. It can be enlightening, to say the least."

"Yeah, I know," Patrick said. He scraped the last piece of peanut butter candy from his cardboard dish and let it dissolve slowly in his mouth. "It would be easier to be alone, wouldn't it?"

Rog licked his spoon. "Easy, maybe. But empty."

"Yeah."

"Are things okay with Yu?"

"They're great," Patrick told Rog. "He's kind of amazing." He related to his mentor what had happened since the call from Ian.

"Wow," Rog said. "He's a keeper. Just like my Eric, even if we never have a baby to raise. It happens to straight people too, right? We have an amazing life together, and I'm a fool to feel like anything's lacking. Right?"

"I don't know."

"Baby girl, you're supposed to agree with me," Rog said with a wink.

"Eric is really sexy," Patrick said. "That facial hair—"

"Oh, that's enough, girl." Rog laughed. "He is, though, isn't he?"

"I'm scared to agree," Patrick said.

Rog smacked his shoulder. "Today has been awesome. We should both get back to our men so we can celebrate. Come on. I'll walk you back to your car."

"Okay, Mama. Thanks."

Patrick felt good as he drove home, and then he opened the apartment door to find Evan on the floor on his belly, a pool of vomit next to his face and a note on the coffee table.

Chapter 20

PATRICK CALLED 911. He pried the orange canister of pills from Evan's hand and groped for the pulse on Evan's neck. He thanked every god he'd ever heard of when he felt the weak, irregular beat beneath his fingers. Evan was breathing, but his lips matched the waxy white tone of his skin. Patrick shook him gently and said his name, crouching to move Evan's head into his lap. Evan didn't respond, and Patrick shook him a little harder. Nothing. He pried one of Evan's eyes open and found his dark iris rolled back.

It felt like forever before sirens sounded outside and red-and-blue light flooded the apartment. Patrick had left the door hanging open when he'd seen Evan, and the emergency medical workers rushed in. Patrick handed Evan off to the woman who reached him first, and then he stood and backed away as Evan's pale, limp body disappeared beneath a sea of EMTs. With a shaking hand, Patrick took the note from the coffee table, unfolded it, and read Evan's small, neat words.

Patrick,

Thank you for what you have done for me. I don't know if there's a chance for me to find love or be happy, but I won't be the one to stand in the way of the love and happiness you have found. I know you were planning to stay behind because of me, and I know I'm not worth it. Now you can go to Japan with Yu, and I won't be in pain anymore. Please don't be sad for me.

Love,

Evan

Patrick didn't realize he'd started crying until one of his tears dropped onto the yellow notebook paper and blurred one of Evan's delicately formed letters. He folded the note and put it carefully into his pocket, then sniffled and scrubbed his hand over his wet face. The medical personnel had lifted Evan onto a gurney and placed an oxygen mask over his face. Two men hoisted him up and carried him toward the ambulance waiting outside. Patrick caught the elbow of the woman who'd first examined Evan, and she turned toward him.

"I found this next to him. I don't know if it will help." He put the orange canister in her hand. "Is he going to be okay?"

She shrugged. "We'll know more when we get him to the hospital and do the tox screen. It looks like he took some pain meds, but we don't know how many or if he took anything else. Do you want to ride with him?"

"Yes," Patrick said quickly. He locked the apartment and hurried down the steps, feeling like he moved through a bizarre nightmare. The EMT showed him to the ambulance, and Patrick thanked her. Evan was still unconscious, but his breath misted the clear plastic mask over his face, and an IV pumped fluids into his arm. He looked a little less pale, or maybe that was just wishful thinking. Hope. But Patrick had to hold on to it, to just keep telling himself he'd gotten to Evan in time. If only he had come home instead of stuffing his face full of ice cream. Stupid, stupid, stupid. He should have known better than to leave Evan alone. Patrick took a deep breath. He hadn't known this would happen, and it didn't matter. He couldn't change the past. He could beat himself up later, for all the good it would do anyone. Now, he needed to focus on Evan. When Patrick took Evan's hand, his fingers were cold, limp, and unmoving in Patrick's.

When they reached the hospital, Patrick was ushered off to the side and forgotten amidst a flurry of activity. After Evan had been wheeled into the emergency ward, Patrick stood looking at the orange light on the wet asphalt of the parking lot. For the moment, there was nothing he could do, so he pulled out his phone and called Yu.

"Patrick? I'm just about to leave the Faire grounds. Do you need anything?"

"I'm at the hospital."

"Oh my God! What happened?"

"Not me. It's Evan." Trying to find and order the words to explain what had happened felt impossible; Patrick just didn't have the energy or the clarity. "Just come. Please."

"I'll be there soon."

Patrick paced in front of the entrance for a few minutes, steeling himself to face what he would find when he went into the hospital. He asked the woman at the desk for any news, but he didn't expect anything yet and got exactly what he anticipated—a tired and not terribly sincere apology. He wandered over and sat in one of the plastic chairs, leaned his elbows on his knees, and stared down at the scuffed linoleum floor.

Yu arrived, and Patrick did his best to explain what had happened. Yu didn't say anything; Patrick didn't need him to because Yu was there and that was enough. Yu had never been one for comforting platitudes. He'd speak when he had something useful to offer, and Patrick had grown to appreciate it. He also appreciated Yu making all the necessary calls. Before long, the hospital waiting room filled with their friends. Shawn brought one of those boxes of coffee and a sleeve of cups, and Eric and Rog brought donuts, but no one ate any of them. Jen and Henry hugged everyone, then sat holding Patrick's hands.

All of them waited while the doctors pumped Evan's stomach, got him stabilized, and moved him to a more permanent room. A balding man came out and introduced himself as Dr. Gunderson. Patrick hurried to stand and shake the doctor's hand. "How is Evan doing?"

The doctor narrowed his eyes. "I need to speak to a Mr. Patrick Harford. He's the only one I have permission to speak with on behalf of Mr. Welliver."

"I'm Patrick Harford. Um, do you need to see my driver's license or anything?"

"That won't be necessary." The doctor gestured toward a set of double doors and led Patrick through them into a quiet hallway. "He overdosed on hydrocodone, which is a synthetic opiate. Maybe some muscle relaxers and alcohol as well. We won't know for sure until we hear from toxicology. The two biggest concerns we face when someone overdoses on a drug that slows the central nervous system are losing the airway and losing cardiac function. We've stabilized Evan's heart rate, and at this point, he's breathing normally on his own. I have to ask: Do you believe Evan intended to harm himself?"

Patrick wondered what to say. After a few seconds, he decided the truth might finally get Evan the help he needed, even if he hated Patrick for it. "Yeah, I think he wanted to hurt himself."

Dr. Gunderson nodded sadly. "We suspected as much. Suicide attempts require a mandatory seventy-two-hour psychiatric hold. Then we'll make an assessment based on the psychiatrist's report. If he's a danger to himself, he may need in-patient treatment, possibly substance-abuse therapy. For now, we'll have a nurse watching him at all times to prevent another attempt."

"Can we see him?"

The doctor nodded. "He's legally an adult, so it's his decision. He's asking for you. I will advise you to keep the visit short. Evan is very tired and still not very lucid."

"I'm staying," Patrick said. "I'm staying as long as he needs me to."

The doctor gave him a room number, Patrick went to get Yu from the waiting room, and they got into the elevator and rode it to the fourth floor. Patrick checked in at the nurse's station, and he and Yu went to the room and knocked softly on the closed door. A young man in blue scrubs answered—probably the nurse tasked with watching Evan.

"We're Evan's friends," Patrick said. "Can we come in?"

The blond man nodded. "He still isn't making a lot of sense, I'm afraid." He stood aside so Patrick and Yu could step into the small room.

Evan reclined in the narrow bed, propped up slightly, hooked up to an IV and a heart monitor that beeped out a slow, even rhythm. Patrick took the few steps to his bedside and smoothed the hair out of his face, needing to touch him, needing reassurance that he was real, solid, and alive. Evan's eyes fluttered open at Patrick's touch, and he grimaced and looked away. "Sorry."

With stinging eyes, Patrick cleared his throat. "You're okay. That's all that matters. You're important to me, and I don't want to lose you."

"I don't wanna ruin your life." Evan slurred his words.

Patrick pulled a chair up beside the bed, sat down, and took Evan's hand. Yu stood behind Patrick and squeezed his shoulder.

"You hate me, Yu?" Evan asked.

"No, I don't hate you. I'm worried about you, and I want to see you get well."

"They gonna lock me up?"

"Probably not," Patrick said. "As long as you're not thinking of trying this again. Luckily you're an adult now, so they don't have to inform your legal guardians." Patrick squeezed Evan's hand tighter, angry at the thought of the people who had done this damage to him.

"Where will I go?" Evan's voice cracked.

"Home," Patrick said. "You'll move in with me. And you'll get the help you need. You need help, Evan. More than I can give you."

Evan choked back a few sobs and sniffled. "I don't want to ruin your life. I-I don't want you putting your life on hold for me. I'm not worth it."

"You are worth it," Yu said, his words clipped off in repressed anger. "Try to think about what would have happened if you'd been successful. What would that have done to us? If you think we wouldn't have cared, that we would have just gone off to Japan as if nothing had happened, you need to wake up. Losing you would have hurt a lot of people, ruined a lot of lives."

"Sorry," Evan said. "I'm sorry. I never wanted to make more trouble for you."

"We're going to get through this," Patrick said. "But to start, you have to believe we care about you and want to help. You have to believe you're worth caring about, Evan. You have to."

"Okay."

"There are people here to see you," Patrick said. "Your friends. If you're up to it."

"Okay," Evan repeated. He didn't seem able to manage much else.

Patrick looked up at Yu, and Yu nodded once before leaving the room to retrieve the others from the ground-floor waiting area. In small groups of two and three, their friends came in to kiss Evan's forehead and tell him they were glad he was all right. They told him to hang in there, that they were there to help, and he need only call. By the time Eric and Rog came to see him, Evan looked ready to fall back to sleep.

"Do you want me to stay?" Patrick asked.

"Yeah," Evan muttered.

"If you're staying, I'm staying," Yu said. Patrick looked at the two chairs the tiny room contained, the one he sat in and the one occupied by the nurse.

"You don't have to do that," Patrick said. "There isn't really room."

"I'm not leaving you here alone," Yu insisted. "I'll sleep on the floor."

Eric put a hand on Yu's shoulder. "You being uncomfortable won't help anyone. And since I doubt you want to sit in your apartment by yourself all night, why don't you come home with us? You can sleep at the house, and we'll all come back first thing in the morning with coffee and breakfast."

"Please, Yu," Patrick said.

"Okay. I'll be back first thing in the morning." Yu bent down and kissed Patrick's forehead, the bridge of his nose, his lips. "I love you. Call if you need me. Call if you want to talk. If you want anything." Yu kissed him again, and then he left with Eric and Rog.

Evan fell asleep soon after, and Patrick tried to get comfortable in the stiff chair with his head leaning against the wall. Miraculously, he managed to doze off, waking only once when the nurses assigned to watch over Evan changed shifts.

Bright morning sun spilling through the cracks in the vinyl blinds woke Patrick early the next morning. He sat up and twisted his neck, trying to work out some of the kinks. Evan still slept peacefully, his fingers wrapped tight around Patrick's hand. Patrick pulled away because he needed to use the toilet. The woman in the nurse's chair offered him a tired smile and a nod. Patrick returned it, amazed he'd been able to sleep at all with a stranger watching him all night. He'd never even thought about it, though; he'd been too worried about Evan and then too elated Evan had pulled through. Then he'd just been too physically and emotionally drained to do anything but pass out.

After using the toilet, Patrick washed his hands and splashed some water on his face. He used a little paper cup to rinse his mouth out, but the tap water did little to banish the sour morning taste. When he went back into the room, he found Evan sitting up in bed, still pale and drawn, but looking much more alert. "Hey," Patrick said.

"I really messed up, didn't I?"

Patrick sat down and took Evan's hand again. "Yeah, honey. You did. But we'll fix it."

"Thanks. I-I don't know what to say to you." Evan's dark eyes sparkled with unshed tears.

"You don't have to say anything. You can say anything you want, or you can say nothing."

"I feel like a tool," Evan said. "I'm so fucking embarrassed."

"It's going to be okay," Patrick said. "We're going to get through this. You're going to get better. Maybe this had to happen. Maybe it was even a good thing, because now you'll get the help you need to heal."

"Yeah."

"You have to want to get better, though, Evan."

"I do. I don't want to hurt anymore, but I'm not ready to give up."

"I'm glad to hear that," Patrick said, "because you're in for a fight."

"I think I'm ready," Evan said, meeting Patrick's gaze with clear, determined eyes.

The nurses changed shifts, and breakfast arrived not long after. The hospital provided a plate for Patrick, and he and Evan picked at the toast, oatmeal, canned peaches, and bland scrambled eggs in silence. The doctor on call checked Evan's chart and gave him a quick exam. Then the psychiatrist arrived, and the older man dismissed the nurse before turning to Patrick. "Can you give me an hour or so alone with my patient?"

"Sure," Patrick said, standing. "I'll just go find a cup of coffee. Want anything, Evan?"

"Coffee would be great."

"Okay." Patrick walked out into the hall, stretched his arms over his head, and then rubbed the small of his back with his knuckles. He certainly wasn't looking forward to another night in that chair, but he wouldn't dare complain. It was certainly preferable to the alternative. For once, he hadn't failed. At least not yet.

Patrick made his way toward the elevators, walking slowly, stiff as hell.

"Patrick? Patrick Harford?" someone said from behind him.

Turning, expecting another doctor or counselor, he froze in surprise when he saw a tall, good-looking man in a black kilt and a tight black T-shirt stretched across his broad chest and wide shoulders. He wore heavy boots, and Celtic tattoos covered his arms and legs. The man had dark brown hair with a slight wave to it that fell around his shoulders, and a neatly trimmed beard to match. Concern shone from his green eyes, and judging by the black bags beneath them, the man hadn't slept in quite some time.

"I'm Patrick Harford. What can I do for you?"

The man hurried over. When they stood facing each other, Patrick's head barely reached his chin, and Patrick had to take a step back and look up to face him.

"Can you take me to Evan Welliver? Please," the man said.

"And you are…."

The man extended his hand, and Patrick took it. "Riordan Quinn. Most people call me Dan. I'm Evan's boyfriend."

"I think 'boyfriend' is a strong word, don't you? You've only known Evan for a few months, right?" Patrick took a step back and crossed his arms over his chest. "How did you know he was here?"

"Ian told me, and I've been driving for almost twelve hours. Please take me to Evan. He should be with someone who cares about him."

Patrick's eyes narrowed and his fists balled without his conscious intent. "Someone who cares about him? Like the person he came to when he ran away from you? The person who lifted him out of his own vomit, brought him here, and slept in a chair last night while he held my hand? Look, I don't know you, and I don't know what your intentions are in regard to Evan. I don't know if he wants to see you or if dealing with more drama is what he needs right now. He needs to take time to work on himself. Besides, he's with his psychiatrist."

Dan looked down at Patrick, stunned. Then he smiled wide and patted Patrick on the shoulder. "I like you. It's no wonder Evan talked about you so much. I'm glad you were here to protect him. Think I can buy you a cup of coffee?"

Patrick still wasn't sure what to think of Riordan Quinn, and he didn't know if his presence would help or hinder Evan, but he agreed to the coffee. The two of them headed to the elevator bank and down to the cafeteria, where they bought breakfast and found a seat by a sunny window overlooking a lawn. Patrick had a lot of questions for this man before he could decide if he wanted him seeing Evan.

Chapter 21

"EVAN SAYS you play in a band at the Faire."

"That's right," Dan said after swallowing the bite of breakfast sandwich he'd been chewing. "My family's been doing it for generations, and it's actually a good living."

"But you just left your show behind to come here?" Patrick arched up an eyebrow.

"That's right, and they understood. Evan needs me, and I'm not leaving until he can come with me."

"Evan has me and people who have tried to help him without asking anything in return," Patrick said. "When he gets out of the hospital, he isn't going anywhere. He needs help, and I'm going to see that he gets it."

"I'll be looking for a place here in town, then," Dan said.

"Don't you think that's a little premature?" Patrick asked.

"No."

"Evan is messed up," Patrick said. Dan had seen the scars on the outside, but Patrick doubted he had any idea what hid within. "He needs to take time to heal himself. He might not be in any state to deal with a relationship for quite some time."

"I'll wait."

Getting annoyed, Patrick blew out a sigh and set his fork down. He looked right into Dan's green eyes and held his gaze. "Everyone Evan has ever trusted or cared about has let him down. If he lets himself trust you, and you decide what's inside him is too ugly or scary or hard to deal with, and you walk away, it will destroy him. I can't let that happen."

"Listen to me," Dan said, staring back at Patrick. "Nothing in this world could make me hurt that boy, and nothing on heaven or earth will make me walk away from him. Not you, not his past or his demons. Nothing. And if he isn't ready for more, I'll be his friend. I'll be his friend for as long as he'll let me. But I'll protect him, and I'll have his back. I'm not going anywhere. Now, we can take care of Evan together, or we can have a pissing contest and keep butting heads. We'll be able to help Evan better if we work together, yeah?"

"We'll see," Patrick said.

Dan laughed. "You're a tough son of a bitch for a little guy."

Patrick didn't find it especially funny. "Don't push me. Not when it comes to my family."

"I understand you, Patrick. I'm not the enemy here."

Patrick still hadn't decided, but he said, "Okay. I'll ask Evan if he's up to seeing you."

The psychiatrist was just leaving when they reached Evan's room. Patrick went inside and found Evan smiling a little. Patrick smiled back.

"That doctor is pretty smart," Evan said. "Not like the stuck-up prick I expected. A lot of the stuff he said made sense."

"Good, I'm glad it went well. There's someone here to see you, but if you'd rather rest—"

Evan sat bolt upright and winced when he tugged on his IV. "Dan? Is it Dan? Dan's here?"

Patrick couldn't help smiling a little at Evan's delight. He liked seeing Evan excited and full of life, and if Dan had caused it…. Well, maybe he'd give Dan a cautious chance. "Yeah, honey. Dan's here." Patrick didn't have to ask if Evan wanted to see him. He just left the room, smiled at Dan, and canted his head back toward Evan's bed. Dan smiled and looked almost as gleeful as Evan had. Patrick closed the door and went back to the cafeteria. He ordered a second cup of coffee and went outside to sit on a bench and enjoy the warm sun on his shoulders.

Yu, Eric, and Rog arrived at the hospital about an hour later. "We thought Evan could use a real lunch," Rog said, holding up two stuffed bags from Burger King.

"We disagreed as to what constitutes a real lunch," Yu said with a smile.

"Well, not everyone is a lunatic foodie," Rog teased back as Eric rolled his eyes. "Come on."

They went to Evan's room, and Rog passed out burgers and fries. Evan introduced everyone to Dan, and they spent the next couple of hours trading stories about the Faire. Finally, Yu said, "Will you be okay if I do a few hours of work?"

"Yeah," Patrick said. "We'll be fine."

"You know, you don't have to stay," Dan offered. "I'm here now. Evan won't be alone."

Patrick prickled a little. "No. I think I should stay."

"It's okay, Patrick," Evan said. "Go home and get a shower. Take a nap in a real bed. It's not like I'm going anywhere." Evan looked over at the ever-present nurse reading a magazine in the corner.

God, a shower! A fucking toothbrush and clean clothes. Patrick couldn't resist. "Fine, but I'll be back with dinner, and I'll be staying the night."

"I should be the one to—" Dan said

"No." Patrick held up a hand and interrupted Dan. "I'm staying."

"Then I'll find the closest motel," Dan retorted.

PATRICK SPENT the next three days at the hospital, leaving only to go home, shower, and change his clothes. Dan stayed too, and Yu came whenever he wasn't working at the forge. Eric and Rog stopped by when they could, as did Jen and Henry. Even Tom came for a visit, and he and Dan engaged in a lively conversation about bagpipe playing. Friends had filled Evan's room with balloons, flowers, stuffed animals, and boxes of candy. People from the Faire who'd never met Evan had sent cards. Many of them had been in his place or close to it—the world could be a rough place for sensitive people who didn't fit society's mold.

At the end of the mandatory hold, the doctors pronounced Evan fit for release. Patrick had talked at length with Evan's psychiatrist, and Evan would be staying with Patrick and attending counseling sessions three nights a week and a support group for substance abuse on Tuesdays. Between Patrick, Yu, and Dan, they'd arranged a schedule so Evan wouldn't ever be alone. Dan found an apartment not far from theirs—one with a second bedroom. They'd argued, but Patrick refused to relent. Evan would be staying with them, on their old couch in front of the fireplace, until Patrick knew beyond a shadow of a doubt he would be all right to leave.

About a week and a half after Evan was released, Dan showed up at the apartment. The wedding was only weeks away now, and Patrick and Yu had to finalize a few things. Dan and Evan would play video games, and then Dan would take Evan to his therapy session, and they'd cook dinner together in Patrick and Yu's kitchen. Before Evan had left the hospital, Yu had gathered their large collection of wine, boxed it up, and locked it in the closet in their bedroom.

Outside, the trees on their street were in bloom, and a warm breeze scattered pink and white petals across the sidewalks and stoops. Yu turned the radio on in their SUV, and they drove with the windows down and the wind whipping through their hair. They passed lots of people out on the street walking dogs, pushing baby carriages, roller-skating, or just sitting on benches.

"Will you think I'm selfish if I say this feels good?" Yu asked.

"No," Patrick said, reaching over to squeeze his knee. "It feels fantastic. We haven't had a lot of privacy with Evan staying at the apartment, and now Dan's there all the time too."

Yu gave Patrick a knowing smile. "Dan gave up a lot to be here for Evan. He told me he used all the money he'd been saving for his lease on the apartment here. It seems he didn't have many expenses, living in a trailer on the Faire circuit, and he had quite a bit put back—money he's chosen to spend to be close to Evan. He doesn't seem to have ulterior motives, not that I'm an expert."

Patrick shook his head. "No, he doesn't. I tried to find something wrong with Dan, you know? Some reason he wasn't good enough for Evan. But I can't. The truth is…."

Yu finished Patrick's sentence. "He's a good man."

"Yeah."

Yu parked the car downtown, and they walked hand in hand toward the bakery. Inside, a smiling woman with her curly dark hair tied up in a messy bun led them to a table covered in a white cloth, and they sat side by side in upholstered pink armchairs. Some pink lilies sprouted from a crystal vase at the center. The French-inspired décor and soft pastel palette reminded Patrick of Tish and Tracy's lingerie shop at the Faire. If the baker gave her creations the same level of love and devotion as the sisters, they had chosen wisely.

"First of all, congratulations on your marriage. My name is Nancy, and I'm one of the owners. Now, if you'll wait right here, I've arranged a plate of different cakes for you to try." She left, and Patrick lifted Yu's hand to his mouth and kissed the back.

Nancy returned with six pieces of cake, each on its own china plate and paper doily, arranged on a silver serving platter. She handed each of them a fork and even poured two small flutes of champagne. "The first cake is a double-chocolate amaretto with hazelnut-cream frosting. Go ahead and try it. Some people find the flavor a little too rich, but it's a very decadent choice." Yu broke a chunk off the deep brown cake with the side of his fork and lifted it to Patrick's mouth.

Feeling himself blush, Patrick opened his mouth. "Oh my God!" he said before he even finished chewing. "Just… oh my God." Nancy smiled, but she didn't look surprised. Patrick hurried to scoop up a bite for Yu. "You have got try this!"

Next they tried a white-chocolate cake with raspberry and rosehip frosting, and so far Patrick couldn't decide. They were both so delicious.

"Our next offering is probably our most popular for weddings," Nancy said. "It's a classic white cake with vanilla buttercream frosting. We can garnish it with a variety of chocolates and fruits, and it's the most versatile for decorating. Beside that is our lemon cake with coconut buttercream. It's very popular for summer weddings."

After that they tried devil's food, then red velvet. Nancy left them alone to talk. Patrick honestly thought the first cake had been the best, but he knew Yu didn't like chocolate, so he didn't suggest it. Besides, Jen would have a chocolate cake, no doubt. "I liked the white-chocolate raspberry," Patrick said. "It was light and not too sweet."

"I liked that one," Yu agreed. "The lemon coconut was good too. Or we could always go with the traditional white cake and have them use raspberries as a garnish."

"I liked the flavor of the rosehips," Patrick said.

"Then let's get that one."

"Are you sure? You want the lemon. I can tell." Patrick took a sip of his champagne and another bite of the chocolate cake.

"And that's your third bite of the chocolate," Yu said. "You want that one. But we both liked the white-chocolate raspberry. Besides, it will complement the catering the Stew is doing for us better. If we were having a spicier menu, Asian fusion or something, I would have to insist on the lemon as the perfect match."

"You'd insist, would you?" Patrick brushed Yu's long hair aside and nibbled on the side of his neck.

"I would," Yu said, tilting his head to give Patrick better access. "I'll only have one wedding, and I want it to be perfect to the smallest detail." He groaned a little; Patrick knew how much he liked being kissed in that spot.

He moved to drag his lips along the edge of Yu's ear. "It will be perfect. You'll be there and I'll be there. That's all I need. We could have the ceremony in a ditch beside the road, and it would be perfect, so get the lemon."

"Let's get both," Yu said. "And please stop kissing me there. I haven't had much time with you lately, and I'm about two minutes away from seriously embarrassing myself."

"Sorry." Patrick adjusted in his chair, his face hot. He had also been suffering from their recent lack of privacy. "You really want to get both?"

"Why not? Like I said, we're only doing this once."

"Okay."

Nancy was delighted when she returned to take their order. "Have you given any thought as to how you'd like the cake decorated? Are there any flowers or colors you're using in your ceremony that you'd like reflected in the cake? Some couples have a theme, and we've done some very creative designs. I can show you some photographs for inspiration."

Yu reached into the pocket of his blazer and took out a sheet of paper. "We'd like them to look like this." He slid his perfect illustration of a round, four-tiered cake covered in red and white roses to Nancy.

"You're a very talented young man," she said. "We can absolutely do this for you. The cakes will be beautiful. Now, I just need to get a few more details and your down payment, and we'll see that your cakes are delivered on the day of your ceremony." She wrote some information down on a little notepad, and Yu gave her his credit card, or their credit card, Patrick supposed. They'd been sharing all their accounts for years. Nancy smiled and shook each of their hands as the three of them stood up. "Thank you for your business, and if you don't mind me saying so, you seem very much in love. You make a beautiful couple."

"Thank you," Patrick said, his ears heating. "We're really excited."

He couldn't stop smiling as they drove to get their tuxes fitted. He smiled until his face hurt while the tailor measured them and made adjustments, and he didn't stop until they got back to their apartment and he realized Evan and Dan would be there. After the wonderful day they'd shared, he wanted to go to bed and make love with his soon-to-be husband, and he didn't want to be quiet about it. Then it hit him like a truck: there wouldn't be any nights like that, not for a long time. Evan wasn't going anywhere; he was nowhere near ready to be on his own, and a month after their wedding, Yu would be leaving for Japan. Patrick had no idea how many weeks or months it would be before he even saw Yu's face, and suddenly he wanted to cry. He shoved it back and buried it, putting on a smile as they entered their apartment. He had to keep being strong, keep making sure the people he cared about would be okay.

The kitchen smelled great, and in the living room, Dan and Evan were sitting on the floor, Dan leaning his back against the couch and Evan between his legs, the Xbox controller held out in front of him.

Evan chewed his lower lip as he mashed buttons furiously.

"Come on, Evie-boy! Come on!" Dan hooted and punched the air. "That's got him, Evie. That's the way!"

Patrick smiled. It was worth it. Evan was healing; he'd live and find his place in a world determined to destroy him. If some temporary unhappiness on Patrick's part was the price, he would pay it. "Evan, are you beating up twelve-year-olds in *SoulCalibur* again?"

"This guy was a punk," Dan said, pointing at the screen.

"What did you guys make for dinner?" Yu asked, leaning against the door frame with his arms crossed over his chest. "It smells really good."

"Irish stew," Dan said. "Mom's recipe. Should be almost done." He kissed the top of Evan's head and wriggled out from behind him. Evan looked up at Dan with a love on his face Patrick couldn't miss, and he squeezed Dan's wrist before he turned his attention back to his game.

Yu sat down on the couch to watch Evan, and Patrick went into the kitchen to help Dan. He took out bowls and spoons while Dan stirred his stew, fished out the bay leaves, and tasted a few slurps of the broth. He added a little more salt and pepper and some fresh parsley before declaring it as good as his mother's. He dished it out, and they carried it into the living room. Patrick lit the fire while Dan sliced some fresh bread from the bakery up the street.

Yu put some music on, and then he took a cautious bite of his stew. His eyes went wide, and he looked at Dan. "This is very good."

Dan laughed. "I'll not be offended that you sound so surprised, then."

Yu delicately sipped from his spoon again. "There's red wine in here. And something else."

"Guinness," Dan said, winking at Patrick. "Don't worry, the alcohol cooks out."

"I know that," Patrick said, sounding a little poutier than he intended.

"Wine and beer," Yu mused. "It shouldn't work, but it does."

"Well, thank you," Dan said, dipping his head. "Evie told me you're particular about what you'll eat."

"Life's just too short," Yu said.

"That it is," Dan agreed. "Live every day like it's your last, I say."

"I have some good news," Evan said. "I called and talked to Tom today. He agreed to let me come back to the Faire in the spring. I don't know if I'll get to work with the horses again. I don't know if Ian and Carlton can forgive me."

Dan reached over and ran the back of his hand down Evan's cheek, and Evan leaned into his touch, closing his eyes for a moment. "I talked to my family. They're interested in getting a gig at your Faire. Spending the season here."

"That would be so cool," Evan said with a dreamy expression, as if Dan described his personal fairy tale.

"I wonder if I should try to get my old job back," Patrick said. "I can't imagine playing my minstrel character with someone other than Jen playing Queen Elizabeth. That will feel weird. I can't imagine the Faire without Yu there." Patrick pushed his bowl away, no longer hungry. All of them fell silent.

"I wish you would believe I'll be here for Evan," Dan said.

"I do," Patrick said. "It isn't that."

"I'm not going anywhere," Dan persisted.

"Let's not talk about this anymore," Evan said. "We're all adults, and we can make our own decisions. And speaking of that, I-I want to spend the night at Dan's apartment."

"Evan—"

"Patrick, I'm grateful for everything you've done, but I'm an adult. I'm not sneaking out to go get wasted or try to kill myself. I just want to spend some time with Dan. It's been over a week, and I'm doing better. I know I still have a long way to go, but I'm okay to spend the night with a friend."

Dan frowned a little, probably at the title of friend, and Yu looked at Patrick with such fierce longing, such an impassioned plea in his eyes, that Patrick swore he felt the heat on his face. He squeezed Evan's hand and said, "I understand. You're absolutely right, and I'm not your mother. I trust you to make the right decisions for yourself."

Evan grinned wide. "I'll go get my things." He'd left most of his belongings back at the Faire, so it didn't take him long to pack. With his small bag slung over his shoulder, Evan leaned down to kiss Patrick's forehead. "Love you."

"Love you too, honey," Patrick said. "I'll see you tomorrow?"

"For dinner," Evan said, still grinning as he grabbed Dan's hand to pull him to his feet. "Yu's turn to cook." He tugged Dan into the kitchen, and then Patrick heard the door close.

Patrick started gathering up the dishes, stacking the bowls on top of each other to take them to the sink.

"Don't you dare move," Yu said in a husky voice, moving toward Patrick on his hands and knees.

"But the dishes…."

"Leave them." Yu took the bowls from Patrick's hands and set them back on the table. He stretched his neck to nip at Patrick's lips and run his tongue along the seam.

"You want me to leave the dishes? Won't they bother you?"

"No. I need you, Patrick. I need you so badly." He pulled Patrick's shirt over his head and let it fall. Then he ran his hands up and down Patrick's waist, across his chest and belly, all the while kissing and suckling up and down Patrick's neck, across his collarbones. "You are so damn beautiful. I've missed being able to touch you, look at you, see every inch of you. Tonight I want to make you scream. Then I want to drink a bottle of wine and make you scream again."

"That sounds good to me," Patrick panted against Yu's mouth as he pushed Yu's blazer from his shoulders and started on the buttons of his pants. Soon they were naked, Yu lying on that old rug in front of the fireplace and Patrick straddling his hips. As Patrick circled his body, grinding against Yu and rubbing their cocks together, he sucked his way down Yu's neck and chest, where he captured a dark red nipple between his lips and flicked the tip of his tongue against the hard bud. Yu groaned and dragged his nails down Patrick's back until he could cup both Patrick's cheeks in his hands and urge them gently apart. He ran his fingers over Patrick's opening, and Patrick shuddered.

"Lube?" Patrick asked.

"Bedroom," Yu gasped, his breath hot against Patrick's neck. "Go. Hurry."

Patrick fetched the lube and stood over Yu, his feet on either side of Yu's hips, looking down at the firelight on his slender, muscular body, his parted lips, cheeks stained dark with arousal, and lids heavy over his dilated eyes. Yu reached down to give the base of his erection a squeeze, and Patrick flipped the cap on the lube. He let some of the cool, clear liquid fall on his fingers and reached behind himself, teasing at his hole with his fingertips.

"No teasing, Patrick," Yu said, dragging his hands up and down Patrick's legs. "Not tonight. It's been too long."

"Okay." Patrick crouched over Yu and positioned himself at Yu's cock. He sank down slowly, letting Yu fill him, throwing his head back and moaning as the head of Yu's cock brushed over his prostate. He had to stop moving or he'd shoot all over Yu just from the penetration.

"It's okay, love," Yu said, circling Patrick's lips with his thumb. "We have all night. I'm not going to last either. Go ahead."

Lost for words, his pulse loud in his skull, Patrick could only nod. He took hold of Yu's shoulders and rode him hard, bouncing up and down on his cock for a few minutes before he came without even touching himself. His seed erupted all over Yu's belly, all the way to the top of his chest. Dizzy, seeing stars and trembling all over, Patrick collapsed against Yu. He wailed against Yu's neck as he convulsed. Yu wrapped his arms around Patrick and held him tight, held him together. With a few upward thrusts, he came inside Patrick.

"Patrick, Patrick. Oh God. I—" Yu thrashed his head from side to side, eyes clamped shut tight. Patrick caught his chin to stop his movements, then kissed him hard. It took a moment before Yu settled down enough to kiss him back. "I love you so much, Patrick."

"I love you too." Patrick raked the sweaty hair out of Yu's face and kissed his eyebrows, then the tip of his nose. He bit Yu's chin lightly. "You look so beautiful when you come, when you're satisfied. I love looking at you like this. How—"

"Don't," Yu whispered, pecking along Patrick's jaw. "Not tonight. Let's enjoy tonight."

Patrick nodded even as he felt a threatening sting in his eyes. "Okay."

"You know, I could put off going to Japan for a few more months. I'm sure my sensei would understand a family emergency."

Patrick turned his head and rested his cheek against Yu's chest, closing his eyes and listening to the slow beat of his heart. "I don't want you putting your dream on hold. I thought you didn't want to talk about it."

"I don't." Yu rolled them to their sides and finally broke the connection between their bodies. "Wine?"

"I'd love wine," Patrick said.

Yu kissed him softly, with a hint of regret. "I'll be right back. Then I'm going to take my time with you."

Patrick smiled as he watched Yu stand and stretch, trying to pretend the ache in his chest wasn't there.

Chapter 22 ·

BETWEEN WORKING and preparing for the wedding, the next few weeks flew by for Patrick and Yu, and before they knew it, it was April. Finally, a week before the ceremony, they had nothing left to do but wait. On Monday they'd driven to a courthouse in Maryland and gotten their certificate. They'd decided to let Evan and Dan watch the apartment and spent the night at Baltimore's Inner Harbor, where they had a seafood dinner and visited an aquarium. They'd spent a wonderful evening in a hotel overlooking the water and returned late Tuesday afternoon. Wednesday morning, they woke early to find Evan and Dan scrunched together on the sofa as usual.

Yu kissed across Patrick's bare shoulders as Patrick stood facing the coffeemaker. Lifting his lips, he said next to Patrick's ear, "Can you fill a travel mug for me? I have to get to the airport to pick up my grandmother. Will we still all have dinner together tonight?"

"Of course," Patrick said leaning his head back against Yu as he opened the cupboard to locate a mug. "I made reservations at Umi. Everyone will be there. Eight o'clock."

"I can't wait." Yu kissed the apple of Patrick's cheek as Patrick pressed the lid onto the travel cup and handed it to Yu. "I have to get going. I'll see you later."

"Love you."

"I love you too." Yu turned Patrick and gave him a final kiss before hurrying out the door.

Patrick spent most of the day tidying up the apartment, assisted by Evan and Dan. After lunch, they took turns showering, and around five, the three of them got ready to go to the LGBT center where Patrick volunteered. Though he'd be staying in Pittsburgh longer than he'd originally planned, he'd given notice that he planned to step down when Yu had told him about Japan, and another young man was ready to take his place. He supposed giving up the meetings would allow him more time to spend with Evan, and more time to work on projects and perform, since he'd soon be paying for the apartment by himself, and he hoped to do so without dipping into the money his father had left him.

He still wanted to use that money to make a home—a place they could stay and make their own.

The meeting room in the center was packed when they arrived. Patrick couldn't believe it. Normally, between ten and fifteen young people attended the support group on a good night, but tonight, there had to be thirty or more. Instead of the usual cookies, coffee, and donuts, cakes, vegetables and dip, homemade casseroles and salads, and bottles of soda and juice filled the long plastic table along the wall. The people sitting in the folding metal chairs got to their feet and clapped when Patrick entered. Heat flooded Patrick's cheeks and ears and tears stung the corners of his eyes. He found himself frozen just beyond the doorway.

Jeremy, the young man who'd volunteered to host the group when Patrick stepped down, approached him with a smile and patted Patrick on the shoulder.

"What are all these people doing here?" Patrick asked.

"They wanted to come," Jeremy said. "You've touched a lot of lives. Tonight, instead of the regular meeting, we all decided a celebration was in order. Of everything you've done."

"Oh my God." Patrick blinked hard to keep from crying. "I can't believe it."

"Come on." Jeremy took hold of Patrick's arm and led him toward the refreshment table which, Patrick noticed, also included pizza and a sandwich platter. "Have something to eat."

As he filled a paper plate on autopilot, still in shock, Patrick looked over his shoulder at Evan and Dan. Both smiled proudly. Neither seemed surprised. Had they known? Been part of this? He'd be sure to ask them later.

After everyone had a chance to eat and socialize, Jeremy moved to the center of the ring of chairs, and the conversation fell to silence. "It's good to see everyone," he said. "I'm glad all of you could make it. I know many of you have moved on and no longer need this group, and that's a good thing, but remember our doors are always open, and you're always welcome back. Many of you are leading happy and successful lives largely due to one person, the person we're here to honor, to say good-bye to, and to wish the best to on the next adventure of his life. Patrick, get your butt up here."

Though he no longer flinched at dancing on a stage in his underwear, Patrick flushed and trembled as he approached the center of the small room and looked out over all the expectant faces. He recognized many of them, though he hadn't seen some of them in months: young people he'd helped find work, find housing, enroll in school…. People he'd lent the strength to succeed just by listening, being a friend. People who had found their place in the world with his help. Dammit, he was going to cry. He hoped Jeremy didn't expect him to make some kind of speech, because he didn't think he could choke anything out.

All these kids, healthy and happy or on their way there. Had he really done that? Him? He had, he realized. In the wake of the few he'd failed, he'd almost forgotten his many successes.

A dark-haired young man—Juan, Patrick remembered—stood and lifted his can of cola. Everyone turned to look at him as he spoke. "A little over a year ago, when I first came here, I was homeless and hooking. For the first few meetings, I sat in the back and didn't say much. I didn't even know why I was here. I thought I was so alone, until I started to hear the stories. Patrick's story. It took a while to sink in, but I learned lots of people were in the same situation, but instead of feeling sorry for themselves, they worked. I learned I didn't have to do it alone, and there was no shame in asking for help. I asked, and I got that help. I got that help from Patrick. It wasn't a picnic, but—Well, the abridged version is now I'm working, going to school, and have a place of my own. I just wanted to say thank you."

"I—my pleasure," Patrick managed, swiping at his nose.

Juan sat down, and a girl named Natasha stood, twisting the ends of her long blonde hair as she told her story. "I thought my life was over when my parents kicked me out. I didn't think anyone cared what happened to me, but then I came here, and Patrick helped me get into public housing until I could save up for a place of my own. It meant so much, just having someone on my side—"

One by one, about a dozen people told their stories. Not all of them were so dramatic—quite a few simply thanked Patrick for his help filling out student-aid forms or letting them use him as a reference—but by the time they finished, Patrick was wiping his eyes on the sleeve of his sweatshirt. He saw some new faces—a girl with a Mohawk, a boy in a dirty sweatshirt, and two young men who might have been brothers or cousins. They stayed quiet but smiled and nodded in agreement with what the others said. Patrick had no idea he'd made such a difference, touched so many lives, and he'd never felt anything quite so wonderful.

Finally, Jeremy took the floor again. "Well, we're almost out of time. If there's nobody else who wants to speak, we pitched together to get a cake—"

"Wait." Evan walked slowly around Patrick, arms crossed over his chest and fingers digging into his shoulders. He stared at his shoes as he spoke almost too softly to be heard. "I owe Patrick a lot, and I want everyone to know. I want him to know. He's given up so much for me— you don't even know. I kind of wish he wouldn't. He's the only person who's ever cared about me. Having someone care when no one else ever has… it feels awesome. And I feel—I just want to say thanks."

Everyone clapped when Patrick reached for Evan and folded him into a hug. Evan hugged back, his arms so tight around Patrick's ribs Patrick could hardly breathe.

"I feel like I don't deserve what you're doing," Evan said, his breath hot and wet against Patrick's ear and cheek.

"You do. Please believe that."

"Trying," Evan gasped. "I mean, if you think I'm worth it…."

"I do. I love you, honey. Come on. Everybody's pretending not to stare."

Evan chuckled. "Yeah." Dan put his arm around Evan and guided him toward the cake on the table, and as Patrick watched them, he couldn't help sensing the mutual care and trust, even if it hadn't grown into love yet. It made him happy to see Evan had found a true friend.

They had just enough time for a quick piece of cake before they had to leave to get ready for dinner. Patrick, Evan, and Dan sat with Jeremy, discussing the future of the center's programs. Evan planned to return to the support group, and Dan vowed to accompany him. In the spirit of the group, they would both seek guidance and provide help and advice to others.

"I want to share my story," Evan said. "I was just like everybody else. I thought it was just me. I want to get better, and if I can help somebody else, it's the least I can do."

"This is hardly an exact science," Jeremy said. "It's more having a hand to hold as you stumble through. For all of us."

"I'll be right here with you, Evie," Dan said, squeezing Evan's knee before looking at Jeremy. "But I could use some help with all this too. Help to help him."

"I'm not a professional," Jeremy warned.

"Oh, I have a professional," Evan said. "Dr. Benson, and she's awesome. But I can use all the friends I can get."

They continued talking as the others deposited their plates and plastic forks in the bins, many of them stopping to shake Patrick's hand and wish him well. He caught up with some of the people who had become his friends, but before long they were alone in the meeting room. Jeremy made Patrick promise to keep in touch before going to collect stray bits of trash. Soon the three of them stood to leave. They'd made it almost to the door when the young woman with the blue Mohawk stopped Patrick. "I was listening," she said, "and I think I need to talk to you."

"Okay," Patrick said. He'd seen the desperation in her eyes before and knew she needed help. As much as he hated to be late for his prewedding dinner, he couldn't walk away. "What's your name?"

"Cindy."

Patrick shook her hand. "Cindy, I'm Patrick. What can I do?"

Cindy's eyes darted between Evan and Dan. "Can we talk alone?"

"Sure. You guys mind waiting by the car?"

"Not a problem," Dan said, wrapping an arm around Evan's shoulders. They left the room as Patrick and Cindy sat down facing each other.

"I'm scared," Cindy admitted, her brown eyes wide and honest as she looked at Patrick.

"Are you in danger?"

"No. I—No, not really."

"Cindy, can you tell me what's going on?"

"This is so embarrassing…."

Patrick took her hand and gave it a squeeze. "Honey, I've heard it all."

Cindy forced a laugh. "You can probably tell I'm a dyke. I've been out, out and proud, since fourteen, and my family's okay, I guess."

"What's the problem?"

"Well, I'm an art student at Carnegie Mellon. A few weeks ago, I went to a party, and… and I don't know how it happened, but I'm pregnant. My parents are going to lose it, and I don't know how I'm going to finish school…."

"A party?" Patrick asked. "Cindy, were you raped?"

She grinned and shook her head. "Nothing like that. Look, I'm not stupid. I'm not about to go to a frat party or someplace I'll be in danger. It was just a get-together in a friend's dorm, about ten of us. We were drinking cake-flavored vodka and cream soda, and, well, I'm not much of a drinker. Everybody else either left or fell asleep; I don't really remember. Jason—he's a biotech major—and me were on the couch, watching *Torchwood* reruns on Netflix. Well, we were watching the episode where Captain Jack Harkness met the *real* Captain Jack Harkness… you know, when they went back in time?"

"I know," Patrick said. "That episode was really emotional. Hot, too."

"I don't even know what happened. Jason's gay. I'm gay, but, well…. It was over in, like, three minutes, and now I'm pregnant. I don't know what to do. I have a steady girlfriend. We've been together two years. I told her, and she forgave me, but neither of us is ready to raise a child."

"Do you want to end the pregnancy?" Patrick asked. He'd been in this situation before and had plenty of pamphlets to offer to Cindy.

"No." She shook her head so hard the rows of silver rings in her ears rattled. "It isn't this baby's fault I got drunk and made a mistake. I-I can't do that. I don't think I could look myself in the mirror."

"Adoption, then."

"Yeah, I thought about that, but I'm not sure. I'd want to know my baby's in a loving home. I can't just hand him or her off without knowing. I don't know what to do. Can you help me?"

Patrick leaned forward to rest his elbows on his knees. Beyond the abortion and adoption literature, he didn't know what he could offer. He might have to refer Cindy to someone more qualified.... "Wait. I might be able to help you. I know a wonderful couple who really want a baby. I can't promise anything, but if you want to meet them...."

"Yes! I want this baby to have a family who will cherish him or her. Want her."

"Why don't you come to dinner with me tonight?" Patrick offered. "It might fall through, but I can introduce you to Eric and Rog."

Chapter 23

UMI WASN'T busy on a Wednesday night, with the exception of Patrick's party. Their group occupied an entire wall of pale, shining wooden tables. They filled the upholstered benches in front of the gorgeous, ukiyo-e paintings on the restaurant's walls. Chopsticks waited on polished stones in front of them. Patrick sat next to Yu and Aouli, with Shawn and Yu's grandmother, Yuki, seated across the table. The fountain burbled softly in the distance as they looked at each other, unsure of what to say. To their left, Henry, Jen, Tish, and Tracy talked excitedly about wedding attire, while a table down, Eric and Rog conversed with Cindy and her girlfriend, Liz, all four of them leaning in and looking serious. At the end of the line, Evan and Dan sat close on an upholstered bench, Dan's arm over Evan's shoulders.

When the waitress came to take their drink order, Yu's grandmother quickly said, "Sake," with a wink at Patrick. She was a tiny woman with deep lines around her eyes and mouth, graying hair, but lively, twinkling eyes and an easy smile. Noting what must have been shock on Patrick's face, she grinned and added, "Young man, I'm eighty-six years old. I might not have many more days left, and I plan to enjoy every one I get. Besides, this is a celebration. My only grandson is getting married."

Patrick bowed his head and stared at the cloth napkin draped over his thigh, his cheeks hot and tingling. After speaking with Yu's mother, he feared offending his grandmother. He didn't know much about Japanese customs, but he knew one little slip could make her see him as a backward simpleton. "I beg your pardon, Mrs. Hashimoto. I didn't mean any offense."

She reached across the table to pat Patrick on the shoulder, and he looked up to meet her gaze. Her eyes crinkled to crescents when she smiled, just like Yu's did. In some ways, they looked a lot alike. Clearly, Mrs. Hashimoto excelled at reading expressions where Yu failed altogether, though. "Don't be so nervous, Patrick. I don't expect you to be Japanese. Remember, I spent many years in America myself. I want you to enjoy yourself. You make my grandson happier than I've ever seen him, and for that I love you already. We're family now. And please call me Yuki."

"Thank you," Patrick said as the tension drained out of his neck and shoulders.

"Yu tells me you're a performer," Yuki said. "A dancer, isn't it?"

Another crest of nerves welled up, and Patrick gripped the edge of the table as it broke over him. How was he supposed to answer that? If he did or said anything to alienate Yu from the grandmother he adored, Patrick would never forgive himself.

Yu placed a hand on Patrick's shoulder, opposite his grandmother's. "You don't have anything to be ashamed of. Your performances are beautiful, and I'm very proud of you." He looked at his grandmother. "Patrick performs in drag. It isn't campy, though. It's really art. It makes the audience think and feel. His shows fill me with wonder, just like I hope to do with my pieces."

"I think that's lovely," Yuki said. "I'm glad you two found each other. You know, I'm taking a pottery class back home, exploring my creative side. My pieces aren't very good, but it's a lot of fun. Perhaps I can show them to you when you come to Japan."

"I'd like that," Patrick said.

She smiled again and sipped sake from the tiny clay cup the waitress brought. At the next table, a pop sounded as Henry opened a bottle of champagne, and Jen hooted, and Tish and Tracy clapped. "To the happy couples!" Shawn said. "And to making it all official on Saturday. Congratulations, bitches!" He seemed to remember Yu's grandmother and lifted a hand to his mouth.

Yuki tapped her sake cup against Shawn's flute. "You're going to have to try a lot harder than that to shock me, young man. I didn't marry Yu's grandfather until I was thirty-two, and I spent my younger days in New York City, Paris, London, and Rome. I bet I could tell some stories that would make *you* blush."

With a wicked grin, Aouli leaned in and took Yuki's hand. "Oh, girl. You can't dangle a morsel like that in front of us and not make with the feast. This I want to hear. Paris, in what, like, the forties?"

"The early fifties, thank you very much."

Aouli fanned himself with his hand. "You have got to tell me about your clothes!"

With the exception of Eric and Rog's table, all of them leaned in to listen to Yuki with rapt attention. She even had some photos in her wallet, the lovely, grainy, sepia-toned kind that made everyone look like a movie star. Three plates of appetizers arrived, and they passed them around, each of them using their chopsticks to lift a few items onto their individual plates. When they'd made their reservations, they'd opted to trust Chef Shu to prepare them a course of appetizers, entrees, and dessert. Like most of Yu's favorite places, Umi prided itself on the freshest seasonal ingredients. Patrick selected gyoza, edamame, and sawara sashimi.

"Yu's grandfather was an artist," Yuki said, a piece of yellowfin held daintily between her chopsticks. "Not professionally. He made his living as a pharmaceutical researcher, but he always wanted to be a painter. I can show you some of his work—watercolors done in the garden, mostly flowers and birds. He was very talented." She closed her eyes for a few seconds and smiled wistfully. "I think he imparted a lot of his passion to Yu. Art is a noble pursuit."

"I only wish my parents agreed," Yu said. Patrick thought about the wedding invitation Yu had finally thrown in the garbage bin by his desk. At this point, he couldn't let himself hope Yu's parents would appear at the ceremony, having acknowledged the error of their ways, like a scene from a cheesy movie. They probably didn't even know when or where the ceremony would be held. How could they?

His grandmother shook her head. "Sad. Michiko was always very driven. She wanted to be the best at everything, and she made me proud. I'm sorry to see it's made her lose sight of what's important in life—like family and doing what makes you happy. I can't believe she's turned into such an uptight snob.

"I'm proud of you. Preserving the past, tradition, is a wonderful way to spend your life. Especially now that you have someone who supports you."

"I never thought I'd find someone," Yu said. "Everyone was always trying to change me into something else."

"You're perfect." Patrick couldn't resist leaning over to brush Yu's hair away and kiss his cheek.

"Oh, get a room," Shawn teased even as he flashed them a full-toothed smile. "Some of us are trying to eat, here."

"I'm happy for you both," Yuki continued. "And I'm looking forward to having family around again. Patrick, I hope you'll visit me now and then while Yu's working. I can show you some sights, and we can have tea together. I'll teach you how to make Yu's favorite takoyaki, and show you the stream where he used to catch fish. I think I even have some of the first wooden swords he made."

"That sounds nice," Patrick said, resting his elbow on the tabletop and his cheek in his hand. "But I'm afraid I won't be coming right away. It might be a few months or so until I can join Yu."

"But why?" she asked.

Patrick looked at Evan and Dan, seated on the far side of Eric and Rog's table, feeding each other and staring into each other's eyes as if no one else existed. "I have obligations here," Patrick said.

"When I married Yu's grandfather, we could barely manage a few hours apart," she said with a wink.

Conversation slowed as their entrees arrived—miso-glazed black cod and garlic teriyaki strip steak—and they all savored a delicious meal and the dessert that followed. When none of them could force down another bite, the party began to break up. Eric and Roger invited Cindy and Liz to their house for coffee, an optimistic sign in Patrick's mind, though he'd become more careful about being optimistic. Aouli and Shawn planned to go to a club, and Evan announced he'd be spending the night at Dan's apartment. He'd been doing that a lot lately and even kept most of his things at Dan's now. Tish and Tracy had to make some last-minute alterations to Jen's dress, and they left, talking excitedly, with Henry trailing behind, looking a little lost. Patrick gave him a sympathetic smile and a wave, and then it was just him, Yu, and Yuki.

The check arrived. Yu reached for it, and he and his grandmother exchanged a few clipped words in Japanese before she said, "Young man, don't make me slap your hand like I did when you were a boy and couldn't keep it out of the mochi. I'm doing fine, and I haven't had anyone to take care of but myself in years. Let me spoil my family a little. It makes me happy."

Yu dipped his head. "*Hai, Obaa-san.* I'm sorry."

She patted his hand before slipping her credit card into the leather folder. "I think I'm going to walk around for a while. You boys can go on without me. It's a beautiful evening, and I feel like exploring. Every city has its own rhythm, and the best way to get in tune with it is just to wander. I'll get a cab back to my hotel when I feel ready."

While a little apprehensive, Patrick knew Yu's worldly grandmother could look after herself, and she wouldn't appreciate him suggesting otherwise. Plus, Shadyside was an upscale neighborhood—and a safe one. Plenty of others would be out enjoying the warm spring evening. Besides, they had one last appointment—one last loose end to tie off—and Patrick just wanted to get it over with.

A MOVING truck, along with two burly men in tan uniforms, awaited Patrick and Yu when they arrived at Wade's shop. As they stepped into the swath of luminescence the headlights cast, Patrick grasped Yu's hand. He knew it was a possessive and immature display, but he couldn't help himself. In hindsight, he wished he'd asked Yu to deny this commission, even if they could use the money.

As soon as he caught a glimpse of the man leaning against the lintel of the open shop, Patrick knew what Yu had seen in James Chandler. He was older, maybe midforties, but his snug black T-shirt and dark jeans showed he kept in very good shape. His even tan made his blue eyes and short silver hair stand out with an almost metallic glint. Patrick felt his lip curling and tried not to compare his own features to James's high cheekbones, strong, cleft chin, and thin but shapely lips. Sure, he was a good-looking man—Who was he kidding? James could have been a *GQ* model, but Yu had chosen Patrick, and nothing else mattered.

Yu and James shook hands. Both of them smiled warmly, and Patrick tried not to read too much into it.

"You're looking very well," James said. "How have you been?"

"Very well," Yu said. "I graduated recently, and I'm going to Japan to study with a swordsmith. I'm also getting married on Saturday. Actually, I'm already married, as of Monday. This is Patrick Harford-Elion, my husband."

They shook hands, and James held firm when Patrick tried to pull away. "You're a very lucky man, Mr. Harford-Elion."

Yu saved Patrick from saying something acerbic by putting his arm around Patrick's waist and saying, "We both are."

James smiled a little regretfully. "I'm glad you're happy. Truly. You deserve it. You deserve a man who appreciates you for who you are. I'm sorry I wasn't that man. I was a fool. I know that now."

Patrick wanted to tell him he was too late, but Yu pulled away and went into the shop with James following. Yu whisked a sheet off a life-sized steel sculpture, and Patrick gasped at the beauty. Like Yu's other pieces, the strokes of the hammer hadn't been polished out, and they added depth and character to the piece. Patrick recognized the subtle dip between the muscles of the belly, the pronounced collarbones and elegant neck. Yu. It looked exactly like him, right down to the earlobes. The steel remained rough and unworked from the knees to the base, but Yu had even sculpted his cock in shocking detail. The figure looked slightly upward, full lips parted in a small smile. In one hand, it held a sword parallel to its right leg, and in the other hand, cupped in front of its heart—a rose.

James ran a fingertip reverently down the statue's chest, and to Patrick it felt too intimate. He bit his lips to keep quiet. "Exquisite. This exceeds my wildest expectations."

"Thank you," Yu said with a small bow. "You can have your men pack it up."

James nodded to the movers, and the two men wheeled a wooden crate into the shop and began encasing the sculpture in bubble wrap. James took out his checkbook and a pen as they lowered the statue into its case for transport. Part of Patrick wanted to tell James he couldn't have it—he could hardly bear imagining the older man fondling Yu's beautiful body—while the other part gloated that he had the real thing.

James handed Yu the check. Without looking at it, Yu folded the check in half and tucked it into the breast pocket of his blazer. "I appreciate your patronage, James. Really."

James reached up as if he wanted to touch Yu's face, but then he let his hand fall. "Really, you say to me. As if you could lie. I—never mind." He took both Yu's hands in his. "I'm glad you're happy. I know you're going to have a brilliant, successful life and career. Yu… take care."

Without another word, James turned and walked to the black Mercedes parked near the truck, got inside, and drove away as quickly as the bumpy grass allowed. The two movers finished securing the crate on the truck, and soon they were gone too.

Patrick moved beside Yu and rested his head on Yu's shoulder. Yu reached over to pin a lock of hair behind Patrick's ear.

"He still loves you," Patrick said.

"Maybe. He loved the idea of me. What he thought he could make me into. Not what was really there."

"I think I hate him," Patrick said, half joking and half not.

Yu chuckled. "He's hardly a bad man. He just doesn't understand himself. James has weaknesses and insecurities he can't see. Even I could see them. He hides behind his money and his power, but he's very lonely and very scared of being judged."

"Stop being sympathetic," Patrick said.

"Poor James. He never had a chance. Not from the first time I looked at you, at that barbeque in Eric and Rog's backyard. Remember?"

Patrick wriggled a little closer and turned his head so his lips brushed Yu's neck when he spoke. "Yeah. I didn't think you were into me. No one did. And then you wanted to take me to dinner. I felt like I'd won the lottery."

"I felt like I did, when I finally realized you weren't going to write me off as too much trouble."

"We're a couple of girls." Patrick laughed and nipped at the skin below Yu's jaw. "God, I'm glad nobody else can hear us right now. Can you imagine Henry or Shawn? Ian?"

"I don't care," Yu said. "You know, five minutes ago all I wanted was to get you home and in our bed…."

Together, they turned to face each other and found each other's lips. "Now?" Patrick asked in a damp exhale, flicking at Yu's mouth with his tongue, tasting the salt of the soy sauce lingering on his lips.

"Like my grandmother said, it is a gorgeous night."

Patrick nibbled across Yu's lower lip, tasting and suckling between words—ginger, tea, and sweet bean paste above the sweetest flavor of all: Yu's unique essence, his smoky spiciness. "I do not… want to think… about your grandmother. You're right. There's nobody else here, and the grass is all sparkly with dew, and I can smell the new leaves and the first of the flowers, and even though your statue was beautiful, you're more beautiful, and... and... God, I want you. I want you as bad as I did the first time you touched my hand."

Yu pulled Patrick tight against him and circled his hips, rubbing their cocks together. "Here on the ground?"

"Yep. Here in the center of all this magic." Patrick glanced up. The stars looked bigger and brighter than usual. It was probably his fantasy-inclined imagination, but Patrick swore he could see the points of light stretching from the burning centers of those stars and streaking across the velvety sky. "Here. Now. And hurry. In a moment, now will be gone, and we'll have lost it forever."

"But we'll have the next now. A new now, with every second. Another and another and another." Without letting go, Yu backed Patrick out of the shop and guided him over toward the trees, where the grass was high and smelled fresh and sweet. Kissing, they dropped to their knees and fumbled their way out of their clothes. The wet ground was warm on Patrick's back, the scent of the soil rich and strong. Moonlight washed over them, accentuating all the bumps and planes of Yu's body as he moved above Patrick, making his hair glisten until it looked liquid and alive. He was so much better than any work of art.

"And you're all mine. In this now. And this one. And the next. All of them."

"Every now. Always. Forever," Yu breathed against Patrick's face.

For maybe the first time, Patrick believed it with every cell in his body, every wispy vapor of his spirit, every loud pound of his heart in his ears.

Chapter 24

SATURDAY COULDN'T have been more perfect if Patrick had custom-ordered it out of a fairy-tale romance. The spring sun was just warm enough to keep them comfortable in their tuxedos, and a playful breeze ruffled their hair and nudged a few petals from the red and white roses decorating almost every inch of the field beyond the Faire's jousting arena, sending scarlet and ivory confetti tumbling between the rows of chairs. The flowers' perfume wafted around them as Patrick stood looking at Yu, more gorgeous in his black tux than Patrick had ever seen him. As they stood off to the right side of the podium, beneath the billowy gauze pavilion festooned with more blossoms, Patrick tried to forget it wouldn't last.

Both couples tried to stay behind the scenes as people began to arrive. The beautiful arbor Yu had made as a gift for Jen and Henry glistened in the sun above the lectern. The seats on the left side of the aisle—Jen and Henry's side—filled quickly with their family members and friends. Patrick and Yu's side looked sparse in comparison. Yuki sat talking to Tom's wife, Susan, in the front row, and Dan sat a few seats over. Joe from the bar where Patrick performed and some of his brothers from their motorcycle club sat behind them, all of them wearing matching leather vests, though one of the men wore a dress shirt and bow tie beneath. Rog's sister and her husband were there. A few of the kids from the LGBT center had come and waited with some of the artisans and vendors from the Faire, and Ian and Carlton had made it back in time, but that was it. Patrick's mother and stepsiblings hadn't showed—hadn't even called to attempt an excuse. Patrick supposed it was just as well. They would have just picked away at his happiness like vultures. Though he should have known better, Patrick kept watching for Yu's mother and father until it was almost time for the ceremony to begin. Of course, neither appeared. Yu didn't seem upset; he just kept looking at Patrick's face and smiling like he couldn't believe Patrick existed.

The time came for them to take their places. Rog, Shawn, Aouli, and Evan, all in black suits and red waistcoats, lined up, and Patrick took his place behind them and smiled at Eric as he clasped his elbow. Then he looked over his shoulder and winked at Yu, who stood with Wade. After some prompting, Rog's niece, Naomi, in a red dress with a white bow at the waist, hurried to take her place at the head of the procession. Her sister, Melissa, already stood ready across the aisle, in front of Tish and Tracy.

Tom, along with two other bagpipers, a fiddler, and a drummer, began playing Mendelssohn's "Wedding March". The atonal wavering notes vibrated through Patrick's insides as Naomi and Melissa stepped forward to scatter red and white rose petals along the path to the podium. As the song ended, both of the wedding parties approached, slowly, a step at a time, until they stood on either side of Tom, who handed his instrument to one of the other musicians and took his place between them.

Tom, in the full Highland garb he wore at the Faire, opened his arms and smiled wide. "Welcome, friends. We are gathered here together on this beautiful spring afternoon to celebrate love and possibility. We're here to witness two young couples celebrating the love and happiness they have found in each other, and to share in their joy as they begin their lives together. We can only feel hope as we witness what the love between these people has fostered and can only feel delight as we imagine how high they will soar on the wings sprouted from that hope."

Tom winked at Patrick, and Patrick clutched a little tighter to Eric's arm. His stomach felt full of butterflies, and his heart so full of light and happiness he worried he'd float away.

"It's a magical and amazing thing to find not only a lover, but the person who completes you, mind, body, and soul," Tom continued. "To find the person who makes you feel whole, the person you know will stand beside you through any storm. Partnership means never doubting you'll find support from at least one person, even when the rest of the world seems against you. It means being fearless, exposing the good and bad within you, the entire truth of your being, and knowing you'll always be accepted. It can mean work. It can mean compromise. It can mean changing the course you'd planned for your life and setting out on an uncharted path. But a marriage, a partnership built on love and trust, means always having a place your heart feels at home. A sheltered and protected place to wait out the tempest, a small space the foul weather can never touch. Jennifer and Henry have found this place in each other's arms. Patrick and Yu have found it in the love and trust they've nurtured."

As they'd practiced, Tish and Tracy stepped aside. Tom turned toward Henry as he approached the dais, and Jen followed behind him on her father's arm. Her mother wept softly in the front row as Jen put her arm on Henry's elbow. They recited the vows they'd written to each other, exchanged rings, and finally kissed to seal their commitment. They made a beautiful couple, and many handkerchiefs appeared in the audience.

Tom turned to Patrick and Yu. "Who gives this man in marriage?"

"I do," Eric said. "To my great honor."

"I do," Wade said with a smirk. "Lad's a fair blacksmith. I'm sorry to lose him. I should get a couple of sheep, at least."

Everyone laughed, and Patrick did too. Of course their wedding would be a little weird. Tish and Tracy stood behind Jen in simple red-satin gowns but wearing their signature elaborate white wigs. Tom wore a kilt, and some of their friends were dressed in fairy wings above their gowns and doublets. Patrick didn't care. It was *their* wedding; it only had to please them. And it did.

Eric and Wade handed off their charges, and Patrick and Yu took each other's hands. Tom looked serious as he spoke to them. "Yu, Patrick. Each of you is placing all your hope on the other. That's a great burden to bear. You can live up to it, but it might not always be easy. If you're ever angry or disappointed, remember this day. Remember the man you love looking at you, giving you his heart, trusting you to take care of it. Remember what a precious gift you've been given, and always act accordingly. Now, are you ready?"

Yu said a soft, "Yes," while Patrick grinned and nodded like a fool.

"Patrick Harford-Elion, do you swear to stand beside Yu Harford-Elion, no matter what obstacles you two might face? Do you swear to love him unconditionally, to accept his strengths along with his weaknesses? Do you vow to make him happy, to love him, to stand at his side for as long as fate allows?"

"I do," Patrick said, his voice loud and clear despite the palpitations of his heart.

Tom repeated his questions, and Yu said, "I do, with all my heart and soul."

"Yu and Patrick would now like to recite their vows to one another," Tom said.

Patrick withdrew a crumpled sheet of notebook paper from his pocket. When he'd written his vows, he'd worried they'd be too mushy and sentimental, but now, holding Yu's hands and looking into his warm brown eyes, he didn't care what anyone else thought. This was for Yu—for them.

"Yu Elion, I loved you from the first moment I set eyes on you. I loved you first for your beauty, but soon after, I loved you for your kind heart and indomitable spirit. You showed me I could always count on you, your love and honesty. I have never doubted what you felt for me, and all I want is to make you feel the same way. I want to be beside you. I want us to face challenges and adversity together. I want to be with you as we pursue our dreams and stand up to our nightmares. I want to make you as happy as you have made me. I swear to always support you, to accept you, to love you for who you are. You're perfect, and I'm blessed to be the one you've chosen as a companion. I vow to work every day, every minute, to be worthy of you and prove my love for you. You have made me keep my belief in fairy tales and happy endings. When I look at you, I still believe the world is full of magic, and I want you to see that magic along with me."

Yu gazed into Patrick's eyes and smiled. "I give you my heart and soul because I know you'll protect them. Everything I have is yours. You are my now; you make the past not matter, and you make the future something to anticipate. I vow to try to do the same for you. I vow to always make you look forward to the next moment, to make you happier than you were a moment ago. All I want is for you to know how much I love you. I promise to never stop showing you how precious you are to me."

When Tom spoke, it startled Patrick. For a few seconds, he'd forgotten they weren't alone, that they were saying these things, baring their souls, to everyone who mattered to them. "By the power vested in me, I now declare you husband and husband. Yu, Patrick... lads, I think you should kiss before one of you explodes."

They kissed, and everyone clapped, but to Patrick, it sounded muffled and faraway as he slid his lips and tongue over Yu's and both of them grinned so hard it made the act difficult. Everything beyond Yu's arms around him looked to Patrick like a watercolor blur: just sunlight, grass and flowers, yellow bleeding into green and green into red and purple, swirling around them like scraps of stray magic. They clung to each other, foreheads pressed together, as the people in the chairs showered them with birdseed.

Jen threw her bouquet into the crowd, and Aouli dodged it at the last second. One of the bikers, a younger man, cleaner cut than the others, picked up the flowers and brought them to Patrick's Polynesian sister. Aouli refused to accept them, though the big, blond man with the crew cut seemed more intrigued than disappointed, even when Aouli rolled his eyes and turned his back.

Everyone eventually made their way up to the Stew, where a buffet-style meal awaited them. Like everyone else, Patrick went through the line and took a steak kebab, a piece of roasted chicken, and a filet of batter-fried fish. He filled the rest of his plate with red-potato salad, spring greens, baked beans with bacon, and a fresh-baked roll. After filling a plastic goblet full of merlot, he went to join his party beneath the arbor draped in red-and-white gauze. The rest of the guests gathered their meals and found places at the tables set up in front of the tavern. Some of the Faire musicians had set up on the tavern's porch—at the exact spot where Yu had proposed—and they provided music while the newlyweds and their guests enjoyed the simple, but extremely tasty feast.

Both couples came to the center of the gathering to cut the cakes when they appeared, and soon the rest of the guests queued up. The waitstaff in their Renaissance garb, who Patrick knew had volunteered, passed around plastic flutes and filled them with champagne.

Henry's best man, a friend since childhood named Jimmy, stood and lifted his glass. As a toast, he told a few funny but innocent stories of their time growing up together. He commented on Jen's beauty and wit before remarking that she must have the patience of a saint. He wished the happy couple well, and everyone saluted them before draining their glasses. The waiters and waitresses quickly gave everyone a generous refill, and Evan stood and smoothed the lapels of his black jacket. His fingers remained curled around the edges so tightly his knuckles went white.

"Hey, Evan," Patrick whispered. "Don't worry about it. Just say, 'To Yu and Patrick,' and lift your glass."

Evan shook his head, took a deep breath, and pulled himself up to his full height. "Half a year ago, Patrick was a stranger to me, and I didn't believe him when he told me he cared about me. How could he when we'd just met? But as I got to know Patrick and Yu, I found two people who had an infinite supply of love to share. I saw how much they cared about everyone around them, and in no time that included me. I also saw a bond between two people like nothing I ever imagined. Yu and Patrick have faced challenges, been put in horrible and unfair situations, and I know it put a strain on them. I've never been at a wedding before, so I'm sorry if I'm doing this wrong or it's too personal. I guess I could tell a funny story, maybe about how Patrick told off Pete at the bar where I used to work, but that isn't what I think of when I think about Patrick and Yu. I just think about love—a love that's so strong there's so much leftover they can't help but share it with everyone. A love that has been stretched thin but never torn. Patrick and Yu have kindness, they have strength, and they have courage, and the way I see it, all of it grows out of their love. I could stand up here and wish them money and success, but they don't need it. They already have everything they need. They're blessed, and so all I can hope is that they'll have a long, long time to enjoy the love they've found and to spread it. I hope many more people will see them, people who never believed things could work out, and change their minds."

Evan lifted his glass. "To the best friends I've ever had, and to two of the best people I'll probably ever meet. To Patrick Harford-Elion and Yu Harford-Elion!"

"Huzzah!" everyone yelled, raising their glasses into the air.

Evan took a miniscule sip of his champagne before sitting down and leaning close to Patrick. "Was that okay?"

Patrick wiped at his eyes before kissing Evan on the cheek. "It was perfect. Thank you."

"I had more I wanted to say. I just didn't want to turn it into something about me. Not when today is about you. But I want you to know how much stronger you've made me feel."

"Eat your cake," Patrick said, grinning and feeling his cheeks warm.

"Wow! This is really good!"

After giving everyone ample time to enjoy their dessert and drain several more glasses of wine, the Faire musicians packed up, and Aouli took their place near the sound system and picked up the mic. "Time for the newlyweds to get their fine asses up here for their first dance as married couples." He fiddled with the dials on the equipment, and music began to play. Patrick and Jen had agreed on the song—David Bowie's "Within You" from *The Labyrinth*, a movie they both loved. "Get your sweet asses up here and dance, bitches!"

Yu stood first, bowed, and offered Patrick his hand. "Mr. Harford-Elion, would you do me the honor?"

"Absolutely, Mr. Harford-Elion. I don't think I'll ever get tired of saying that."

"You're so adorable." Yu leaned in to nip the shell of Patrick's ear and run his tongue along the edge.

"Oh Jesus," Aouli said into the microphone. "Save it for the honeymoon, boys!"

The two couples made their way to the patio. As Patrick wrapped his arms around Yu's shoulders, it didn't take him long to forget they had an audience. He let their chests and bellies press together, let Yu lead him as he breathed in the scents of Yu's skin and hair: sandalwood and the ocean; fragrances he knew well, that made him feel safe and at home but still excited him. He closed his eyes and dropped the side of his face to Yu's shoulder. Yu dipped his head and sang the lyrics next to Patrick's ear. Patrick had never heard him sing before, and his voice, like everything else, was strong and clear with a trembling undercurrent of delicacy and elegance.

"I'll be there for you, as the world falls down...."

"I know," Patrick whispered. "I know you will." He took Yu's cheeks in his hands and kissed him as the song came to an end.

"Okay, break it up, lovebirds," Aouli announced. "There are still children present!" The next song they'd chosen, the Cure's "Just Like Heaven" began to play. "All right, boys and girls! This isn't a spectator sport! We need all of you up here. Get those asses off the benches and on the floor!"

Though Patrick and Yu and Jen and Henry continued dancing, no one rose to join them. After a minute or so, Yu's grandmother, in her formal kimono, stood up, crossed the grassy sward, and bowed to Eric. He returned her bow and took her hand to lead her to the patio. Tracy and Ian joined them, then Tom and his wife. Soon almost everyone danced on the porch or the grass beyond it, just as the sun set and the sky glowed with rose and gold. Rog danced with Naomi while Tish danced with Melissa. Jen's mother danced with Joe, and Shawn danced with Carlton, who proved a very good sport. The young biker invited Aouli, but Aouli crossed his arms over his chest and pretended to be busy with the sound equipment.

Looking over, Patrick saw Evan dancing with Dan. Even though the top of Evan's head only reached Dan's chin, Evan appeared to lead, and Dan just let him, looking down it him with what Patrick could only describe as pure adoration. They looked mismatched, Evan willowy and lithe in his dark suit with his white-blond hair spilling over his shoulders like something out of a gaslight fantasy, and Dan in his black kilt and chunky boots with his sleeves rolled up like a barely civilized Celtic warrior, knot-work tattoos and all. But the way they moved together, the way they smiled every time their eyes met, told Patrick they belonged together just as he did with Yu.

Led by Aouli, they performed all the obligatory wedding rituals: the dollar dance, mother-son and father-daughter, the silly line dances, and even the Time Warp. Long after twilight, the celebration began to break up as people with jobs and children excused themselves and others settled at tables to take advantage of the open bar. The servers began cleaning up. Henry disappeared for a while, only to reappear at the edge of the lawn on a white charger with flowers braided into its mane. He held out his hand to Jen, who clearly hadn't anticipated this surprise, and everyone cheered as she mounted up behind him. The couple waved as they rode off into the night. Eric and Rog agreed to give Yuki a ride back to her hotel, and Evan left with Dan. Soon only some of Yu and Patrick's Faire acquaintances, and the members of Henry's family who couldn't abide wasting free booze, remained.

"Are you ready to leave?" Yu asked Patrick.

"Yeah. I don't think they need us here anymore."

"Good." Yu took Patrick's hand and led him through the dewy grass, far beyond the light of the tavern, down the hill in the direction of the tournament field and Wade's forge. The octagonal white tent near the woods glowed like a frosted-glass lantern. Inside, Patrick found more champagne on ice—Veuve Clicquot, his favorite—dozens of candles, and the scent of roses thick on the air. An actual bed with a white iron frame stood on a lush red carpet at the center of the tent. Yu pushed a button on the small radio atop a wooden crate, and soft music began to play.

Yu slowly pulled off Patrick's bow tie and kissed his neck, making jolts of electricity race down Patrick's spine, raising his pores to gooseflesh. He shrugged out of his jacket and let it fall to the ground, and Yu caught his lips as he started on the buttons of Patrick's shirt. Patrick barely had the presence of mind to try to get Yu out of his suit, but luckily Yu helped him, and soon they stood with skin pressed to and sliding against silky skin. Patrick was oddly nervous, and he didn't know why. They'd had sex before, and this didn't feel different, but—

"It's different."

"Why?" Yu asked as he tickled the sides of Patrick's waist with his fingertips.

"I-I don't know. Maybe because we only have each other, forever now… I want to be enough for you."

Yu popped the button on Patrick's trousers and slid his hand inside to stroke Patrick's length through his boxer briefs. He knew just how to touch Patrick; that hadn't changed, and he soon had Patrick throwing his head back and arching into Yu's grip. "I don't want anyone else," Yu panted against Patrick's cheek. "I'm just so glad you're mine… all mine. You are so much more than enough. You're everything I've ever wanted. Patrick, Mr. Harford-Elion, I love you."

"I love you." Yu's gentle touches pushed Patrick's anxiety away until it was gone. They worked their shoes and pants off and got onto the bed. Patrick hadn't noticed the rose petals until they crushed beneath their twining bodies, releasing their scent. "You did all this for me…."

"I'd do anything for you." Yu dragged his lips down Patrick's chest until he could pull at a nipple and flick it with his tongue. Patrick arched off the bed, hips in the air and precome dappling his belly. Yu kissed his way down Patrick's waist and across his belly until he reached Patrick's stubbly pubic hair. He buried his face between Patrick's thigh and torso and took a deep inhale of Patrick's scent. Slowly, he gripped Patrick's pulsing cock at the base and ran his tongue up the length, pausing to lap at the sensitive groove on the underside of the head. Then he opened his mouth and swallowed Patrick down in a quick, clean stoke. The muscles of Yu's throat undulated around Patrick's hard dick as he swallowed and acclimated. Patrick clamped his eyes shut, fisted the sheets, and tried to hold back his release.

Yu slid his lips and tongue slowly, decadently, up Patrick's shaft, resting one hand on Patrick's hip, though Patrick knew Yu wouldn't stop him from thrusting if he wanted to. For now, Patrick felt content to let Yu tease him, pulling away to kiss Patrick's belly and inner thighs as soon as Patrick's balls started to contract.

"I love the way you taste," Yu breathed into Patrick's belly button. "I could touch and taste you forever."

"I want to taste you too," Patrick said, wetting his lips at the thought. "Turn over?"

Yu gave the tip of Patrick's cock a lingering peck before shifting on the bed and bracing himself on his knees, his belly brushing Patrick's nose. Patrick ran his face against Yu's silky treasure trail, then took a pass with his tongue, tasting Yu's sweat and the underlying flavor of his smooth, golden skin. Then he grasped Yu's thighs to pull him closer, so he could pull one of Yu's balls into his mouth and caress it with his tongue. Yu let out a puff of air as he held Patrick's shaft and peppered light kisses around the base. Neither of them sucked, just tasted and explored, tongues running up each other's lengths and lips pulling gently at heated skin. By the time Yu drew Patrick back inside his mouth and throat, Patrick was already too far gone to hold back. He couldn't even concentrate on reciprocating anymore; he just held the crescents of Yu's ass, threw his head back, and cried out as he came, tingling all over, light sparkling behind his eyes.

It took Patrick a while to drift back down from his ecstasy enough to realize Yu had lifted his weight and stretched out beside Patrick, stroking Patrick's belly and kissing down his arm as Patrick basked in his afterglow. Still catching his breath, Patrick rolled to face him and found his lips, tasting himself on Yu's tongue. He grasped Yu's shoulder to urge him over to his back, and Patrick nipped his way down his ribs, leaving little red ellipses on his skin and making Yu's belly flutter. Yu twisted his fingers into Patrick's hair and very gently urged him lower.

This time Patrick didn't tease. He knew from the flush on Yu's face and the way his breath caught that he was close, so Patrick let his pretty uncut cock slide between his puffy, sensitive lips and into his throat. He cupped Yu's balls and bobbed his head, feeling Yu's hot, hard flesh slipping over his tongue. In only a few minutes, Yu's flavor exploded into Patrick's mouth as Yu came with a sharp cry. Patrick swallowed all he had to give and held Yu in his mouth as he softened. Yu whimpered rhythmically as his hands opened and closed in Patrick's hair.

Patrick sat up and wiped his mouth on the back of his hand. Yu looked beautiful with his lips shiny and swollen, his cheeks dark, and his lids low and relaxed over his dilated eyes. Patrick kissed him softly, and Yu pulled Patrick down to his chest and wrapped his arms around them. They rested, both grinning, caressing, and toying with each other's hair.

"Thirsty?" Yu asked.

"And hungry. Even after that huge meal."

"Good." Yu wriggled out from beneath Patrick and opened a cooler. He took out a plate of tiny, triangular sandwiches and a bowl of chocolate-covered strawberries. After setting them carefully on the bed, he popped the cork on the champagne and filled their flutes.

They finished their snack and the bottle of wine. It was just enough alcohol to make Patrick feel warm, relaxed, and amorous without feeling hazy or dulling his senses. When they kissed again, Yu's lips tasted of chocolate and the lobster and watercress from the sandwiches. Both had gone perfectly with the champagne. Yu set their dishes on the ground, then grasped Patrick's hips and rolled Patrick on top of him. Their renewed erections pressed together between their bellies until Yu opened his legs and wrapped them around Patrick's waist.

"Yu?"

"I want you, Patrick. I want you to come inside me, and then I want to come inside you. Don't worry. I have more food and wine to keep your strength up."

Patrick chuckled against Yu's lips. "I'm not worried. I love this. I could do this forever. Food or not."

"We will do this forever. Every chance we get."

"Well, then, let's get started."

Chapter 25

DROPPING JEN and Henry off at the airport had left Patrick drained. He was thinking about a cup of tea, some cookies, and maybe a nap as he trudged up the steps to their apartment. He dropped his car keys into the ceramic dish on the kitchen table and went in the living room to find Yu sitting at his desk, drawing.

"Hey," Patrick said, wrapping his arms around Yu's shoulders and resting his cheek on the top of Yu's head. He needed Yu, and Yu might not intuit it from Patrick's tone of voice. "Can you stop working? Sit with me for a while?"

"Sure. I was just passing the time. I'm not taking on any new commissions at this point."

Because he'll be leaving in a few weeks. "I was sad to see Jen and Henry go," Patrick admitted as they settled together at the corner of the couch. "It's a great opportunity for them, but I'm really going to miss them. I have other friends, but…. Now that they've worked everything out with Cindy and Liz, Eric and Rog are going to have a baby to take care of soon, a person who'll need them a lot more than I do. And even a few months without you is going to feel like forever. Everything's changing. People are going away, out of my life. I'm feeling sorry for myself. I can't help it. Growing up, I didn't have anyone. I guess I still have Evan, but he spends most of his time with Dan when he's not working at the Faire. I feel like I'm losing all the people I need."

"Not me."

"Not forever; I know that. But for a while. Maybe months. I'm going to be alone again."

"No, you won't." Yu pinched Patrick's chin and made Patrick meet his gaze. "I can't do it, Patrick. I'm not going until you can come with me. I'll wait."

"No. No, Yu. That isn't what I want. This is your dream. Don't put it on hold for me. I just need to wallow in self-pity and get it out of my system. I know I'm being a baby. I can suck it up for a few months."

"I can't."

"You shouldn't try to lie when you don't even understand the concept," Patrick said, sounding much more bitter than he'd intended. "I know you don't mind being alone. You'll just work and sleep and be completely content."

Yu rubbed his eyes with his thumb and finger. "There was a time when that would have been true. I convinced myself no one would ever understand or accept me, so I was better off without them. It isn't like that with you. The idea of spending all that time without you, of imagining you here upset and lonely, it's more than I can take. You have my soul. How can I make swords without my soul?"

"I don't know what to say. I don't want you to lose this opportunity. What if someone else takes your spot?"

Yu was about to answer, but the door opened, and Evan and Dan stepped into the kitchen, carrying bags of groceries and laughing and talking. They set the bags down and began putting the food away as Dan announced, "Dinner's on us tonight."

Patrick wasn't hungry, but he didn't tell them, muttering a thanks instead. He loved Evan and Dan—he did—but he didn't feel like being around them at the moment. They seemed so happy as they worked together in the kitchen, teasing each other and tickling each other's ribs. "I'm going to take a nap," Patrick announced. "I'm a little out of it."

"Okay," Evan said. "We'll wake you when dinner's ready. You won't want to miss it!"

"Do you want me to come with you?" Yu asked.

"If you're tired. I really do want to sleep for a while. I don't mind if you'd rather draw."

"Okay." Yu kissed Patrick's forehead and went back to his desk.

Patrick went into their room, stripped down to his shorts, and left his clothes on the floor at the foot of the bed. He was too worn out to parse the details of Yu offering—demanding, really—to put off his trip to Japan. He hardly felt like he could move, so he collapsed on the bed and rolled toward where the pulpy afternoon light seeped in through the cleft in the curtains, giving the room a fuzzy glow. The boxes Yu had already started to fill stood stacked in the corners, crowded in next to his weapons and sculptures and Patrick's shoe boxes and dress forms. They needed more space....

MAYBE TWO hours later, after the sun had set, Yu came in to wake Patrick for dinner. He handed Patrick a mug of coffee and lay down beside him, draping an arm over Patrick's belly and a leg over his thighs. "Dinner will be about a half an hour. You can take your time drinking that."

Patrick smiled, still tired, and ran his fingertips through the soft, sparse hair on Yu's forearm. They sat in silence, watching the shadows cast by the streetlight that had replaced the sun. When Patrick finished his coffee, they went into the living room, taking their places around the coffee table as they had almost every night since they'd opened their home to Evan and Dan. A rack of lamb, fragrant with rosemary, garlic, and thyme sat on a platter surrounded by sprigs of fresh herbs. There was red potato gratin, white asparagus, and fresh sweet peas. Even a bottle of red Côtes du Rhône and four glasses. Evan must have seen Patrick's eyes linger on it, because he said, "Don't worry. I just want a glass with dinner, just like I had at the wedding. One bottle of wine is hardly enough to get four guys drunk, okay?"

"Okay," Patrick said, sitting down on his heels. "So, what's the occasion?"

Evan reached into Dan's lap to take his hand. "Well, I was going to wait until after we ate, but.... Dan and I want to move in together. I want to move in with him."

"That's a little sudden," Patrick said, even as he realized the irony. He'd asked Yu to move in with him after the first night they'd spent together and gotten angry when Yu had worried it was a drastic step.

"Why? I spend most of my time there anyway," Evan said. "You guys need the space. We're *friends*, and I don't want that to change, but we don't need to live together. You should live with your husband, and I should live with—I should live with the man I love. Why should we wait? We want to be together *now*. This is what we both want, and we know we're imposing on you."

"You're not," Patrick said without much conviction. He knew Evan was an adult, and if he wanted to live with his boyfriend, Patrick couldn't stop him.

Evan rolled his eyes. "Please. You guys shouldn't have to hurry to have sex while we're out at the store. We shouldn't have to rush and sneak around either."

"But what will happen to you if it doesn't work out?" Patrick asked, worried. "Where will you go?"

"Let's talk about this after dinner," Dan said calmly. "There's no sense in letting all this get cold."

Patrick reluctantly agreed and nodded. Though the food was excellent, he found he had little appetite. He didn't know what he wanted, what he was supposed to want. Was it selfish for him to want to believe Dan would take care of Evan, that he could go to Japan with Yu? He didn't want to pass Evan off, though, so he could move on to a more fun life with less responsibility. That was exactly what his mother had done when she'd left Patrick with his drunken father and run off to California, and he'd always considered it pure selfishness. Was it any less selfish to be so damn glad Yu wasn't leaving him, to hope maybe he'd just change his mind and they could make a home here, where their friends and family lived?

Being alone scared the shit out of him, and it shouldn't. He'd taken care of himself since he could remember, and he'd made it on his own....

"Evan, I don't want you leaving because you feel guilty. I asked you here, and this is your home, for as long as you need it or want it."

Evan took a small sip of his wine and reached across the table to clasp Patrick's hand. "I did need it. I don't now. Patrick, I'm never alone. I have people watching me every second: you, Dan, the knights at the Faire, Jeremy at the support group, even Tom. I don't even resent it. I know I still have a lot of trust to earn back, and I'm trying. You need to give me enough rope to hang myself so I can prove to you I won't. I won't, Patrick. I don't want to die. I never really did. I just wanted to stop hurting and stop being a burden, and I'm doing that. Slowly, but I'm learning to get past the pain and make a place for myself."

"If it doesn't work out, you'll have nowhere to go," Patrick repeated.

"That's not going to happen. Do you really think I'd turn him out on the street, even if things didn't work about between us?" Dan asked.

"I don't know you that well," Patrick said a little testily.

"I hope to God you know me better than that," Dan answered, mimicking Patrick's tone. "You took care of Evie, and I'm grateful to God he had you. You earned the right to be protective, but you have to let him leave the nest."

"I can't stop him from doing anything," Patrick said, staring down at the uneaten food on his plate.

Evan squeezed Patrick's hand a little tighter. "What you think is important to me. I don't want to lose you as a friend. It's hard for me to believe Dan won't leave—everyone always has—but it's a chance I want to take. I need to take it, even if it ends up hurting—"

"Evie—"

Evan held up his hand. "No. I can't just hide away from everything that might hurt me, or I'm going to miss out on living. Besides, I'm working now. Saving money. If I have to, I can make it on my own. Just like you did. I'm not looking for a sugar daddy anymore."

"Jesus, I hope not," Dan said. "I'm a drummer in a Celtic band at the Renaissance Faire. You may have noticed I don't drive a Mercedes. Probably never will."

"And I don't care." Evan leaned over and kissed Dan's whiskered cheek. "I don't care if we live in a tent somewhere."

"This sounds awfully familiar," Yu said with a smile and a glint in his eyes. "I remember a discussion about us living in a ditch. I remember you telling me you didn't care."

"Still don't," Patrick said, finally smiling and letting the tension drop from his shoulders. If Evan and Dan didn't care about money, if they felt the way he had about Yu, maybe they could make it. They had to be allowed to try. "So you're doing this, then? When?"

"All it's going to take is me throwing the two pairs of underwear, T-shirt, and jeans I shoved under the couch into a plastic bag," Evan said, rolling his eyes. "I don't exactly need a U-Haul."

"As soon as we can, we'll go pick out some things, furniture, dishes and whatnot. Give the place some character. Make it ours." Dan grinned wide at the idea of such domestic bliss, and Patrick's heart melted a little more.

"You know, our electronics—the Xbox and TV—won't work in Japan," Yu said. "If you would like, you guys can borrow them while we're gone."

Evan sat up a little straighter, his eyes widening. "So you're going? I hoped you would."

"Eventually," Patrick said cautiously.

"I thought you'd planned to go at the end of May," Dan said.

"We might wait," Yu said.

"Why?" Evan asked. "That's almost a month away. By then, I think you'll see me and Dan are fine. His family's coming up to perform at the Faire for the season, which is kind of stressful—"

"They're going to love you," Dan said. "You're about to find out what it means to have a real family, and a big, doting, protective one."

"I already know how it feels to have a family," Evan said, looking between Patrick and Yu. "It might be small, but it's awesome. Best family in the world."

"Families don't abandon each other," Patrick said.

Evan rolled his eyes. Patrick would be glad when he outgrew that particular gesture. "You're not abandoning anyone. We'll talk; you'll send pictures; you'll come home to visit, and maybe we'll even come visit you. I'd fucking love to go to Japan. And then you'll come home, and maybe we'll still be here, and if we're not, we'll get together when we can. We'll always make time to get together."

"I still have to think about this," Patrick said.

DAN'S APARTMENT was a little dated and a little shabby, but it was clean, and the building was safe and secure. Despite the faded wallpaper and scuffed wooden floors, the secondhand shelf full of books, plush sofa, plaid curtains, candles in jars on the windowsills and a thick, moss-green rug made the place feel cozy—like a home. The small galley-style kitchen was beyond the living room. The two large windows and yellow paint on the cabinets made it bright and warm, as did the mismatched dishes and pots and pans sitting on shelves because there wasn't room in the cabinets. There also wasn't room for a table, but the living room had plenty of space for a rustic round table with cracking ivory paint. A bouquet of May flowers sat at the center, in a ceramic vase made by the potter at the Faire. Evan's katana hung in a prominent place above the TV, and Dan's tribal drums, bagpipes, flutes, and other instruments sat neatly along the walls.

"This reminds me of our apartment," Yu said, and Patrick smiled.

"You're here," Evan said, moving away from the sink where he'd been peeling potatoes to hug each of them. "Thank you so much for coming. Um, I'm afraid you've already seen pretty much everything but the bedroom and the bathroom. We're still working on the place." Still, Evan looked proud.

"It's wonderful," Patrick said. "How's work going?"

Evan indicated the sofa, and they all sat down while Dan took over with the potatoes. "Good. Exhausting. Dan's sister Mara is teaching me to play the fiddle. It's something I've always wanted to do, but I've still got my other responsibilities, and I'm helping out with the horses again. And I still have the group at the center. It's good, though."

"It sounds good," Patrick said. "Staying busy is good, especially with things you enjoy."

"Yeah. I'm hoping to get good enough to go on the road with Dan's family when the Faire ends in the fall."

"That sounds like a lot of fun," Patrick said.

Evan grinned and shook his head, his pale, shaggy hair brushing his eyelashes. He had more color in his cheeks than Patrick had ever seen, and he'd put on a few pounds, though he'd probably always be on the lithe side.

"You really seem happy," Patrick said.

"I am, so I wish you wouldn't worry and look so miserable."

"I am not miserable," Patrick protested.

"Yeah, okay," Evan said. "Here, there's something else I want to show you."

Evan got up, went into the bedroom, and returned with a small, sable-colored animal held between his elbow and chest.

"What is that?" Patrick asked. "A weasel?"

With a smile, Evan sat back down, and his pet crept up his arm to sit on his shoulder, burrowing a twitching pink nose into the hair below his ear. "It's a ferret. His name is Lancelot. I've always wanted a pet, and my therapist thought he'd be good for my anxiety. Ferrets are good travelers, and they don't need much space, so he can come on the road with us and live in our caravan at the end of the season here."

Lancelot scampered over to Patrick and Yu and gave them a few sniffs before darting under the couch. "He's cute," Patrick said.

"Dr. Benson likes the idea of me taking on some responsibility," Evan said. "She thinks I won't want to get wasted as much since I know Lancelot's depending on me."

"But if you go on the road, you won't have your doctor or even the support group anymore," Patrick said.

"Patrick—"

Thankfully, a knock on the door interrupted the awkward conversation. Eric and Rog came in with Cindy, and Rog set an aloe plant on a stand by the couch. "Housewarming present."

Ian, Carlton, Tish, and Tracy arrived soon after, and most of them sat on the floor around the Xbox while Evan and Dan finished preparing their very early dinner. Then they stacked the table with potato salad, deviled eggs, chips, dip, rolls, a platter of meats and cheeses, and a vegetable tray. It made a perfect late-May meal, and they enjoyed it picnic style, cross-legged on the rug, with the exception of Cindy. Though she wasn't even showing yet, Rog insisted on surrounding her with pillows on the couch and bringing her food like a waiter. Still, he never stopped smiling, and Eric smiled as he watched him fussing around like a mother hen. Patrick couldn't imagine what he'd be like when the baby came, and he felt a pang. Everyone was smiling—happy. They'd be happy without him. None of them needed him nearly as much as he'd imagined.

But that was okay. Better than okay. The people he loved would be fine; they'd be happy.

"Patrick, honey, what's wrong?" Tish asked, setting her glass of chardonnay on the floor.

"I think I miss you guys already."

"Are you having second thoughts?" Yu asked.

Though his eyes stung, Patrick took Yu's hand and kissed the back. "Hell no. Just thinking too much. We have so much to look forward to, but we're going to miss out on things too. The baby. Seeing Evan play a show with Dan's family. Seeing the day when Tracy finally convinces this foul-mouthed son of a bitch to settle down...."

"Hey, you little shit!" Ian protested while everyone else laughed. Ian shrugged and turned his attention back to sneaking food to Lancelot.

"And someday Tish will meet a guy...."

Everyone went quiet, and for a second Patrick didn't know why. Tish blushed.

"Jesus, Queen Titania!" Tish said. "I thought you knew. I thought everyone knew, but especially you. I thought that was why you asked me to make your first corset all those years ago."

"I just thought you did nice work," Patrick said, feeling like a tool.

"God, I knew in thirty seconds," Cindy said, patting the cushion beside her until Tish sat down. "So, what kind of girls do you like?"

They talked and giggled in hushed tones while everyone else caught up and finished their meals.

"We don't have much time left," Evan said, opening and closing his fingers around the hem of his T-shirt, "but would you like to hear me play something?"

"I'd love that," Patrick said, and everyone else clapped softly.

Evan took a battered case from the closet and an equally battered violin from inside. Dan pulled a chair out from the table and wedged a djembe between his knees. After a few false starts, Evan began playing a melody Patrick knew well, his notes clear and confident. The little ferret scampered up Dan's leg and across a shelf until he could stretch across the sunny windowsill behind Evan. If Patrick hadn't known better, he'd have said the little fellow liked the music.

"Ooh, I know this one!" Tracy squealed with delight.

Eric ginned and took Rog's hand. "We all know this one."

And they all sang "Wild Mountain Thyme" while Evan fiddled and Dan accompanied him on his drum.

"Oh the summertime is coming

And the trees are sweetly blooming

And the wild mountain thyme

Grows around the blooming heather.

Will you go, lassie, go?"

After the song ended and the last note of Evan's fiddle faded to nothing, they all sat quietly, many of their eyes glittering. Patrick squeezed Yu's hand tighter, and Dan pulled Evan onto his lap. Tracy nuzzled closer to Ian, and Eric kissed Rog on the forehead.

"We had some damn good times," Eric said.

"And we'll have more," Tish replied.

"Hell yeah," Carlton said, lifting his beer bottle. "To good times!"

"Good times," everyone said, lifting their drinks into the air.

"To the future," Rog said.

"To friends," Evan added, "and family." He looked at his watch. "It's time to go."

Patrick and Yu hugged everyone and told them they loved them. Patrick cried more than a little, but he wasn't ashamed. Maybe he was feminine or too gay, but what the hell? These people loved him anyway.

Evan drove them to the airport. Patrick had given him the old Horizon; the lady still had plenty of life in her, he was sure. Evan dropped them off at the All Nippon Airlines terminal and hugged them both again. Then he hugged Patrick a second time and gave him a soft, platonic kiss on the lips. "Thank you for not giving up on me."

"No, honey," Patrick said, pulling Evan tight, not quite ready to give him up, "you never needed me. You're fierce. But I'm glad we're friends."

"I love you, Mama."

"Love you too."

"Well, safe travels." Evan got back in Patrick's old car and sat behind the wheel, watching them until they reached the doors. Patrick took a long, last look at Evan's smiling face before he turned to enter the airport.

Now amidst all the chaos and possibility, Patrick grew excited about everything they would discover. He'd taken care of the people he loved; they would be fine. Now, now was their time. He caught Yu's hand and dragged him toward the security checkpoint and then on to the gate to await their flight. He could barely sit still as they waited to board. Finally, they were shown to their seats, and he clutched Yu's arm as the plane sped down the runway and climbed into the sky. Blue firmament and wispy white clouds streaked by beyond Patrick's small window. He watched, heart pounding, nervous but exhilarated, before turning to look at Yu. Yu's eyes sparkled, and he smiled, and for once, he intuited Patrick's wonder.

"I've flown to Japan many times, but with you here, it feels new and wonderful. I can't wait to show you everything for the first time."

"Me neither." They ascended higher and higher until the ground became a tiny patchwork quilt beneath them, then just a brownish blur, then endless ocean, sparkling, jewel-like all the way to the dip in the horizon.

Patrick felt free. He had only himself and Yu to think about. Finally, they had wings. Wings to carry them anywhere, strong wings to always keep them aloft. Wings that sparkled in Patrick's imagination as he held Yu's hand and prepared to face their life's next adventure.

AUGUST (GUS) LI is a creator of fantasy worlds. When not writing, he enjoys drawing, illustration, costuming and cosplay, and making things in general. He lives near Philadelphia with two cats and too many ball-jointed dolls. He loves to travel and is trying to see as much of the world as possible. Other hobbies include reading (of course), tattoos, and playing video games.

For more info, visit Books by Eon and Gus:
http://www.booksbyeonandgus.com

How the story started

ON
TINSEL
Wings

AUGUST LI

http://www.dreamspinnerpress.com

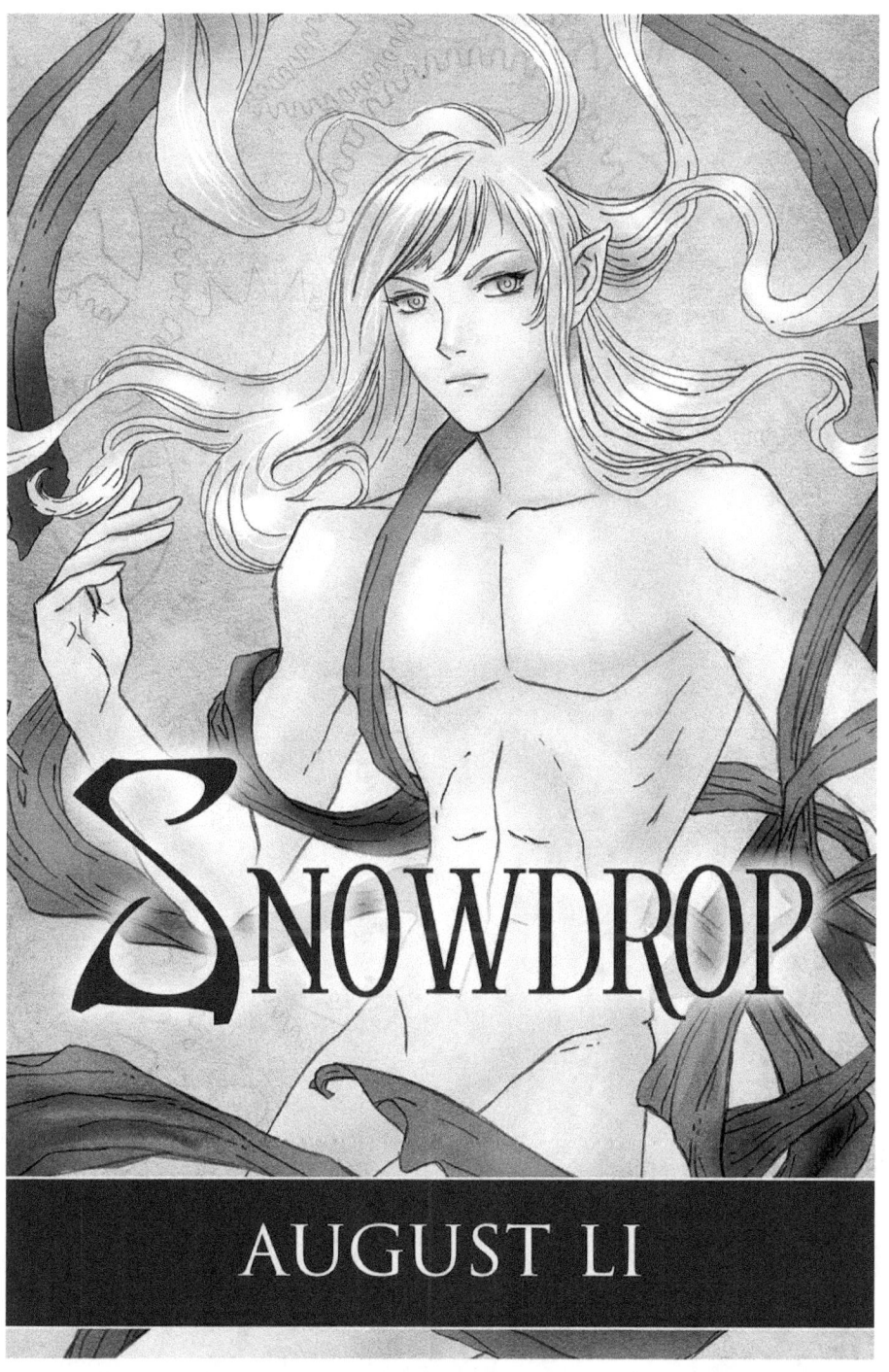

SNOWDROP

AUGUST LI

http://www.dreamspinnerpress.com

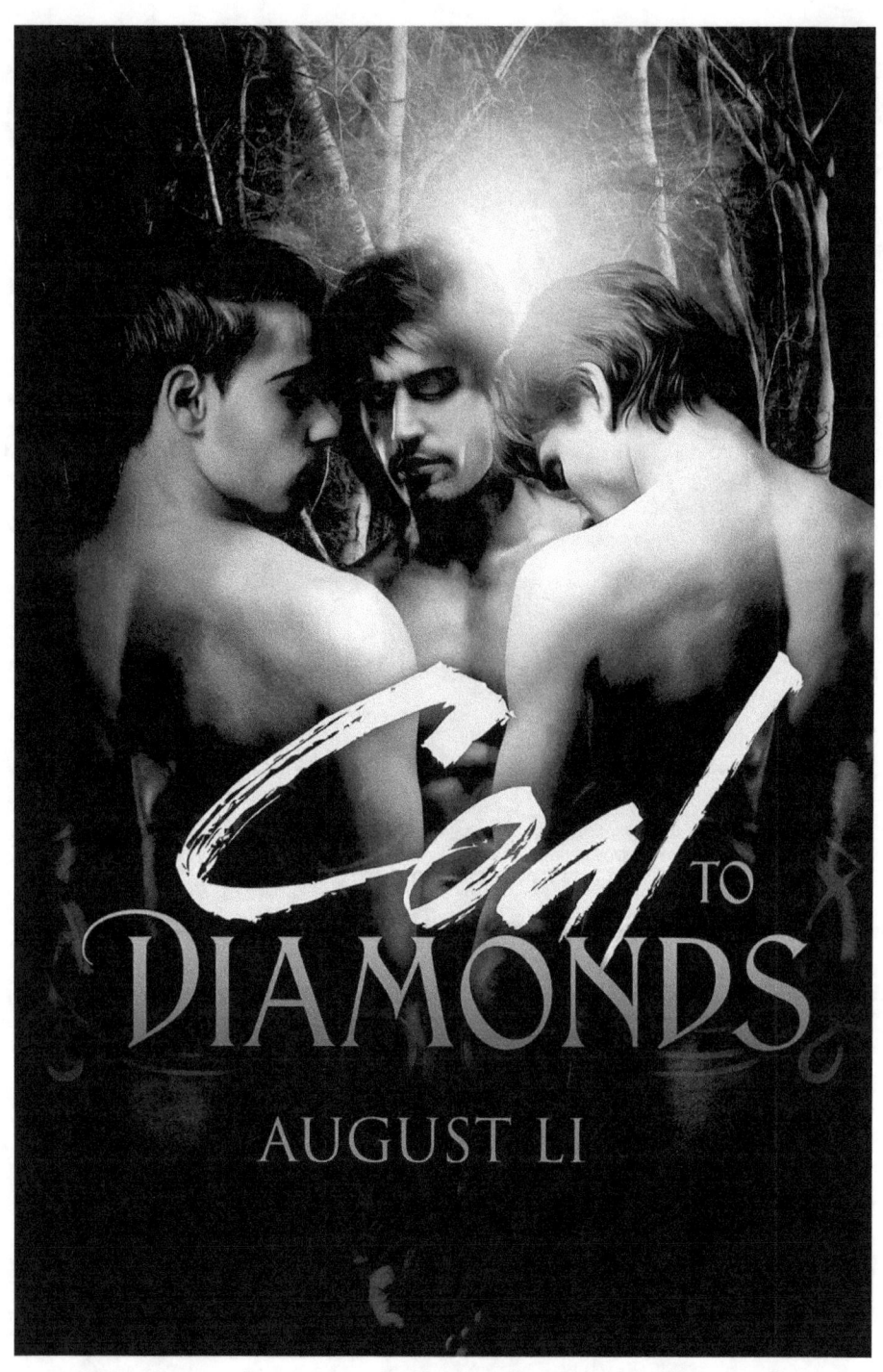

Coal TO DIAMONDS

AUGUST LI

http://www.dreamspinnerpress.com

Wine
AND
Roses

Other Paths: Book One
A TALE OF THE
BLESSED EPOCH
AUGUST LI

http://www.dreamspinnerpress.com

AUGUST LI

ΠΕΣΚΑΥΑ

http://www.dreamspinnerpress.com

EON DE BEAUMONT

RUM & GINGER

http://www.dreamspinnerpress.com

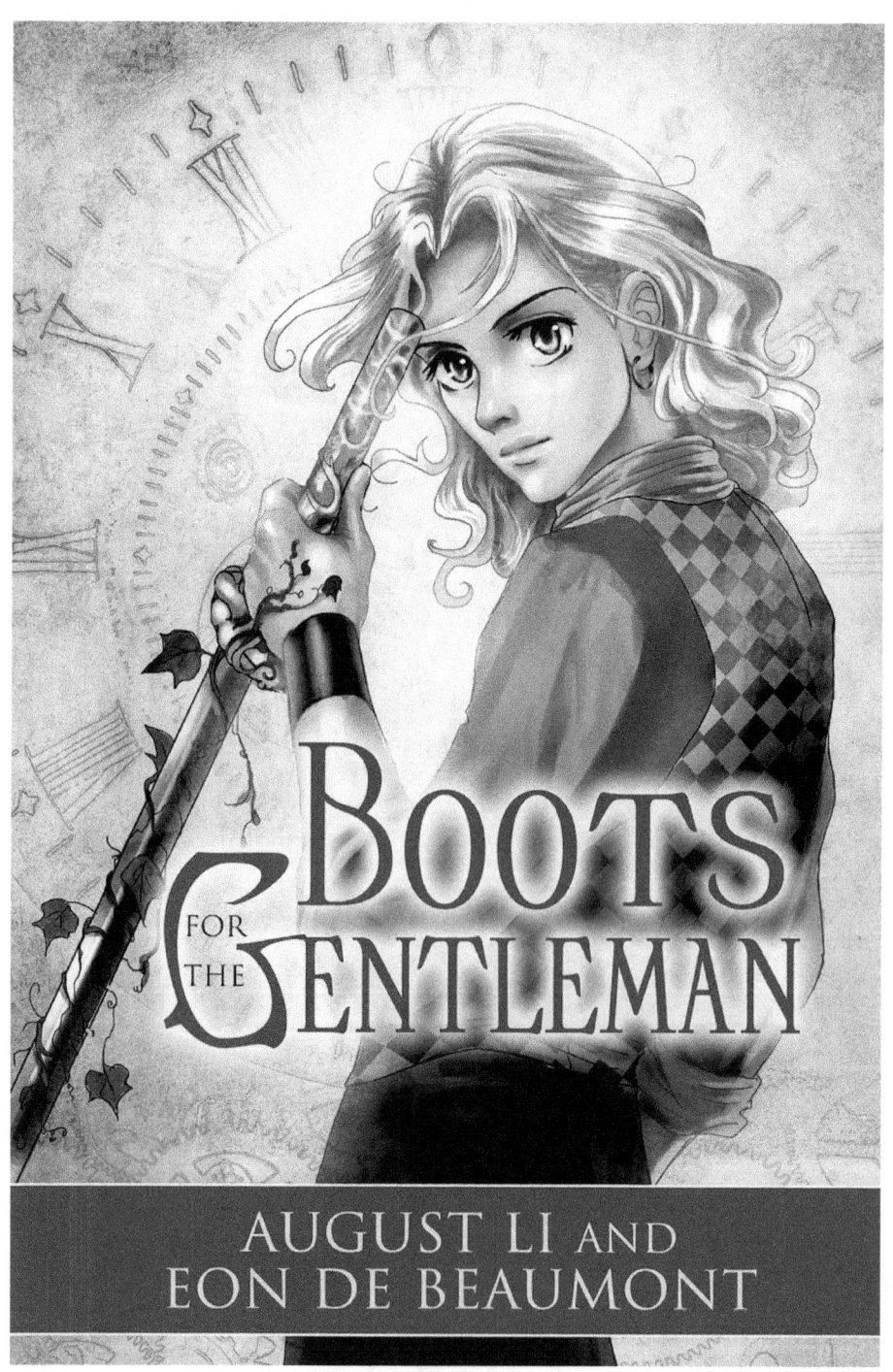

BOOTS FOR THE GENTLEMAN

AUGUST LI AND
EON DE BEAUMONT

http://www.dreamspinnerpress.com

A GRIMOIRE FOR THE BARON

AUGUST LI AND EON DE BEAUMONT

http://www.dreamspinnerpress.com

ONLY
LOVE

GARRETT LEIGH

http://www.dreamspinnerpress.com

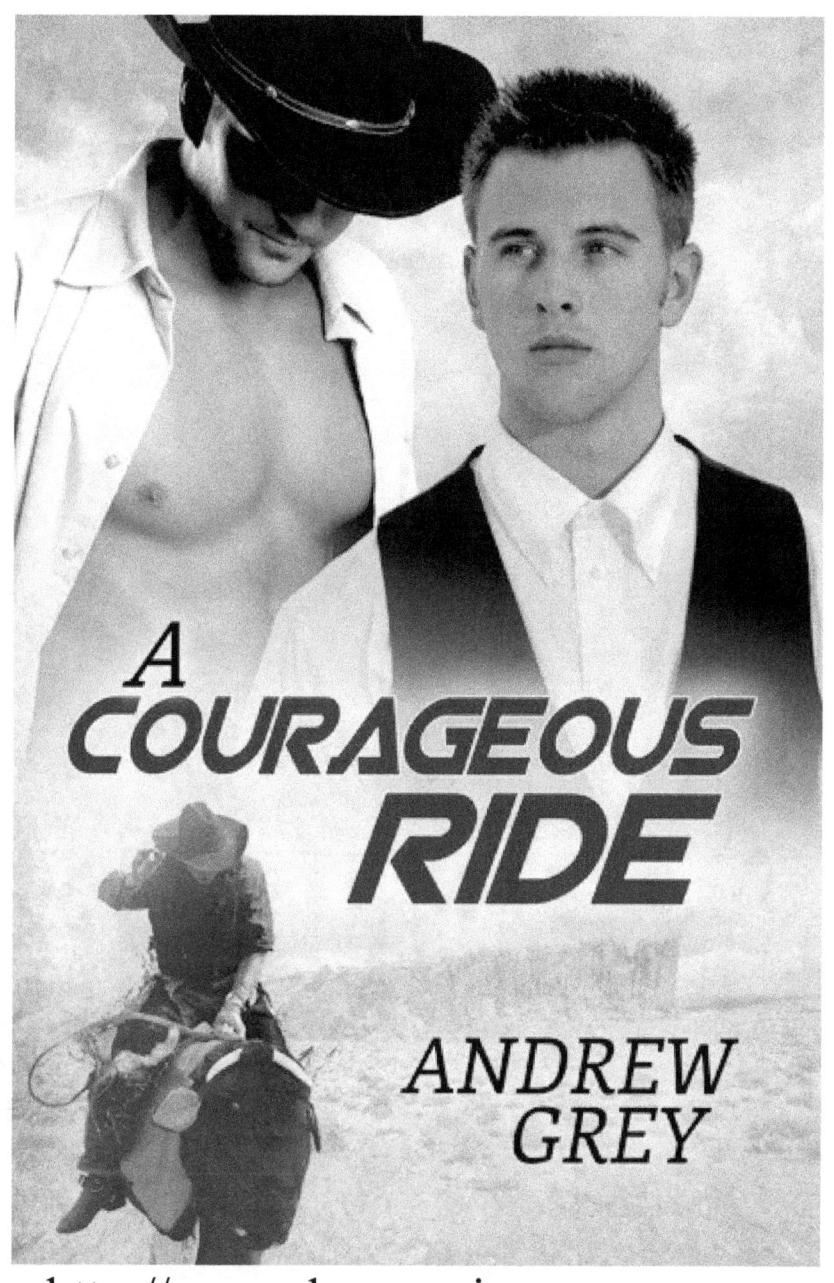

A
COURAGEOUS
RIDE

ANDREW GREY

http://www.dreamspinnerpress.com

★★★★★
"...an emotionally
articulate and
gripping novel."
–*The Novel Approach*

SPENCER

JP BARNABY

http://www.dreamspinnerpress.com

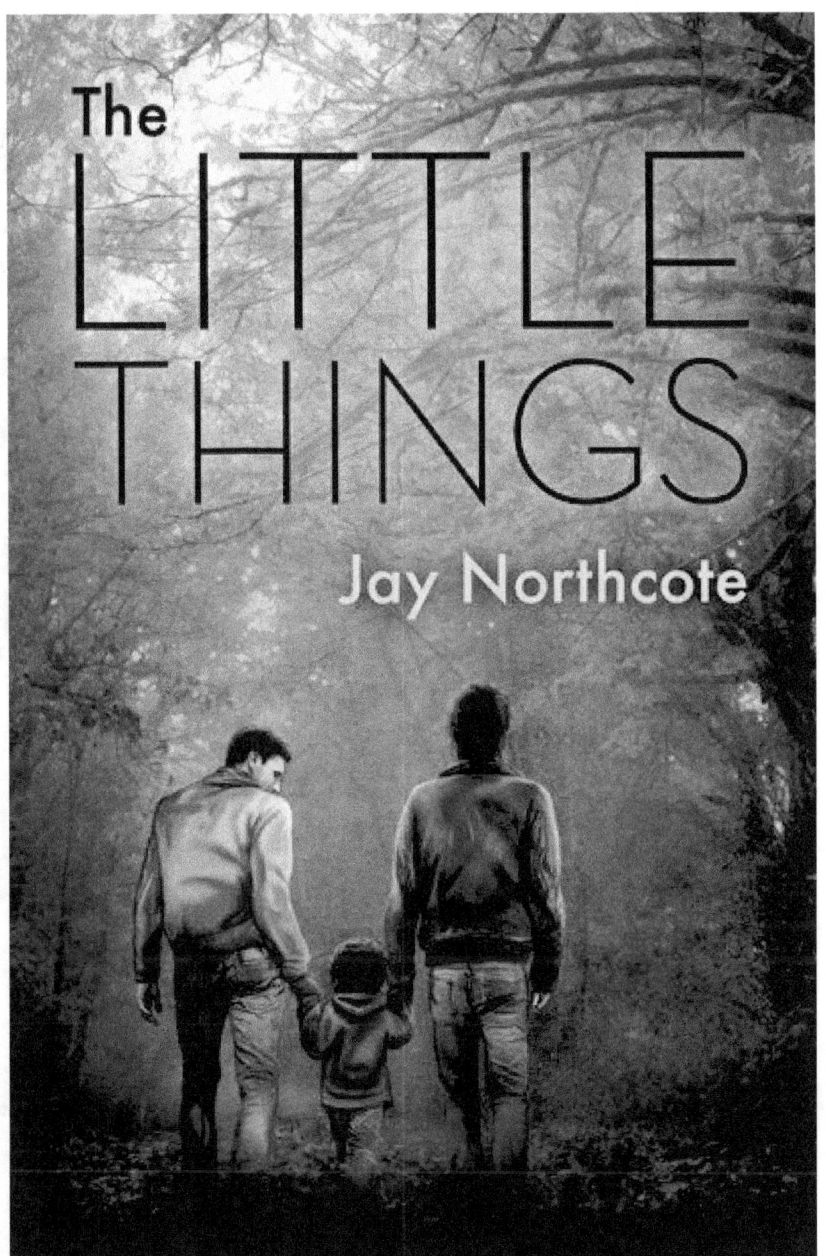

The LITTLE THINGS

Jay Northcote

http://www.dreamspinnerpress.com

CATCH MY Breath

M.J. O'SHEA

http://www.dreamspinnerpress.com

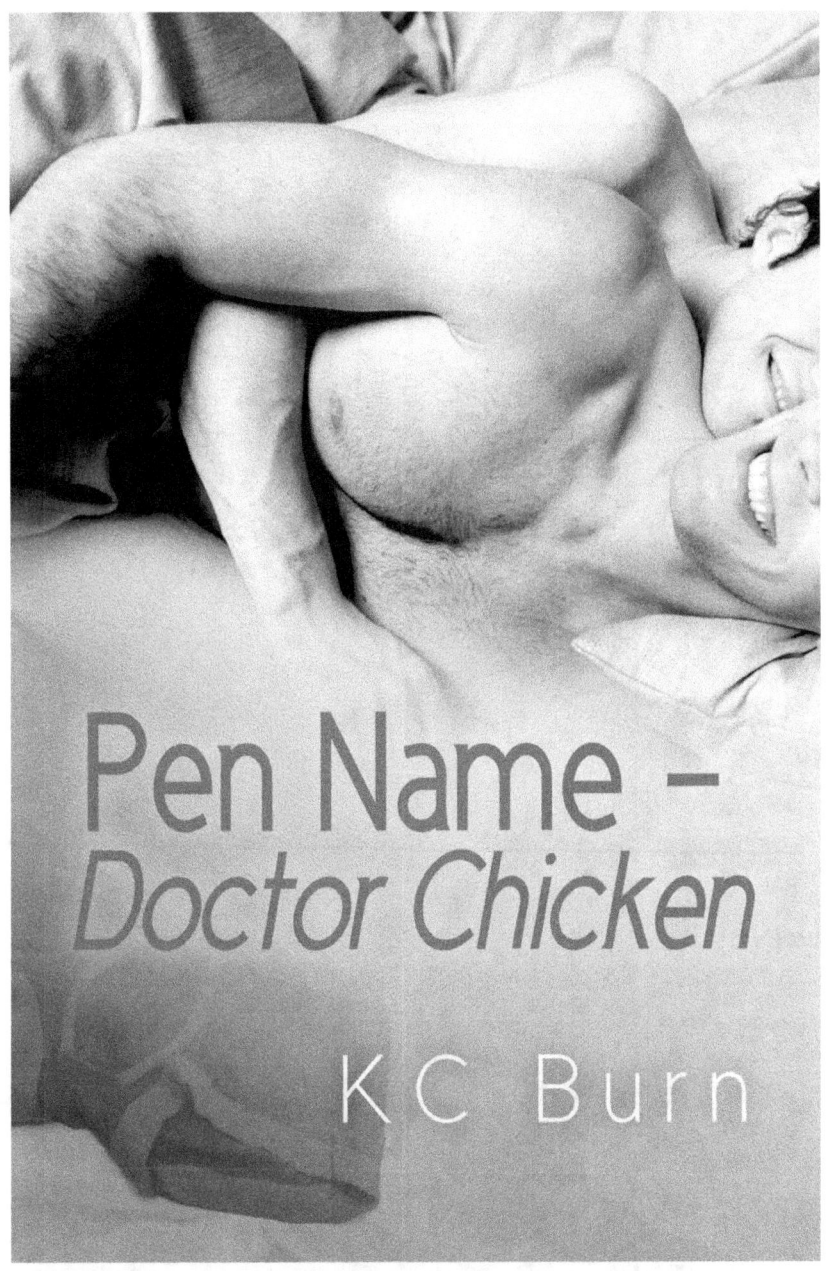

Pen Name –
Doctor Chicken

KC Burn

http://www.dreamspinnerpress.com

www.ingramcontent.com/pod-product-compliance
Lightning Source LLC
Chambersburg PA
CBHW070057030726
47506CB00002B/499